KOYESTA ONLINE - BOOK 1 - EARLY ACCESS

PAIGE FALLBRIGHT

JOHN ELIJAH CRESSMAN

MAVERICK-GAGE PUBLISHING

ISBN: 978-1-954524-22-4 (Paperback)
ISBN: 978-1-954524-23-1 (Hardcover)
ISBN: 978-1-954524-24-8 (Audiobook)
AISN: 978-1-954524-12-5 (Amazon Kindle)

Front cover image by Christina Myrvold
Editing By TC Tunstall

Printed by Maverick-Gage Publishing in conjunction with IngramSpark, in the United States of America.
First printing edition 2022.
Maverick-Gage Publishing
Allentown, PA

info@maverick-gage.com
www.maverick-gage.com
John Elijah Cressman
www.johnecressman.com

Created with Vellum

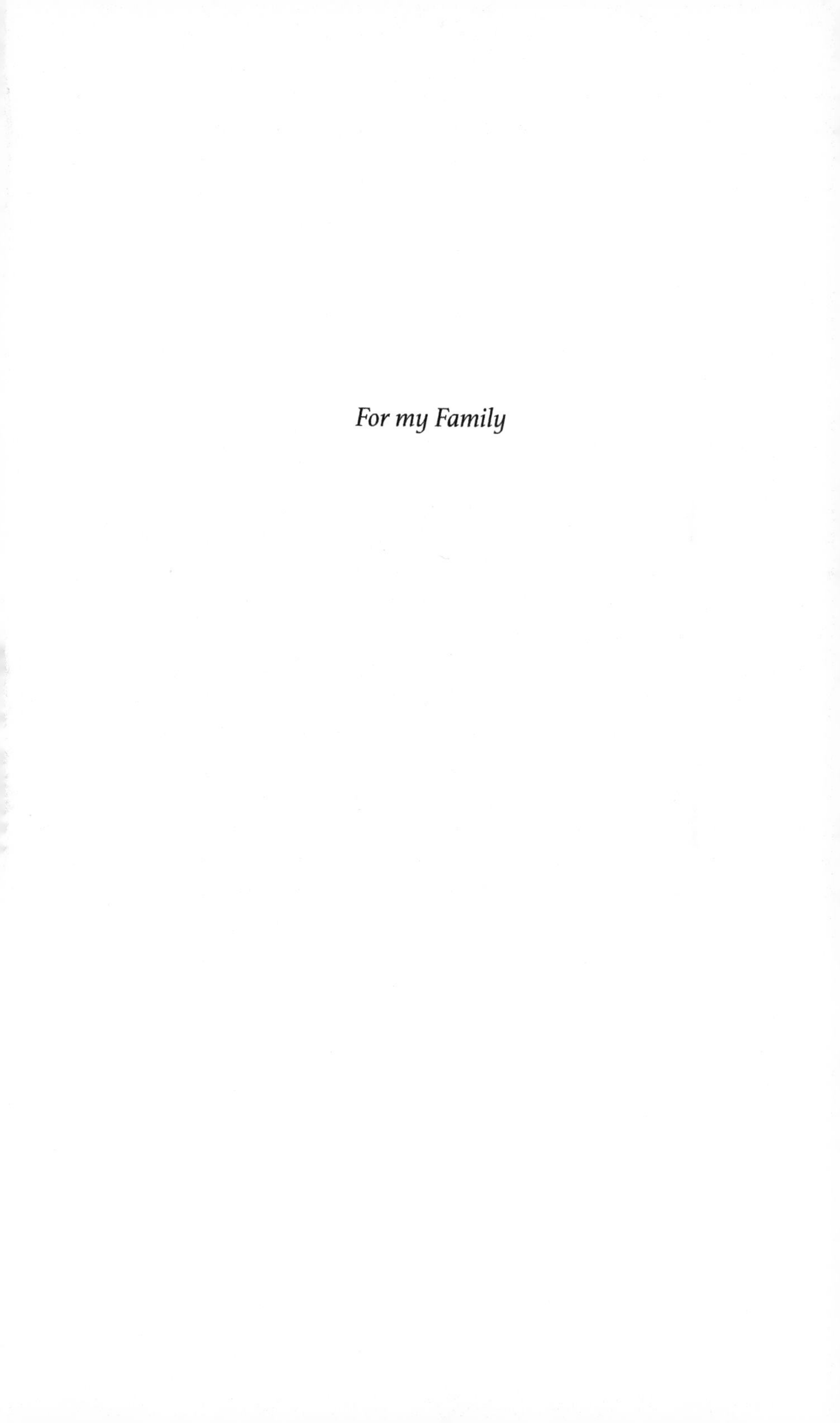

For my Family

1

"I won!" Cole cried excitedly, causing Madison to glance up from her tablet in annoyance. She was just getting to the good part of the novel she was reading and the interruption had broken her concentration. At the same time, she was curious. No one in her family ever won anything.

Judging by the excitement on her twin brother's face, it must be something he really wanted. She smiled despite herself, shaking her head slightly. Madison slid the tablet onto the coffee table next to her and focused on her brother. "What did you win?"

"I won the Koyesta Online Contest!" he replied enthusiastically, his face split with a huge grin. "I really won!"

Madison didn't want to curb her brother's excitement, but she was more cautious than he was. Especially when it came to the internet. She gave him a serious look. "It's not something from a Nigerian prince is it?"

"No! Of course not!" Cole looked at her incredulously.

Then his expression turned sheepish. "I never actually sent him money!"

"Because of me!" Madison reminded him. "You were ready to!"

Her brother had shown her an email from a Nigerian prince who claimed to want to send him money because of some reason or another. All he wanted was the money to cover the bank transfer fees - oh, and he was willing to take payment in electronic gift cards.

"I was not," Cole replied and then shrugged. "It wasn't like I had any money to send anyway."

"True." Madison sighed. Their parents were divorced, and their single mom was working two jobs to help them get through college. Neither Cole nor Madison had wanted their mom to work the second job to help them, but she'd insisted. Nothing they'd said had dissuaded her and they'd finally been forced to accept her help.

Turning her attention back to her brother, she softened her expression. "You're sure it's not some sort of scam?"

"No way!" Cole said, his enthusiasm returning. He turned his phone around, so the screen was facing her. "See! It's legit!"

Of course, from six feet away, Madison couldn't make out any words on the screen. It looked like his email app but she couldn't even be sure of that. She rolled her eyes and stretched out her hand. "Let me read it."

Cole rushed forward and slapped the phone into her open palm. Bringing the screen up to eye level, she read the email on the screen.

Dear Cole Faller,

Congratulations! You have won 1 of 4 First Prizes in the Koyesta Online Early Access Contest! Only 1000 people will get the opportunity to explore the exciting world of Koyesta starting June 15th and you and 3 of your friends will be among the first!

Your First Prize package includes the following for you and up to 3 of your friends:

1 Year of Koyesta Online subscription (a $199 value)

1 Excelsior Electronic Systems (EES) Excalibur Virtual Reality Rig (a $2299 value)

1 Koyesta T-Shirt (a $19 value)

1 Koyesta Travel Mug (a $24 value)

$250 cash to cover taxes

1 Early Access to Koyesta Online starting June 15th (priceless!)

Prize must be claimed by June 10th or will be forfeit and another winner will be drawn.

Please follow the link below to our website to enter your information and the contact information for up to 3 lucky friends.

As a reminder, to encourage you and your friends to explore the world of Koyesta, you will have a chance to win real prizes by completing in-game activities up until the official release date. Exact prizes will vary based on activity and accomplishment.

Thank you for entering the contest and happy adventuring in Koyesta Online.

Sabre Online Enterprises

Note: Participants are responsible for all taxes for any prizes earned during the Early access period. Sabre Online Entertainment does not guarantee that any participant will win a specific prize or any prize at all. See official rules and terms of use on our website.

Madison read through the email and then read it again. It seemed legitimate. She looked up at Cole. "And you entered this contest? This isn't something they sent you unsolicited, right?"

It was Cole's turn to roll his eyes. "Of course, I entered it! It's going to be the most awesome game ever! Michael and I have only been talking about it for like... a year now!"

Scrunching her face up in concentration, Madison thought she remembered them discussing some sort of game. But then again, they were always discussing some game or another. Finally, she shrugged. "Which game is this?"

Cole's eyes went wide. "THE game! Koyesta Online! The one with a new immersive headset! It's supposed to be just like being there!"

Madison let out a sigh. She loved her brother but sometimes, she thought he was a bit too trusting. She shook her head. "Cole, you can't trust marketing hype. I mean... it's just that... hype..."

Shaking his head vigorously, her brother snatched his phone back and tapped the screen several times. Then he thrust it back with a list of videos from the most popular video site. "Just watch these! It's not hype!"

She took the offered phone and scanned the videos. They were mostly official trailers for the game. Madison looked up at Cole. "You know you can never trust official trailers. They're like movie trailers. They show you the best stuff and then the rest of the movie is junk."

Cole shook his head. "Just watch."

"Fine, I'll watch one," she told him. While she always

tried to support her brother, online gaming really wasn't her thing. It was hard to get enthusiastic about it.

Nevertheless, she could see he was really excited about it so she nodded to him and looked down at the playlist. She hit play on the first video and dramatic music began to play through the phone's tiny speakers.

"Turn it sideways and make it full screen!" Cole insisted.

Sighing again, she did as he asked, and the video became full screen as she switched to landscape.

"The world of Koyesta is in trouble," the announcer's deep voice boomed as the camera panned over an amazingly real landscape with a walled medieval-looking city. As the camera angle moved, Madison saw fields and people moving far below, almost like the real world.

"A call for brave adventurers has gone out to all corners of the world," the announcer continued, and the camera began to show short snippets of different races. She had read some fantasy books and seen the more popular fantasy movies, so she recognized some of them.

Dramatic music with an upbeat tune played as the clips moved from one scene to another, showing the different races. There were dwarves in their mines, halflings gathered around a table in a tavern, really small people tinkering with some sort of machinery. Then the image changed to beautiful elves high in a forest tree dwelling before quickly changing to the plains where other elves, dressed in what looked like Native American leathers, stalked through the tall grass with bows.

The music changed again to a darker tune, but still just as dramatic. The camera switched to a dark swamp and a large greenish creature Madison didn't know. Then it went to a torchlit cave as two even larger creatures came around the corner. Were those supposed to be ogres? Next the camera panned to an enormous underground city with strange, alien-looking architecture. Dropping down into the city, it showed more elves. But these were different from the other elves. They were a deep violet color, with glowing red eyes and sharper features. They just looked more... sinister.

"Will you answer the call?" the announcer asked in his deep, bass voice as a group of adventurers struck a heroic pose and the camera zoomed on them.

The image stayed on the adventurers as some additional text came up on the screen, but Madison ignored it and held out the phone to her brother. She nodded. "It looks amazing. But you know how those trailers are."

"They have come out in several articles and said that was all real footage," Cole argued. "That's what the game actually looks like."

"If that's true," she said. "Then you will have a blast!"

"Oh yeah!" Cole grinned.

"The email said you can invite 3 friends," she reminded him. "Did you pick them out yet? I assume Michael will be one of them?"

Michael was their cousin and was the same age as them. He and Cole had been inseparable since they were young and did nearly everything together. At least, everything online.

They lived an hour and a half apart, so didn't get together as often as they wanted. Nowadays, they mostly connected by playing online games together. This would probably be another one they'd share.

Cole nodded enthusiastically. "Oh yeah! I texted him when I got the email but he hasn't gotten back to me."

"Probably in the pool," Madison thought aloud. She knew Michael's parents had put in an above ground pool recently. Since then, she'd swear Michael had become part fish.

"Probably," Cole agreed, a little disappointment on his face.

"Who else?" Madison asked.

Cole looked down, not quite meeting her eye. "I... uh... well, I mean..."

"Just spit it out," Madison said with a small chuckle. "Is it Ethan? Hunter?"

"Actually," Cole said, looking up at her. "I was hoping you would do it with us."

Madison wrinkled her forehead. "Me? Why me? You know I don't really..."

"I know," Cole interrupted. "You don't like those games. You like the gem games and stuff. No, I mean... there are... real money prizes for this early access period. They want to encourage people to explore and stuff. Some of the prizes are big money. Enough to pay for a year of college."

That got Madison's attention. She and Cole had both gotten summer jobs to help pay for tuition next year. Not to mention, their mom was working a second job to help them out as well. She raised an eyebrow. "Like... how much money?"

Cole shrugged. "They don't come right out and say. It's

very vague. It depends on what you do and if you're the first person to do it, that sort of thing."

It sounded like some sort of marketing scam to her. And yet, if it were true and she could play a game to make some money until her job started on the July 4th weekend, maybe it was worth it. Maybe.

"I'll think about it," Madison told him.

"Think quick," Cole told her. "I have to give them the names of my 3 friends this week."

2

Madison did think about it. She actually lay in her bed that night, weighing whether she should try Cole's game or just chill out until her job at the restaurant started.

High school graduation was just behind her and the last few weeks had been brutal as she studied for her finals. Now, she really did want to relax a bit before she started working. Besides, she had books to read.

Her current book was about a guy who was abducted by aliens and dropped on a world where magic was real and there were all sorts of aliens that looked like creatures from Earth legends. There were elves and dwarves, even a foxgirl. It looked like a good read but she had barely gotten through any of it.

Then there were the other things she had to do. In addition to the chores around the house, she and Cole needed to help her grandparents. They had some health issues, mostly just getting old, and needed their help around their yard.

She also wanted to see her cousin, Rose, who was an hour's drive south from them. She was a year younger than Madison and still had one more year of high school before she'd be joining Madison at college. At least, for the first couple of years.

Madison stared up at the ceiling and sighed. Did she really want to get sucked into her brother's gaming world? Was there really a chance that they could win some of those prizes?

Before she'd gone to bed, Madison had actually looked up the Sabre Online Enterprises website on her computer, as well as the Koyesta Online website. She found more trailers, which looked equally impressive. Unfortunately, there wasn't a lot of information about the game itself, the game world or the so-called prizes.

Sure, they mentioned prizes for the early access winners, but nowhere could she find what the prizes actually were. She could devote some time to this game with Cole and all they might walk away with was a free hat or mouse pad.

On the other hand, maybe it was just what she needed. Much like her books, maybe the game would give her a little escapism and help her relax. Or would it stress her out more? She knew she sometimes got a bit too competitive with things. She was a bit too much like her parents.

Her father was a nuclear engineer and even though she didn't see him that often, she knew she'd inherited some of his brains. Her mom was also smart, but not in the same way. Mom was... Mom.

Mom was tenacious and a real go-getter. She owned her own business, which she started from scratch, just put herself through college for a second degree and was now working a second job to make sure she and Cole had enough money for college.

She thought about her older sister, Jade. She was in her third year of college. She'd gotten a scholarship, but it hadn't paid for everything. Jade still needed money for books, food and - of course - anything fun she wanted to do on the weekends.

Jade had gotten an internship over the summer and was currently working at some company. She hadn't really told Madison much about it, other than it was an office job.

Madison sighed again. It was getting late, and she really needed to sleep but this might be one of those nights when her brain wouldn't shut off.

Growling softly in frustration, she threw the covers off her and padded over to her computer desk. She sat down in front of it, switching it on. If she couldn't sleep, the least she could do was try to do a bit more research before she gave Cole her answer.

BLEARY-EYED, Madison wandered down the stairs and into the kitchen. Cole was already there, eating what she guessed was his second bowl of cereal. He looked up at her as she walked in and frowned, forehead wrinkling in concern. "You okay?"

Madison stared back at him for a moment before answering. "I'm fine. I didn't sleep well."

"How come?" Cole asked as he shoveled another spoonful of cereal in his mouth.

"I was thinking about whether or not to play the game with you," she told him as she collapsed into the chair across from him.

Cole immediately looked up from his cereal, eyes wide with excitement. He didn't even finish chewing. "And?"

"Don't talk with your mouth full," Madison said, making a face.

Rolling his eyes, Cole finished chewing and then made a face. "Yes, Mom."

Madison glared back at him. She hated when he said that.

"So?" Cole asked, the anticipation in his voice evident even to her sleep-deprived mind.

She considered briefly making him wait, but given his level of enthusiasm, she didn't want to be cruel. Plus, she was too tired to play games at the moment. "I'll do it!"

Cole stood up, pushing back his chair and raised his hands in the air. "Yes!"

Groaning at his level of energy given her sleepless night, she held up a finger. "One condition."

Narrowing his eyes, Cole slid back into his chair and looked across the table at her. "What condition?"

"I'm not going to be the only girl," she replied, crossing her arms over her chest. "If you want me to be in your group, then you have to have Rose too."

"Rose?" he repeated as if the name left a bad taste in his mouth. He furrowed his brow. "She doesn't even like video games."

Struggling out of her chair, she walked over to the cabinet and pulled out a bowl, then fished a spoon from the silverware drawer. Dragging herself back over to the kitchen table, she once more collapsed onto the chair. "I'll text her later. If she knows I'm doing it, I think I can convince her to join."

Cole bit his lip as the wheels turned in his head. He stared down into his bowl of cereal as if the bits of frosted flakes somehow held the answer he needed. Finally, he looked up. "Fine. But if she doesn't want to do it, you still play with us."

Madison hesitated and Cole pressed on. "Come on. It's a chance to check out... like... a real virtual world... and win money doing it!"

"You know that's an oxymoron, right?" she asked. "A real virtual world."

He shrugged. "Maybe. But some leaked info from the beta testers say this is just like being in a real world. Like, it's that good."

Dumping a large helping of frosted flakes into the bowl, Madison then grabbed the milk and downed the flakes. She picked up her spoon and gestured at her brother with it. "I'll believe it when I see it."

She looked down at the frosted flakes and cursed silently. Madison normally tried to eat healthier but, at the moment, she was just too tired to make herself something else. She frowned, but then shrugged and took a bite. When she was done chewing, she looked at her brother.

"You know I start my job on July 4th weekend," she told him. "I can play with you until then. Once that starts, my job comes first."

Cole nodded. "I haven't found a job yet."

"You have to keep looking," she told him.

"I know, I know," he said. He bit his lip again. "I was hoping that if we won some money, maybe neither one of us will have to work. If we win enough, maybe Mom won't either."

Madison knew it was wishful thinking, but she didn't want to curb his enthusiasm. She nodded and mumbled an affirmative sound as she chewed another mouthful. She didn't really believe it, but she wasn't about to burst his bubble.

"The letter said something about claiming the prize by the 10th. When does the early access begin?" she asked after swallowing her mouthful of frosted flakes.

"The 15th!" Cole said enthusiastically. "That's in like 10 days! I can't wait! Neither can Michael!"

"You already told him?" she asked, realizing it was a stupid question. Of course, he had. There was no way he wouldn't have shared this with Michael already. In fact, he'd probably told him about it before approaching her.

"Uh, yeah!" Cole replied in a tone that told her she should have known. "He's crazy excited."

"So then, I just need to convince Rose to join us," Madison said between mouthfuls.

"Exactly! But I need an answer by the 10th! Oh, and I'll

need a bunch of information and she'll have to fill out some online forms," Cole rattled off in rapid succession.

"I'll text her after breakfast." Madison groaned but nodded. She stifled a yawn. "Or maybe after I go back to bed."

3

A day before the early access began, the group met at Rose's house. Madison, Rose, Michael and Cole were all sitting at a patio table next to her pool as Rose's younger brother, Hunter, and her mom and dad played with their second cousin, Lacie.

"She's so cute!" Madison said, unable to suppress it any longer. Lacie wasn't a baby anymore, but she was still an adorable toddler. She sighed and turned back to the group.

"My mom wasn't so sure, but Dad finally said it was fine," Rose told them, leaning forward in a conspiratorial fashion. "Let's hope it stays that way."

"What's the big deal?" asked Michael, leaning back and taking a sip of his soda.

Rose brushed some of her blond curls out of her face and rolled her eyes. "Since some of us aren't eighteen yet, I still need to get permission. Remember that? Remember when you had to ask for permission to do stuff."

"Nope," Michael lied with a grin. "It was too long ago. That was like... wow... a year ago. Who remembers that far back?"

"He doesn't remember that," Madison snickered. "But he remembers every level in whatever new game he's playing."

"You only have so much brain," Michael replied with a shrug and threw a sideways glance at Cole. "You have to focus on the important stuff."

Michael and Cole both chuckled and fist bumped while Madison and Rose both rolled their eyes. Madison stopped just shy of saying "Boys!"

"What is this game anyway?" Rose asked. "There's nothing to read on the website. I mean it's a fantasy game, right? Like that movie with the dwarves and the dragon?"

Cole and Michael exchanged looks, both nodding. "There's no video feeds. And now that I see the VR gear, I understand why."

Madison remembered opening up the package, which the company had sent to them via next day air. She wasn't sure exactly what she'd expected, but that hadn't been it. It looked like a headband with lots of LED lights and two wires coming out of it.

Michael wrinkled his brow. "Those EES rigs are weird-looking, but they're supposed to be state of the art."

"Yeah," Rose said with a frown. "That's what freaked out my mom. She doesn't like the idea of brain stimulation. She's so old fashioned."

"My dad thinks it's cool," Michael said. He looked around, as if seeing if someone was listening to them. "We didn't tell my mom."

Madison and Cole exchanged looks. Cole gave the group a sheepish smile. “We didn’t tell our mom exactly how it works either.”

Rose let out an exasperated breath, glancing over at her mom in the pool. “Probably a good thing.”

“What class are you all going to be?” Michael asked after taking another sip of his drink. “Did you decide yet?”

“I’ll be the tank,” Cole announced. “So, a fighter or a knight - whatever they have available.”

“I read that they have some sort of pet class,” Michael said. “I might try that.”

“Pet class?” Rose perked up. The girl loved animals. She volunteered at a local pet shelter on weekends and, as far as Madison knew, still planned on going to school to be a veterinarian. Oh yeah, Rose loved animals.

Madison looked past the pool to where a small chicken coop had been built by her uncle - all because Rose wanted chickens. They also had two dogs and a houseful of their own cats, plus some cats they were fostering for the shelter until long-term owners could be found.

“A pet class is a class where you have an animal, elemental, or even a construct, that fights for you,” Michael explained. “But you like animals, so if they have druid, you should go for druid.”

“Druid?” Rose asked, brow furrowed. “Like in England?”

“Huh?” Michael asked, scratching his head.

“You know,” Rose retorted. “They say druids may have built Stonehenge. Those druids.”

Michael and Cole exchanged looks and then burst out

laughing. Cole shook his head. "Where do you learn all that stuff?"

"That's what happens when you don't use your brain for memorizing game levels and actually learn real-world stuff," Madison pointed out. She held out her own fist to Rose and her cousin fist bumped her.

"Anyway," Cole said, obviously stirring the conversation away from Michael and his obsession with video games. He looked at Madison. "What about you? What class are you going to be?"

Madison shrugged. She had been scouring the internet to find out more about the game, but the company was really keeping things under wraps. There wasn't even a map of the fantasy world that they were supposed to be entering. "I don't know. There's no information out there..."

"Duh," Michael said, interrupting her. "That's the way they want it. They want everyone to experience it first-hand. I hear they'll even be cracking down on anyone who posts any game information. It's part of the license agreement you click on before you can play."

"How do you know that?" Cole asked him.

"Uh, someone on one of the online groups posted it," he explained. "I guess he tried to log on already."

"And he actually read the terms of use agreement?" Rose chuckled. "I don't even read those."

"Right!" Madison agreed. She cleared her throat. "Anyway, I was thinking of maybe someone who uses magic. Remember that RPG game we played together..."

"Dungeons and Dragons," Cole supplied helpfully.

"Right, Dungeons and Dragons," Madison continued.

"I was a blue dragon sorcerer, and I could shoot lightning..."

"From your butt," Michael chuckled, and Cole snickered too.

"From my mouth," she said, glaring at both of the boys.

"Breath weapon," Cole corrected. "It's called a breath weapon."

Madison sighed in frustration. "As I was saying, I want to be something like that. Where I can... you know... throw magic out."

Cole looked thoughtful. He glanced at Michael, but their cousin was sipping his soda. "This might work. The group, I mean."

Rose and Madison cocked their heads at Cole. Rose furrowed her brow. "What do you mean?"

"Well, usually, you need three class types to succeed in most games," Cole elaborated. "A tank, a healer and dps."

"DPS?" Madison asked. She thought she remembered hearing that abbreviation, but she couldn't recall it at the moment.

"DPS... Damage per second," Michael explained.

"Right." Cole nodded. "The tank holds the monster's attention, the healer - you know - heals, and the two dps, or damage dealers, burn it down."

Rose and Madison both nodded, the concept seeming somewhat straightforward.

"So, if I'm a fighter, that means I'm the tank. If Rose is a druid, she'll be the healer..." Cole stated.

"Oh, a druid is a healer?" Rose asked. "And they get animals?"

"Generally," Cole said. "I mean, a druid is generally a nature person, so they get spells that have to do with plants and animals."

Rose brightened. "Oh, that sounds like fun."

Nodding, Cole continued. "That means Rose would be the healer, and then if Michael and Madison are both pet classes, then we have the magic formula."

Madison looked at Rose and they both shrugged. They'd figure it out.

"What was that about the money?" Rose asked, her eyes darting to her parents in the pool. "We will be winning some money, right?"

Cole shrugged slowly. "I mean, we CAN win money. But there are no details on what we have to do to win money. Hopefully, there will be some sort of system message or something that tells us."

Rose leaned in again and lowered her voice. "That was kind of my selling point with this thing - that we'd be making money. Otherwise, my mom wanted me to find a part-time job."

"I'm sure we'll win something," Michael said. "I mean, we just pick a big city and there should be tons of quests. One of them is bound to win us one of the prizes."

"I hope so," Rose said with a worried expression. "Otherwise, I'll have to get a job."

The group went quiet for several minutes. The only sound was the sound of Lacie giggling in the water and the cooing sounds Rose's parents made to the toddler.

Finally, Cole looked at his phone. He looked at Madison. "We should get going so we can stop at the store and pick up the groceries and put them away before Mom gets home."

Madison looked at her own phone and nodded. She looked up. "We're all meeting online tomorrow at 8am, right?"

"8am?" groaned Michael. "That's too much like school."

"Hey, you guys wanted to play all day," Madison snapped. "Let's get an early start and then we can have the evening free."

"Oh," Rose said suddenly. "How do we know where to start so we can all see each other?"

Cole nodded. "I got an email. They've registered us as a team, so the game will automatically put us all in the same starting city. They said we can go our separate ways after we appear, but each team starts off together."

"Cool," Rose replied. "I'll see you guys tomorrow then."

"See you tomorrow," Madison told them.

4

"Welcome to the land of Koyesta," a voice boomed as Madison entered the game.

It was the strangest sensation. She felt like she was floating weightless in the darkness for a moment before things began to fade into existence.

Suddenly, Madison was standing in an enormous room that seemed to have no walls but stretched on into infinity with marble pillars spaced every ten feet. The architecture of the pillars reminded her of pictures of Roman or Greek pillars.

She glanced from side to side but there was nothing but pillars for several hundred feet before they disappeared into a swirling mist. It was the same all around her. Just the same emptiness surrounded by swirling gray mist.

"Where am I?" she muttered then stopped as the voice that came out of her mouth sounded strange and hollow.

Madison glanced down at herself to see a transparent, wavering form that vaguely looked humanoid. It was also transparent. She gasped. Was she a ghost? Some sort of spirit?!

"You are on the cusp of the underworld, my child," came a clear, female voice from behind her.

Startled, Madison spun towards the voice and came face to face with a shimmering golden image of a woman. A woman who was twenty feet tall. Madison swallowed involuntarily.

The woman was beautiful, like, supermodel beautiful. With flawless skin and long, wavy hair that cascaded down to the middle of her lower back. The huge woman smiled down at her.

"Who are you?" Madison asked, her voice cracking. She cleared her throat and then tried again. "Who are you?"

"I am Mordra, the mother of all things, mistress of the tapestry of life," she replied, still smiling. "You were dead, but Thorakar, the Father of Skies, and King of the Gods, has decreed that your work is not done in Koyesta."

"I'm dead?" Madison asked. She brought her hands up to her face and sure enough, she could see right through them. She certainly looked like a spirit. Was this how the game started? Was she dead?

"Yes, my child," the goddess replied. "But we have stopped you from your final descent. Your work in Koyesta is not complete. I will send you back."

"Cool," Madison replied and looked at the large woman expectantly.

The goddess frowned, somehow still managing to look absolutely gorgeous.

"Is something wrong?" Madison asked.

"The threads of your journey, of your life, are missing," the goddess replied. She shook her head. "The great serpent has devoured your history. I will need to build a new life and a new body for you to return to. I will ask you questions, and we will weave you back into the tapestry of life."

Madison nodded. She guessed this was the character creation that Cole had told her about. "Go ahead and ask."

"When you were on Koyesta," she said. "What race were you born of?"

Suddenly, a holographic picture of a large man and woman dressed in furs stood before her. Next to the image was some text in golden letters.

Barbarian
Making their home in the harsh frozen tundra of the Southlands, these mighty warriors are the strong and fiercest of humans.

Madison reached out to touch the image but as she moved her hand, the image shifted. Suddenly, she was looking at slim, ebony-skinned elves with long tapered ears and sharp features. The two had pale, ivory hair and glowing red eyes. They looked... sinister.

Deep Elf
Cast away by their lighter brethren for the worship of the dark goddess, Solestria, these deep elves retreated deep into the hollow earth where the magical radiation from the dark sun warped and twisted them into creatures of evil.

Madison shook her head and quickly gestured past the various races to see if dragons were a playable race. She got to the end and it cycled back to Barbarian.

She sighed. Not off to a good start. But she remembered one of the races looked a bit like dragons. Gesturing through the various races, she stopped on a lizard-dragon hybrid race.

Drakkar
Originally the spawn of dragons and humans, Drakkar have become their own race. Hailing from the island of Aragorath, they worship the dark dragon goddess, Yaramoth. They work to bring all things into the void with Yaramoth and feed her never-ending appetite.

Madison frowned. She liked the idea of being part dragon, but she didn't want to be evil. Could she be good? She turned to the waiting goddess.

"If I chose an evil race, do I have to be evil? Can I be a good Drakkar?" she asked.

"Your path is your own," Mordra replied. "But know that if you break from your people, you may not be welcome back among them."

Madison nodded. If she chose to be a good Drakkar, the other Drakkars wouldn't like her. She shrugged. That was fine. It sounded like they were from some island anyway. She may not even run into them. Finding no way to select Drakkar, she turned back to the goddess. "I want to be a Drakkar."

"You are a Drakkar." Mordra nodded. The goddess did

something in the air and threads appeared briefly and then disappeared.

Suddenly, Madison felt like ants were crawling up and down her body. She shivered and opened her mouth to scream as she moved her arms across her body to brush them off.

She stopped as she saw her hands. They were no longer translucent. Instead, they were long, slim and taloned. She blinked. She had scaled hands. Madison moved her fingers and then giggled as the talons moved in response to her will.

Looking down at the rest of her body, she saw that she was bipedal but completely scaled. She was a Drakkar!

Then a strange sensation in her butt caused her to look behind her. There, emerging from the base of her spine was a lizard-like tail. She tried to move it and it responded to her thoughts, moving first left, then right. She shuddered. "That is so weird."

"What was your profession when you were previously alive," the goddess asked, seeming oblivious to Madison's fascination with her new body.

A new series of holograms came up and she realized this was where she picked her class. Swiping through the various classes, she read each description carefully.

Originally, she had wanted to be a sorceress - someone who could do magic. But, in this game there were several classes who could do magic. There was a wizard, a sorcerer, a necromancer and an enchanter.

Each had different abilities, but she had no idea which one would be the best. Necromancer was definitely out. She didn't want to be summoning dead people. That was just gross and disturbing. Wizard and Sorcerer both looked good, but Enchanter intrigued her.

Enchanter
Specializing in magic of the mind, Enchanters are able to manipulate the thoughts of others, as well as being able to create illusions and manipulate force itself to create constructs. They are the only class capable of enchanting metals for magical items.

Madison read the description several times. She bit her scaly lip, the sensation strange and a bit unsettling. She really did FEEL herself biting her lip. It was weird. Very weird. This took virtual reality to a whole new level.

She wanted to experiment more, but her movements were limited at the moment. She would need to finish up creating her character before she could play around and see the limits of this virtual reality.

Looking at the hologram, she read the description of the Enchanter again. It wasn't quite what she had in mind, but she really liked the idea of being able to create illusions and manipulate people. She smiled. She wondered if the spells would work on her brother. She sighed. Probably not.

Making up her mind, she turned to Mordra. "I am an Enchanter... er... Enchantress."

Mordra nodded and created more threads from nothing that glowed briefly and then disappeared. "You are an enchantress.

"What god or goddess do you worship?" Mordra asked.

Madison hesitated as holograms of gods and goddesses appeared. She wasn't sure how she felt about choosing one. She looked over at Mordra. "Do I have to choose one?"

"No, my child," the goddess replied. "Not all denizens worship a deity and some worship multiple deities."

"I'll go with none for now," she announced.

"You are agnostic, understood." More threads appeared and then disappeared.

"What special ability were you born with?" the goddess asked and more images appeared that she had to cycle through.

Gesturing through the abilities, several of them stuck out. In the end, she decided to go with an ability called Draconic Ancestry.

Draconic Ancestry

The dragon blood in your veins is especially strong, toughening your scales and giving you small wings that you can use to glide from heights, taking no damage from falls. Your dragon blood also grants you the use of your ancestral dragon's breath weapon once per day.

No sooner had she told the goddess her choice when she felt that strange ants on her skin feeling in her back as large, bat-like wings sprouted from her back.

"Cool," she muttered and with a thought caused the wings to furl and unfurl. She grinned. "Very cool."

"What was the color of your dragon ancestor?" Mordra asked.

Dragons appeared before her and she paged through

them until she found what she wanted - a blue dragon. And its breath weapon was lightning!

"Blue!" she said without hesitation. "Definitely blue!"

Almost instantly, her greenish scales turned a deep azure blue with an almost incandescent look to them. It was actually very pretty.

She went through the remaining tasks quickly, knowing that her brother and cousins were probably waiting on her.

Finally, she gave her last answer and the goddess created a thread that disappeared again. Mordra turned to her and spoke. "You are ready to return to Koyesta. Your threads are woven into the tapestry of life now. Should you fall in battle, the threads will lead you here and you may return to your world through that portal."

A glowing golden portal opened next to Madison so suddenly that she jumped back. Feeling stupid, she stood up straight and looked at the portal. Through it, she saw what appeared to be a small medieval village.

"Go now," the goddess said. "Return to Koyesta. It needs you more than ever."

Stepping into the golden portal, the world around her dissolved and she was suddenly somewhere else.

5

Madison shivered as she appeared on a rocky shoreline, a cool wind blowing in from the ocean. She squinted reptilian eyes as the sun momentarily blinded her, so much brighter than the area she had just been in. Shielding her eyes from the warm sun with a scaled hand, her forked tongue snaked out of her mouth involuntarily. As it did, she smelled the salty air, slightly tainted with a scent of fish.

She blinked. Madison was actually feeling the warm sunshine on her scales and she could actually smell the ocean - through her tongue! She shook her head. How was this possible? How could she be getting all of these sensations?

"Please tell me that's not you, Madison?" came a booming voice from behind her.

Spinning and dropping into a crouch, Madison was immediately assaulted by a translucent screen that appeared in front of her vision. A heads-up display, or

HUD, she realized. On the screen were several options, including challenging a player to a duel.

As she mentally wondered how to dismiss the annoying screen, it faded away. Had she done that? She would figure it out later. At the moment, she was faced with a nearly seven-foot-tall muscle-bound man with a huge, two-handed sword resting on his shoulder.

The young man looked like some sort of action movie star, with bulging muscles and body fat so low that every single muscle fiber seemed to be visible. He had a chiseled jaw, thick eyebrows and long, wavy brown hair that hung down just below his shoulders. On his chest was a blue tattoo of a raven clutching an axe in one claw and a sword in the other.

He was clad only in a kilt of green and blues and sandals, giving him a Celtic or Scottish look. Other than those simple clothes, the only other thing he held was the gigantic sword and a metal bracer on his right hand. Looking closer, Madison saw a rope that went from the metal bracer to the hilt of the sword. She wondered what that was for? Was that so he wouldn't lose it?

"It's you, isn't it?" the man said in his deep voice.

Squinting at the man, she realized there was a familiarity to the man as well. Something about the nose and the eyes. She blinked at him. "Cole?"

"Cole?" the man chuckled. "I am Sir Brothar Snowbear!"

Madison rolled her eyes. "It is you, Cole! Your name is... Brothar? Like Brother?"

"No," the big man said, shaking his large head. "Brothar... like BRO... THAR!"

She shook her head slowly at him, but he was unfazed. He stretched his arms out wide and breathed in. "How cool is this! I can smell the ocean and... uh... cooking fires, I think." Excitedly, he pointed down to his feet. "I can actually feel the grains of sand in my sandals!"

A human approached them, dressed only in a leather loincloth and sandals. He was maybe five feet, ten inches with short, brown hair. He was slim but cut like Cole's avatar, a chiseled six-pack showing on his slender physique. In his left hand, he carried a wood club but otherwise didn't seem to have any other belongings. Wandering behind him was a tiger cub. At least, it looked like a tiger except it was dark gray with slightly lighter grey stripes.

If the slight resemblance to her cousin and the cat trailing him hadn't given him away, the huge grin he broke into when he saw them did. "Cole? Madison?"

Cole stood up to his full height and flexed his muscles. "BRO-thar Snowbear... shorty!"

Michael chuckled. "Bro-thar! I like it! I am Zachatolus Catfriend."

Cole rolled his eyes at their cousin. "Zachatolus? Catfriend?"

The smaller man just shrugged and grinned. He bent down and picked up the cat. "Check him out. I called him Buddy!"

Cole and Madison exchanged looks and it was obvious that they were resisting rolling their eyes at their cousin. Michael had a big gray cat named Buddy and apparently, he needed one in the game too. Only this one wasn't a real cat, just a simulation.

Holding the now-purring cub, Michael looked at Madison. He cocked his head and then grinned even bigger. "You have wings! How did you get wings?!"

Cole twisted his head to look at her and then walked around and looked at her back. "Whoa! You do have wings! Do they work?! Can you fly?!"

With a thought, Madison unfurled her wings and beat them a few times before folding them back up on her back. "The special ability said something about gliding and not taking damage when I fall, but I don't think I can actually use them to fly."

"Aw," Michael said. "That stinks."

"Yeah," Cole agreed. "That would have been really cool."

Her brother held out his right arm, showing off the metal gauntlet. "My special ability is the Crow Clan. They are able to attach their weapons to rope or chains and throw the weapon and then pull the monster it hits back to them. Sort of like the mortal fighting game and that guy who yells Get Over Here!"

Michael grinned. "Cool!"

Madison was about to ask Michael what his special ability was, but a quiet voice called out to them. "Cole? Michael?"

The three of them turned to see a short, blond-haired young woman who was barely five feet tall. She was extremely petite, but not quite as cut as Michael or Cole. The woman's hair was curly and fell halfway down her back. Poking through her hair were long, tapered ears. Elf ears.

Like Michael, the elf wore a leather loincloth, but

she also had some sort of leather sports bra-looking piece of clothing covering her small breasts. Both the loincloth and the top had leather fringe hanging down, reminding Madison of Native American garb. As if to complete that look, she wore leather moccasins, had red and white face paint and carried a hatchet or tomahawk in her hand.

Madison instantly knew who it was. Other than her ears, she was the spitting image of Rose. “Rose!”

The elf broke out into a smile, then she cocked her head and looked at Madison. Her eyes widened. “Madison?!”

Sighing, Madison nodded. “It’s me.”

Rose did a double take but then shrugged. “You look cool! I like the blue scales.”

Madison smiled. “Thanks!”

Looking at the two boys, Rose pointed to each of them in turn. “Cole? Michael?”

They grinned in acknowledgement.

“WAIT?! WHAT?!!” Rose exclaimed suddenly as she caught sight of Michael’s pet. “You have a tiger cub?!”

Rushing over to the cub, she began to pet him and scratch his chin. “What’s his name?”

“Buddy,” Michael replied with a grin.

Rose nodded. “Like your cat.”

Michael bobbed his head.

“What’s your character’s name?” Cole asked Rose.

“Plays-With-Animals,” Rose replied with a shrug. “I think these elves are like Native Americans. So, I tried to think of a name that would fit.”

Cole nodded and then turned to Madison. Towering

over her, he looked down. "What about you? You never told us your name."

Seeing that everyone had turned to look at her, Madison gave them all a sheepish smile. "I didn't really know what to pick. I went with Draconia Manasinger."

Her brother nodded in approval. "That sounds very in character. I approve."

Rose pouted at them. "I wanted an animal. How come he gets one and I don't?"

Cole shrugged. "I think druids have spells to like... charm animals. You can eventually get different animals to be your companions. Michael will only ever have the one. Right, Michael?"

Michael nodded, holding the furry, purring bundle in his arms. "Yeah. Buddy is soul bound to me. That means he will respawn with me. But he's the only animal companion I can have."

Rose frowned. "How do I find out what spells I have? Oh! Something popped up!"

"Yeah," Cole said with a nod. "I think the HUD is controlled by your thoughts. Just think about it and it comes up."

Rose's eyes moved back and forth and Madison assumed she was reading something in her HUD. Apparently, their HUDs were only visible to themselves. Probably a good thing. While Rose read her spells, Madison brought up her own HUD and looked at the information presented.

Name: Draconia Manasinger
Class: Enchanter

Level: 1
Health: 16
Mana: 42
Stamina: 100%
Experience: 0
Needed for Next Level: 1000
Race: Drakkar
Sex: Female
Strength: 70
Agility: 90
Reflexes: 95
Hardiness: 70
Intellect: 100
Wisdom: 95
Charisma: 55
Languages: Common, Draconic, Artoshian, Valharian
Special Ability: Draconic Ancestry
Skills:
Weapon
Blunt 1Hand
Blunt 2Hand
Small Blades
Magic
Abjuration: 1
Alteration: 1
Channeling: 1
Divination: 1
Evocation: 1
Meditation: 1
Other
Runes: 1

History: 1
Archeology: 1
Spells:
Minor Force Shield
Minor Telekinetic Asphyxiation

Madison furrowed her brow as she looked at all of the information. It was a bit overwhelming, and she wasn't sure what most of the stuff did. It appeared like she could mentally "click" on things and get more information. She was about to do just that when Rose spoke.

Eyes coming back in focus, Rose pouted again. "There's no spell for charming animals!"

"You might get it later, at a higher level," Cole told her, holding up his hands in a placating gesture. "Don't worry, we'll level up quickly since we have a balanced group."

Rose bit her lip but nodded. "Fine. Let's level up then."

They all looked around at the beach they had found themselves on and then at the medieval village. Madison raised a scaly eyebrow. "Maybe we should check out the village first."

"Good idea!" Cole agreed. "There's probably quests in there for us to do!"

After a moment of affirming nods, the others followed Madison into the small town.

6

Their motley crew strode into the village, looking less like adventurers and more like homeless renaissance faire performers. Madison did finally remember to look down at herself to make sure that she was wearing something to cover her private parts. Luckily, she was wearing something similar to Rose - only hers was threadbare cloth instead of leather.

The streets of the village consisted of hard-packed dirt and wide enough for two carts to pass, side by side. The buildings were simple, mostly single-story structures, decorated in the Tudor style. They looked worn but serviceable, probably indicating the village had been here for a while.

Villagers were garbed simply. The women wore simple dresses in dark colors, while the men wore pants and tunics. Any of the villagers who looked their way scowled and then hurried away.

"I don't think they like us," Rose noticed.

"They are probably intimidated by my manliness," Cole replied, starting to strut. He did his best Schwarzenegger impression. "I am... pumped up!"

Michael chuckled but Madison and Rose looked at each other and rolled their eyes. Then Madison noticed that the people scowling didn't really seem to be looking at Cole. They were looking at her.

Suddenly, she remembered that she was one of the "evil" races. She grabbed Cole's arm just as two men in chain mail came running around one of the buildings!

"Enemy!" one of them cried. "You never should have come here!"

"Devil-beast!" yelled the other.

Before anyone could react, the first of the two guards reached her and swung his sword. Just before it hit, she saw her brother going for his sword while her cousins stared wide-eyed at what was happening.

Fisherton Guardsman slices you for 197 damage.

Madison screamed as the blade sliced across her scales, cutting through them and into her soft flesh beneath. She felt it as it cut through flesh and organs, obviously doing enough damage to kill her. As she collapsed to the ground, her vision fading to darkness, she just managed to glimpse Michael grabbing Cole before everything went black.

You have died.
Your equipment has suffered damage.

Note: Because you are not yet level 5, there is no death penalty.

The next moment, Madison was back at the strange place she had started. She immediately looked down and saw that her body was completely healed. She felt the area. It wasn't even tender.

She shook her head and gritted her teeth. That had REALLY hurt! If she were to get sliced by a sword, Madison was certain it would feel very similar. She shuddered. It was all too real.

Was that how everything worked with this virtual reality world? Everything felt the way it would in real life? That seemed terrifying. What if you fell into lava? Or drowned? Did the game simulate all of that?

Pushing off the question for another time, Madison looked around. She was definitely in the same place where she'd started. The pillars and the fog were there, as was the golden gate, but there was no sign of the goddess who had interacted with her the first time.

She looked at the gate. Madison hesitated. Should she go through it? What if she came back to the same spot? Would she be killed again? She bit her scaly lip.

Sighing, she realized she couldn't stay here forever. She'd go through the portal and then make a run for it back to the beach. It had seemed safe there. At the very least, no one had attacked them. It was as good a plan as any - go through the portal and run for the beach! Taking a deep breath, she took several steps and plunged into the shimmering portal.

There was a moment of vertigo and then Madison

appeared elsewhere. She spun to begin running but realized she was already at the beach.

"It's probably our respawn point," a voice said from behind her.

"Ahh!" she screamed, spinning towards the voice. She relaxed as she saw her brother and cousins.

Rose bit her lip and then gestured to the ground. "We dragged your body over here for you."

"My.... body...?" Madison repeated and looked down.

Sure enough, her blue-scaled body was lying there with a huge slice through the chest. She swallowed and tried not to be sick. Madison looked up. "Why did I just leave a body?"

"You must have gear on your old body," Michael said, gesturing down to it. "Loot it and it should disappear." He looked suddenly embarrassed. "Um... also... you're almost naked right now."

Cole snickered. "Huh... I didn't even notice."

Rose chuckled and bobbed her head. "Uh... yeah. That's like... a thong."

Embarrassed, Madison looked down to see that they were right. She wore what some people might think of as a string bikini - a TINY string bikini - that barely hid anything! She went to cover herself with her arms and somehow the game interpreted that as she needed to be covered. Her wings unfurled and wrapped themselves around her, obscuring her front from them.

"Whoa," Michael gasped. "Nice! They're like a built-in cloak or something."

"Michael! Cole! Turn around!" she demanded. Chuckling, the boys did so.

With their backs to her, she looked pleadingly at Rose. "Help me get dressed!"

Rose looked around in confusion and shrugged. "How?"

Bending down, Madison reached to her loincloth to pull it off her dead body and immediately a menu came up.

Your Corpse
Worn Bottom
Worn Top
Cracked club
Loot all (Yes/No)

Madison looked at the list of items and with a thought looted them all. As she did, her previous body dissolved into glittering dust that fell to the ground and slowly faded away. That was fine with her. She really didn't need a copy of her body lying around for everyone to look at.

Looking down at herself, Madison saw that she was still in the thong. She growled in frustration. "I looted my stuff. Why isn't it showing on me?!"

Cole half turned his head. "It's in your inventory. Just equip it."

"Equip it how..." she started to say but her HUD popped up with a list of items and a representation of herself. Currently, she had 3 items in her inventory list and nothing on her body. With a thought, she equipped everything and was suddenly dressed. She also held a club in her hand. "Oh... uh... you can turn back around now."

The two boys turned and nodded. Cole grimaced. "Sorry. I didn't even think about your faction. Drakkars are the evil alliance. You'll probably be kill on sight in all the good towns and villages."

Madison sagged. "Are you serious?"

Cole looked at Michael and they both nodded. Michael gave her an apologetic look. "You'll have to raise your reputation with the town before they let you walk around."

"And how do I do that?" she grumbled. She had been so happy with being a Drakkar. Now, she was starting to regret her choice since they were in the "good" lands.

Cole brightened, he held out one of his meaty fingers. "One, doing quests. Right now, that's probably out since you won't be able to get to a quest giver in the city.

"Two," he held up another finger. "Usually, there are some enemies of the village or area that killing will give you reputation with the town." He frowned. "But that might be a lot of grinding."

He held up a third finger and looked thoughtful. "Third, there may be some outlying quest givers who might be neutral enough to talk with you but still give town faction."

Madison looked at her brother hopefully. "Which do we do?"

Michael nudged Cole in the ribs with his elbow. "We can go into the town and ask around. It shouldn't be too hard to learn if there are town enemies. When we find out, we can come back, get you, and we all go start grinding reputation."

Madison let out a frustrated breath. "Fine. Go ahead. I'll wait here."

"Don't worry," Cole said in his deep voice. "I'll be back!"

"You want me to stay with you?" Rose asked Madison.

"No, go ahead with them." Madison shook her head. She looked out across the beach and then at the club in her hand. "I think I might take out my frustrations on those crabs."

Michael chuckled and Cole nodded. "Just be careful. They're probably level 1 crabs - the same level as you."

Nodding, Madison shooed them away with a gesture. "Sure. Sure. Just go find out what we have to do so I don't get killed again."

"Ok," Cole said and then waved the others to follow him. Michael and Rose hurried after him, Rose throwing one last look over her shoulder at Madison.

Watching them disappear into the town, Madison sighed and hefted her club. She was frustrated and she needed to work it out. She glanced back at the beach and saw the large crabs scurrying around the water.

"Ok Mr. Crabs," she said, turning towards the beach. "Time to die!"

7

Madison's first attempt at killing a poor, defenseless crab did not go as expected. Apparently, the crab was a level 1 creature and was nearly as powerful as she was. The thing didn't attack her as she approached. It ignored her, content to go about its business hunting for things on the beach.

The crab was just under a foot wide. It was larger than the crabs she'd seen at the beach in Ocean City, but not as large as the king crabs she'd seen pictures of. Its shell was a mottled gray color with flecks of a lighter gray around the borders. It had two normal-sized claws, rather than one big claw and one little claw, like some crabs. It seemed in every way something she'd see in the real world.

She smiled confidently. She should be able to crush the thing with one blow of her club. It wasn't until she slammed her club down on the thing's shell that the problems ensued.

You crush Beach Crab for 3 damage.
You have become better at Offense (+1%).

Immediately the crab turned, and her HUD appeared red in her vision. The crab raced forward and tried to pinch her with its claws.

Beach Crab pierces you for 1 damage.
Beach Crab misses you.
You have become better at Defense (+1%).

Madison yelped as one of the claws found an opening in between her scales. The thing really hurt! Growing angry at the crab, she slammed her club down on the top of its carapace but the blow slid off.

You miss Beach Crab.
You have become better at Offense (+1%).

Frustrated, she pulled the club back for another strike. As she did, the crab darted in for another go at her.

Beach Crab pierces you for 1 damage.
Beach Crab pierces you for 1 damage.
You have become better at Defense (+1%).

"Ahh!" she growled in pain as both claws found their mark on her ankle. She tried to dance back from the crab, but it scrambled towards her, intent on revenge.

She smashed her club down on it again. This time, it hit with a satisfying crunch.

You crush Beach Crab for 5 damage.
You have become better at Offense (+1%).

Unfortunately, the crab was still alive. She gritted her teeth. "What is this? Super crab?"

Beach Crab misses you.
Beach Crab misses you.
You have become better at Defense (+1%).

The crab retaliated with both of its claws but this time - thankfully - they couldn't penetrate her scales.

"Die, crab!" she yelled and brought the club down again on its shell.

You crush Beach Crab for 3 damage.
You have become better at Offense (+1%).

Again, there was a satisfying crunching sound as her club impacted the thing. And yet, the crab was still alive. It scrambled forward and snipped at her.

Beach Crab pierces you for 1 damage.
Beach Crab pierces you for 1 damage.
You have become better at Defense (+1%).

"Argh!" she winced, taking two more pinches from the claws. She kicked at the crab with her clawed feet, but it scurried away. "Stupid crab!"

She once again brought her wooden cudgel down on the thing's head but her aim was slightly off and it skidded off the side of its carapace.

You miss Beach Crab.
You have become better at Offense (+1%).

The crab did not miss.

Beach Crab pierces you for 1 damage.
Beach Crab pierces you for 1 damage.
You have become better at Defense (+1%).

"Ow!" she growled. "Die already!"

Madison brought the club down on the crab again, managing a solid hit in the center of its shell.

You crush Beach Crab for 5 damage.
You have become better at Offense (+1%).

The crab looked a little worse for wear, but that didn't stop it from retaliating with its dual pincers of pain.

Beach Crab misses you.
Beach Crab pierces you for 1 damage.
You have become better at Defense (+1%).

Screaming at the crab, Madison brought the club down as hard as she could. This time, there was a louder cracking sound as she made contact with the creature.

You crush Beach Crab for 5 damage.
You have become better at Offense (+1%).

You have killed Beach Crab.
You have gained experience!

"Ha!" she laughed aloud as the crab stopped moving. She pointed her club at the dead crab in the sand. "That'll teach you!"

Madison realized she could feel her heart thudding in her chest and her breath was coming quickly. She shook her head slowly. This game really was like real life. Well, except for the fact that the crab probably would have gone running away in real life and not tried to kill her - even if she did hit it first.

Smiling at her victory, she looked down at the dead crab and her HUD popped up.

Beach Crab Corpse
Crab Meat (x2)
Crab Carapace (x1)
Loot all (Yes/No)

Unsure what to do with either of those items but hesitant to leave them, Madison looted everything. When she finished, the crab's corpse dissolved into glittering dust, similar to her own corpse when it had been looted. The dust remained on the ground for a few seconds before it too faded away.

The pain from her wounds had faded, but she felt something wasn't quite right. She brought up her HUD and looked at her statistics.

Name: Draconia Manasinger

Class: Enchanter
Level: 1
Health: 8
Mana: 42
Stamina: 65%
Experience: 100
Needed for Next Level: 900

It looked as if she were down to half of her Health. As she looked at the number, it ticked up from 8 to 9. Good, she was regenerating her Health on her own. That was good. She wouldn't have to wait for Rose to come back and heal her.

Looking at her Stamina, she saw that it was at 65, no... 66... 67. Even as she watched, the Stamina seemed to recover a point every second. Interesting, that meant it regenerated much more quickly than Health, which was still hovering at 9.

Scanning further on her character sheet, Madison saw she had gained 100 experience for killing the crab! She did a little happy dance, then looked around to make sure no one had seen her. Nope. No one but the crabs and a few seagulls.

She needed 900 more experience for her next level. If each crab gave her 100 experience, she just needed to kill 9 more crabs.

Madison hesitated. The pain from those crabs was all too real. She bent down and examined her ankles. There didn't seem to be any lasting wounds but the memory of the crab's claws was still fresh in her mind.

Suddenly, Madison felt stupid as she looked at her

character sheet. She was supposed to be an Enchantress. A magic user. And she'd been whacking the crab with a club. That was something her brother should do with that big sword of his. She rubbed her forehead.

She needed to start acting - and fighting - like a mage. She sighed. Maybe then she wouldn't get so beat up.

Looking at the spells she had access to, she read each of their descriptions.

Minor Force Shield
Mana: 10
Duration: 5 minutes/level
Description: Creates an aura of force that surrounds your body, granting you additional armor and phantom Health.

Minor Telekinetic Asphyxiation
Mana: 8
Duration: 5 seconds
Description: Afflicts the target with an enchanted hand that continues to choke them, doing damage and weakening the target.
Note: Requires the need to breathe. Does not work on undead or automatons.

Madison read the descriptions several times to make sure she understood them. Unfortunately, both were lacking in details. How much armor did she get from the Shield Spell? How much Health? How much damage did the asphyxiation do? How much did it weaken them?

She checked her Mana.

Mana: 42

That was enough for one shield spell and four of the choking spells. Would that be enough? She had no idea. And unfortunately, there was really only one way to find out. She checked her Health.

Health: 12

It would still be a few more minutes until she was full Health and she didn't want to cast the shielding spell until it was back at max. That way, she could see exactly how much phantom Health she received from the spell.

Madison hefted her club and looked out at the many crabs that scattered the beach. She shook her head and smiled. "So many crabs. So little time."

8

Once again, things didn't go as expected for Madison. Her choking spell barely did any damage and that was when it worked. Half the time, she would cast it and it would fizzle. This became extremely frustrating.

When she'd picked Enchanter, she had envisioned casting mind-blowing spells and dealing death to her enemies from afar. The reality was very lackluster. But she stuck with it and eventually figured out a method.

She would first cast her shielding spell on herself. Then, she would cast the choking spell on a crab. The spell did only a few points of damage, but she noticed that it did weaken the crabs to a point where they missed nearly half the time. Combined with her shield and extra Health, she made short work of the crabs.

By the time her friends returned, Madison had earned second level. That was when she was in for a nasty surprise. She hit 1,000 experience on her 10th kill. She was immediately enveloped in a pale golden aura that gave her shivers down her spine.

The nasty surprise came when Madison looked at her character sheet.

Experience: 1000
Needed for Next Level: 8000

Madison cried out in frustration. She would need 7,000 more experience to reach the next level. At 100 experience per crab, that was 70 crabs. That was when her brother and cousins showed up.

"Everything... okay?" Cole asked in his deep voice.

Making a face, Madison crossed her arms over her chest. "I made level 2 and now I need 7,000 more experience to make level 3!"

Chaos erupted among the others.

"You made level 2?"

"How'd you make level 2?"

"Did you get any good loot?"

"Show me how to level too!"

The rapid-fire questions took Madison by surprise and she held up her hands to quiet everyone down. When they stopped talking, she put her hands on her hips. "One at a time. Rose, you first."

"How did you level? Can you show me?" she asked enthusiastically. "I need to get more spells!"

"I killed crabs," Madison said with a shrug. "It's easy. You just go out there and whack them. Cole, you're next."

"Oh." Cole grinned. "Ah... I was just going to say good

job making level 2. I was going to ask what you did but you just answered that."

Giving him a nod, she turned to Michael and raised an eyebrow.

Michael just grinned. "What Cole said."

Madison let out a frustrated breath and looked at the others. "Did you find out anything?"

Once more chaos erupted as everyone tried to talk over each other. At one point they all stopped talking, looked at each other as if to let the other person talk, then when no one did, they all started talking again.

"One at a time, please," Madison said, rubbing her forehead. She had a headache, and it wasn't from them. It had been slowly growing but now it was definitely noticeable.

Cole spoke up. "We learned that there are a group of gnolls that have been harassing the village. They've killed a few villagers on the outskirts, attacked a few merchant caravans and generally make a nuisance out of themselves."

Madison furrowed her brow. "What are gnolls?"

"Dog-headed people," Michael replied, then looked thoughtful. "Well, not really people. They have arms and legs, but they're covered with fur... with dog heads."

"And killing them will make the villagers like me?" Madison inquired.

Cole shrugged. "I don't know if 'like' is the right word. Maybe... hate less."

Madison leveled a glare at her brother, and he grinned. "I thought you said killing them would earn me faction or something..."

"Reputation," Cole corrected. "And it will. But it might not be enough to get you to 'like' status. More like 'we don't hate you enough to kill you on sight' - I hope."

She sighed. "I guess that's better than nothing."

"Actually, I have an idea," he told his sister. "The militia captain gave us a quest to prove that we killed some of the gnolls... uh... what were they called? Blackbeard? Blackburrow?"

"Blackmange gnolls," Rose supplied helpfully.

"Right." Cole nodded. "We need to return 10 Blackmange claws to him and we'll get some experience and reputation with the city."

"But I can't get the quest," Madison protested. "I can't even get in the town."

"Even if you could get the quest," Michael added, "you couldn't turn it in."

"Right," Cole told them. "But if we start killing the gnolls and saving the claws. Once you get enough reputation where you can actually walk into town, we will give you all the claws to turn in. Then boom, a massive jump in reputation."

Madison shot her brother a puzzled look. "You can do the quest more than once?"

"It says 'repeatable' on it," Rose said, her eyes moving back and forth as she read her HUD. "So, I guess so."

"That sounds good then," Madison said with a smile. It would be nice to be able to walk through the village without getting killed. Otherwise, she'd be stuck outside the village every time the others went inside.

"Oh wait, let me do something," Cole said and his eyes went glassy as he did something with his HUD.

Madison received a message in her own HUD.

Brothar Snowbear has invited you to join a group.
Do you wish to join (Yes/No)?

She was confused for a second before she remembered that Brothar was the silly name Cole had given to his character. She mentally selected yes.

You have joined a group.

As soon as she saw the message, she also saw little translucent icons appear on the left side of her vision. Under each icon was the person's name, as well as red and blue bars that she guessed showed their Health and Mana.

"This way, we'll share experience and we can also share quests," Cole said. "Hold on."

Brothar Snowbear has shared a quest with you.

You have received a new quest "Blackmange Bounty"
Fisherton Militia Captain Bartem does not have enough guards to protect the village and go after the marauding Blackmange gnolls. He has asked you to thin their numbers and bring back a claw from each one you kill.
Return 10 claws to Captain Bartem for a reward.
Reward: 10 copper rook, Minor Item (x1), +100 reputation with Residents of Fisherton, +100 reputation with Guards of Fisherton.
Accept quest (yes or no)?

Madison read the quest and quickly accepted. She piqued an eyebrow at her brother. "What's a copper rook?"

Cole groaned and the others did too.

"What?" Madison asked.

"It's like... a penny," Rose said. "There's copper, silver and gold."

"Don't forget platinum and mythryll," Michael said with a roll of his eyes.

Her brother sighed. "We looked at a couple of the shops. Everything's expensive. Most things cost silver and gold."

"And copper is the lowest money?" Madison asked.

Cole nodded. "So, we'll need to like... find a treasure or kill a boss or something if I ever want to buy armor. Even the armorsmithing kit is like 2 silver. That's 200 copper."

"I guess we need to go kill gnolls and loot their corpses," Michael suggested. "They might drop coins and probably loot we can sell. They might even drop armor pieces."

"That's what I'm hoping," Cole agreed.

"I just want experience so I can get that spell that allows me to get some pets," Rose said.

"Then we better get going," Cole said, looking around and then up to the sky. "How long do you think we've been in game?"

"About an hour," Madison replied. "If you include the part where we chose our character."

"We still have several hours before we have to break for lunch," he said. "We should use that time to find the

Blackmange hideout and scout it out - kill as many as we can."

"That sounds like a plan." Michael grinned. "Buddy is hungry for some dog!"

"Do you have any idea where to look?" Madison asked.

"I talked to the captain," Cole told her. "He said there are more raids to the west. I'm thinking they must have a hideout to the west."

"I have a skill called Tracking," Rose said. "Maybe I can find... you know... tracks that will lead us to their hideout."

Cole bit his lip as he looked down at Madison, his massive frame towering over her. "We'll have to skirt the town and then stay just off the road in case we run into any patrols."

Madison rolled her eyes. "Because they'll kill me if they see me."

"Sorry," he said with a small shrug.

"Not your fault," she said. "I'm the one who wanted to be a Drakkar."

"Oh," Cole said, smacking his head. "As we learned with Madison, this is the bind point. If any of us die, this is where we'll reappear. Depending on how far away we die, it'll be a long run in our underwear."

"Thanks for reminding me," Madison murmured, remembering her embarrassing episode. Hopefully, that wouldn't become a common thing. "Let's just go kill some gnolls before lunch!"

9

The group circled the town and then headed down the west road. The others walked on the worn, dirt road while Madison was forced to walk twenty yards off the road whenever they caught sight of any passersby. It was frustrating but hopefully it wouldn't take long for her to earn Reputation with the townsfolk and be able to actually be seen by them.

When they had walked about ten miles from the village, they came to a set of burned and abandoned farms. There were creatures moving about in the farms and even from where she stood, Madison could tell they weren't human.

Cole motioned the group to crouch and led them to an overgrown piece of fencing. When they'd all gathered, he peeked over the edge of the fence. Curious, the others peeked as well, trying to get a view of what was going on in the destroyed field.

A quick glance told Madison they'd found the gnolls.

Or, at least, some of the gnolls. Black and brown-spotted dogmen were running around the field. They were an odd sight - a strange juxtaposition of man and dog.

The lower part of their bodies looked like a dog who was standing on his hind legs. The upper part of the body looked humanoid, complete with hands, fingers and opposable thumbs. To top off the strange sight, the creature had the head of a dog. Madison cocked her head. To her they favored rottweilers, at least in the head.

"Okay," Cole whispered. "I have an ability called Taunt. It will make the creature focus on me. The plan is, I get its attention, spin it and everyone burns it down."

Michael nodded but Madison and Rose exchanged looks. "What?"

Cole sighed. "I will taunt it, so it focuses on me. I'll turn it around so that it faces me and has its back to you. Then everyone beats on it or casts spells at it until it dies. Got it?"

Madison looked at her brother. "Why didn't you just say that to begin with?"

Michael chuckled and her brother just shook his head. Then he glanced between the two girls. "Do either of you two have any buffs?"

"Buffs?" they both asked in unison.

Michael snickered and Cole sighed again. "Spells that will help us. Specifically, spells that will help me since I'm going to be taking the brunt of the damage."

Madison nodded, remembering her shield spell. "I have one that will increase your armor and give you some additional health."

"Cool. That will help," Cole said with a smile. He turned to Rose. "How about you?"

Rose's eyes were glassy as she looked at her HUD and then she nodded. "This one sounds like it will help. Skin of the Tree. It says it makes your skin hard like wood. It says it gives you more armor and more health."

Michael scratched his head. "Sounds like they do the same thing."

"They probably won't stack," Michael noted.

"Let's test them and find out," Cole said. "Cast both of them on me and we'll see if they work together or if one overwrites the others."

Madison quickly cast her spell on him, watching a glowing aura flow from her hands to Cole and then settle over him like a protective cocoon before disappearing.

"Let me check," Cole said. "Yep. I have 6 more health. Okay, Rose, now you."

Rose started doing something and green energy began to coalesce around her hands. It seemed to be reaching a peak and then suddenly it sparked and then disappeared.

The blond elf pouted. "It fizzled."

"That happened to me too in the beginning," Madison explained. "The more you cast it, the less it fizzles."

"That's annoying," Rose complained.

"Just try it again," Cole encouraged.

Rose tried again and again it fizzled. Luckily, on the third try it worked and Cole was surrounded by green light. It lingered on him for a moment and then his skin turned a dark brown. At the same time, it thickened and became pitted - like tree bark.

"Whoa!" Michael said, looking at Cole. "You look like ten-day old pizza."

Cole held up his arm and looked at it. He shrugged. "I don't care, as long as it helps."

Her brother's eyes went glassy, and he frowned. "They don't stack. The barkskin overwrote the shielding spell. But it's okay. It gives me 11 more health. That'll work."

"So, mine's more powerful?" Rose smiled.

"Looks that way," Cole said with a wink at his sister. "Okay. Let's go kill stuff!"

Standing up, the group was startled to see one of the gnolls standing on the opposite side of the fence, sniffing at the air. The dogman jumped back, barked and then pulled a rusty dagger from his belt and lunged forward.

"Over here, cat breath!" Cole yelled but the gnoll continued towards Rose.

Rose screamed and backpedaled away from the gnoll. As she scrambled to get away from it, Cole yelled "Get over here!" and threw his huge sword at the gnoll. It hit the dogman in the back, eliciting a yelp of pain.

Brothar Snowbear impales Blackmange Gnoll Pup for 9 damage.

Cole then jerked back on the rope connected to his sword and yanked the gnoll back to him. The dogman yelped again as he was pulled away from Rose, only to get whacked again by Michael. At the same time, Buddy - his tiger cub - bounded forward and sank his teeth into the gnoll's leg.

Zachatolus Catfriend crushes Blackmange Gnoll Pup for 2 damage.
Buddy bites Blackmange Gnoll Pup for 3 damage.

"Come here, you flea-bitten mutt!" Cole yelled and this time, the gnoll turned to face him just as Cole pulled his sword free. It stabbed her brother in the arm with its dagger.

Blackmange Gnoll Pup pierces Brothar Snowbear for 2 damage.

"Ow!" screamed Cole, flinching away. "That actually hurt! What the heck?"

Madison tried not to smile. She had meant to tell them about that but had completely forgotten. But it was kind of funny watching her brother in his big, barbarian body feeling the same pain she had from those stupid crabs.

Remembering what they were here for, Madison rushed forward and brought her club across the gnoll's head. Its head snapped to the side and the creature collapsed to the ground.

You crush Blackmange Gnoll Pup for 4 damage.
You have become better at Offense (+1%).
You have killed Blackmange Gnoll Pup.
You have gained experience!
Your reputation with Residents of Fisherton has increased.

Your reputation with Guards of Fisherton has increased.
Your reputation with Blackmange Gnolls has decreased.

"That really hurt," Cole repeated, rubbing the spot where the gnoll had stabbed him. He stopped and turned an accusatory gaze on Madison. "You could have warned us."

Suppressing a smile, Madison shrugged. "Sorry, I forgot."

Cole made a face that indicated he didn't believe her but before he could say anything else, Michael let out a frustrated breath. "That stinks! That thing was only worth 25 experience! That's a lot of gnolls just to hit level 2."

Madison checked her own experience.

Experience: 1025

Sure enough, Michael was right. It was a quarter of the experience she had gotten from the crabs. She started to wonder why that was but Cole answered.

"We're grouped, so it's splitting the experience," he told them. "It's pretty standard. But, we can kill more as a group so in the long run, it will be more experience for the same amount of time."

"That makes sense," Madison said, thinking about how long it had taken her to kill the crabs. Together, they'd taken down the gnoll much more quickly.

"Rose," Cole said, looking over at the elf. "You can't run away during a fight."

Rose gave them a guilty look. “Sorry. It scared me at first.”

“That one was easy,” he explained. “But there will be much stronger ones and we all have to work together.”

“I won’t run again,” Rose assured them.

Michael reached down and touched the gnoll’s corpse. “Let’s see what this puppy was carrying.”

Blackmange Gnoll Pup Corpse
Rusty Dagger
Gnoll Claw
100 Koyesta Coins
Loot all (Yes/No)

The screen popped up for only a second and then someone must have hit loot because it suddenly disappeared, just as the gnoll’s body dissolved into golden dust.

“Wait!” Cole said. “What was…”

Congratulations! You were the first group on the server to kill a Blackmange Gnoll Pup. You have been rewarded Koyesta Coins.
You may check your rewards by going to Character Menu-> Profile -> Rewards -> Early Access Awards

“Did we just get a prize?” Rose asked, eyes wide. “What are …uh… Koyesta coins?”

Michael’s eyes went glassy, followed by Cole’s. A moment later, both of them had disappointed looks on their faces.

Cole frowned as his eyes came back into focus. "It looks like it's some sort of internet money."

"Cryptocurrency," Michael corrected.

"You mean, like Bitcoin?" Madison asked. She was proud that she actually knew what cryptocurrency was and that she's read some articles on it.

Michael nodded. "Yeah, like Bitcoin. Only Koyesta is very new and not worth much."

"How much is 100 Koyesta coins worth?" Rose asked, furrowing her eyebrows.

"$10," Michael said with disappointment.

"That's all?" Rose asked, crestfallen. "Geez... $10 apiece for an hour. I guess that's like working at a fast-food place."

"No." Cole sighed. "We got 100 coins to share between us."

"Oh," Rose said, furrowing her brow. "So, that's like $2.50 an hour."

"Yeah." Cole frowned.

Seeing them all looking down, Madison tried to think of something positive to say. "That's true. But look at it this way, that was $10 for one fight. That's not bad."

Cole perked up. His eyes went glassy for a moment and then he smiled. "Good point! We got a reward for being the first group to kill that mob. It may be that no one else is in this area and so any new Blackmange gnolls we kill could net us similar money. If we can find their base, I'm sure there are all kinds of different gnolls. We could make a hundred bucks... maybe more."

Rose brightened. "That would be better."

Michael looked up from scratching his tiger cub.

"Yeah, but the ones at the base will be higher level than these. We should try to level up on these so we're all at least level 2 before we go after the base."

Nodding, Cole looked around at the many gnoll pups running around, oblivious to the fate of the gnoll her group had just killed. "Okay then! Let's kill some gnolls!"

10

A half hour later, the group had killed 37 more gnolls before the rest of them gained level 2. They would have had to kill a few more, but a larger, named gnoll appeared. This one had been stronger and had been carrying a rusty scimitar. Despite the Bark-skin, it had almost killed Cole before they brought it down.

Killing the named gnoll had earned them another 100 Koyesta coins and they all felt better about that. At the same time, Rose had learned that she could wield scimi-tars. She'd gotten an evil grin when she realized she could use it.

Cole explained that in some games, this one included, you could only effectively use a weapon you had a skill in. Unconvinced, Madison had tried it and found that it liter-ally just felt wrong in her hand. It was if she wanted to do nothing more than put it down. Even worse, no matter how hard or how often she hit a gnoll pup with it, she never did more than a single point of damage. She returned it to Rose.

When they had all hit level 2, they retreated back to the road and took a little breather. Looking at them, they looked like either a bunch of medieval homeless people or a pack of vagabonds.

Other than a few rusty daggers and the scimitar, they'd found several pieces of rusted, molded or threadbare armor. The named gnoll had even dropped a ring mail bracer - which Cole now wore. The other random pieces now adorned them, making them look more comical than fierce.

"Now what?" Rose asked. "Do we go find different gnolls?"

Cole nodded. "That would be my choice. I'm just not sure which way to look. Are you able to try your tracking skill?"

Rose brightened and hopped to her feet. "Oh, right. Let me check."

Her cousin spent the next ten minutes wandering around the road, looking at something none of them could see. Occasionally, she'd make a frustrated sound. Finally, she walked over to them. She gave them a disappointed look. "I don't see any gnoll tracks on the road."

Looking up from rubbing Buddy's belly, Michael gestured around with his free hand. "Maybe they don't use the road. They probably come from the forest."

Cole stood up and scanned the area. He bit his lip, looking thoughtful. "Does anyone remember which direction the named gnoll came from? What was he called Frappy? Fippy? Ripley?"

"I don't remember its name. Something Blackpaw, I think," Madison said. She pointed opposite the road. "But it came from over there. I was facing it when it came out of the woods."

"We should go over there and let you try tracking," Cole declared. He hoisted his huge sword and started in that direction. "And we can kill some gnolls on the way there."

A few minutes and six gnolls later, the group stood around while Rose once again scanned the earth. Finally, she looked off into the woods. "There are definitely tracks from that direction. Lots of them."

Cole grinned, pointing into the forest with the arm that wore the ringmail bracer. "Then that's the direction we go."

Eager to find different gnolls and make more money, the rest of them eagerly followed her brother into the forest. That is, until he stopped a few feet in. He turned and gestured for Rose to go in front. "You lead. You're the only one who can see the trail."

Rose looked around the forest dubiously, slowly walking in circles as her eyes searched the ground. After looking around again, she nodded and started through the trees. "I've got the trail again, come on."

The group followed Rose through the forest for almost fifteen minutes before they came upon a large clearing. Cole's huge hand snaked out and stopped Rose before she walked into the clearing. He put his finger to his lips and then pointed at the far side.

The group gathered behind some foliage and looked

out to where Rose had pointed. Michael furrowed his brow. "Is that some sort of cave?"

"What's it supposed to be?" Cole asked, sharing his cousin's confusion.

The clearing was about fifty feet wide and mostly oval shaped. At the far end was a cleared patch of the forest that led back to a cave. It appeared that the stone around the cave had been carved into a shape.

Madison cocked her head one way and looked at the cave entrance. After a moment, she cocked her head the other way. Then she smiled. "I think it's supposed to be a dog head... or maybe a gnoll head."

Rose nodded and pointed. "See, the entrance is its mouth and those are ears on either side."

Michael and Cole both squinted. Finally, Cole shook his head. "If you say so."

"That probably has lots of new gnolls," Rose suggested. She rubbed her fingers together. "More money!"

Cole nodded but continued to look around the clearing and at the cave entrance. "We don't know what level those guards are." He glanced at the gnolls that ran across the clearing on regular intervals. "We should take out one of those scouts or runners, or whatever they are. See how tough they are."

"Okay." Rose shrugged and started to step out.

"No," Cole said, sizing up the situation.

Michael pointed to the far end. "Down there would be better. Pull them into the forest."

"That's what I was thinking too," her brother agreed. "Come on, let's circle around."

The group circled around to the edge of the clearing on the right-hand side. Cole then walked 10 yards into the woods before stopping. He turned to his sister.

"Madison, you go to the edge of the forest," he told her. "Cast that strangle spell..."

"Minor Telekinetic Asphyxiation," Madison corrected him.

"Whatever," Cole continued. "Cast as soon as one of them comes in range, then turn around and run back here."

Madison looked at him dubiously. "Are you sure you can get it off me when I get back here?"

Cole smiled. "Sure... yes... maybe... I'm like 99%... maybe 90% sure..."

She gave her brother the evil eye but he just grinned. "Fine. I can pull it off you. But just in case it doesn't work the first time, cast your shielding spell on yourself."

Nodding, Madison did exactly that. She cast Minor Force Shield on herself then quickly went to the edge of the forest and waited. She didn't have to wait long. A larger gnoll, about the size of the named gnoll they'd fought earlier, came running towards her.

Waiting until it came into range, she cast her spell.

Blackmange Scout takes 4 choking damage.
Blackmange Scout is choking.

The gnoll clutched at its throat for a moment before turning angry eyes on her. It immediately began sprinting towards her. With a squeak, she spun around and ran for the rest of her group. She could hear the gnoll scout behind her and ran faster.

Breaking into the group, she ran past them and then spun around, ready to get hit.

"Fight me, cat breath!" Cole taunted and the gnoll turned towards him, clawing at him with both hands.

Blackmange Gnoll Scout claws Brothar Snowbear for 5 damage.
Blackmange Gnoll Scout claws Brothar Snowbear for 4 damage.

Flinching at the pain, Cole chopped at the gnoll, slicing a gash across it, then backhanded it with his ringed bracer, rocking its head to the side.

Brothar Snowbear slashes Blackmange Gnoll Scout for 8 damage.
Brothar Snowbear slams Blackmange Gnoll Scout for 3 damage.

"What was that?!" Michael yelled as he slammed his club into the gnoll's shoulder. At the same time, Buddy ran forward and bit the gnoll's leg. It yelped in pain.

Zachatolus Catfriend crushes Blackmange Gnoll Scout for 3 damage.
Buddy bites Blackmange Gnoll Scout for 3 damage.

"New skill." Cole grinned. "Gives me a pummeling attack."

"Ugh, no fair!" Michael growled. "I need a better weapon and you get an extra attack!"

"I AM a tank," Cole replied.

"I like my weapon," Rose said with a smile, slicing her scimitar against its back.

Plays-With-Animals slashes Blackmange Gnoll Scout for 6 damage.

"That's so unfair," Michael complained.

"What?!" Rose retorted. "You have a tiger cub!"

Michael looked down at the feisty cub and grinned. "I do!"

Madison moved in and brought her club down on the back of the gnoll's head.

You crush a Blackmange Gnoll Scout for 4 damage.

It yelped at the various blows but continued to attack her brother.

Blackmange Gnoll Scout claws Brothar Snowbear for 5 damage.
Blackmange Gnoll Scout claws Brothar Snowbear for 5 damage.

"Uh... ow!" he said, looking at his Health dropping. He slashed his sword diagonally across the gnoll's midsection.

Brothar Snowbear slashes Blackmange Gnoll Scout for 8 damage.

Zachatolus Catfriend crushes Blackmange Gnoll Scout for 3 damage.
Buddy bites Blackmange Gnoll Scout for 3 damage.

Suddenly, the gnoll spun and tried to run past Madison.

"No! No!" Cole yelled. "Don't let it run!"

Plays-With-Animals slashes Blackmange Gnoll Scout for 6 damage.
You have killed Blackmange Gnoll Scout.
You have gained experience!
Your reputation with Residents of Fisherton has increased.
Your reputation with Guards of Fisherton has increased.
Your reputation with Blackmange Gnolls has decreased.

They quickly checked the loot and received a set of ringmail boots, a gnoll claw and another prize notification.

"Another 100 coins!" Rose said, her eyes refocusing. "That's $30 total, so $7.50 each. Still not so great."

"There's more where that came from," Michael said with a grin and reached down and patted Buddy on the head as the little tiger cub tried to gnaw on his sandal.

11

Over the two hours, the group killed dozens of gnolls, with everyone managing to hit level 3. They all gained additional health and mana and once again, their skills began to improve. Madison noticed that her skill level seemed to be capped at five times her character level. At the moment, that meant she could only improve to rank 15.

They also managed to kill several more new types of gnolls and two named gnolls, bringing the money they'd earned up to 7,000 Koyesta coins, or $70. Split four ways, that was only $17.50 each, which for four hours of work, wasn't much.

On the plus side, they'd all upgraded their weapons and Cole was now clad in a complete set of the rusty ring mail armor the gnolls wore. It was stretched tightly across his massive chest and bulging arms, but he did manage to make it fit.

Rose and Michael both had a few scattered pieces of

rawhide armor now. Neither had the skill to wear the ring mail, so rawhide was the best they could do. Unfortunately, no armor had dropped for Madison. She still wore the same threadbare garments she'd entered the game with. It was getting frustrating.

"I'm hungry," Michael said after their latest kill. "Let's break for lunch and come back in an hour. Then maybe we can go into the dog's mouth."

They all looked at the intimidating entrance with the burly gnoll guards who stood watch. So far, they'd been picking off stragglers as they roamed too far away from the others. It was a strategy that had served them well so far but if they wanted to go further in, they'd have to stretch their comfort zone.

Madison's stomach growled, or rather, her character's stomach growled, and she nodded. "I'm hungry too. Let's do that. Meet back here in an hour?"

Cole pointed further into the woods. "Let's log out a little further away, so we don't log back in to any surprises."

The group followed him further into the woods and then one by one, they went into their HUDs and chose the logout option. Madison watched the others fade away into golden sparkles and then she too logged out.

The game world faded away and she blinked her eyes as she felt the familiar feeling of her bed. She reached up and removed the VR headband that had been around her forehead and then sat up from the bed.

Stretching, she reached down and picked up her phone to check her messages. Before she even had a chance to unlock her phone, she furrowed her brow. Her phone said 9:41am. That wasn't right. They'd started at 9am and they'd been in for almost four hours, maybe a little more. Something must be wrong with her phone.

"Holy - !" she heard Cole's voice shout out from his bedroom. She heard shuffling and then footsteps as he came rushing into her room.

"Madison!" he said, wide-eyed. "Do you see what time it is?!"

Madison frowned. "What time do you think it is?"

"It's 9:41...well... 9:43 now!" he replied excitedly as he checked his phone. "How is that even possible?!"

Knowing the simplest answer was usually the most correct, she shrugged. "Something's up with our phones. Maybe they lost connection or something."

Cole shook his head. "No, my computer and the clock in the hall both have the same time."

"That's... that's not possible," she replied. "We were in the game..."

"For four hours! I know!" Cole exclaimed. "That's so crazy!"

The phone in her hand rang at almost the same time Cole's phone rang. She didn't even have to look down at the caller id to know it was Rose. She had a special ring tone for her cousin.

"It's Michael!" Cole said, sliding his finger across his phone and bringing it to his ear.

Still confused, Madison hesitated a moment longer and then answered the call before it went to voicemail.

"Hey," she said.

"Madison! OMG! We were in that game for like... four

hours... but it's only been 40 minutes! What's going on?" came Rose's excited voice.

"I don't know," Madison replied. "But I'm going to go to their website and find out."

"Me too!" Rose agreed, her voice excited, bordering on hysterical. "I'll call you back!"

The line went dead and Madison overheard part of her brother's conversation.

"Right! It's so cool! Like a day in the game would be like six hours!" she heard Cole tell Michael.

Seeing that her brother was engaged with Michael, Madison sat down at her desk, brought up her computer and went to the company's website. After a bit of reading, she found what she was looking for.

Koyesta Online will be the first VR MMORPG to use the Excelsior Electronic Systems (EES) Excalibur accelerated neural stimulation technology. This will allow players to experience an unprecedented level of immersion and play while still leaving them time to enjoy life.

There was a footnote to the paragraph and Madison scrolled down to the bottom of the website to read it.

Please read the full warning and disclaimer for the Excalibur headset on the EES website.

Madison followed the link to the EES website and, finding the Excalibur headset page, scanned through it until she found what she was looking for.

Excalibur uses EES's proprietary version of the military's accelerated neural stimulation technology. This allows players to experience virtual reality at up to 6x the speed of normal brain stimulation.

Note: Please consult a physician if you experience any side effects from accelerated neural stimulation.

Frowning, Madison read the section several times. See a doctor if you had side effects? What kind of side effects? What could go wrong?

She was about to start doing some research on the side effects of accelerated neural stimulation when Cole shook her.

"What?" she asked with a glance behind her.

"Michael and Rose want to play longer since we've only been on for less than an hour." Cole gave her a big grin. "Come on!"

Madison bit her lip. Should she say something about the side effects? No, she decided. Not until she read more.

"What about lunch?" she asked, then she rolled her eyes as she remembered it wasn't even 10am.

"Do you feel hungry?" Cole asked with a knowing smile.

She cocked her head. Actually, she didn't feel hungry at all. "No."

Cole's grin widened. "I think our AVATARS were feeling hungry."

"Are you serious?" Madison asked, furrowing her brow. "We'll feel hunger too?"

Her brother shrugged. "I guess we have to eat in game. Come on, let's get in!"

"You don't have a problem with the accelerated virtual reality?" she asked, her tone serious.

"Are you kidding?" Cole asked. "It's awesome! We can play like... 4 or 5 times as long now!"

"You think that's safe?" she asked.

"Yeah. Haven't they been using stuff like that for the military?" Cole shrugged. "That was that whole news story about Area 51 technology that went around the social networks for like a year."

Madison remembered it vaguely but had dismissed it after the words "alien technology" and "Area 51" had come up. At that point, she relegated it to the realm of conspiracy theory and ignored it.

"Just do me a favor," she told her brother, meeting his eyes. "If you start to have any weird side effects, let me know. Okay?"

"Side effects?" he asked, forehead wrinkling. "Like what? Like having too much fun?"

She let out an exasperated breath. "Just tell me if you feel strange after we play for a while, okay?"

Cole looked thoughtful. "The time difference will be weird to get used to. I mean, I really feel like I was in the game for hours. It's so weird that we were only in there for less than an hour."

"I know," Madison agreed. It did feel weird. She had hours of memories from something less than an hour. No wonder the military was using it for training. They could train someone in a fraction of time.

Idly, she wondered if that technology would make it to colleges before she graduated. Being able to learn and graduate in a sixth of the time would be awesome. Of course, the colleges would probably still charge full price for the courses.

"The others are waiting for us in game," Cole said impatiently, leaning towards the door. "While we're out here talking, they're in there waiting forever for us."

"Fine," she said, standing up from her desk. "Let's go back into the game."

Cole didn't bother replying, he just ran out the door and back into his room.

Walking over to her bed, she lay down on it and pulled on the headband. She took a deep breath and hesitated before clicking on the on switch but after a moment, went ahead and turned it on. Immediately, the real world faded away.

12

"So realistically," Rose said, once they were all back in. "We made like $17/hour for the first hour. That's good. Better than we can make at our side jobs."

"True," Michael agreed. Madison knew he had a job at a restaurant, but only worked on weekends and when they needed him. "Plus, it's a lot more fun."

"Oh yeah," Cole agreed, and fist bumped Michael. "And speaking of which, we should fight our way into the gnoll den. There's got to be different types of gnolls inside, and probably named ones as well. Probably even a boss or two."

"Can we handle them?" Michael asked. "We're only level 3."

"We won't know until we try." Cole shrugged. "If they get too high level, we can always retreat and farm gnolls around them until we hit level 4 or 5."

"Cool," Michael said with a grin.

Cole turned to Rose and Madison. "Is that okay with you?"

Rose nodded. "If it means making more money, that will make my parents happy. And that means I can keep playing."

"Fine with me," Madison replied. Just then her stomach growled, followed by Rose's stomach and then Michael's and Cole's.

Michael laughed. "That was a chorus of hungry stomachs."

"It's our characters," Cole said. "We must have to eat in game. Chances are, at some point, we'll start suffering penalties if we don't eat."

"Where do we get food?" Rose asked.

"Probably back at the village," Cole answered. "There might be berries or other stuff we can eat out here, but nothing's dropped so far."

Madison remembered the crab meat she had looted at the beach. "I have crab meat."

Everyone turned to look at her. "What?"

"I looted crab meat from the crabs I killed on the beach," she explained.

"Is it edible?" Cole asked.

Madison shrugged. "It just said crab meat."

"Try examining it," Michael suggested. "It should give you some stats."

Nodding, Madison brought up her inventory and examined the crab meat.

Spoiled Crab meat (x10)
Type: Component

Skill: Cooking
Wt: .1 lb / 1 lb
Description: A tender, flaking white meat from a crab, used in many recipes. Unfortunately, this meat has spoiled. Eating it now would not be advisable.

Madison read off the description to the group.

"Sounds like you can make food with the cooking skill," Cole said. "But I'm not sure how that would work. By itself, I don't think we can do anything with it at the moment - especially since it's spoiled."

"So, no food for now," Rose said, holding her hand to her stomach.

"We could go back to the village and get some food," Madison suggested. "Didn't you say we can sell the other gear we've been collecting for the gnolls. That might give us enough money to buy some food. Then we won't get any penalties while we're in there fighting."

Cole considered her words and nodded. "Good idea. My inventory is almost full anyway."

"That's because you're carrying most of the stuff," Rose pointed out.

"It's the curse of being the biggest and strongest." Her brother flexed his huge arms. "I don't even work out."

Madison rolled her eyes. "Come on, let's head back to the village."

"Right," Rose said, shaking her head at Cole.

Her brother looked at his huge muscles and shrugged. "What? It's true."

"Uh," Michael said, looking around. "Which way was it back to the village?"

Everyone froze and looked around. Madison looked around at the various trees, which all looked very similar. She pointed to where she thought they'd come from. "It's that way, right?"

Rose scratched her head and pointed a different direction. "I thought it was that way."

Cole shook his head and pointed yet another direction. "No, it's that way.... I think."

"We're lost." Michael chuckled. "The first day of a new game and we're lost."

"Wait," Madison said, holding her hands up. She pointed to Rose. "Can't you use your tracking to find out where we came from?"

Rose brightened. "Let me try!"

The petite little elf looked all over the ground before looking up in disappointment. "We don't have any tracks."

Cole sighed. "They probably faded when we logged out."

"Does that mean, we really are lost," Rose said nervously.

"I don't think it's that hard," Michael said, pointing to the clearing. "We arrived here around the middle of the clearing... over there." He pointed to the spot Madison had previously indicated they had used to enter the clearing. "Then we circled over here to draw out the stragglers. Right?"

Madison nodded. "Yes. I think you're right."

Michael nodded. "It was definitely the middle part because it was opposite the entrance to the burrow."

"True," Cole agreed.

"If we go opposite to the burrow entrance and then head that direction," Madison started.

"We should get back to the road," her brother finished. "Good memory, Michael."

Michael grinned.

With Michael leading, the group followed him around the edge of the clearing until they were directly across from the entrance to the gnoll den. Doing an about face, they began hiking through the forest.

After a while, the forest suddenly gave way to a familiar clearing. Everyone gave a little cheer, though at this point, their stomachs were starting to really hurt from the hunger. It was like the worst hunger pain Madison had ever felt. All she wanted to do was eat something - anything - to make it stop.

"That's interesting," Cole said, looking out at the farm area.

"What?" Madison asked.

"The gnolls we were killing earlier didn't respawn," he explained. "Nothing has."

Looking at the clearing, Madison couldn't help but agree. "What does that mean?"

"I'm not sure," Cole said. "It means either they have a really long respawn time or they don't respawn at all."

Rose shrugged. "What does that mean for us?"

"First," Cole explained, "that means we can't just keep killing these things for reputation. There might be a finite number of them. It also means, if we clear out the gnoll den, it won't respawn."

"Cool," Michael said. "That means we'll be the first and only group to clear it."

"That's good and bad," Cole pointed out. "It means we can't just farm them to increase our level. Once they're all dead, we'll need to find something else to level up on."

"But that's good, right?" Rose asked. "Killing new monsters means we can make more money if we're the first to kill them."

"True," Cole agreed. "But it also means, we may have to go further and further from the village - and our bind point."

"Let's worry about that after we clear out the gnolls," Madison told them. "Right now, I feel like something is burning a hole in my stomach."

Michael nodded. "Yeah. Me too."

"Me three," Rose said. "Let's get to the village and find something to eat!"

They walked back to the road and once again, Madison had to walk just off the road, in case they met any villagers. Last time, there had been only two villagers closer to the village. This time, they ran into a small patrol of three chain-mail-clad guards.

The guards stopped a few feet away from her group. They were dressed similarly to the ones who had attacked and killed her in the village and Madison shrank further back into the forest.

Two of them were human, but the middle one was obviously a dwarf. The two humans carried pikes while the dwarf had a large battle axe in his hand. The dwarf held out a hand. When he spoke, she noticed the dwarf had what she thought was a Scottish accent. "Identify yourselves and state your intentions."

Madison peeked out from around the tree she was hiding and strained to hear the conversation.

"We are adventurers heading back to Fisherton," Cole said. "We've been hunting down gnolls all day."

The dwarf spat. "Filthy creatures, gnolls! A pox on the lot of them. Well, if you're hunting gnolls, then you're a friend to Fisherton. Just be careful if you venture into their den. Rumor has it, the gnoll war leader has a powerful shaman backing him up."

"Thank you. Good to know," Cole said.

"As you were then. And make sure you don't cause any trouble in town," the dwarf said and eyed them all. "We don't look kindly on troublemakers."

Turning his head, he waved the other two forward. "Come on, you poor excuses for guardsmen, we have more area to patrol. The sooner we get back, the sooner we can hit the tavern."

Madison heard the other two soldiers groan and then they followed the dwarf as the group continued walking down the road. She waited until they were out of sight before moving closer to the road.

"What was that all about?" she called out.

Cole shrugged. "No idea. Just a patrol, I guess."

"What was that about a powerful shaman?" Madison asked.

"Probably a rumor or hint or something," Michael answered. "It might mean there are two bosses, the warlord guy and the shaman."

"That's good, right?" Rose asked. "That's more money."

"And more loot," Michael retorted with a grin.

"Let's sell our stuff and then get back to killing gnolls," Madison said.

"Right," Cole agreed. "And speaking of which, give us all your loot so we can sell it for you."

"You don't think I will be able to get into the town yet?" Madison asked.

Her brother shook his head. "We killed a decent number of gnolls, but probably not enough to raise your reputation that much. Maybe by the end of today."

"Let's hope," she groaned and began pulling items from her inventory and distributing them among the rest of her party.

"We're going to start hitting those farms on the outskirts," Cole said. "Why don't you stay here while we run into town. We'll meet you back here as soon as we're done."

Madison sighed. "Fine."

"We won't be long," Rose assured her.

With that, they said their goodbyes and headed into the town, leaving Madison alone on the road. She let out a frustrated breath and then waded back into the forest to wait for her friends.

13

It took all of about two minutes for Madison to get bored with waiting. Looking around the forest, she decided to explore a bit. After all, this virtual world was so real, it was like being on another planet.

Remembering how they'd almost become lost earlier, she knew she should mark her path. Since the Hansel and Gretel method didn't work - and she had no breadcrumbs anyway, she decided to channel her inner Saknussemm from Jules Verne's Journey to the Center of the Earth.

The only weapon she had was a club. That wouldn't help her mark the trees. Walking back to the road, she found a rock with a sharp edge. Walking to the nearest tree, she carved her initials "MF" into the tree with the rock.

Stepping back, she admired her handiwork. She nodded to herself. If the group returned before she did, Cole should recognize her initials. Hopefully, he'd think to look for other marks and follow her trail.

Walking back into the woods, Madison walked a hundred yards and then marked another tree. She made sure her initials were on the same side of the tree so that if her brother was trying to follow her trail, they'd be able to see the marks easily.

With her plan in place, she began making her way through the trees, stopping every hundred yards to carve another set of initials. After ten sets of initials, she stumbled upon some berry bushes she hadn't seen before. Curious, she walked over to them and examined the berries.

Madison had been hiking and camping with her mom and grandfather many times. She wasn't an expert at wild berries by any stretch of the imagination, but she was familiar with some edible berries her grandfather had pointed out on their hikes. These looked like wild blackberries.

You have become better at Foraging (+1%).

Plucking a berry off in the bush, she examined it with her HUD.

Fresh Wild Blackberry (x1)
Type: Food
Wt: .01 lb / .01 lb
Description: Found in wooded areas and sometimes grown in civilization, these wild berries provide sustenance to animals and humanoids alike.

Just reading the description made Madison's stomach

growl. She quickly gathered a handful, earning more increases in the Foraging skill. She ate as she gathered, quickly becoming full.

Madison wasn't hungry any longer, but who knew how long that would last. And who knew if she would find more bushes. She decided to take as many berries with her as possible. After all, she could always share them with the others when they met up.

Getting to work, she picked the bushes clean, earning a skill up in Foraging along the way.

You have earned rank 2 in Foraging.
New ability discovered: Plant Perception.
Plant Perception
Type: General
Mana: N/A
Stamina: N/A
Duration: Passive
Range: 100ft
Description: Edible plants now stand out to your keenly trained eye, making them easier to see when you are within 100ft.
Warning: Not all edible plants are good.

Congratulations! You were the first player on the server to reach rank 2 in Foraging. 2,000 Koyesta Coins has been added to your account.
You may check your rewards by going to Character Menu-> Profile -> Rewards -> Early Access Awards

She grinned at the message and opened up her character menu to look at the reward. Her grin grew even larger as she read the amount. She'd earned $20, just for picking a bunch of berries. And how long had that taken in real time? Seconds? A minute at most?

Dismissing her HUD, she started to look for more bushes when a voice from behind her caused her to jump.

"Well, look what we have here, boys," came a familiar voice with a Scottish accent. "An enemy of the Alliance!"

Spinning, Madison came face to face with the three guardsmen that had stopped her group back on the road. Panicking, she looked for a direction to flee.

"We can take its head back and put it on a pike!" one of the human guards said.

"Stop talking and kill it!" the dwarf growled.

Now in full panic mode, Madison scanned the area, unsure which way she could run. The guards stalked forward, weapons out and she did the only thing she could think to do.

"Don't kill me! I surrender!" she cried out.

The guards stopped and blinked.

"Uh," said the human guard on her left, a confused look on his face. "Is it allowed to do that?"

"It's an enemy of the Alliance," muttered the guard on the right. "We kill enemies of the Alliance."

The humans started forward and Madison squealed, getting ready to turn and run.

"Hold, fools!" the dwarf bellowed. "Enemy or no, we aren't savages. We don't kill enemies who surrender."

The two humans stopped and turned to the dwarf. "Uh… what do we do with it?"

"We take it back!" the dwarf retorted. "Throw it in the

cage. Let the Captain interrogate it."

Cage? Madison started to panic. Maybe she should just let them kill her and then respawn.

"Bind its hands!" the dwarf ordered, and the two men grabbed her roughly and pulled her hands behind her. One of them took a long piece of leather and bound her wrists tightly. Had she been human, it would have chafed. As it was, with her scales, she was at least spared that pain.

"You will follow me," the dwarf told her, glaring at her. "The boys will be behind you, so if you try anything... you'll regret it."

Madison nodded and that seemed to satisfy the dwarf. "All right, let's take the prisoner back to town."

Flinching as the two guards prodded her with their pikes, Madison started forward. She began to wonder if it would have been better just to let them kill her. She could have respawned by now and been on her way back. Now she wasn't sure what would happen to her.

They marched back to the road and the dwarf stopped suddenly, forcing her to stop and then get pricked by the pike tips as the men behind her didn't react quickly enough.

The dwarf spun and pointed to the tree with her initials on it. "What does that mean? Is that some sort of arcane symbol? The sign of your clan? Will others be coming?"

Madison cursed herself for not realizing what the game characters would think of her marks. The guards must have seen her mark and followed the trail right to her. Brilliant, Madison! Really brilliant!

"It's... uh... my..." She started to say initials but realized they were her real-life initials, not the initials of her character. She thought quickly. "It was the mark of my clan."

The dwarf squinted at her. "There are more of you out there in the woods?"

She shook her head. "No, I am the only one here. I did it... uh... out of habit."

"Hmm," the dwarf mumbled, eyeing her up and down. "I don't believe you, but that's up to the Captain to decide."

Without another word, the dwarf spun, and they resumed their march back to the town. As they walked through the farms that she and her group had circumvented, Madison saw the farmers stop their work to stare at her. They all wore looks of disgust.

When they finally entered the town, the first thing she saw was her brother and cousins coming towards her. She was pretty certain that the guards were much higher level than any of them and they'd easily kill her group.

Not only that, if her experience with the gnolls was anything to go by, attacking the guards would only give them negative reputation with the town. That was something she couldn't allow.

Michael looked over and caught sight of her. His face grew red, and he reached for his weapon, taking a step towards her. Madison gave him a pointed stare and shook her head. She silently mouthed "No." Michael stopped, but it was obvious he was torn on what to do. She gave him another shake of her head.

Cole saw her then and started forward, but she caught

his eye and gave him the same shake of her head. He frowned but gave her a nod.

"What are they doing to her?" Rose cried out as she too saw Madison and the guards. Cole put a hand on her shoulder and then bent down and whispered in the elf's ear. She looked like she was about to cry but kept her eyes on Madison until the guards ushered her into one of the buildings. The barracks no doubt.

Marching her into a large room, the dwarf stopped in front of a sturdy but plain-looking oak desk. Behind the desk was a bald man of middle years. He looked up at the group as they came in, eyes flicking to Madison, before dropping down to look at the dwarf.

"Sergeant Rhormir," the man said, his voice authoritative. "It seems you have a prisoner."

"Yes, Captain," the dwarf replied, coming to attention. "We apprehended the prisoner in the woods north of Old Pass Road."

The Captain raised an eyebrow. "You apprehended it in the woods? Doing what?"

"It was marking trees," said one of the human men.

"And eating berries," added the other one.

The dwarf rolled his eyes and the Captain's face flushed. "Did I address either of you, Privates?"

"Uh, no sir," they answered in unison.

"Then stay quiet," the Captain ordered, turning his attention back to Rhormir. "Is that true? It was marking trees and eating berries?"

"Aye, sir," the Sergeant answered.

"Strange behavior for a Drakkar," the Captain said. He nodded towards the door in the back. "Put it in the cage and I will interrogate it after my meeting with the mayor. Did you check on the two farms?"

"Aye, sir, we did," the dwarf replied. "Both burned to the ground."

The Captain sighed. "The mayor is going to want more patrols, but we just don't have the manpower. And we certainly don't have the men to post guards at each farm."

Standing up, the Captain shook his head. "Let me go tell the mayor the news. I'll be back to deal with the prisoner."

With that, the Captain moved from around the desk and left through the door she'd entered from. At the same time, she was prodded by the men's pikes and followed the dwarf through the rear door and into a hallway.

They walked to the end of the hallway where she saw a large cell. The walls were wood, like the rest of the building, but the front of the cell was a mesh of thick iron strips. The iron was rusted in places, but would no doubt still keep her in.

There was a single barred window that let a bit of light in, but otherwise the only illumination came from a torch, opposite the cell. She frowned. Not exactly cozy.

Taking a large keyring from the opposite wall, the dwarf unlocked the door to the cell and then she was prodded into it. No sooner had she crossed the threshold than the door was slammed behind her and then locked.

"Don't try anything," the dwarf said and then, gesturing to the men, disappeared down the hallway.

Once again, Madison was left alone. Only this time, she was a prisoner.

14

"Madison!" came a deep voice from behind her.

Spinning towards the window, Madison saw her brother's face looking in through the bars. Or rather, the face of Cole's avatar. He had his face pressed up against the bars and was looking around. "How'd they'd catch you?"

Madison sighed. "I started to explore the woods and I marked the trees with my initials. I think the guards saw that and followed my trail to me."

"Oh wow," Cole said. "That's some good AI... you know, artificial intelligence."

"I know what AI is, Cole," she snapped.

"Sorry," he said. Cole backed up and looked at the bars. "I might be able to bend them but even if I did, you'd never squeeze out of them. I'd have to rip them away completely... and I don't think I can."

"You shouldn't do it anyway," she told him. "I'm sure a

jailbreak would give you negative reputation. Then you'd be in the same situation I'm in."

Michael pressed his face up, next to Cole. "Try to make a break for it and let them kill you. Taunt them if you can. Just get them to kill you so you respawn."

"What about my stuff?" she protested. She felt herself flush. "My clothes especially."

"Give them to us," Cole said. "Give us all your gear. Then you'll have nothing on your corpse. We can wait for you by the respawn spot and give it to you."

She bit her lip, realizing she'd be in her little string bikini until she died and respawned. She looked down at herself and furrowed her brow. Did it really matter? She was all scaly anyway. Sighing, she moved herself against the wall and started a trade with Cole.

She started to put everything in the trade window when she suddenly got an idea as she was moving the gnoll claws into the trade area. "Wait a minute! What about the gnoll claw quest?"

"Huh?" Cole asked.

"That gnoll claw quest," she repeated. "That's from the militia captain, right?"

"Yes," Cole said. "He was in the front room when we met him. He gave us the quest to help Fisherton by killing gnolls."

"Right," she said. "He's supposed to come and interrogate me. Maybe I can turn in the quest and earn enough faction that they like me."

Cole and Michael looked at each other dubiously. Cole shrugged, barely visible in the window. "I don't know. It might not work since your faction isn't high enough."

He paused and looked thoughtful. "Although, we shared the quest with you... so... maybe."

"Someone lift me up!" she heard Rose's voice from the other side of the wall. "I want to see her too!"

Michael disappeared and suddenly Rose's head appeared. She wobbled for a second before grabbing onto the bars. "What did you do, Madison?"

"Would you believe drunk and disorderly?" Madison replied with a grin.

"Ha," Rose retorted. "Not unless you ate some special mushrooms out in the forest."

"I'll tell you later," Cole told the elf. "Quick, everyone give me your gnoll claws. We're going to give them to Madison."

Her brother and cousins disappeared for a moment and then Cole reappeared. He opened up a trade window. He added all of their gnoll claws and then accepted the trade. Checking her inventory, she saw that she had 141 gnoll claws.

"Will 141 be enough?" she wondered aloud.

"The quest is for 10 claws, so that's 14 turn-ins," he replied. "It doesn't say how much faction each turn-in gives you. Hopefully it will be enough. If not..." He bit his lip. "And you have to die and respawn, we'll lose all the money and items from the quest."

Madison frowned and bit her lip. "Maybe I..."

She heard the door at the far end of the hall open. They were out of time. "Someone's coming. Go!"

Cole locked eyes with her and gave her a little nod. "Good luck."

Then he disappeared and she heard them moving

away. Turning around just in time, the Captain walked down the hallway holding a wooden chair. It was probably the same chair from his desk.

He placed the chair a few feet from the bars, probably just out of arm's reach, and sat down. She got a good look at the man then.

He was older than she'd originally thought, maybe mid-fifties if he was in the real world. He had salt and pepper hair cut short, with a bit of extra gray along the sides. His face was angular but unremarkable, framed in a short, well-groomed beard.

Like the other guardsmen, he wore a chainmail tunic, but his armor looked a bit better maintained. In fact, everything about the man said he liked things clean and orderly. Even his leather boots were shiny and well maintained.

He wore a thick leather belt that matched his boots and strapped to the belt was a simple sword on one side and a dagger on the other.

"You were a soldier," she guessed.

The Captain raised an eyebrow. "Are you observant, or is that what you learned from your intelligence?"

"You're neat and orderly," she replied. "And your boots are shiny. The only people I know who shine their boots are soldiers."

"Half right. Soldiers and courtesans." He looked down at his boots and chuckled. The smile faded and his expression grew grim. "Why are the Drakkar interested in Fisherton? What is your mission here?"

Madison bit her lip. He thought she was an enemy spy and technically, she was one of the "evil" races but yet, she wasn't. But how could she convince him of that? It wasn't like she could just explain that she was a player, and this was where the game made her start.

She thought of a movie she'd seen and smiled. Maybe a little lie would help her. "I'm not from where the rest of my people are from."

"Oh?" the Captain inquired. "Where are you from?"

"I was... ah... marooned here when I was a child," she told him. "I've been living in the forest since then."

"Oh really?" he asked.

She nodded. "I've been foraging in the forest for food, just trying to survive. I've been making my way south. I came upon your town and was hoping I could make a home here."

"You?" the Captain asked, forehead wrinkled. "Wished to make a home here?"

"I've been lonely," she replied. She knew she needed to sell her story and began thinking about how it actually would have felt to be marooned, drawing from her memories of a few movies about castaways. "I hadn't seen anyone until I came upon the village. It got so bad, I started talking to..." She was about to say volleyball but knew he wouldn't understand it. She thought quickly. "... a rock that I called Winston. I even drew a face on it. It never talked back though."

The Captain sat back and rubbed his beard. "Go on."

"I found out that the town was being attacked by gnolls," she said. "I've been killing them, hoping that if I helped the town, maybe you'd... you know... let me stay."

"Let's assume you are right about gnolls bothering

Fisherton," the Captain said. "How did you find out about them?"

"I was there when they burned the farms," she said. "I saw the fire and came to investigate. There were too many of them at the time, but I've been slowly hunting them down since then and killing them."

"Oh really?" the man said suspiciously.

"I heard you were offering a reward to anyone who helped to thin their numbers," she continued but he interrupted.

"Heard from who?" the Captain asked, eyes narrowed.

"I... ah..." Madison stammered, realizing she had no good way to explain quest sharing with her group. Then an idea hit her. "I was hiding near the road and heard some people talking. Adventurers, I think. There was a big guy, a human with a cat and an elf, I think."

The man rolled his eyes. "I remember that lot."

"I heard them talking about it, so I thought maybe if I helped too," she said, trying to sound as pitiful as possible. "I thought maybe you'd accept me too."

"And you say you've actually killed some gnolls?" the Captain asked. He appeared genuinely intrigued.

"Many," she replied with a smile.

"Many?" he asked, his eyes narrowing again. "How many do you claim to have killed?"

"141," she replied.

"Ha!" the man laughed. "You had me going there. I was actually starting to believe you. Had you chosen a more realistic number, you might have had me."

"I can prove it," she shot back.

The Captain raised an eyebrow. "Oh? How?"

"I collected their claws," she said.

The man stopped laughing and stared at her, he stretched out a hand. "Let me see."

Counting out ten of the claws, she produced them from her inventory and handed them to him. If he thought it was strange that she was producing them from thin air, he didn't show it.

Quest "Blackmange Bounty" Complete.
You have gained experience!
Your reputation with Residents of Fisherton has increased.
Your reputation with Guards of Fisherton has increased.
Congratulations! You were the first group on the server to complete the quest Blackmange Bounty. A Reward has been added to your account.
You may check your rewards by going to Character Menu-> Profile -> Rewards -> Early Access Awards

Madison smiled at the extra reward. Checking, she saw that they had earned 500 Koyesta coins for completing the quest! While she was in her HUD, she saw that the quest had given her 100 experience as well. She hoped that was group experience and not just her getting it.

"This is only ten," the man said. "You said 141, I believe."

Nodding, Madison counted out 10 more and handed them to him, then repeated that in increments of 10 until she had given him 140. After each turn-in of 10, she'd gotten an additional quest message and each time her reputation had gone up. She looked at him hopefully.

The man looked between her and the pile of gnoll claws. He bit his lip, clearly having some sort of internal debate. Finally, he looked up at her.

"If you've killed this many gnolls, then you have done our town a great service," he told her. "If it were up to me, I would be inclined to release you and let you continue your extermination of the vermin."

Madison sighed. "But it's not up to you."

"I'm afraid not," he said. "I already informed the mayor. It will be up to him on whether I release you."

"Can you ask him?" Madison pleaded, trying not to sound too desperate.

"I can and I will," the man said, rising to his feet. "My gut tells me there is something else going on and that the burning of the farms was just a prelude." He scratched his beard. "Yes, I will go see the mayor now. I will be back."

Without another word, the man turned on his heel and walked quickly down the hall and disappeared through the door.

Madison leaned back against the wall. She sighed. "I'll just wait here then."

15

She didn't have to wait long. Fifteen minutes later, the Captain returned. He walked down the hallway and sat down in the chair he had left. He looked at Madison with an unreadable expression for nearly a minute before speaking.

"I talked with the mayor," the Captain said.

Madison waited for the man to continue but he seemed to be struggling with some inner thoughts. She resisted the urge to say "And what did he say?" Instead, she just waited in silence.

"He believes we should use you to help with our gnoll problem," he said finally, again pausing in a way that made Madison believe that perhaps he didn't feel the same way. She waited for a moment before he continued. "He asked me to release you and spread the word that you are welcome in the town..."

Excitedly, she looked up at him. "Really?!"

The man held up his hand. "On one condition."

Madison raised an eyebrow. By his tone, she had a feeling she wasn't going to like the condition.

Making a face, as if he had just eaten something sour, he continued. "He will let you stay in the town on the condition that you enter the gnolls' lair and kill their leader."

Unconsciously, Madison swallowed.

"Personally, I think it's a death sentence," the Captain said. "I had a scout, gods rest his soul, who was keeping tabs on them. He reported the gnoll commander was surrounded by elite gnoll guards. You may have killed a lot of gnolls, but not gnolls like that.

"There's also some sort of shaman at the commander's side," he continued. "According to our scout, most of the trouble started when the shaman showed up - seemingly out of nowhere - and began to have the commander's ear.

"If you plan to go after the commander, you'll most likely have to deal with him as well," the Captain explained.

It seemed overwhelming when he explained it like that. It was almost as if he didn't want her to go after them. Luckily, although Madison knew she certainly couldn't do it alone, she wouldn't be alone. After all, hadn't they been planning on going inside the lair anyway? With Cole and her cousins, hopefully they could handle it.

"The choice is yours," he said. "You did the town a favor by killing the gnolls, so I'm willing to give you the benefit of the doubt and release you. But if you want to stay, you'll have to do as the mayor asks."

You have received a new quest "Blackmange Assassin"

Mayor Adli Deeppockets has offered you the chance to be accepted in the town of Fisherton. To do so, you must kill the command of the Blackmange gnolls.
Kill the Gnoll Commander
Reward: 10 gold, +1000 reputation with Residents of Fisherton, +1000 reputation with Guards of Fisherton.
Accept quest (yes or no)?

"I'll do it," she said quickly and accepted the quest.

The Captain took a deep breath and let it out. He nodded. "I thought you might."

Standing up, he took the keys and unlocked the door. "Grab that chair and follow me."

Happy to be out of the cell, Madison grabbed the wooden chair and followed the Captain out the door at the end of the hallway and into the small office where she had first met the man.

He took the chair from her and motioned her to the other side of the desk, while he sat down and opened up one of the desk drawers.

"By the way, my name is Bartem," he said, gesturing to the chair on the opposite side of the desk. "Have a seat."

"I'm M..." Madison stopped. She had been about to say her real name. "I'm Draconia Manasinger."

"A pleasure, Draconia," he said with a slight nod. He pulled out a leather pouch and set it on the desk in front of him. It clinked with the sound of many coins. "You were right about the bounty on the gnolls. I did offer it to whoever killed them, and I stand by my word."

He opened the bag and pulled out a silver piece and laid it on the table. He then counted out 4 stacks of 10 copper coins. "The reward was 10 coppers for every 10 claws. That's 140 copper, so 1 silver and 40 coppers - unless you want it all in copper?"

Madison grinned at the coins. "No, the silver's fine!"

He nodded and pushed the coins to her. "Here's the reward for killing the gnolls. I think I already expressed how grateful Fisherton is for your help in culling their numbers. It might make them think twice before they burn any more villages."

Reaching down to the floor, Bartem pulled up a burlap sack and put it on the desk, sliding it over to her. "I took some of our tack and two canteens of water from our stores. If you're going after the gnolls, you'll need food. I also took the liberty of picking up some clothing for you, seeing how your current clothing is little more than rags. Consider it part of your reward."

Madison grinned at the man, touched by his thoughtfulness. She resisted the urge to open the sack then and there. Instead, she just thanked the man. "Thank you so much!"

He waved away her thanks and stood up. "Do you truly intend to try to go after the gnolls?"

She nodded. "Yes."

Captain Bartem shook his head then gestured to her to follow him back into the hallway. "Come with me. There might be something else I can do to help you."

Standing up and grabbing the money and the sack, Madison followed him through the backdoor and into the hallway. He stopped in front of the first door to their right and brought out a worn iron key. He stuck it into the lock and gave it a twist until there was an audible click. He swung the door open to reveal a room filled with scattered weapons and other knick knacks.

"I'd give you weapons and armor from my own stores, but besides being against regulations, we barely have enough as it is," Bartem told her. "But these are all items we confiscated during altercations or brawls. If, say... four of the items went missing... who's to say what happened to them."

With that, he turned his back to the room and began whistling an unfamiliar tune. When she didn't move, he turned his head and nodded towards the room meaningfully.

Grinning, Madison stepped into the room and began to scan it for anything useful. The first item that caught her attention was actually the biggest item in the room - a two-handed sword in a sheath. She grabbed it for Cole, knocking over a woodcutter's axe and a quiver of arrows in the process. She flashed the Captain an embarrassed smile. "Sorry."

She also found a six-foot-long staff that seemed like it would give her more reach than the club she carried. The further away she was from the enemies, the better. As she retrieved the staff from the corner, her eyes fell on two metal rods that looked like bars from a prison cell.

The rods were about two and a half feet long of iron and one end was wrapped in leather. She cocked her head. Were those metal clubs of some sort?

Tentatively she picked one up. It was heavy. Too heavy for her to use effectively. But maybe Michael could use them! He was still using the club he'd started with.

Smiling at her choices, she stashed them in her inventory and stepped out of the room. "I got everything. Thank you."

"For what?" The man winked at her, giving her a look of innocence. "Oh my, someone left the door to the storage area open. I'd better lock it before something goes missing."

Madison realized he was probably breaking some rules by allowing her to take the items but guessed that his sense of honor wouldn't allow him to let her fight the gnolls without help. Whatever the reason, she was grateful for the new gear.

After locking the door and replacing the key in his pocket, he escorted her back out into the office.

Bartem shut the door to the hallway and turned to face her. "I wish you the best. Not just for your sake, but for Fisherton's sake too. Go with the gods and I pray that your mission is successful."

"Thank you," Madison said with a smile. "And thank you for all of your help."

The Captain waved her thanks away. "More than deserved. I'd kill those gnolls myself if I didn't have duties here. It's good to see that even a Drakkar is willing to protect our town from the gnoll scourge - uh, no offense intended."

"None taken," she said with a shrug.

"I'll spread the word about your deeds," he said as he walked her to the door. "My guards have already been informed and won't hassle you, but I wouldn't expect any warm welcomes from the townsfolk. They may need a bit more time to warm up to you."

Opening the door to the outside, he gestured to her. “Good luck, Draconia Manasinger. And happy hunting.”

“Thank you, Captain Bartem,” she replied and strode out of the militia building, once more a free woman.... a free woman with some new loot! Madison couldn’t wait to show the others!

16

"You're free!" Rose yelled, appearing from the side of the militia building and running towards her. She reached Madison and threw her arms around her in a tight hug. "We were so worried."

Madison felt something brush against her legs and looked down to see Buddy, rubbing himself against her and purring. She smiled.

"Nah," Cole said, coming over. "I was planning a jailbreak if they didn't let you out."

"Shhh!" Madison said, glancing around on the narrow street. "Don't say that too loud."

Cole looked sheepishly around, stopping in front of Madison. "Glad you're out. Did the quest turn-ins do the trick? You were still grouped, so we all got experience."

"And a reputation bump," Michael added. "They're nicer to us now."

"Tell us what happened!" Rose demanded, disengaging her bear hug and stepping away.

Madison, still conscious of being the "evil" race, glanced around the street. Villagers were staring at her and whispering to each other. "Let's head out of town."

"You're finally not kill on sight and you want to leave?" Cole asked.

"I'm not exactly Miss Popular," Madison pointed out, gesturing around. "More like, barely tolerated, now."

The others looked around and must have finally noticed all of the staring villagers. Cole nodded. "Good point, let's go."

As a group, they turned and headed west, out of town. Cole moved in front of Madison, while Rose and Michael moved to either side, partially hiding her from view until they'd left the small town.

Once they reached the outskirts, where acres of fields separated them from the farmhouses, everyone relaxed.

"Alright," Rose said, nudging Madison with her shoulder. "Tell us what happened."

Nodding, Madison related the events of the jail and her conversations with Captain Bartem. She finished by remembering she had items for them. "Oh! And I have gifts!"

"Gifts!" Rose exclaimed, bouncing on her feet. "What kind of gifts?"

Madison gave her an embarrassed smile. "It's some new weapons and they didn't have a scimitar. Sorry."

Rose looked disappointed but then shrugged. "It's okay. I like this scimitar."

"So does that mean you have something for me?" Michael asked hopefully.

Turning to smile at him, she pulled the iron rods and

handed them to him. His eyes widened and he snatched them from her. "Oh wow! These are like metal arnis sticks."

Michael began twirling them around in an impressive display and then stopped. "I wonder if this means I can attack twice now?"

Madison shrugged. "Maybe."

Cole shook his head. "I don't think so. I wasn't able to really do any other attacks until the skill became available. That must be how they limit low-level characters from being too powerful if controlled by someone who is already an experienced fighter."

Michael sagged. "Bummer."

"At least it looks cool." Cole grinned.

"True." Michael returned his smile.

Pulling the greatsword from her inventory, she handed it to Cole. "This was there too."

Cole took the sword gingerly and slid it out of its sheath. His eyes went glassy and then he smiled. "It does 2 more damage than my starter sword. Thanks!"

"Oh... and hold on," she told them as she fished out a quilted tunic and leggings from her sack. Before trying them on, she looked at them through her HUD.

Quilted Tunic
Type: Cloth
Location: Chest
Skill: Light Armor
Size: Medium
Armor: 2
Quality: Average

Quilted Breeches
Type: Cloth
Location: Legs
Skill: Light Armor
Size: Medium
Armor: 2
Quality: Average

Both were better than the poor-quality armor she had now that didn't actually give her any armor. She equipped both and a moment later she looked more like an adventurer and less like a hobo.

Reaching into the bag, she also pulled out a pair of odd-looking shoes. Madison frowned.

"Are those clogs?" Rose asked, cocking her head.

Madison shrugged. They looked a bit like clogs. They had a thick wooden sole to which a similarly quilted fabric upper had been riveted or nailed. She turned them over in her hand. "They do kind of look like them."

Bringing them up in her HUD, she was surprised to see that yes, they were some sort of quilted armor, similar to her tunic and breeches.

Quilted Pattens
Type: Cloth
Location: Feet
Skill: Light Armor
Size: Medium
Armor: 2
Quality: Average

"They actually count as armor," Madison told the group and slipped them onto her feet. They felt a bit weird at first, but after taking a few test steps around the road, she nodded. "They'll work."

She pulled out her staff and equipped it, taking a look at the stats.

Pine Quarterstaff
Type: 1-Handed Crushing
Hand: Right
Skill: 1-Handed Crushing
Size: Medium
Dmg: 4
Quality: Average

"Nice staff. Better than the club you were using," Rose commented.

"Right!" Madison agreed, giving the staff a few practice swings.

"Anything else?" Rose asked.

"Some food and canteens," she replied and then remembered the coins. "And some money! I got 1 silver and 40 copper!"

"Very nice!" Rose commented. "How much do we have total now?"

"After buying the food," Cole said, eyes going glassy as he looked up something in his HUD. "12 silver, 69 copper."

"Is that good?" Madison asked.

Rose frowned. "Everything in town is expensive."

"At least," Michael added. "Everything we want... like weapons and armor. The food wasn't too much."

"Yes," Cole agreed. "It seems like the things that the townsfolk would use - tools, foodstuffs, that sort of thing, are priced pretty low. Anything an adventurer would need is priced much higher."

"Armor and weapons WERE expensive in the medieval ages," Madison told them. "That's why only royalty had suits of armor."

Cole grinned. "Good thing I took Blacksmithing as a skill. All I need is a blacksmithing tool kit and some ore and I can make my own armor."

"Ooh!" Rose cooed. "You could make me a better scimitar."

"Probably." Cole shrugged. Then a serious look came over his face. "The quest you got from the Captain, can you share it?"

Madison opened up her HUD, went to her journal and brought up the quest. Sure enough, at the bottom of her vision was a "Share quest" option. She mentally selected it.

Cole grinned. "Nice. That should make us welcome in the town."

"So, we go kill the commander now?" Rose asked with a grin.

"Uh no," Michael answered. "The commander is probably in the most guarded part of that burrow. We'll have to slowly fight our way to him. And given how the guards reacted when they found your little doodles on the tree, we should probably expect that they'll react like real enemies."

"What do you mean?" Rose asked, her tone going from enthusiasm to worry in a heartbeat.

"I mean, the AI in this game seems very sophisticated," Michael explained. "Once we start attacking the base itself, they'll probably set up some sort of defenses to make it more difficult for us. Maybe even traps and ambushes."

"The AI is smart," Madison said. "We'll have to be smarter."

"That's the plan," Cole agreed. "We'll need to test their defenses and see how they react. Hit and run tactics might work the best."

"Unless they come at us with their entire army," Michael said.

"Let's hope they don't do that!" Cole retorted.

"So then, what's the first step?" Madison asked.

"We should decide soon," Michael said, pointing at the sky. "Because it looks like it's getting dark."

Everyone looked up. Cole frowned. "Well, that stinks."

"Why?" Rose asked

"Because we can't see in the dark," Cole replied.

"Can we use torches?" Madison suggested.

"We'd have to go back and buy some," he replied.

"And those were one of those expensive things," Rose remembered.

Madison scratched her head. "How long is an hour in real time?"

"About 6 hours," Rose said quickly. Everyone looked at her and she shrugged. "What? I calculated it."

Michael whistled. "Nice."

"Okay," Madison said. "So nighttime is probably what... 8 or 10 hours... that's like an hour and a half. I say we use the rest of daylight to get to the gnoll place, then take an early lunch and come back first thing tomorrow morning, game time."

Michael nodded. "That sounds good."

"Sure," Rose agreed.

Cole frowned but then shrugged. "That's fine, I guess. But we'll need to figure something out for nighttime, since that's a lot of play time we'll miss."

"Everyone think about it while we're gone and see if we come up with any ideas," Madison suggested.

Everyone agreed and they quickly retraced their steps to the gnoll burrow. This time, there were no gnolls running about at the farm, nor were there any outside the burrow. They crept quietly through the forest as the sun continued sinking beneath the horizon.

Rose pointed out that she could see just fine, even once the light was almost gone. Madison noticed the same thing, though she did notice her night vision seemed to fade after 100 feet or so. Cole and Michael were literally in the dark. They had no night vision and bumped into trees and nearly tripped on roots as they made their way to the gnoll burrow.

Stopping on the outskirts of the clearing, they crouched down and looked towards the burrow entrance. A line of gnolls now stood watch, with torches mounted on poles, like tiki torches. It was obvious they were expecting trouble.

Cole scowled as they looked into the clearing from the cover of the trees. "It looks like they're onto us. Killing the gnolls earlier must have alerted them."

"What does that mean?" Rose asked, eyes wide.

"It means they'll be ready for us," Michael explained. "It means things just got a lot tougher."

Cole cursed his breath.

"Cole!" Madison snapped.

He shrugged and at least attempted to look embarrassed. "Let me think about a strategy while we break."

There was a murmur of agreement and they all prepared to log out.

"One thing we know now though," Madison pointed out before they logged.

"What's that?" Cole asked.

"The gnolls can't see in the dark either," she said, pointing at the torches. "Otherwise, they wouldn't have those."

The others turned and looked back at the gnolls. Cole scratched his head. "Good catch. Maybe we can exploit that somehow."

"Think about it while we break," Rose said.

"Right," Cole agreed.

"See you guys in an hour and a half," Madison told them and then used her log-out option. As she did, the world faded away.

17

They logged back in after lunch just as the sun was starting to rise in the sky in Koyesta. They crept back to the edge of the clearing and peered towards the entrance. A few things had changed since the last time they'd been logged in.

The torches they had seen previously had mostly died out. They were little more than flickers at this point. Additionally, the ten gnolls they'd seen before had been reduced to only six. Four of the six were propped up against the side of the entrance, sleeping.

"There's only two alert guards!" Michael whispered. "If we get in quick, we can take them out before the other four get a chance to wake up fully."

Cole nodded. "This might be our best chance to get in quietly."

"What if they cry out for help?" Madison asked. "Or raise an alarm."

"If they raise the alarm," Cole replied after thinking

for a moment. "We retreat back here and see what they do."

Madison bit her lip. Given the Fisherton guards' reactions to her carvings, she wondered if the gnolls might be craftier than they thought.

Even as she thought that, there was barking from the entrance as a large gnoll came out of the entrance and began barking and snarling at the others. Its demeanor reminded Madison of a drill sergeant.

The gnolls who had been sleeping sprang to their feet, tails between their legs and heads down. The drill sergeant cuffed one of the slower moving gnolls. The blow sent the other gnoll stumbling, causing the others to snicker. They stopped quickly when the sergeant glared at them.

"I guess that's their boss," Michael whispered.

"Or their dad," Rose joked.

"Whoever it is," Cole complained. "He just ruined our surprise attack."

"Wait," Madison said, getting their attention. "Something's happening."

They turned their attention back to the entrance just in time to see a dozen gnolls emerge. The new group immediately split into two groups of six and jogged into the forest. Unlike the other gnolls, these all carried bows.

"Archers?" Michael asked.

"Hunters," Madison guessed, remembering their own struggle for food.

"Interesting," Cole said. "You might be right."

"So even they have to eat," Rose commented.

"It would seem so," Cole said.

"We should go after the hunting parties," Madison said. "Cut off their food supply."

Cole nodded. "Good idea."

"They'll probably send out more hunting parties then," Michael pointed out. "Probably with more gnolls."

"Then we kill those too," Cole said. He looked at Rose. "You didn't get a better healing spell yet, did you?"

Rose shook her head, pouting her lips. "Still the same one."

"I hope it's enough," Cole sighed. "Six at a time is a lot."

"Hey," Michael said with a grin. "What's the worst that could happen? We die? We'll just respawn and come back and try again."

"Fair enough." Cole shrugged. "Let's go!"

Using her tracking skill, Rose led the way through the forest until they caught up with one of the hunting parties. When they found them, the gnolls had just taken down a deer, and were gathered around it. Cole didn't hesitate.

"Charge!" her brother yelled, rushing forward with his sword raised.

The gnolls were surprised at the large barbarian suddenly rushing towards them and they hesitated. Cole's sudden charge also surprised the rest of them and they hurried to catch up with him.

Rose cast her protection spell on Cole just as he waded into the gnolls. With a mighty sweep of his sword, he sliced through three of the gnolls' bows, effectively disarming them. The stroke ended by carving into another of the gnoll's arms. Madison and the others caught up to him just as the gnolls began to react.

"Fight me!" Cole began yelling, taunting the six dogmen. They turned to face him, eager to put an end to their enemy.

Michael arrived first, followed by Buddy. Both attacked the injured gnoll in the middle as it went for the dagger at its side.

Zachatolus Catfriend crushes Blackmange Gnoll Hunter for 8 damage.
Buddy bites Blackmange Gnoll Hunter for 6 damage.

Madison arrived next and slammed her staff down on the thing's head.

You crush a Blackmange Gnoll Hunter for 6 damage.

Rose arrived last, slicing her scimitar across the back of its legs.

Plays-With-Animals slashes Blackmange Gnoll Hunter for 7 damage.

Then it was the gnolls' turn to retaliate. The three whose bows had been destroyed tossed their destroyed weapons to the ground and grabbed the long knives at their belt. The other three took a step back and fired their arrows point blank at Cole.

Blackmange Gnoll Hunter pierces Brothar Snowbear for 6 damage.
Blackmange Gnoll Hunter pierces Brothar Snowbear for 7 damage.
Blackmange Gnoll Hunter pierces Brothar Snowbear for 5 damage.

"Ugh!" her brother growled. "That really hurt!"

With three arrows sticking in him, Cole swung his great sword at the injured gnoll hunter, slicing it down the front from shoulder to groin. The thing howled in pain.

Brothar Snowbear slashes Blackmange Gnoll Hunter for 11 damage.

Her group attacked again, focusing on the same gnoll in an attempt to bring it down.

Zachatolus Catfriend crushes Blackmange Gnoll Hunter for 7 damage.
Buddy bites Blackmange Gnoll Hunter for 7 damage.
You have killed Blackmange Gnoll Hunter.
You have gained experience!
Your reputation with Residents of Fisherton has increased.
Your reputation with Guards of Fisherton has increased.
Your reputation with Blackmange Gnolls has decreased.

The gnoll hunter collapsed and Madison changed her

target to the one next to it, swinging her staff down on top of its head, right between the ears. The dogman yelped.

You crush a Blackmange Gnoll Hunter for 7 damage.

Instead of attacking, Rose took the opportunity to cast her healing spell on Cole. He didn't acknowledge her spell, but focused on the remaining gnolls, yelling out taunts again.

Plays-With-Animals heals Brothar Snowbear for 11 damage.

By now, all of the hunters were armed and retaliated against the big man.

Blackmange Gnoll Hunter pierces Brothar Snowbear for 4 damage.
Blackmange Gnoll Hunter pierces Brothar Snowbear for 5 damage.
Blackmange Gnoll Hunter pierces Brothar Snowbear for 7 damage.
Blackmange Gnoll Hunter pierces Brothar Snowbear for 6 damage.
Blackmange Gnoll Hunter pierces Brothar Snowbear for 5 damage.

"Argh!" Cole grimaced as the gnoll's weapons found their mark. Growling, he swung his big sword across the chest of the injured gnoll, leaving a long gash.

Brothar Snowbear slashes Blackmange Gnoll Hunter for 12 damage.
Zachatolus Catfriend crushes Blackmange Gnoll Hunter for 5 damage.
Buddy bites Blackmange Gnoll Hunter for 9 damage.
You crush a Blackmange Gnoll Hunter for 7 damage.

Rose once again cast her healing spell on Cole, healing some of his wounds.

Plays-With-Animals heals Brothar Snowbear for 10 damage.

Barking and growling, the gnolls had their own turn, stabbing and firing their arrows.

Blackmange Gnoll Hunter pierces Brothar Snowbear for 4 damage.
Blackmange Gnoll Hunter pierces Brothar Snowbear for 7 damage.
Blackmange Gnoll Hunter pierces Brothar Snowbear for 4 damage.
Blackmange Gnoll Hunter pierces Brothar Snowbear for 7 damage.
Blackmange Gnoll Hunter pierces Brothar Snowbear for 6 damage.

Her brother was looking a bit worse for wear, bleeding now from a dozen wounds. But, still he kept fighting. This time, in addition to slashing the creature with his sword, Cole slammed the hilt into its face.

Brothar Snowbear slashes Blackmange Gnoll Hunter for 11 damage.
Brothar Snowbear slams Blackmange Gnoll Hunter for 6 damage.

The force of the blow to the face snapped the gnoll's neck back at a bad angle. There was a cracking sound and the gnoll dropped bonelessly to the ground. That left four.

You have killed Blackmange Gnoll Hunter.
You have gained experience!
Your reputation with Residents of Fisherton has increased.
Your reputation with Guards of Fisherton has increased.
Your reputation with Blackmange Gnolls has decreased.

Michael and Madison both attacked the next one, while Rose continued to pour healing into Cole.

Zachatolus Catfriend crushes Blackmange Gnoll Hunter for 7 damage.
Buddy bites Blackmange Gnoll Hunter for 3 damage.
You crush a Blackmange Gnoll Hunter for 4 damage.
Plays-With-Animals heals Brothar Snowbear for 13 damage.

If the gnolls had any feelings for the two gnolls who had fallen, they didn't show it. Unless they figured the best retort was fighting back.

Blackmange Gnoll Hunter pierces Brothar Snowbear for 5 damage.
Blackmange Gnoll Hunter pierces Brothar Snowbear for 4 damage.
Blackmange Gnoll Hunter pierces Brothar Snowbear for 5 damage.
Blackmange Gnoll Hunter pierces Brothar Snowbear for 5 damage.

Her brother staggered under the blows but stayed up. As a paladin and a barbarian, he had more health than any of them. Madison just hoped it would be enough.

Brothar Snowbear slashes Blackmange Gnoll Hunter for 13 damage.
Zachatolus Catfriend crushes Blackmange Gnoll Hunter for 8 damage.
Buddy bites Blackmange Gnoll Hunter for 6 damage.
You have killed Blackmange Gnoll Hunter.
You have gained experience!
Your reputation with Residents of Fisherton has increased.
Your reputation with Guards of Fisherton has increased.
Your reputation with Blackmange Gnolls has decreased.

The third gnoll went down under an onslaught from her brother, Michael and Buddy, leaving Madison to pivot and swing her club like a baseball bat at a gnoll's head.

You crush a Blackmange Gnoll Hunter for 7 damage.
Plays-With-Animals heals Brothar Snowbear for 10 damage.

The three remaining gnolls hesitated, looking down at their fallen comrades. It wasn't a long hesitation, but it cost them.

Brothar Snowbear slashes Blackmange Gnoll Hunter for 12 damage.
Brothar Snowbear slams Blackmange Gnoll Hunter for 5 damage.
Zachatolus Catfriend crushes Blackmange Gnoll Hunter for 7 damage.
Buddy bites Blackmange Gnoll Hunter for 8 damage.
You crush a Blackmange Gnoll Hunter for 9 damage.
You have killed Blackmange Gnoll Hunter.
You have gained experience!
Your reputation with Residents of Fisherton has increased.
Your reputation with Guards of Fisherton has increased.
Your reputation with Blackmange Gnolls has decreased.

Barking and yipping, the last two gnolls realized they probably weren't going to make it. They sliced at her brother, missing and then ran in different directions.

The sudden movement caught Madison's group by surprise and although they all managed blows against the fleeing gnolls, they couldn't coordinate their efforts. Half of them struck one creature while the rest attacked the other.

Brothar Snowbear slashes Blackmange Gnoll Hunter for 13 damage.
Zachatolus Catfriend crushes Blackmange Gnoll Hunter for 9 damage.
Buddy bites Blackmange Gnoll Hunter for 7 damage.
You crush a Blackmange Gnoll Hunter for 8 damage.
Plays-With-Animals heals Brothar Snowbear for 11 damage.

The blows weren't enough to bring either of the gnolls down and they were suddenly left with a choice as to who to go after.

"Don't let either get away to warn the burrow!" Cole yelled. "Michael, you and Rose go after that one! Madison and I will get the other one!"

Running after her brother, they ran through the trees after the creature. It was only ten feet in front of them, but it seemed to be maintaining the distance.

Suddenly, Madison remembered her spells. She cast her Minor Telekinetic Asphyxiation on the gnoll, causing it to gasp and cough as it pawed at its throat. Nearly stumbling as it tried to catch its breath, the two of them quickly caught up with it.

Brothar Snowbear slashes Blackmange Gnoll Hunter for 12 damage.
Brothar Snowbear slams Blackmange Gnoll Hunter for 6 damage.

You crush a Blackmange Gnoll Hunter for 9 damage.

The gnoll seemed more intent on getting away than fighting and tried to slip by them. It was a mistake.

Brothar Snowbear slashes Blackmange Gnoll Hunter for 13 damage.
You crush a Blackmange Gnoll Hunter for 8 damage.
You have killed Blackmange Gnoll Hunter.
You have gained experience!
Your reputation with Residents of Fisherton has increased.
Your reputation with Guards of Fisherton has increased.
Your reputation with Blackmange Gnolls has decreased.

Madison's staff blow to the neck seemed to be the last straw. The gnoll clutched at its throat and then fell to the ground. Dead.

Reaching down, Madison looted the gnoll.

Blackmange Gnoll Hunter
Rusty Sword (x1)
Rusty Shield (x1)
Loot all (Yes/No)

She looted the items and Cole shook his head. "Not that I'm complaining, but if it had a sword and shield, why didn't it use them?"

Madison shrugged and they turned to walk back to

the other gnoll bodies. After only a few steps, they received a message that let them know Michael and Rose had gotten their gnoll.

You have killed Blackmange Gnoll Hunter.
You have gained experience!
Your reputation with Residents of Fisherton has increased.
Your reputation with Guards of Fisherton has increased.
Your reputation with Blackmange Gnolls has decreased.

Madison grimaced, still breathing hard from chasing the gnoll. "One group down. One to go."

18

The next group proved only slightly more difficult than the other group. Better yet, after the first gnoll fell, Madison gained level 4! By the time the last gnoll fell, the rest of her party had gained level 4 as well. And with level 4, came new spells and abilities for most of them.

"Sweet!" Cole said, still glassy eyed from looking at his HUD. "I have a new ability called Healing Hands. It allows me to heal damage once per hour. I also have a new skill called Smash."

"What does it do?" Madison asked.

"COLE SMASH!" her brother said in a low voice, mimicking the big green superhero from the movies. Given how big her brother's avatar was, he was really only missing the green skin. When no one laughed, he shrugged. "I don't know. But it's one more attack."

"Oh yeah!" Michael said, obviously looking at his own character sheet. "A new attack skill called kick!"

"That's nice!" Rose said. "So, you can... kick things?"

Michael nodded with a grin. "And Michael was kung fu fighting! He and Buddy were fast as lightning..."

The others rolled their eyes.

"What?" Michael said. "Surely you've heard the legend of the great Beastmaster ninja and his faithful cat?"

Rose put her hands on her hips. "And you're him?"

Michael nodded and gave her a knowing smile. "Some say it is so."

Rose cocked her head and looked down at Buddy. The gray, striped cub was hopping around after a butterfly at the moment, looking super cute. She furrowed her brow. "Is it me, or is Buddy bigger?"

Taking a hard look at the tiger cub, Madison realized Rose was right. "You're right! He is bigger!"

Michael nodded nonchalantly. "As I level, so does he. Or, at least, his stats go up."

"That's cool!" Rose said. She pouted. "When do I get a pet?!"

"Did either of you two get new skills or anything?" Cole asked.

"Ooh!" Rose said as she looked at her character sheet. "I got a new skill called Forage!"

"I have that!" Madison told her. "It lets you find edible food in the forest."

"That's cool!" she said. "Oh! And I have new spells too! Five of them!" Her eyes went glassy as she read through her spellbook. "One is called Camouflage. Then there's two cure spells: poison and disease. One is called Minor Gateway. It says it sends me to my bind point."

Rose hesitated and looked directly at Michael. "The last one that allows me to Call the wind...."

"Pass gas, you mean?" Michael snickered.

"Uh!" Rose threw her hands up. "I knew that's where your mind would go! No! It does damage and a stun, possibly pushing the creature backwards."

"That sounds like what happens when Cole passes gas. It stuns me and pushes me back!" Michael chuckled.

Cole snorted but Madison ignored the two boys.

"That sounds interesting," Madison said. "You can stun something without everyone having to close their eyes. For the gateway, is it just you or can you send someone else?"

Rose frowned. "Just me."

"Well," Cole sighed. "We now know that there is poison and disease in the game."

"Snakes and spiders?" Michael asked.

"And other things, no doubt," Cole replied. He looked at Madison. "How about you?"

Madison smiled. "I got some spells too!"

Cole gestured for her to continue. "And?!"

"And there are five of them," Madison teased.

"And what do they do?!" Cole asked in an exasperated tone.

"Color Blast, which stuns everyone around me," she said. "Unless you have no eyes."

Michael scratched his chin. "That probably includes us - unless we close our eyes right before you do it."

"That might work," Cole said. "We'll need to test it before we try it in combat. How long does it last?"

Madison looked at the spell description and frowned. "Only 4 seconds."

Cole nodded. "Might be good in a bind but not sure how useful it would be otherwise. What else?

"This one sounds interesting," she said. "Daydream. It puts a creature into a trance for 24 seconds - unless they are attacked."

"Crowd control," Michael said with a grin and Cole nodded.

"That might be a game changer," he said. "If we get multiple enemies, you cast that on the ones we're not fighting and they're effectively out of the fight for half a minute. If you can keep it up, it will seriously cut back the damage I take."

Madison nodded. It made sense. Any gnolls she put into a daydream, wouldn't be attacking. Then, they could focus on one or two at a time. She read off the next spell. "Animated Guardian I. It animates a sword and shield to serve me."

"For how long?" Michael asked.

Animated Guardian
Mana: 10
Duration: Special
Description: Enchant a weapon and shield to serve as a faithful servant. This animated servant can fight, guard or accept simple commands. The construct remains until the energy that holds it is dispelled through damage.
Note: Once summoned, the caster can swap weapons with the construct if better weapons are available.

Madison read the spell description again and shrugged. "It doesn't have a duration. It stays until the magic that binds it together is destroyed through damage."

Michael whistled. "That's nice! I'm not sure how much damage it will do, but it will be some extra damage. Like having another person in the group."

"Then there's one called Siphon Energy. It lets me siphon energy from a construct to replenish my mana," she told them. "I guess I can take some of the animated guardian's energy from him."

"Turn him into a walking battery," Michael said. "We'll name the animated guardian... copper top!"

Rolling her eyes, Madison read the last spell. "The last one is the same as Rose's spell. Minor Gateway."

Cole rolled his eyes. "So, the girls won't have to walk back to the village if they don't want to."

Rose and Madison exchanged looks and then gave each other high fives. They both turned to the boys and gave them superior looks.

Michael chuckled and then raised an eyebrow. "But do you have a cute tiger cub pet?"

Rose stuck her tongue out at him.

"So now what?" Madison asked. "Do we head back to the entrance?"

"Yes," he said. "We'll try out your new spells on the guards at the gate. If we can daydream most of them, it should make it easy."

"We hope," Michael snickered, bending down and scratching Buddy behind the ears. The tiger cub purred in response.

Using Rose's Tracking skill, they easily found their way back to the entrance. As before, there were six gnolls standing guard. This time, none of them were sleeping. The gnolls actually looked alert.

"This is going to be interesting," Cole said. "Go ahead and summon your guardian thing."

Madison nodded and took the sword and shield from her inventory. She laid them on the ground before her and then cast her spell. White and blue sparkles flared from her hands and then settled onto the two items. After a moment, the sword and shield floated into the air until they rested at the height where they might if a real human was holding them.

"That's freaky," Rose said, moving her hand in between the sword and shield. She shivered. "I feel something tingly but otherwise there's nothing there."

"Okay, focus," Cole said. "We rush in and I taunt them. Everyone focuses on the same one I do. Madison, you Daydream the others. Got it?"

Everyone nodded and Rose cast her protection spell on Cole, turning his skin into bark.

"Okay, on your mark, get set... charge!" Cole yelled and burst from the trees.

The group closed in on the gnolls quickly, but they had plenty of time to get ready. They assumed some sort of "V" formation in front of the entrance with the spears ready.

Cole went in fast and, reaching them, swiped his

sword across the first line of spears, shattering them. But the remaining gnolls were ready and stabbed at him.

Blackmange Gnoll Guard pierces Brothar Snowbear for 6 damage.
Blackmange Gnoll Guard pierces Brothar Snowbear for 7 damage.
Blackmange Gnoll Guard pierces Brothar Snowbear for 6 damage.

Closing, Cole smashed the flat of his blade down on the center gnoll's head and then slammed the pummel of his sword into its snout.

Brothar Snowbear bashes Blackmange Gnoll Guard for 6 damage.
Brothar Snowbear slams Blackmange Gnoll Guard for 7 damage.

Michael and Buddy reached them next. Her cousin jumped up and delivered a painful-looking flying kick to its chest, staggering it. He then followed up with a blow from his iron stick to its neck. At the same time Buddy pounced on the gnoll's leg biting it, while simultaneously scratching with one of his paws.

Zachatolus Catfriend kicks Blackmange Gnoll Guard for 6 damage.
Zachatolus Catfriend crushes Blackmange Gnoll Guard for 7 damage.
Buddy bites Blackmange Gnoll Guard for 7 damage.

Buddy claws Blackmange Gnoll Guard for 4 damage.

Rose reached them next, slicing across the gnoll's chest with her scimitar.

Plays-With-Animals slashes Blackmange Gnoll Guard for 8 damage.

Madison reached them last because she had slowed down so she could cast her spell. Before she did, she pointed to the center gnoll and looked at her Animated Guardian. "Kill!"

Silently, the shield and sword glided forward. As soon as it was in range of the gnoll, it slammed its shield into the thing and then slashed its sword across the creature's legs.

Animated Guardian slams Blackmange Gnoll Guard for 7 damage.
Animated Guardian slashes Blackmange Gnoll Guard for 6 damage.

After a moment, her spell went off and rainbow sparkles surrounded the gnoll on the far left.

Blackmange Gnoll Guard is Daydreaming.

The gnoll's jaw went slack and its weapon dipped. Its eyes went dull as it just stood there and stared off into space. Madison grinned. It had worked! She began to cast the spell again, this time aiming it at the one on the far right.

Blackmange Gnoll Guard pierces Brothar Snowbear for 6 damage.
Blackmange Gnoll Guard pierces Brothar Snowbear for 7 damage.
Blackmange Gnoll Guard pierces Brothar Snowbear for 6 damage.
Blackmange Gnoll Guard pierces Brothar Snowbear for 4 damage.
Blackmange Gnoll Guard pierces Brothar Snowbear for 5 damage.

Her brother grimaced as spears and daggers stabbed out at him. Growling, he brought his greatsword down on the center gnoll's shoulder, biting in deep.

Brothar Snowbear slashes Blackmange Gnoll Guard for 11 damage.

"They're tougher than the hunters," Cole growled.

Zachatolus Catfriend crushes Blackmange Gnoll Guard for 8 damage.
Buddy bites Blackmange Gnoll Guard for 7 damage.

"It's still going down!" Michael grinned as he and Buddy attacked it.

Plays-With-Animals heals Brothar Snowbear for 11 damage.
Animated Guardian slashes Blackmange Gnoll Guard for 7 damage.

Madison's spell went off and the one on the far right sagged, staring off into nothing. "Two down!"

"Good!" Cole said, right before a flurry of blows hit him.

Blackmange Gnoll Guard pierces Brothar Snowbear for 5 damage.
Blackmange Gnoll Guard pierces Brothar Snowbear for 8 damage.
Blackmange Gnoll Guard pierces Brothar Snowbear for 5 damage.
Blackmange Gnoll Guard pierces Brothar Snowbear for 5 damage.

Cole slashed his sword down, lopping off the creature's head, its lifeless body toppling to the ground. He then spun and slammed the flat of his blade into the side of the next gnoll's head before slamming him with the pommel.

Brothar Snowbear slashes Blackmange Gnoll Guard for 11 damage.
You have killed Blackmange Gnoll Guard.
You have gained experience!
Your reputation with Residents of Fisherton has increased.

Your reputation with Guards of Fisherton has increased.
Your reputation with Blackmange Gnolls has decreased.
Brothar Snowbear bashes Blackmange Gnoll Guard for 7 damage.
Brothar Snowbear slams Blackmange Gnoll Guard for 5 damage
Zachatolus Catfriend kicks Blackmange Gnoll Guard for 7 damage.
Zachatolus Catfriend crushes Blackmange Gnoll Guard for 7 damage.
Buddy bites Blackmange Gnoll Guard for 5 damage.
Buddy claws Blackmange Gnoll Guard for 6 damage.
Plays-With-Animals heals Brothar Snowbear for 10 damage.
Animated Guardian slams Blackmange Gnoll Guard for 6 damage.
Animated Guardian slashes Blackmange Gnoll Guard for 8 damage.

Madison cast her Daydream spell on the next gnoll, causing him to go slack jawed too. She smiled. Combined with her guardian attacking, she felt like she was really contributing to the combat.

One of the gnolls was dead and three were daydreaming. That left only two gnolls who were actually fighting.

Blackmange Gnoll Guard pierces Brothar Snowbear for 7 damage.

Blackmange Gnoll Guard pierces Brothar Snowbear for 6 damage.
Brothar Snowbear slashes Blackmange Gnoll Guard for 9 damage.
Zachatolus Catfriend crushes Blackmange Gnoll Guard for 8 damage.
Buddy bites Blackmange Gnoll Guard for 6 damage.
Plays-With-Animals heals Brothar Snowbear for 10 damage.
Animated Guardian slashes Blackmange Gnoll Guard for 7 damage.

Casting her spell on the final fighting gnoll that wasn't being hit, she growled in frustration as her spell fizzled. She immediately began to recast it.

Blackmange Gnoll Guard pierces Brothar Snowbear for 7 damage.
Blackmange Gnoll Guard pierces Brothar Snowbear for 8 damage.

Her brother took two more hits but then retaliated with his full arsenal of attacks, slashing, slamming and bashing their current target. It didn't survive.

Brothar Snowbear slashes Blackmange Gnoll Guard for 11 damage.
Brothar Snowbear bashes Blackmange Gnoll Guard for 7 damage.
Brothar Snowbear slams Blackmange Gnoll Guard for 5 damage.

You have killed Blackmange Gnoll Guard.
You have gained experience!
Your reputation with Residents of Fisherton has increased.
Your reputation with Guards of Fisherton has increased.
Your reputation with Blackmange Gnolls has decreased.

Since the only gnoll not Daydreaming was now their target, Madison quickly switched her spell to the first one she had cast the spell on. She wasn't sure how close the time was to expiring, but she wanted to make sure it didn't rejoin the fight.

The remaining gnolls went down very quickly. With only one gnoll attacking at a time and the others staring dumbly out into space, they focused on their target until it went down while Madison kept the others stupefied.

"Good job, Madison," Cole said as the last gnoll fell. "Good crowd control."

Madison smiled. It was nice to be an important part of the group, instead of someone who just whacked things with her staff. A girl could get used to this.

19

The group quickly looted the corpses and moved to the entrance of the cave. They peeked around the sides of the cave, looking into the tunnel that led down.

"Do you think anyone heard us?" Rose asked.

Cole shrugged. "I don't hear anything."

Madison craned her head to get a better look down the tunnel, but her vision was obscured as the tunnel dipped down. "I don't see any other gnolls."

"Let's go down," Michael said enthusiastically.

"Uh..." Rose muttered, screwing up her face. "We want to go down into the spooky tunnel without knowing what's waiting for us? Isn't that like... something people do in a horror movie?"

"Probably." Michael grinned even wider.

"We should scout it out," Rose said.

Cole nudged his head toward the opening. "Go ahead."

Rose looked at him wide-eyed. “Me? Why me?”

“Aren’t you the one who can see in the dark? If you don’t carry a torch, they have less chance of seeing you,” Cole pointed out.

The little elf girl’s mouth moved but no words came out. Finally, she shut her mouth and stepped out into the opening of the cave. “Fine! But if I die... it’s your fault!”

Cole shrugged and then motioned her forward.

Gritting her teeth, she started into the cave hesitantly.

“I’ll go with you,” Madison volunteered. “I can see in the dark too.” She gave Cole and Michael a dark look. “I mean, if the boys are too afraid to go down, we girls can do it.”

She grabbed Rose’s hand and the two of them started forward. Outside the glow of the torches, the tunnel was dark. Luckily, Madison’s reptilian eyes allowed her to see much better than a human in darkness.

The two of them continued down the sloping passageway but stopped when they heard barking and yapping further down the tunnel.

“Are they coming this way?” Rose asked.

Madison shrugged. “I can’t tell. We’ll have to keep going.”

“I was afraid you’d say that,” Rose replied.

They continued on, hugging the sides of the tunnel until they turned a corner and saw light up ahead. Rose, who was on the opposite side of the cave, made biting motions with her teeth. Madison frowned. Was that supposed to mean gnolls?

Keeping low, Madison crossed to the opposite side of

the tunnel and slowly moved aside her cousin. "What do you see?"

"Gnolls," the elf whispered. "Seven, no eight."

"That's a lot," Madison said. "Two more than we've taken on."

Madison glanced around the part of the room she could see. "There might be more in there too."

Rose shook her head. She had a better vantage point than Madison and appeared to be able to see more. "That's all of them."

"Okay," Madison said. "I have an idea. Let's go back."

"What idea?" Rose asked.

"I'll tell you when we get back," Madison said and then quietly crept back into the darkness of the tunnel and back towards Michael and her brother.

They made it back and quickly explained the situation. Cole frowned as he heard their report.

"That's a lot of gnolls," he said. "A lot for me to tank until you get them mezzed."

"Mezzed?" Madison asked, brow furrowed.

"You know, mesmerized," he grinned. "Like, in a daydream..."

Madison rolled her eyes. "Anyway, I have a plan."

"Let's hear it," Cole said.

"I go first," she started. "I'll get to where I can see them. Then, I'll ... uh... mez... one and at the same time, send my armored guardian after another. That'll leave us six. And we've dealt with six before.

The rest of the group exchanged glances. Michael nodded his head. "That'll work. Let's just hope you can hold off the gnoll long enough."

"Once we take down the first one," Cole told them. "I'll taunt that one off. It'll be a little rough, but I think we can do it. Good plan."

Madison beamed. Considering that she didn't play this type of game that often, she felt proud of herself for coming up with the idea. She just hoped it worked!

"One problem," Michael pointed out. "If we're using torches, they'll see the light coming."

Shaking her head, Madison motioned for Rose to come over. Her cousin hurried over and stopped in front of her.

"Rose will lead you," Madison told them. "She'll be your eyes. Cole, you can put a hand on her shoulder and Michael can put a hand on your shoulder. She'll lead you down to the point where there's light. You should be able to take it from there."

Michael and Cole exchanged looks and then nodded.

"That sounds good," her brother said. Then he turned to Michael. "Remember, hand on my shoulder. If you find your hand between two pillows, remember - those aren't pillows."

Madison let out a breath and rolled her eyes while the boys had a chuckle. "Are you done?"

"Yes, Mom," Cole said and stuck his tongue out.

She made a face and stuck her tongue out in return. It was actually a bit freaky looking, even to her, since she now had a forked tongue.

Cole made a face. "That's gross."

"Yes, yes," Madison said. "It is... let's just get going, okay?"

"Okay," Cole said. "Let's get going. Madison, lead the way. Rose, you're our eyes."

Madison led the way back down the passage. They went down the slope and then all the way to the turn in the passage. From their position, the boys signaled that they could see into the light. That was good. Once she kicked things off, they'd need to rush around the corner.

Putting her hand at her side where they could see it, she counted down on her fingers. 5... 4... 3... 2... 1.

Madison cast her spell at the nearest one she could see.

Blackmange Gnoll Guard is daydreaming.

The gnoll she targeted went slack jawed and glassy eyed while the one next to it spun and, seeing her, barked to the others.

"Kill it!" she ordered her Animated Guardian and the sword and shield glided forward, slicing at the gnoll as it ran towards her.

Animated Guardian slams Blackmange Gnoll Guard for 6 damage.
Animated Guardian Slashes Blackmange Gnoll Guard for 8 damage.

The gnoll guard staggered and then began pawing and scratching at the guardian.

As it did, her brother came barreling around the corner and began yelling his taunts at the gnolls as he unleashed his full arsenal of attacks on the closest gnoll.

Brothar Snowbear slashes Blackmange Gnoll Guard for 10 damage.
Brothar Snowbear bashes Blackmange Gnoll Guard for 7 damage.
Brothar Snowbear slams Blackmange Gnoll Guard for 6 damage.

"Your mama has fleas!"

"Your daddy's in the pound!"

"You deserve the cone of shame!"

"No treats for you!"

"Bad doggie!"

Michael and Rose ran around the corner on his heels, attacking the same gnoll.

Zachatolus Catfriend kicks Blackmange Gnoll Guard for 6 damage.
Zachatolus Catfriend crushes Blackmange Gnoll Guard for 7 damage.
Buddy bites Blackmange Gnoll Guard for 7 damage.
Buddy claws Blackmange Gnoll Guard for 4 damage.
Plays-With-Animals slashes Blackmange Gnoll Guard for 8 damage.

Like the fight with the guards above, this went as expected. With Madison keeping the gnolls occupied with her Daydream spell and everyone else focusing their damage on one gnoll at a time, they cut through the ranks easily.

They were down to the last two when the one they

were focusing on suddenly spun and ran out the opposite entrance to the cave, barking.

"Kill her! Kill her!" Cole yelled but it was too late. The fleeing gnoll disappeared into the opposite side, barking and yapping in pain. Moments later, other barking and growling could be heard further away.

The group exchanged looks. Cole looked around the room and then down at the bodies. "Loot and run! Loot and run!"

The barking grew steadily closer from the opposite tunnel. The party looted the six corpses littering the floor. Cole and Michael grabbed torches from the walls, and they all ran up the tunnel as fast as they could.

When they got to the top, Madison called for them to stop. "Give me your torches!"

"What?!" Cole gasped, out of breath from the run.

"Give me your torches now!" she repeated.

The boys did so, and she moved the Animated Guardian's shield so it was flat. It didn't resist. She set the torches on it. "Keep going that way!"

Without a word, the Animated Guardian glided towards the far edge of the clearing. Madison pointed the opposite way. "Come on, we go this way."

"Nice!" Michael grinned. "Decoy!"

"It's light," Cole said, following Madison. "You think they'll see the torches."

"No idea," Madison puffed. "But it was all I could think of."

The group made it into the woods about the same time as a large group of gnolls came rushing out of the entrance.

Crouched down in the bushes, Madison lost count at twenty. The gnolls looked around and then one of them spotted the torches moving through the forest in the opposite direction.

Barking and pointing, the gnolls rushed off after the Animated Guardian. Moments later, they had disappeared into the woods.

"Come on," Cole said. "Let's put some space between us in case they come back to the area and search around."

They all nodded and moved away from the gnoll lair, anxious to put some distance between them before the dogmen returned.

20

Madison and her group retreated nearly a mile away before stopping. The group took up positions behind trees and waited to see if the gnolls would follow them. After fifteen minutes, they started to relax.

Madison received a message that her Animated Guardian had been dismissed, so she assumed the gnolls had caught up with it and killed it. Belatedly, she realized her guardian had carried away their only shield. Without a new shield, she wouldn't be able to summon another one.

She turned to her brother. "So, now what?"

Her brother shrugged. "I'm not sure. This AI seems pretty smart. I'm not sure what it will do next."

"Search the woods?" Rose asked in a worried tone.

"I think we would have heard them or seen them coming by now," Michael said. He was sitting cross-legged with Buddy nestled in his lap, sleeping. He stroked the tiger cub's fur. "Right?"

"Maybe," Cole said with a shrug. He glanced back the way they had come.

"If the AI is so smart," Madison said. "It might make similar choices to us, right?"

Cole and Michael nodded their heads.

"What would you do if you were in charge of defending the burrow?" Madison asked. She didn't play these games and wasn't sure what would be considered valid strategies. If it were her, she would have searched around the forest. She might even have led a retaliatory strike against the town or burned some more farms.

"I'd probably set up booby traps," Cole said. "Or some sort of ambush. Lure them in, then box them in and kill them."

"Great," Rose said.

"But these are fairly low-level monsters," Cole commented. "If they were adept at tactics, it would be impossible for low-level players to kill them."

Madison considered his words. She cocked her head. "I wonder how smart they're supposed to be."

"I'm sure they're no Einsteins," Rose retorted, getting a snicker from Michael.

"True," Cole said with a nod. "Some of their tactics might depend on whatever their intelligence is supposed to be."

"You said that you might set up booby traps, right?" Madison said.

Her brother nodded. "Yeah... lure them into the lair,

then do a covered pit with spikes or something like that. Depends on what materials I had at my disposal. Why?"

"Why don't we set up booby traps?" She smiled. "Maybe dig a pit, fill it full of sharpened sticks and lure them to it."

Cole gave Madison a wicked grin. "That's evil! I didn't know you had it in you!"

Madison rolled her eyes. "It's just a game."

Michael nodded approvingly. "Oh yeah… it starts with a few booby traps in a game and the next thing you know, you're lowering lotion down to someone in your basement going - it puts the lotions on its skin."

Rose and Cole chuckled, and Madison glared at her cousin.

"I think it's worth a try," Cole said. He looked around. "The problem is, without a shovel, it will take a LONG time to dig a pit."

"What about those branches where you bend them back and attach spikes, and then when someone trips the rope, they whip around and stab them," Rose asked.

"I like that idea!" Michael said, waking Buddy. The cub looked around, yawned and then closed its eyes and settled back down for a nap.

"No rope," Madison said, sagging back against a tree. She had thought she was being clever, but they didn't have the resources to do what they needed to. Suddenly she had an idea. "How much money do we have left?!"

Everyone turned to her. "What?"

"I've got an idea," she said. "We need rope and shovels. Can't we just go back to the village, get them and then come back and make our traps?"

The others exchanged glances and Cole facepalmed. "That's perfect! In fact, it will be cheap because shovels are things the NPCs use. Same with rope. Good idea!"

Rose smiled smugly. "Or you boys can stay here while us girls gate back to the village, get the stuff and come back. It will take half the time."

"I forgot about that," Cole admitted. "You're right. It would take half the time."

Rose put her fist out and Madison fist bumped her. Rose smiled. "Girl power!"

It was her brother's turn to roll his eyes. "Yeah, yeah. Girl power."

"More like.... Girls go to town on a shopping spree," Michael snickered.

Rose stuck her tongue out at Michael but shrugged. "Actually, that's not a bad idea."

"Focus!" Madison said, snapping her fingers in front of Rose. "We barely have any money. We can't spend it all at once." She paused, looked at Cole and then winked. "Unless we see something really cool!"

"Totally." Rose grinned.

"I think we just went broke," Michael commented with a frown.

"You might be right," Cole agreed. His eyes went glassy for a second. "Since you're going back, take our loot and sell it."

Madison nodded and the two boys began to pull things out of their inventory and pass it to Rose and Madison. By the time Cole had emptied his inventory, both girls were so weighted down, they could barely move.

"OMG!" Rose said. "I feel like I have weights strapped to every part of my body."

"Me too," Madison growled.

"What happened to girl power?" Cole snickered. Then he became serious. "You're probably overburdened. Just go sell before you do anything else, and you should be fine."

"Easy for you to say," Rose groaned. "I feel like Grandpa with his cane."

Madison felt her pain, literally. It really did feel like she was Atlas, with the world on her shoulders. "Come on, let's go and sell all this stuff."

Madison and Rose both began casting their spells. The spells took much longer than their other spells, nearly thirty seconds. Finally, she finished, and the forest faded away to be replaced by the sounds of seagulls and the smell of the ocean. Looking around, she realized they were back on the beach where she'd arrived.

"Cool!" Rose said with a smile, but the smile quickly faded. "We're here. Let's go sell this stuff before my avatar has a hernia."

"Amen to that," Madison said, and the two girls slowly limped towards the nearest store.

FIFTEEN MINUTES LATER, they had sold all of their items to the three stores in the area, all except for a half dozen spears Madison decided they should stick down at the bottom of the pit.

They found and bought several coils of rope and four

shovels. As Cole had guessed, those items had probably been meant for the NPCs, so were priced low enough that the NPCs could afford them.

What surprised Madison the most, was the way people no longer looked at her in fear or disgust. Most people just gave her a curious stare or paid her no mind.

Rose, on the other hand, had people smiling at her, waving or even saying greetings to her. She seemed like the most popular person in town. Rose beamed at all of the attention and waved and replied back to the people. *Must be nice,* Madison thought to herself.

"They sure are nice now," Rose said, waving to another passerby who tipped his cap to her.

"To you at least," Madison frowned.

"Aww," Rose said, playfully jabbing Madison with her elbow. "I'm sure they like you too... deep down."

Madison looked around at the people, none of which showed the same friendliness towards her. "It must be VERY deep down."

"But they're not trying to kill you," her cousin noted.

"Thank God for small favors," Madison agreed.

She briefly wondered if her new status was the work of Captain Bartem. Had the man spread the word about her? Or if it was somehow a result of the reputation system and having killed all of the gnolls was finally paying off. She shrugged to herself. It didn't matter.

While she would have enjoyed a little goodwill from the townsfolk, she was just happy to walk around without the glares and stares. So long as they weren't trying to kill her or tying her to a stake and burning her, she was good.

Some more townsfolk said hello to Rose. Madison

smiled as her cousin continued to get all of the attention. Let Rose have the spotlight. She deserved it.

Who knew, maybe after they killed all the gnolls, the town would welcome them all as heroes. Of course, they had to actually kill all the dogmen first.

Their tasks done, the two of them headed out of the village and back to where the boys waited. They had traps to build and gnolls to kill.

21

When Madison and Rose returned, they found that the boys had been keeping tabs on the gnolls. Unfortunately, there had been some new developments.

"Twelve of them guarding the entrance?" Rose asked, wide-eyed.

"I don't think we can take that many." Madison grimaced. "Not even with my spell. And now we don't even have my Animated Guardian."

"You're right," Cole said with a grim nod. "That's too much damage for me to tank."

"You think we can peel some away?" Michael asked. "Take on a smaller group, then go back for the rest?"

Madison shook her head. "I don't think they'll fall for that. I mean, if the computer has any brains."

"AI," Michael corrected. "AI."

She made a face. "Computer. AI. Whatever. I think

they'll be smarter next time. Like the last time, one of them went for help."

"You have a point." Cole nodded. "It might be some sort of learning AI. We do something, it reacts and learns."

"Wait?! You mean, it will just keep getting smarter," Rose whined. "How are we going to beat it?"

"A frontal assault won't work," Michael said nonchalantly. "That's just a one-way ticket back to the beach - minus all our stuff."

Madison remembered something about the room where they'd seen the gnolls. She replayed the scene in her mind. Yes, the room had been different. A different stone, smooth and more refined. Nothing like the tunnel they'd traveled down to get to the room. She nodded to herself.

"Maybe there's a backdoor," Madison suggested excitedly. "When we were down in the burrow, in that room, did anyone notice anything?"

"Like the tons of gnolls that were trying to kill me?" Cole replied.

Michael shrugged. "I was focused on the fighting."

Madison looked to Rose, who just shrugged. "Sorry, I was healing."

Sighing, Madison bit her lip. "I don't think that the room we were in was built by the gnolls."

"Oh?" Cole asked, eyebrow raised. "Do you think the gnolls stole it from some other monsters?"

She shrugged. "I don't know. I just know that it looked carved by like, I don't know, someone with a good knowledge of carving things out of stone."

"Stonemasonry," Rose supplied helpfully. "My dad had to hire one to do something with the area around the pool. He had to hire a landscaper too."

"Stonemason," Madison said with a nod. "Right, so maybe like humans built it and then the gnolls took over and made it their home."

Cole scratched his head. "I mean, it could be. This is all new, so we know nothing about it. There could be some sort of backstory. Maybe some ancient race created an underground complex. Who knows? I don't know that it means there's a backdoor."

Madison thought for a second before continuing. "Maybe not. But if there is, that entrance might not be as guarded. The gnolls may not even know about it."

"That's a lot of if's," Cole pointed out.

"What else are we going to do? If we can't do a front assault," she reasoned. "Then we can't really proceed, right?"

"She has a point," Michael said, turning to Cole. "Unless you're going to pull some insanely genius strategy out of your butt?"

Cole held out a finger. "Want to know what's up my butt... pull my finger!"

"Focus!" Madison said. "Do we search for another entrance or do a full-frontal attack?"

"You never go full frontal," Michael said in a deep voice, earning a snicker from Cole.

Madison rolled her eyes and let out an exasperated breath. She was starting to enjoy the game, but she didn't want to make a bunch of suicide attacks. Dying had sucked. She didn't want to do it again. Not to mention, she finally had some nice clothes and a staff. She didn't want to lose them.

Sighing Cole leaned back against the tree. "Madison is right. Unless we want to try a suicide run, we should at least look for a back way."

"What if we don't find one?" Rose asked.

"There's got to be other monsters around here, right?" Madison asked. "Can't we... you know... go kill more until we're stronger and then come back."

Cole shrugged. "We can. Grinding for levels is boring and not usually the most efficient. We might be able to go back to the village and see if anyone has quests for us to do. We might get more experience that way - plus more reputation."

"But first we look for the backdoor," Madison said.

"You never go full backdoor," Michael said in the same deep voice. Cole chuckled and the girls just rolled their eyes.

"Come on," Madison said, grabbing Rose by the hand. "Let's start looking while the boys misquote movies."

The two girls started walking in the direction Madison thought would allow them to circle around the entrance. After all, if there was a back entrance, then it would be in... the back. Then again, it could be a side entrance. She sighed. It was probably going to be a lot of searching.

Madison heard the boys fall in behind them and smiled. She knew they would. She just hoped she was right. If she wasn't, she knew she wouldn't hear the end of it.

"Come on," she told Rose. "Let's look this way."

Eventually, Madison convinced them to spread out in

a line and look for anything unusual. She'd seen police do it on detective shows when they were searching for bodies in the forest. The concept seemed sound: space people apart so you covered more ground, but hopefully didn't miss details.

With only a little complaining, the boys had joined in and they'd begun sweeping the area, looking for anything out of the ordinary. Again, it seemed like a sound plan to Madison.

Unfortunately, the forest was hilly in the area they were searching. This made it hard to keep their line straight, as well as see much if they were at a low point.

After a couple of hours of game time, Madison was willing to call it quits and admit she'd been wrong. They crisscrossed the area that they thought was behind the entrance to the cave and there was no sign of anything strange.

They'd found numerous berry bushes, wild blackberries and wild raspberries. And try as the boys might, every time they tried to pick a berry from the tree, it squished in their fingers. Both of them got messages about not having the proper skill.

Rose and Madison, on the other hand, were able to pick all the berries. Once the berries were actually off the bushes, they could be traded to either boy. They just couldn't pick berries themselves, it appeared.

The only other things they had found were two holes in the ground where smoke was coming out. Judging by the smell of the smoke, one was the chimney for a brewery. The smoke had a very pronounced hops smell that had a hint of baking bread - probably the yeast they used.

The second was definitely a cooking fire. Whatever the gnolls were cooking smelled good. Madison just hoped it wasn't something gross... like humans.

Her group started to move on from the chimneys, but Madison just stood there and stared at them, an idea forming.

"Come on, Madison," Cole said, waving her to follow them.

"Hold on," she replied, looking around the area. She nodded as a smile spread across her face.

Cole shook his head. "I know that look. Whenever you get that look, I usually get in trouble."

"Not this time." She grinned. "I have an idea!"

"Oh?" Her brother arched an eyebrow.

"We put the traps here!" she said excitedly.

Michael came over to Cole's side and looked around. He frowned. "Here?"

Rose smiled, bobbing her head at Madison. "Yes! That's a great idea!"

Cole and Michael exchanged looks. "What are we missing?"

Madison opened her mouth, but Rose cut her off. "A squirrel built a nest in the chimney of our firepit over the winter. The first time my dad tried to use it, the entire deck filled with smoke because the squirrel had blocked the entire chimney. It got REALLY smokey, REALLY fast."

"Ah," Cole said, looking down at the chimneys.

"We make the traps," Madison explained. "Then block

the chimneys. When they come to investigate and they fall for our traps, we get them!"

The group looked at each other and nodded. Michael grinned. "Yeah! That'll work."

Rose bit her lip. "You think they'll suspect a trap?"

"Only one way to find out," Madison said with a smile. "Plus, we can hide and wait to see how many come and whether they fall for the traps. If not... I guess we will go back to the town and see what quests we can do."

"Alright," Cole agreed. "Let's do it!"

22

Despite the group's enthusiasm, they soon found that their plan was doomed to failure. At least, the part about digging traps. As they quickly learned, there was only a foot or so of topsoil before they hit rock. In hindsight, it did make sense. The gnolls WERE in a cave after all. The ceiling had been stone.

"That was a waste of time," Michael said, breathing hard. Tossing the shovel to the side, he sat down heavily on the ground.

Madison gave everyone an apologetic look. "Sorry, it seemed like a good idea."

She felt bad that she had wasted everyone's time. Now they were back at square one, with no plan other than a suicidal frontal assault.

"You couldn't have known," Cole said, giving her a smile. "None of us thought of it either."

"Uh...guys," Rose said, waving them over. "What is.... Ahhhh!"

One moment, they were looking at Rose waving her hand for them to come over, the next she disappeared. It was as if she had been sucked down into the ground.

Scrambling to her feet, Madison rushed over to where her cousin had disappeared. She stopped suddenly, just inches from a hole that had opened up where Rose had just been standing. Was that some sort of sinkhole?

Madison stared down into the darkness as the boys came running over and stopped just short of the pit.

"What the heck?" Michael said, looking at it. "Did it collapse or something?"

Unable to see far into the darkness of the pit, Madison called out to her cousin. "Ro...!"

Cole's hand shot out and covered her mouth. He put his finger to his mouth and then pointed to the nearby chimneys. "Shhh! The last thing we want is for them to come and investigate."

Pulling his hand down, Madison glared at her brother. "She could be hurt!"

"It's just a game," he told her. "If she dies, she'll respawn. If gnolls come up here and we all die, it will be much harder to get our stuff."

Madison knew her brother was right, but she was still concerned about her cousin. She cocked her head as she thought she heard something.

"I'm... mostly okay..." came a faint voice. "Come... down. You have to... see this."

The voice was faint, but it did sound like Rose. She sounded pained. Madison looked up at the guys. "Did you hear that? She's hurt."

Cole and Michael nodded; both shared their concern. Her brother looked around and walked over to the closest tree. "Throw me some of that rope you bought."

Pulling a coil of rope from her inventory, she tossed it to Cole. He tied the top around the tree, tested it several times and then walked back to them. Looking down the hole, he dropped the rest of the rope down into the hole.

"Let's go!" Cole grinned.

Michael looked at Buddy and frowned. "How am I supposed to get Buddy down?"

Madison furrowed her brow in concentration, then smiled and pulled out another coil of rope. "Tie him to you with the rest of the rope."

Cole shook his head. "See if you can tie him onto me. I have enough strength to lower both of us."

Michael nodded and cut a piece of rope from the coil on the ground. He began talking soothingly to the tiger cub as he began tying the rope to him.

"I'll go see if Rose is okay," Madison told them. She reached down and grabbed the rope before her brother could respond, and then swung herself over the edge. Slowly, she began lowering herself down the rope into the inky blackness below. Above her, her brother looked down disapprovingly for a moment before going back to helping Michael.

With the rope between her legs, Madison lowered herself hand over hand. It quickly became dark and even with her enhanced sight, there was really nothing to see except the smooth sides of the hole. Madison squinted at the sides. They were too smooth. They couldn't be natural. At least, they couldn't be natural in the real world. Who knew what was natural and what was not in this game world.

She lowered herself at least thirty feet before the sides of the cave abruptly disappeared. She was suddenly hanging in the middle of nothing, and it was far too dark to see anything.

"I see you," Rose's voice came from below. It was a loud whisper, but it echoed around the darkness. "You're about twenty feet above the floor."

"Okay, give me a moment and I'll come the rest of the way," Madison replied and continued her descent.

"The rope ends... like... ten feet above the ground," Rose called softly.

Sure enough, a few seconds later, the rope disappeared from between Madison's legs. Holding on tighter with her hands, she lowered herself to the end of the rope. Close to the bottom, the light from the hole above dimly illuminated a small wood elf below her. Rose.

"Go ahead," she said. "Drop down."

Madison let go of the rope and her stomach lurched as she fell to the earth. She managed to land on her feet. As she did, she bent her knees to absorb the impact, and used her hands to prevent her from face planting into the stone floor.

You take 3 falling damage.

"Ow," she said. "3 Falling damage."

Her cousin chuckled mirthlessly. "I took 53 falling damage."

"Ouch," Madison grimaced. "That must have hurt."

"It did," Rose agreed. "Luckily, I'm a healer. Why didn't you use your wings?"

Madison looked over her shoulder at her wings and shook her head. She'd completely forgotten about them.

"Look out below," came Michael's voice moments before he landed with a thud next to Madison. He wasn't quite as graceful as she had been but did manage not to smack his head against the floor.

Groaning, he managed to move just before Cole's huge form landed where he had just been. Whether her brother's size or better muscles made a difference, Cole landed easily on the floor, bending just slightly at the knees.

Cole immediately began to grimace and wiggle around. He spun around and pointed to the tiger cub on his back. "Okay. Okay. Get Buddy off of me while I still have flesh on my back!"

Buddy was unhappy and trying to climb off of Cole, leaving scratches up and down her brother's back. Michael rushed over and scratched the cub behind the ears while saying soothing words. He looked up at Madison and Rose. "Untie him. Don't cut the rope, we'll need it to haul him back up."

The girls quickly untied the cat and he scrambled to the floor, happy to be off of Cole's back - though not quite as happy as Cole was for Buddy to be off his back. Her brother grimaced and turned his back to Rose. "Can you heal this... please."

Casting her spell, she healed Cole.

Plays-With-Animals heals Brothar Snowbear for 11 damage.

Cole smiled and sagged a bit. "Ah. Much better. That cat has sharp claws!"

"He IS a combat pet," Michael pointed out.

Madison took the opportunity to look around. Her eyes were adjusting to the lack of light and she was able to make out details about the room they were in. And it was a room.

Like the room the gnolls had been in, this chamber had been carved or fashioned from smooth stone. Part of the far wall had collapsed and there was rubble strewn on the floor nearby. On the right wall, was a doorway with a smooth stone door blocking it. On the left wall, in exactly the same spot, was another doorway. This one too was blocked with a stone door.

And yet, the room and the doors were not what caught the eye. It was the stuff piled in the corners of the room.

There were a dozen crates, several chests, some sacks and then just some loose coins lying around the right wall.

"Woah," Michael said, obviously seeing it too, even in the dim light. "Is that what I think it is?"

Rose nodded. "It's treasure! We're rich!"

Madison nodded, but frowned. In the movies and stories, treasure usually belonged to someone - or something. She looked around the rest of the room but saw no monster or anything about to jump out.

Her brother seemed to be having the same thought. He squinted into the dark and walked over to the right door and put his ear to it. After a moment, he lifted his head up and backed away - eyes glued to the door.

"Uh, guys," Cole said, keeping his voice low. "I heard gnolls on the other side. I think we're in their treasure vault."

23

"Their treasure vault?!" Rose whispered. "Are you kidding me?"

Cole shook his head. "What else would it be?"

"Didn't you say something about this being older architecture?" Michael asked Madison, gesturing around the room. "Maybe this is a treasure vault from whoever made this place originally."

Madison walked over to the treasure pile, bent down and examined the crates. Some of them had the name "Fisherton" painted on them. The paint wasn't worn. It looked fairly fresh. She shook her head and was about to say something when a prompt appeared.

You have received a new quest "Hey, Those Are Ours!"

You've found crates of goods that the gnolls have stolen from recent trade caravans bound for Fisherton. You have a choice of whether to return the crates to the citizens or keep them for yourself.

Return Crates to Fisherton
Reward: +100 reputation with Residents of Fisherton, +100 reputation with Guards of Fisherton, Unknown for each crate returned.
Keep the Crates
Reward: Goods, Unknown of each crate kept.
Accept quest (yes or no)?

"Did you guys just get that quest?" Madison asked and, glassy eyed, they all nodded. She accepted the quest.

"I guess that answers that question," Michael said, disappointed. "So much for keeping a cut for ourselves."

"That stinks!" Rose said.

"It doesn't say anything about the money," Cole pointed out.

They all looked at Cole, his eyes still glassy. "What?!"

Her brother smiled. "Read the quest again. It says return the crates. It says nothing about the money."

"Oh!" Rose grinned, clapping her hands together. "Let's gather it all up."

"Hold on," Madison said, holding up a hand. "If we take anything or move anything, the gnolls will probably notice."

"So?" Michael shrugged. "We will be long gone by then."

"Right," she said. "But what about killing the boss gnoll."

Cole nodded. "She's right. If we give away that we were here, they will go on high alert. We may not get another chance."

"Another chance at what?" Rose asked.

"Getting the commander." Madison nodded, having thought the same thing. It wasn't as important for the others but finishing that quest would hopefully give her more reputation in town and she wouldn't be ignored.

Michael shrugged. "So how do we get him?"

Madison scratched her scaly head and looked at the right door. "If you had a big treasure and you were the leader, would you keep it near you or put it in some other part of the complex?"

"What?" Rose asked, screwing her face up in confusion.

"Like in the spy movies and stuff," Madison pointed out. "The bad guy usually has a vault in his office or study - you know, basically wherever they spend a lot of time. And that's where he keeps his valuables, plans for world domination and all that stuff."

Cole furrowed his brow. "You think the gnolls on the other side could be the commander and his flunkies?"

She shrugged. "Maybe."

Michael nodded. "That makes sense too from a design standpoint. Put the treasure behind the big boss so players have to work for it. It would be like a reward for killing him."

"Makes sense," Cole agreed. "The question becomes, how do we exploit this to our advantage. Even if we opened that door right now, the commander would probably call in the other troops and we'd be overwhelmed."

Madison smiled. "Unless they were busy with something."

"Like what?" Rose asked.

"Like their chimneys were suddenly blocked," Madison replied.

"Yeah, but that would alert them that someone was here and had blocked the chimneys," Michael commented.

Madison bit her lip but then smiled. She pulled a hatchet out of her inventory. "Maybe we can make it look like a tree fell and blocked them. That should prevent them from suspecting us."

"That might work." Cole nodded.

"What if they come in here in the meantime?" Rose asked and pointed at the rubble that had fallen onto the floor when the roof had collapsed under Rose's weight. "They'll see that and the hole and know something's up."

Michael pointed at the far wall. "We can move the rubble over there. A little more rubble won't be noticed."

"But there's still the hole," Rose reminded them.

"We can cover it up with branches," Cole suggested. "It's far enough away from the door and the crates that they shouldn't notice."

"What about that door?" Madison asked. "What if they're just walking across the room to get to the left door."

Cole walked over to the left door and stuck his ear to it. He furrowed his brow in concentration for a few seconds, then moved his ear to another spot on the door, then another. Finally, he backed away.

Her brother cocked his head, then brushed off dust from the door, revealing symbols that Madison couldn't make out from where she stood.

"I don't hear anything," her brother announced. "But

there's some weird writing on the door. I can't make it out."

Madison and the others walked over to the door and examined the writing that Cole had revealed.

"Can anyone read it?" he asked.

Rose and Michael both shook their heads, but Madison stared at the writing. At first, the symbols didn't make sense but then they seemed to wiggle and form themselves into English. She blinked, unsure she had just witnessed it.

You have read Artoshian.
Congratulations! You are the first player to read Artoshian. A Reward has been added to your account. You may check your rewards by going to Character Menu-> Profile -> Rewards -> Early Access Awards

She grinned as she saw the message. No, she wasn't hallucinating, the writing was now in English. "I can read it. It's Artoshian, it was one of my language choices."

The others saw the message too and all smiled. Another reward.

"Another $10," Rose said. "Good job!"

"You had language choices?" her brother asked. "During character creation?"

"Yes, I got Common and Draconian for free. And then I chose Artoshian and Valharian. They were supposed to be dead languages from two now-extinct races. I figured they might come in handy if we explored some old ruins."

Cole nodded in approval. "Nice. So, what does it say?"

Madison read it and then turned to him, giving him a

halfhearted smile. "It says, Private Quarters of the High Priestess."

"High priestess, huh?" Michael said. "Maybe there's treasure in there too. We should check it out."

"One thing at a time," Cole said. "Let's see if we can kill the gnoll commander first. Then we can see what's behind door number 2."

Michael nodded and scratched his head. "How do you even open the door?"

Madison looked to a slightly raised area just to the left of the door. She could make out writing on it. Brushing off the dust, she revealed more of the strange writing that wiggled until it became English. "Open/Close"

"What?" Rose asked.

"This panel," Madison said, pointing to it. "It says open/close."

"Try it!" Michael told her; excitement written all over his face.

"Not yet!" Cole said again. "One thing at a time. The last thing we want is something coming after us from two fronts."

Michael looked disappointed but he nodded. "Yeah, that wouldn't be good."

"Right," Cole agreed. "Let's focus on getting the quests we have done. Besides, they should both be more money, right?"

Rose looked up and nodded. "Yes! More money."

Madison was a bit surprised at Rose's sudden mercenary streak. Her cousin wasn't a materialistic person, but Madison guessed it had more to do with her mom and dad than with her.

No doubt, they wouldn't approve of her playing the game as much if she wasn't making money doing it. In fact, they may not end up approving anyway, if she spent too much time on it. Madison made a mental note to talk with her cousin later and talk about it more.

"Okay then," Rose said. "What's the next step in our master plan?"

"First, let's move this rubble," Madison said. "Then, we climb back up, cover the pit and cut down the tree."

"Then what?" Michael asked.

"Then we come back down here and ambush the commander when the other gnolls go up to clear the chimneys," Cole said.

"That sounds like a plan." Michael grinned. He looked down at Buddy. "When we climb back up, who's carrying Buddy up?"

Everyone looked at Cole. Her brother rolled his eyes and groaned.

24

The group quickly chopped down the smallest tree they could find that would do the job. Cole had wanted to go large. His thought was that the larger it was, the longer it would take them to move it. Madison pointed out that they would actually have to move the tree themselves in order to get it in place. So smaller was better.

After felling the tree, they dragged it, so it covered up the chimneys, then stuffed some extra branches down the chimneys, just to make sure. Once they were done, they quickly scrambled down the rope and back into the treasure vault. Everyone except Madison.

Remembering her wings this time, she jumped down the pit and as soon as there was room, she unfurled her wings. Her bat-like wings caught the air and slowed Madison enough that she landed without taking any damage.

"Cool!" She grinned. Madison stood up and looked at the others. "Are we ready for this?"

"As ready as we'll be without a few more levels under our belt!" Michael chuckled.

The group gathered by the door. Like the door on the opposite side, this door had a panel that had the writing for open/close written on it.

"Okay," Cole said quietly. "Madison, you're going in first...."

"Me?!" Madison squeaked a bit too loud and then lowered her voice. "Me? Why me?"

"I want you to go in first, let them get close, and then stun them," he told her.

"But that only lasts a few seconds," she protested. She knew what would happen after it wore off, they'd all come after her!

"Right," Cole confirmed. "But that should give you time to mez at least 3 of them. I want you to mez the boss first, then the next meanest-looking one and so on."

"We're not going to take out the boss first?" Rose asked.

Her brother shook his head. "No, kill the adds, then kill the boss. The last thing you want is adds banging on you while you're trying to take down the boss."

"Adds?" Madison asked. She thought she knew what it meant, but she wanted to be sure.

"Additional mobs, adds for short," Michael explained. "It basically means any monsters that aren't the boss. Sometimes bosses summon other monsters, sometimes there are other monsters with the boss - they're all adds."

Madison and Rose nodded. A thought suddenly

occurred to Madison. Something Captain Bartem had told her. "There might be a shaman with the boss too."

Cole's head snapped around to look at her. "A shaman? How do you know?"

"The captain told me," she replied, recalling the conversation. "He said his scout said all the trouble started when the shaman showed up and got in tight with the commander."

Cole and Michael exchanged looks. Michael shook his head. "A shaman's probably a healer. That's not good."

"No, it's not," Cole agreed. He frowned and scratched his head. "Okay, new plan. You still go in and stun everyone. If there's a shaman there, you mez everyone while we start beating on the shaman. You just need to keep the others mezzed and out of the fight."

It sounded pretty easy, basically what they'd been doing. She just needed to keep the commander and whatever guards he had from joining the fight until her group was done with the shaman. Madison nodded. "Okay."

"Good!" Cole smiled. "Everyone knows what to do, right?"

"Oh," Madison said. "Don't forget to cover your eyes until I yell out."

The rest of her group nodded.

"Alright," her brother said. "We'll charge in on 3. Ready? 3... 2...1..."

Cole slammed his hand on the panel and the door slid open more smoothly than Madison would have expected. She rushed in first, looking around the room to gauge the best place to set off her spell.

The chamber she entered was about 30 feet long by 20

feet wide. There were fur rugs of all sorts littered across the floor, making it appear like some sort of crazy, mish-mash plush carpet. The walls were smooth stone like the treasure vault. Unlike the treasure vault, the walls in this room had all sorts of crude drawings on them. Madison wasn't sure, but thought the images were drawn in blood.

Madison shifted her gaze around the room. Lying around on the carpet were a half dozen gnolls, including one that looked much larger than the others. She also caught sight of two burly gnolls by the door on the opposite side of the room armed with swords and shields. Probably guards.

The large gnoll who had been lying on the carpet, who she guessed was the commander, and the burly gnolls reacted first. The commander jumped to his feet while the guards rushed towards her, drawing swords.

Trying not to panic, Madison's mind did some quick calculations, and she ran towards a spot at the edge of the group of sitting gnolls. She just hoped everyone would make it inside the radius of her spell before she had to cast it.

Running forward, she skidded to a halt just as the commander, who had pulled a sword from a scabbard on his belt, prepared for a strike. The guards were still a few feet away and the gnolls from the carpet were scrambling to their feet as well. It was now or never.

Unlike some of her other spells, Color Blast was instant. No sooner had she mentally decided to cast it when an intense strobe-like bombardment of color sprang from her body, temporarily turning the room into the strangest disco ever.

A moment later, everyone in the room looked like they were dazed from a punch. They wavered on their feet but didn't fall. It was actually a bit comical. Then she remembered the plan. "It's done!"

Immediately, she began casting her Daydream spell, first on the commander. As she did, her party came rushing through the door. Cole stopped suddenly, almost causing the other two to run into him. He scanned the room. "Which one is the shaman?"

Finishing her spell, Madison looked around too. "No idea. Maybe he's not here!"

"Fine, everyone on the gnolls sitting on the floor first!" he yelled and darted at the still seated gnolls. The others quickly followed, and they were quickly ganging up on one of the gnolls.

Brothar Snowbear slashes Blackmange Gnoll Advisor for 11 damage.
Brothar Snowbear bashes Blackmange Gnoll Advisor for 6 damage.
Brothar Snowbear slams Blackmange Gnoll Advisor for 7 damage.
Zachatolus Catfriend kicks Blackmange Gnoll Advisor for 7 damage.
Zachatolus Catfriend crushes Blackmange Gnoll Advisor for 7 damage.
Buddy bites Blackmange Gnoll Advisor for 5 damage.
Buddy claws Blackmange Gnoll Advisor for 6 damage.
Plays-With-Animals slashes Blackmange Gnoll Guard for 8 damage.

The advisors recovered from the stun just as Madison finished mezzing the second guard. Barking and growling, they began attacking with small daggers that they pulled from sheaths on cords around their necks. The knives looked almost ceremonial, but still appeared very functional.

With the commander and his guards incapacitated, she turned to the other advisors and began casting her spell. Her group managed to kill the first advisor and then moved onto the next one. By that time, Madison had two of the advisors daydreaming and was about to cast her spell on the next one in line. That was when she caught movement from the corner of her eyes.

The door to the treasure vault was still open and she saw a shorter gnoll garbed in skins step into the room. The newcomer had pierced ears with multiple earrings in them. Some of the earrings had leather feathers tied to them, others had strings of beads.

Yet, it wasn't just the earrings and skins that made the gnoll stand out, it also appeared to have mostly gray fur. It also appeared a bit more grizzled than the others. Madison guessed it was older than the gnolls she'd seen so far.

In the gray-furred gnoll's left hand was a carved, wooden staff decorated like a miniature totem pole but with gnoll faces. Atop the staff was the skull of some small creature, from which hung feathers attached with cords of leather. Everything about the gray-furred gnoll screamed shaman.

The shaman took a few steps into the room, stopped and seemed to take in what was going on in the room. It shook its head slowly and then it did something Madison was not expecting.

"I'm afraid I can't allow you to kill the commander just yet," the shaman said in a decidedly female voice. "I still need him for my purposes."

Then, the shaman lowered its staff and began mumbling a spell.

25

Madison began to cast her Daydream spell on the shaman but suddenly her stomach twisted and she dropped to her knees as her body suddenly ached all over and she felt as if she had a fever.

Dark Shaman hits you with 12 disease damage.
You are diseased.

Her spell dying as she lost focus, Madison struggled to get back on her feet to resume her spell. Blinking her watery eyes, she tried to focus on the shaman, but the room was spinning.

She managed to see that the shaman was casting her spell on someone in her group and Madison called out. "Shaman! Disease!"

Groaning, Madison slowly stood and looked at the shaman. She pushed back the nausea and vertigo. The shaman finished off her spell and Madison looked over her shoulder to see her brother suddenly look ill.

Gritting her teeth, she forced herself to cast her Daydream spell on the Dark Shaman. If she was mezzed, the shaman couldn't cast. Right?

Her spell went off but instead of the shaman freezing in place, she just looked at Madison and snickered.

Dark Shaman resists Daydream.

Resisted? How had she resisted? Growling in frustration, Madison brought up her spellbook. She only had two other spells that might work. Color Blast might stun her, but without warning the others, they would be stunned too.

The only other offensive spell she had was Minor Telekinetic Asphyxiation. It was a choking spell, but would it prevent the shaman from casting? So far, she'd only used it on crabs. And as far as she knew, the crabs didn't talk to begin with.

Suddenly pain wracked her body again, threatening to overwhelm her.

Disease hits you with 9 disease damage.
You are diseased.

Madison began to panic. The spell was still doing damage. How long would it last and how much damage would it do? She knew she had to try something else, and quickly!

She cast her choking spell and targeted the Dark

Shaman. Her spell went off and Madison grinned at the message.

You hit Dark Shaman with Minor Telekinetic Asphyxiation for 4 damage.
Dark Shaman is weakened.
Dark Shaman is choking.

The gray gnoll's eyes went wide as she coughed and gasped, ruining her next spell. Madison smiled and prepared another Daydream spell.

Suddenly a wave of warm relief passed over her and her nausea, vertigo and muscle aches were gone. She involuntarily let out a sigh of relief.

Plays-With-Animals casts Cure Disease on you.
You are no longer diseased.

"Madison!" Cole yelled. "Mez these while we go on the shaman!"

Happy just to be feeling better, Madison started to cast her spell on one of the advisors when she saw the Commander beginning to move. She cursed.

"Language!" Cole gasped in mock horror.

"The commander is moving!" she yelled back.

Cole cursed. He began moving towards the shaman. "Start re-mezzing! I'll have to tank the advisors while we go after the shaman."

Madison nodded absently. Her mind was already on the commander and the guards. She needed to hurry and get them Daydreaming again before Cole was overwhelmed.

A Gnoll Commander is Daydreaming.

Having gotten the gnoll commander back under control, she quickly cast her spell on the two guards and then on the advisors. She was about to get one of the remaining advisors, but an idea struck her as she looked at the guards.

Both were carrying swords and shields. Madison cocked her head. Could she cast her spell on items someone was holding? Curious, she cast Animated Guardian on the sword and shield in the guard's hands.

Staring out blankly, the guard didn't seem to care that its sword and shield suddenly floated out of its hands and came to rest in front of Madison. She smiled and pointed to the shaman. "Kill!"

The guardian rushed to obey. Not having time to watch it, Madison resumed mezzing the gnolls. She occasionally caught glimpses of the fighting in her HUD.

Brothar Snowbear slashes Dark Shaman for 10 damage.
Brothar Snowbear bashes Dark Shaman for 7 damage.
Brothar Snowbear slams Dark Shaman for 7 damage.
Zachatolus Catfriend kicks Dark Shaman for 8 damage.
Zachatolus Catfriend crushes Dark Shaman for 6 damage.
Buddy bites Dark Shaman for 6 damage.
Buddy claws Dark Shaman for 6 damage.

Plays-With-Animals heals Brothar Snowbear for 11 damage.
Dark Shaman casts Poison.
Brothar Snowbear takes 10 poison damage.
Plays-With-Animals casts Cure Poison on Brothar Snowbear.
Brothar Snowbear is no longer poisoned.

This continued for several minutes while Madison continued to keep the Commander, Guards and half of the Advisors mezzed.

Madison was so intent on her job that she didn't even realize she was running low on Mana until her HUD flashed a red message.

You are low on mana.

Eye going wide, Madison checked her Mana and confirmed that it was low. It was so low, she only had enough for two more Daydream spells.

"I'm out of mana!" she called out. "I have enough for two more daydreams!"

"I'm almost out of mana too!" Rose cried. "Maybe one or two more heals or cures!"

"Keep the commander mezzed!" Cole shouted. "Keep me healed as long as you can! The shaman's almost done!"

Madison saw they were right. The shaman was bloodied from multiple wounds and yet still somehow standing. She couldn't last much longer.

Brothar Snowbear slashes Dark Shaman for 12 damage.
Zachatolus Catfriend crushes Dark Shaman for 9 damage.

Buddy bites Dark Shaman for 9 damage.
Animated Guardian slashes Dark Shaman for 8 damage.
You have killed Dark Shaman.
You have gained experience!
Your reputation with Fey of the Dark Realm has decreased.
Plays-With-Animals heals Brothar Snowbear for 12 damage.

The shaman let out a strangled cry and then collapsed back against the wall. She slowly sank to the floor, leaving a long, bloody smear. Then, something strange happened.

The shaman's body began to shimmer with dark light. Before their eyes, it changed and morphed until a humanoid body remained. It looked like the body of a woman, but with the head of a raven. Black, unseeing eyes stared up at them.

"What the heck?" Michael cried out in shock. "What's that?"

They didn't have a chance to contemplate it as the gnoll advisors continued their attacks.

"We have to retreat!" Madison said.

"Where?" Cole asked. "They'll follow us!"

Desperately looking around, Madison's eyes fell on the panel next to the door. It opened and closed the door from this side. What if they broke it? Could the door be opened from this side then?

"The door!" she yelled. "Open it and then smash the panel, we can close it from the other side."

Cole looked at the door and nodded. "Go!"

Madison nodded and started towards them but then

saw the Gnoll Advisor corpses on the ground near her. She raced over and looted them and then started towards the others.

Blackmange Gnoll Elite Guard slashes you for 8 damage.
Blackmange Gnoll Elite Guard bashes you for 9 damage.

The blows staggered her for a second and before she knew it, the second guard was biting at her and scratching her with its paws.

Blackmange Gnoll Elite Guard bites you for 5 damage.
Blackmange Gnoll Elite Guard claws you for 4 damage.
Blackmange Gnoll Elite Guard claws you for 4 damage.

"Ahh!" she screamed and backpedaled away from the gnolls.

"Get over here!" Cole yelled. He targeted the two elite guards and yelled his taunts.

"Over here, flea-bag!

"Cone of shame for you!"

Madison managed to scramble to her brother but by then, the Gnoll Commander was no longer mezzed. He attacked her just as she reached the door.

Blackmange Gnoll Commander slashes you for 13 damage.
Blackmange Gnoll Commander slashes you for 12 damage.

"Ow!" she screamed as the sword slashed across her back twice.

"Over here, you neutered mutt!" Cole called to the Commander. The big gnoll spun and growled.

"Come on, Cole!" she yelled.

Cole shook his head. "I can't! They'll be too close! You guys go!"

"No, Cole!" she yelled.

"I can't hold them! Run, you fool!" he yelled.

Her brother was going to die, and they wouldn't be able to retrieve his corpse without fighting them again, but this time they would have no element of surprise. She desperately wracked her brain for something, but she only had enough Mana for a single spell. Just one spell.

Knowing what she needed to do, Madison stepped over to the gnolls surrounding her brother. As loud as she could, she screamed. "CLOSE YOUR EYES!"

You cast Color Blast.
Blackmange Gnoll Commander is stunned.
Blackmange Gnoll Elite Guard is stunned.
Blackmange Gnoll Elite Guard is stunned.
Blackmange Gnoll Advisor is stunned.
Blackmange Gnoll Advisor is stunned.

In the aftermath of the intense color strobe, Madison blinked and looked at the gnolls. They were all stunned, staggering on their feet in front of her brother.

"Hurry!" she yelled and started towards the door. She stopped, looking back at the gnolls. She chuckled. Somehow, when the stun had gone off, they had all ended up in a straight line in front of where her brother had been. An evil grin spread across her face.

"Come on, Madison! Come on!" Rose yelled.

"One second," she said, still grinning. She stepped sideways so she was in line with the gnolls. Then she released her breath weapon.

Her mouth opened and she felt crackling electricity surge all over her body and gather at the back of her throat. Then, in a blinding arc of blue-white electricity, a lightning bolt shot from her mouth and into the line of gnolls.

You use Ancestral Breath Weapon: Lightning.
You critically electrocute Blackmange Gnoll Commander for 213 damage.
You have killed Blackmange Gnoll Commander.
You have gained experience!
You critically electrocute Blackmange Gnoll Elite Guard for 197 damage.
You have killed Blackmange Gnoll Elite Guard.
You have gained experience!
You critically electrocute Blackmange Gnoll Elite Guard for 199 damage.
You have killed Blackmange Gnoll Elite Guard.
You have gained experience!
You critically electrocute Blackmange Gnoll Advisor for 198 damage.
You have killed Blackmange Gnoll Advisor.
You have gained experience!
You critically electrocute Blackmange Gnoll Advisor for 207 damage.

You have killed Blackmange Gnoll Advisor.
You have gained experience!
Quest Updated.

After each experience gain, there was an additional message telling them their reputation with Residents of Fisherton and Guards of Fisherton had increased, while their reputation with Blackmange Gnolls had decreased.

Madison closed her mouth and looked down at the smoking bodies. She grinned and looked at her group. "Did you see that?"

Cole, Michael and Rose just stared at her wide-eyed.

Michael looked from the dead gnolls to Madison and then back to the gnolls. "And you didn't lead with that... why?!"

26

The group got over the shock quickly and they rushed back in to loot the corpses. Cole stopped in front of the body of the misshapen crone head of a raven. “It says corpse of Dark Fey Raven Hag.”

“What’s that?” Rose asked.

Cole shrugged. “No idea. This, I guess.”

“When it died, it changed into that,” Michael recalled. “That means it’s probably some sort of shape shifter.”

“Weird,” Rose commented, looking at the creature. “It was the gnoll’s friend?”

“That’s the problem with this being a new game,” Cole pointed out. “There’s no game lore wiki or FAQ.”

“Old school,” Michael said with a grin. “We’ll have to figure it out ourselves.”

“It said something about not letting us kill the commander, that it wasn’t done with the gnolls yet or something like that,” Madison recalled, remembering what the shaman/raven hag had said when it had first come in.

"So, they were... allies?" Rose asked.

Madison frowned and then brought up her HUD. She scrolled through the messages until she found what she was looking for. She read it to the others.

You have killed Dark Shaman.
You have gained experience!
Your reputation with Fey of the Dark Realm has decreased.

"There's no negative gnoll reputation," Cole noted. "Good catch."

"What does that mean?" Rose asked.

"It means they probably weren't allies," he explained. "If they were, killing it would have given us negative reputation with the gnolls."

"Yeah and killing the gnolls would have given us negative reputation with the Fey," Michael pointed out. "I just went back and looked. It's all just Blackmange gnolls until we killed her."

"So then why..." Rose started but barking sounded at the door.

Everyone went quiet. There was a pause, then more barking.

"They're probably asking something like - everything okay in there?" Cole whispered.

"Why aren't they just coming in?" Madison asked.

"They're either afraid to enter without permission or they damaged the opening mechanism on the other side.

It may only be openable or closable from this side," Cole answered.

There was more barking, this time louder and this time, Madison thought she could hear more than one voice. There was another pause and then some barking and then the sound of metal hitting stone.

"Uh oh," Michael said, his brow furrowing. "I think they're trying to get through the door. We need to make like a tree... and leave."

"Get the rest of the loot and head back into the treasure vault," Madison said, and the others nodded.

"I'll break the opening mechanism on this side," Cole told them. "That'll slow them down for a bit."

The group quickly looted the bodies. As they did, the sound of metal on stone got louder and faster. Something else was strange too. The bodies didn't disappear.

"The bodies are still here," Madison said, feeling like Captain Obvious.

"That's weird," her brother said, stopping to look at them. "Maybe because they're bosses or something?

"Or," Michael said, scratching his head. "Maybe they're part of the plot or quest."

"Either way..." Madison started but more sounds at the door distracted her and made her lose her train of thought.

"I think they're using a pick on the door," Michael said, cupping his hand to his ear. "And there's probably more than one of them at it now. We don't have much time."

"Hurry!" Madison said, turning her back on the bodies.

Her brother smashed the opening mechanism for the door on this side, then they all went into the vault and shut the door from the other side.

"Now what?" Rose asked. She looked up at the rope. "Back up?"

"Let's take as many crates as we can," Madison said, pointing to the crates stacked against the wall. "Remember the quest?"

"And the money!" Rose and Michael said simultaneously. They looked at each other and giggled.

"Jinx!" Rose called.

Michael stuck his tongue out at her. "Just get the money."

"How are we going to get the crates up the rope?" Madison asked.

"With muscles." Cole flexed his muscles like a bodybuilder in a contest. Once again, he used his Arnold voice. Then he smiled. "And our inventories. See if you can put one in your inventory and then climb up."

Nodding, the group did as he said. They did it at the same time and then all groaned at the same time.

"I'm encumbered!" Rose squeaked, her shoulders sagging. "I feel like there's a camel on my back!"

Madison frowned. "It's like when we were carrying everyone's equipment..."

"Only worse!" Rose agreed.

Her brother groaned but then twisted his torso and moved around. "I see what you mean. I feel like I have a heavy backpack on or something. But I think I can still climb. How about you, Michael?"

Michael was moving very slowly. He shook his head.

"No way. I can walk really slowly with this crate, but I won't be going anywhere quickly."

Rose and the rest of them replaced the crates. Madison looked at her brother. "You're the only one who can carry them. You'll have to carry them up one at a time."

Cole looked at the half dozen crates. He groaned. "This is going to take a bit. I can't climb with more than one crate."

The group gathered up the coins, while Cole climbed up the rope with the crates. As he was climbing up with the second crate, there was a crash in the other room. There was lots of barking and then banging on their door.

"I think the jig is up," Michael said. "They're onto us!"

"We should leave the crates," Rose said, looking up the rope. "And just get out of here."

Madison thought for a second. She snapped her fingers and looked between Michael and her brother. "Can you guys get back to the village with two crates?"

"We might have time to... oh... I know what you're thinking," her brother started, looking down from the rope. "That should work. But you probably won't be able to move."

"I know," Madison said and shot a look at Rose. "We can each take two crates and then use our minor gateway."

Rose frowned. "Your brother is right. We won't be able to move."

"We don't have to," Madison said. "Or rather, we won't have to until we get there. Once we get to the beach, you can give me your two crates and then run and get the captain."

Her cousin brightened. "That sounds like a good idea."

The sound of metal on stone started on the opposite side of their door. Michael put his hands over his ears. "I feel like that's the most annoying sound ever."

"It will get more annoying if we're still here when they break in," Cole called down. "Strap your cat to you and let's go."

Michael looked aghast. "You mean... you're not going to..."

"I'm carrying a freaking crate," Cole growled. "You'll have to carry Buddy."

"Oh yeah," Michael said with a sheepish grin.

"Uh," Rose broke in. "Can you guys find your way back to the village without me?"

"Sure...we can..." Cole started, almost at the top of the rope. He looked down at Michael, giving his cousin a questioning look.

Michael shrugged. "I wasn't really paying attention."

Her brother sighed. "I'm not completely sure I remember the way back. To be honest, all the forest looks the same to me."

Michael flashed a grin at Rose. "Uh... I think that would be a no."

Madison sighed. "Give me all the crates."

"But you're not going to be able to walk at all," Rose said. "Just leave some."

"Just give them to me," she told them. "I'll just stand on the beach until you guys get there. So, you know, hurry back."

"We will," Rose promised.

One by one, Madison put the crates into her inventory. The first crate felt as if she had a giant backpack full of books, strapped to her back. When she picked up the second one, she felt like she was trying to lift Cole over her head. By the time she got to the fourth crate, Madison felt as if she were trying to lift a car and it was about to fall down and crush her.

"You okay?" Rose asked.

"Do... I... look... like... I'm... okay," Madison growled through gritted teeth. "I feel like I'm about to be crushed to death."

"Just remember," Cole pointed out. "It's not real, it's just in your head."

"I'll....do something... to... your... head." She grimaced back.

A chip of stone sailed past them and they realized they were out of time. The gnolls were almost through the door. Madison looked at them. "Go!"

Then she began casting her spell. The spell had a long cast time, and she watched as her brother and cousins shimmied up the rope. Then, just as they started to pull the rope up after them, everything faded away.

A moment later, she was on the beach, startling a group of kids playing nearby.

"Ey," one of them said, wide-eyed. "You're the dragon lady. The one who's been killing gnolls!"

"I... am..." Madison answered, trying to turn her grimace into a smile. "If... you run... and get... the captain... I'll give... you each... a silver."

"A silver?! Honest?!" the oldest one said. "You hear that, Parker, Hunter?! Come on!"

The three boys ran off into the town yelling, "Captain! Captain!"

Madison tried to smile, but the suffocating weight just made her grimace. She prayed the captain would come quickly.

27

The group gathered later that evening in the local tavern, called the Tipsy Pelican. The tavern, actually more of an inn, was one of the largest buildings in the town. And if not, it was certainly the loudest.

While the outside was stone with wooden trim, the inside was all wood. It had various pieces of boats and nautical gear hanging on the walls and obviously catered to the people of the town who were fishermen. And judging by the crowd, that was quite a few.

The air was thick with smoke and the smell of stale beer, neither of which appealed to Madison. But unlike in real life, the smoke didn't bother her at all. In fact, even Rose, who really hated smoke, didn't seem to be bothered.

The noise in the tavern dimmed slightly when they walked in and then a few people from the tables let out a little cheer. It seemed word of their exploits had gotten around the town. Even Madison was now accepted -

though she did notice she still wasn't quite as admired as the others.

The group took a table in the corner and the boys immediately ordered ale from the barmaid who stopped over. The woman was in her middle years but had the lines of someone who had lived a hard life.

She was dressed in a stained dark-gray skirt and blouse, over which she wore a stained apron. Her hair, dark brown and streaked with gray, was pulled back in a ponytail. Looking down at the woman's hands, Madison saw that they were cracked and scarred. She guessed the barmaid did more than just wait tables.

"You're drinking?" Rose asked disapprovingly. She looked from one boy to the other. "You're not old enough."

Michael shrugged. "This is a game. It's not real beer. It's not real food either."

"Oh." Rose brightened. "So, I can eat whatever I want here, and I won't gain weight."

Madison rolled her eyes. In real life, Rose was even slimmer than her elven body in the game. The last thing she had to worry about was gaining weight.

"Do we even know how much money we actually have?" Rose asked.

Michael watched the barmaid as she started making her way back to the table with their ales. He licked his lips. "125 gold, 303 silver, 211 copper."

"You counted it already?" Rose frowned at her cousin.

"Nah," Michael said with a grin. "When I picked it up, it told me the full count in my HUD."

"Oh," Rose replied, going quiet as the barmaid

returned and set two pewter mugs in front of Cole and Michael. Both boys wore huge grins.

"Can I have a menu please?" Rose asked.

"A menu, darling?" the barmaid chuckled. "Sorry, this ain't no fancy city inn. Just a simple oceanside tavern with a few rooms for rent. Would you like to know the specials?"

Rose nodded. Madison guessed "specials" meant whatever they were actually serving that night. It turned out she was right.

"We have fried sea bass and tatters, or we got fish soup," the barmaid told him.

Her cousin frowned at the options. Madison guessed neither of those were things Rose would normally eat.

"No thank..." Rose started to tell the barmaid, but Michael held up his hand.

Michael leaned into Rose and spoke softly. Madison could barely make out his words. "You need to eat something, or your character is going to get hungry."

Throwing an annoyed look at her cousin, Rose sighed. "Bring me the... fish soup."

"One fish soup," the woman said. "Anyone else?"

Madison guessed the fried fish and tatters were like fish and chips. Even if they weren't, they'd at least fuel her character for a while. "I'll take the fish and tatters."

"Me too," Cole said. He brought his mug to his face and took a long sip of it before setting it back down.

Chuckling, Madison pointed to her brother. "Nice mustache."

"Huh?" Her brother cocked his head at her for a moment before it dawned on him. Grinning broadly, he swiped his sleeve across his mouth, wiping away the foam mustache he'd accumulated.

"What about you, honey?" the barmaid asked Michael.

Michael shrugged. "I'm fine."

Madison rolled her eyes again. "Didn't you just say we needed to eat?"

"I'm fine."

"He'll take the fried fish and tatters too," Madison told the woman.

The barmaid looked from Michael to Madison and then back to Michael. She shrugged. "One fish soup and three fried sea bass with tatters. Will that be all?"

Madison bit her lip. "Do you have anything other than ale?"

"We got mead," the barmaid answered. "It's my husband's own brew."

"I'll take one of those!" Madison said.

Rose leaned in. "What's mead?"

"It's an alcoholic beverage made from honey," Madison answered.

"I like honey!" Her cousin brightened. Rose turned to the barmaid. "I'll take a mead too."

Michael snapped his fingers. "Can I get an extra fish soup for my cat?"

The barmaid looked down at the tiger cub curled up under the table. She rolled her eyes and shook her head. "So, two meads, two fish soups and three sea bass and tatters?"

"That's about it," Madison replied.

Taking one last glance around the table, the barmaid spun and disappeared into the crowd.

"Okay," Cole said. "She's gone. Let's divvy up the loot."

"How much loot do we have?" Michael asked. "I really didn't loot anything in the gnoll dungeon."

"I thought maybe the captain guy would give us something when we turned in the crates," Rose said with a pout. "But at least we earned some real money!"

Madison smiled. That much was true. They'd gotten nearly two hundred dollars for being the first ones to complete the two quests. With the other Koyesta coins they'd earned from killing unique gnolls, they were now over $300. Split four ways, that was $75 each. Not a bad day. And the day wasn't over yet.

"Hello? Earth to Madison?" Cole said, snapping his fingers near her head.

Madison frowned at her brother in annoyance. "What?"

"You looted quite a few of the gnolls," he repeated. "What did you get from them?"

Bringing up her inventory, she read off the items.

Studded Rawhide Gorget (x2)
Spiked Rawhide Pauldrons
Spiked Rawhide Gorget
Runed Shaman Staff
Carved Pine Totem
Obsidian Earrings (x2)

"That's it," she told them. She paused and looked at the items in her inventory again. The icons for each item had a faint shimmer around them. She squinted. "That's weird. Those items all glow."

"Glow?" Michael said excitedly. "Like... a magical glow?"

"Examine them and see if they have any special properties!" Cole told her.

Madison sighed and mentally clicked on each item, reading the stats she received.

Studded Rawhide Gorget
Enchanted Item
Type: Leather
Location: Neck
Skill: Medium Armor
Size: Medium
Armor: 2
Quality: Average
Strength: +1
Description: Given to the elite guards of the commander, these otherwise ordinary-looking rawhide gorgets were enchanted by the Dark Shaman to give the guards extra strength in battle.

Spiked Rawhide Pauldrons
Enchanted Item
Type: Leather
Location: Shoulders
Skill: Medium Armor
Size: Medium
Armor: 2
Quality: Average

Strength: +3
Slam Attack + 1
Description: The Dark Shaman enchanted these spiked pauldrons for the commander to give him an extra edge in battle.

Spiked Rawhide Gorget
Enchanted Item
Type: Leather
Location: Neck
Skill: Medium Armor
Size: Medium
Armor: 2
Quality: Average
Strength: +3
Description: A stronger version of the studded gorgets given to the elite guards, the spiked version was enchanted specifically for the commander.

Obsidian Earring
Enchanted Item
Type: Earring
Location: Ear
Skill: N/A
Size: Medium
Quality: Average
Reflexes: +1
Description: A set of these enchanted earrings were given to the gnoll commander as a gift by the Dark Shaman. The obsidian gems set into the silver hoop flickers with magic.

Runed Shaman Staff
Enchanted Item
Type: 2-Handed Crushing
Hand: Both
Skill: 2-Handed Crushing
Size: Large
Dmg: 9
Quality: Average
Mana: +5
Hardiness: +5
Description: Found with the Dark Shaman, this staff bears runes of unknown origin. Their meanings and purpose can only be guessed.

Carved Pine Totem
Type: Totem
Hand: Either
Skill: N/A
Size: Medium
Quality: Average
Mana: +10
Description: This piece of charred pine has been carved into the likeness of a raven. When held, a strange warmth radiates from it.

"Ooh," Michael smiled. "That's a nice haul!"

"I call dibs on the pauldrons!" Cole said.

"Why do you get them?" Michael asked.

"They add to the slam attack," her brother replied with a grin.

Michael shrugged. “That’s fine. I get the earrings then.”

“Hey!” Rose protested. “What about us!”

“You like your scimitar, right?” Madison asked. “Why don’t you take the totem? It increases your magic, and you can hold it in your offhand.”

“That means you could use it too,” Rose countered.

Madison shook her head. “I’ll take the staff. It gives me some mana but also it’s a heavier weapon so it will do more damage.”

The group went back and forth with the items but in the end, the spiked pauldrons and gorget went to her brother. The earrings and one of the studded gorgets went to Michael, while the other studded gorget and totem went to Rose. Madison got the runed staff.

By then, the barmaid had returned with their food and conversation stopped while they devoured their dinner.

28

What Madison ate of her dinner was actually extremely good. She wasn't a huge fish and chips person, but the sea bass and tatters were well made and seasoned just right. Rose took one sip of her soup, made a face and then pushed it away. Making sure the barmaid wasn't looking, she slid it onto the floor for Buddy. Her cousin then proceeded to eat half of Madison's fish and tatters.

But that wasn't the most interesting thing. Apparently, the game had some sort of alcohol effect programmed in. On the first sip, she received a notification.

You have consumed Tipsy Pelican Mead.
Strength +1
Agility -1
Reflexes -1
Hardiness +1
Intellect -1

Wisdom - 1
Charisma - 1
You have gained a new skill: Alcohol Tolerance
You have become better at Alcohol Tolerance (+1%).
Congratulations! You were the first group on the server to consume Tipsy Pelican Mead. A Reward has been added to your account.
You may check your rewards by going to Character Menu-> Profile -> Rewards -> Early Access Awards

She smiled at the rewards but then a warm sensation flooded her body. Madison also started to feel... good. She blinked. "Uh... did you guys get a new skill when you drank your alcohol? Are you feeling any... you know... effects?"

The two boys looked at each other and grinned. Cole laughed. "I'm up to -10 Intellect! -10 Wisdom! Alcohol tolerance at 11 already!"

"Hah!" Michael retorted with a grin. "I'm up to -12, alcohol tolerance: 13!"

"What? How?" Cole growled.

Michael shrugged. "Your avatar is bigger. Probably needs more. Have you started seeing double yet?"

Rose looked aghast. "Are you guys getting drunk?"

"No!" "Yes."

The boys looked at each other, having given different answers. They laughed and turned back to Rose.

"Yes!" "No!"

The boys laughed again. Madison furrowed her brow. Was their speech starting to slur? She pushed the mead away, as did Rose.

"Relax," Cole told them. "It's just game stuff. We're not really drunk in real life. It's like when the shaman cast that disease spell. I mean, I felt sick. Really sick. But it was just a game effect."

"I'll pass. You should too," Madison said, giving the boys a disapproving look.

Cole waved off her concern. "We're just going to log for the evening anyway, so we'll be fine in the morning."

Madison opened her mouth to retort but Captain Bartem chose that moment to walk up to the table. He was smiling as he looked down at them. "Excellent! Our new town heroes are celebrating their success! Do you mind if I join you?"

Without waiting for an answer, the captain pulled a chair from a nearby table and sat down with them. He waved over at the barmaid. "Kaitee, another round for our heroes. Tell Samuel we want the good stuff! Oh, and tell Karl I want a steak!"

The boys grinned and exchanged looks, then both of them flashed an innocent smile at Madison. "It would be rude not to accept."

Madison fumed silently. She'd just managed to earn a good reputation with the town. She didn't want to screw anything up by refusing the captain's hospitality. Instead, she just smiled back at the captain and when he wasn't looking, turned a glare on her brother and cousin. Rose bit her lip and said nothing.

"I just want to tell you again what a great service you did for Fisherton," Bartem said, turning back to the group. "I wish I could do more for you, but unfortunately, the militia's budget is limited."

The group exchanged looks and then they all smiled back at the captain. They'd purposefully not told him about the extra coin they'd found. As it was, they had a nice little haul when combined with the 10 gold each of them had received from turning in the quest. Then there was the real-life money they'd earned by being the first to do the quest.

"We were glad to help," Madison replied.

"I'm glad you feel that way," the captain said as Kaitee, the barmaid, returned with five new mugs. She sat them on the table and took a step back.

"The steak will be a bit," Kaitee said. "Karl had to run over to the butcher to get it."

"Karl's the cook. He makes a mean steak though it's almost sacrilege to eat steak instead of fish in this town," Bartem explained to them. Then he turned a smile on the barmaid. "Thanks, Kaitee."

The barmaid nodded and then turned and walked over to another now-empty table to clear away the dishes. The captain reached down and took a long draw of his drink and then looked up.

"I'm afraid I have another request," the captain said. "You've cut the head off the beast, so to speak, and you even killed the shaman - whatever that was."

The group had told him about the gnoll shaman who had turned into a raven-headed crone when she had died. The captain had questioned them about her and any documents or orders she might have carried. Unfortunately, there hadn't been anything so obvious on the body. For now, the identity of the creature, and its purpose, remained a mystery.

"My fear is," the man continued. "That either another gnoll will step into the commander's shoes or another one of those raven women will infiltrate the gnoll burrow and take control."

"You want us to finish off the gnolls," Madison guessed.

Captain Bartem leaned back, took a long sip of his drink and then set it on the table. "That's precisely what I want you to do. And I need you to do it quickly, while they are still disorganized."

You have received a new quest "Cleansing the Burrow"
Captain Bartem fears a new leader may emerge in the Blackmange gnoll tribe. He wants you to prune their numbers so they can never again be a threat to Fisherton.
Kill Blackmange Gnolls
Blackmange Gnolls Killed (0/50)
Reward: +500 reputation with Residents of Fisherton, +500 reputation with Guards of Fisherton, +1000 reputation with Captain Bartem.
Accept quest (yes or no)?

The group exchanged smiles, even the boys - who were starting to look very tipsy. Another quest hopefully meant more real-life money. Madison quickly accepted the quest. "We will do our best."

"Oh yeah," Cole said, smiling a little too broadly. He was obviously feeling the effects of the new alcohol. She rolled her eyes at him.

"Excellent!" the captain said with a smile. He took

another draw from his mug. "I also have some news. I talked with Araman, sort of our local sage..."

"A sage?" Madison asked, perking up. A sage could mean books or knowledge about this world. That could give them a big advantage and help them understand more about this game and where they might need to go to make more money.

"Yes, he's an old gnome who moved here a few years back. Lives on the southside, on the beach," Bartem told her. "Anyway, he said the structure you were describing is most likely an ancient Artoshian ruin that the gnolls stumbled into. Funny, no one in town I spoke with ever remembers a ruin nearby."

"They may have found it by accident," Madison said. "The entrance was actually rough stone, like a cave."

"Yeah," Rose agreed. "It was all rough all the way to the bottom of the tunnel. They may have been expanding the tunnel and accidentally uncovered it."

Madison nodded. "That's what I was thinking."

"Me too," Cole said, suppressing a giggle. Her brother looked at Michael who giggled back at him.

"-23," he muttered and then they both chuckled.

"Guys!" Madison hissed but the captain waved away her concerns.

"They earned a few brews. You all did," the captain told her. He stood up with his mug. "I will let you enjoy your celebration in peace, while I go enjoy my steak and ignore the glares from the other townsfolk. Thank you again and I'll make sure Kaitee puts this last round on my tab!"

The captain walked over to the table Kaitee had

cleared earlier and sat down. He caught the barmaid's eye and held up his mug.

Madison whipped her head around at the boys, glaring at them with narrowed eyes. They looked at her and burst out laughing. She ground her teeth. "What's wrong with you two?!"

"Whaaaaat?" Cole asked, the word slow and slurred.

Rose shook her head and smiled. "Let them have their fun. It's about dinner time so I'm going to log and come back in the morning. Are we going to go back to the gnoll place then?"

"I hope so," Madison told her, glaring at the boys. They just laughed again.

"Okay, I'll see you later," Rose said. "Or I'll call you after I eat and we can set a time to come back in."

Madison smiled. "Sounds good! See you back here in a bit."

With that, Rose's eyes went blank and then she slowly faded away. Both boys looked at her fading and burst out laughing.

"Ugh! Boys!" Madison growled. "I'll see you two back in the game in the morning... well... morning in the game!"

The boys just laughed again.

"Cole!" she snapped. "I will see you for dinner!"

With that, she brought up her HUD and logged out to the sound of the boys laughing and reaching for the beers that she and Rose hadn't touched. Then the world faded away and she was back on her bed, looking up at the ceiling.

29

Her brother logged out a few minutes later and seemed completely unaffected by the in-game alcohol. Cole walked over to her room and pretended to walk a straight line. Then he gave her an "I told you so" look and stuck out his tongue at her. "See! Nothing! It's just a game effect!"

"Then why even do it?" Madison shot back. She rubbed her temples, where a mild headache was beginning to form. Luckily, it was a dull ache and not a sharp or throbbing headache.

Cole grinned. "Why not? Besides, we got some extra money from being the first to try the mead and that thing the captain ordered, Samuel's Special Brew or something like that."

Madison looked down at her phone. It was nearly dinner time. "Let's eat and then we can log back in later."

Her brother shrugged and then turned around. Looking over his shoulder, he grinned and winked at her as she started towards the door. "Dibs on the bathroom!"

Sighing, Madison shook her head and went downstairs to use the bathroom down there. The game seemed to override your sense of your body, including your feeling of hunger and the need to relieve yourself. They needed to be careful, or a particularly long episode could cause... an accident.

Going downstairs, they saw that their mom was home. She said hi, but then turned her attention to her computer. Her mom owned her own business and had been complaining recently of withholding taxes or payroll taxes or some sort of taxes. There was also some sort of visit by the state that she had to prepare for. Madison really tried not to think about taxes. They were just depressing.

Madison and Cole ate and then Cole called Michael to talk about the game. Madison, still curious about the Artoshians - or was it Artoshia - went back upstairs to search around on the internet to see if anyone had posted anything about it.

A half hour later, she gave up in frustration. No one was posting anything, other than more game-type experience stuff. It seemed everyone was keeping game-world details to themselves.

She thought she understood. There was real money involved at the moment. People weren't about to give another group something that might allow them to complete a unique task before they did. It was still frustrating.

Feeling a need to satisfy her curiosity, she logged back

in. After a moment, she appeared back outside the front door of the Tipsy Pelican. Madison blinked and looked around. It was dark out; the sun's glow was just starting to light the horizon. The inn was closed, she realized, so the game had moved her outside. Interesting.

Luckily, her eyes allowed her to see perfectly fine in the dim light and she began walking up and down the streets of the southside of the small town, looking for what she wanted. She found it after twenty minutes, just as the sun peeked over the ocean.

The small building, she stopped in front of had a faded copper sign in the shape of a scroll. It was worn from the elements and the once-shiny copper had faded to a dull, pale green. The building had light coming from the window and Madison felt herself grow excited. The person she was looking for was up. At least, she hoped it was him.

Walking to the door, she rapped on it and then stepped back. She heard what she thought were dogs barking but nothing else. She waited a minute and then knocked again. She was about to knock a third time when the door opened.

"It's the wee hours of the morning!" a high-pitched voice complained. "There better be a dragon attack or a gnoll raid going on or I'm going to be upset!"

The man who answered the door was tiny. He couldn't be more than three feet tall but with slightly oversized hands and feet. Also, his head looked proportionately larger than a human head. His nose as well. It was almost as if he were a caricature of a small human.

What had Captain Bartem called him? A gnome? Yes,

that was it, the little man was a gnome. He was wearing a gnome-sized sleeping gown and long cap with a yarn ball at the end - obviously his sleeping clothes. And at the moment he was frowning.

"Are you Araman?" Madison asked.

The little man blinked, as if seeing her for the first time. His eyes narrowed. "Who wants to know?"

"I'm..." Once again, she almost said Madison. She sighed and started over. "I'm Draconia. I'm the one who found the ruins."

Araman's frown faded as he looked her up and down more closely. "You're a Drakkar."

"Yes," she replied hesitantly.

"I can't say I've ever seen a live specimen," he replied. He looked her up and down like a butcher might inspect a piece of meat. Either uncaring or unaware he was in his sleeping robe, Araman stepped out of his house. He made a circle around her, continuing to inspect her. As he completed his circuit, he nodded. "Blue. An unusual pigmentation."

Remembering the trait she had chosen, Madison explained. "It is from my dragon ancestry. I come from blue dragons."

"Ah," the gnome nodded. "Blue dragons. Desert hunters. Loners. Breathes lightning, if I remember correctly."

Madison nodded, having breathed lightning herself recently.

"Fascinating, yes, very fascinating," Araman said and then stopped and shook his head. "But that doesn't explain why you're disturbing an old gnome so early in the morning!"

"Sorry," she apologized. "Your light was on and I really need to ask questions about the Artoshians."

The gnome huffed but then shrugged. "Yes, I suppose you would. When Captain Bartem talked to me, he said he was going to ask you and your group to go back to the ruins. Well, let's not talk here... come in, come in."

Not waiting for a reply, the little gnome spun and hurried back into his house. He left the door open, so Madison assumed he wanted her to follow. She did.

"Shut the door behind you please," he said, moving further into the room.

Madison stepped into the house, shut the door and then turned towards the gnome. Araman was on the opposite side of what looked like a living room. She noticed that both the door and the rooms seemed made for human-sized people. That probably meant the house hadn't been built for him.

She looked around the room. There was a fireplace against the right wall. On the floor in front of the fireplace was a woven rug. On the rug, a few feet back from the fireplace were two chairs. Both were leather bound and looked extremely well crafted. Both looked expensive and also appeared to be a matching set.

Between the chairs was a small round table that currently held a silver serving tray. The tray contained a single glass or porcelain cup and a silver kettle from which steam rose.

One of the leather chairs was obviously gnome-sized and was no doubt the chair the gnome used. The second chair was human-sized and was currently occupied by two dogs. Madison didn't recognize the breed.

There were two doors and one doorway in the room. The doorway on the far side of the room looked to lead into a kitchen or cooking area. Then there was the door she just came through and the final door near it, which she guessed led to the gnome's bedroom.

The rest of the wall space was obscured by bookshelves, all filled with books. There were different-sized bookshelves and different-sized books. Large books, small books, thin books and fat books.

Madison felt her eyes go wide at all the books. She wondered if they were actually readable in-game. If so, had someone in the real world actually written all of those books?!

Araman walked over to the larger chair and spoke to the dogs. "Dixy! Roxy! Down!"

The dogs looked up at him briefly and then laid their heads back down. Apparently, they were quite content about their place in front of the fire.

The gnome rolled his eyes and repeated their names. "Dixy! Roxy! Down!"

This time, the dogs didn't even look up. Araman shook his head. He walked into the kitchen area, made some noise as he did something, and then came back with two biscuits in his hands.

Returning to the dogs, he held up the biscuits. Immediately, the dogs' heads shot up, their eyes locked on the biscuits.

"Dixy! Roxy! Down!" Araman said, gesturing down with the biscuits. This time, both dogs obeyed, hopped down and sat in front of the gnome. The entire time, they didn't take their eyes off the biscuits.

The gnome walked over to his chair and sat down. He gestured with the biscuits. "Come!"

Both dogs hurried over, eyes still on the biscuit. Araman gave them a stern look. "Lie down!"

The dogs obeyed, lying down but keeping their heads up and their eyes on the biscuits.

"Good dogs!" Araman said and then tossed each of them a biscuit. The dogs caught the biscuits in their mouth and immediately began crunching on them.

"You'd better sit down before they finish," the gnome said and gestured to the chair.

Madison quickly got to the chair and slid onto it. "Thank you."

Araman reached down, petted each dog on the head. "Good puppies!"

After a minute of petting the dogs, the animals laid their heads down and closed their eyes. The gnome sat back in his chair and looked over at Madison. "So, what is it you want to know?"

30

"I need everything you know about the Artoshians," Madison blurted out.

The gnome chuckled. "Everything I know. Well, that would take quite a while. How about if I give you a summary and we can go from there?"

"That sounds great," she replied, a little embarrassed about her initial response. Madison was thinking too much like she would if she were in a library or in front of a search engine.

"Excellent," Araman said with a nod. He settled back in his chair and looked into the fire. "Well, as most of us know, the Artoshian culture thrived from about 3,000 BC until well, sometime during the Fey war."

"BC?" Madison asked quizzically. She guessed BC didn't stand for Before Christ, like it did in the real world.

The sage raised an eyebrow. "Before Cataclysm. Although some older scholars refer to it as BB, Before the

Breach. Do they call it something different in your culture?"

Thinking quickly, Madison came up with the first thing that came to mind. "We refer to it as BF, Before Fey."

"Ah," the sage acknowledged with a nod. "I'll have to make a note of that. Anyway... where was I?"

"Artoshian culture thriving..." Madison remembered.

"Ah yes, the Artoshians were elves, of course, we all know that," Araman continued. "But not like the elves we know today. Not, that was before the split that drove them apart."

"The split?" Madison asked. She was feeling a bit overwhelmed with the gnome information dump. She was wondering if she should have just asked for a book on the matter.

"77 AB, After Banishment, when the curse the Fey had cast on the Artoshians finally manifested itself fully," Araman replied. "Now we have the high elves, the wood elves and the night elves. Before that, there was only one type of elf and they called themselves the Artoshians."

"Ah yes." Madison nodded.

"Ahem." The sage cleared his throat. "Where was I?"

"The Artoshians," she supplied helpfully.

"Oh yes! The Artoshians were one of the two dominant cultures back then. They built huge cities, only one of which survives to this day - Quauroux, to the north. The humans occupy it now, of course. They renamed it to Queensford, after Queen Tami II. Back in 4017 AB - After Banishment - if I remember correctly."

He paused and looked at Madison, who - not knowing what else to do - nodded. She made a mental note that there was a city to the north called Queensford. From the sound of it, it might even be the capital of this area.

"Yes," the gnome continued. "Everyone knows the stories of the Great Breach and the invasion of our Realm by the dark Fey. It was the Artoshians and the Valharians, once enemies, who finally put aside their differences, and came together and finally sealed the breach."

Madison remembered that she knew the Valharian language as well.

"Who were the Valharians? Humans?" she asked.

"It was a human empire," the sage agreed. "I mean, we all know the Valharian emperors were human from about 2,000 BC forward. But I am sad to admit, there were gnomes and other races involved in that evil empire. Your people included."

The gnome looked at Madison and she nodded, despite not having known that. She really knew nothing about them - other than being able to read their language. It was interesting to find out that the Drakkar had been part of the Valharian empire.

From what it sounded like, they had been evil and the Artoshians had been good and led by the elves. Then, the Fey invaded and the good nation, or collection of nations, had joined with the evil empire and they'd killed the Fey.

"Unfortunately, the final battle decimated both sides. Both empires were mortally wounded and collapsed shortly thereafter. With the emperor and the ruling council both dead, the Valharian empire collapsed immediately. With no strong leader, the evil races began fighting over the scraps of the empire until somewhere around 54 AB. By then it was all over, and we see no more records of the Valharian empire."

Madison nodded. "What about the Artoshians? What happened to them?"

"They returned to their great cities and tried to mend their wounds," Araman answered. "They might have even been able to do it. At least two thirds of their people had been wiped out but unlike the Valharian empire, they were still united. At least, until the..."

Remembering what the sage had said earlier, Madison hazarded a guess. "The curse?"

The gnome nodded gravely. "Some of the high elves have said they believe the curse was meant to turn them all into twisted versions of elves, like the Fey who invaded. But it didn't quite work the way the Fey expected - or perhaps it did and what happened was always their intention. Perhaps the Fey's intention was always to fracture the elven nation. Who can say?"

"So, they split and that was the end of them?" she asked.

"The curse twisted a third of the remaining elves into violet-skinned, evil-hearted versions of high elves," Araman told her. "They tried taking control of the Artoshians but the other two races of elves that were created from the curse - the wood elves and the high elves - banded together and forced the night elves underground, into the Hollow Earth."

"The Hollow Earth?" Madison asked. Was that like Journey to the Center of the Earth?

"Yes." The man nodded. "That's where they live to this day, though obviously they still raid the surface elves from time to time." Araman paused and looked at Madison. "Does that information help you?"

She bit her lip, remembering the Dark Fey they'd killed and how it had been shape shifted into a gnoll. Madison debated on whether she should tell the gnome about it. She wasn't sure of the significance of it - if there was any at all.

Madison decided to test the waters. "Are there any Fey left?"

"After almost 5,000 years?" the sage asked. "No. The Fey who were trapped on this side of the veil were hunted down and killed. I don't think there's been a Fey sighting for... well... at least four thousand years?"

Biting her lip, Madison let out a breath. "What if I told you we killed a Fey in the gnoll burrow. One that had taken the form of a gnoll shaman."

Araman chuckled and waved her comment away. "I wouldn't even jest about something like that."

"It's true," Madison said, giving him a serious look. "We were fighting the Commander when this gnoll shaman showed up. We killed it but when it died, it transformed into a raven-headed old woman."

Madison stopped short of telling the gnome that she'd read the name in her HUD. It seemed non-player characters (NPCs) didn't respond to them when they just disappeared from the game, nor did they respond when players said anything that related to game mechanics.

"You're joking, of course," the gnome said nervously. "Did the captain put you up to it?"

Shaking her head, Madison made her face as serious as she could. "I'm not joking. I'm sure it was a Fey."

The gnome laughed nervously, his face growing paler. He shook his head. "It can't be. All the Fey on this side have been dead for millennia. If you encountered one... that would mean..."

Araman trailed off and didn't speak for nearly a minute. Madison waited but after a minute, she pressed him. "What would it mean?"

"Well," the gnome said, getting a faraway look in his eyes. "One, perhaps the Fey are immortal, or extremely long lived, and this is a remnant of those Fey who were left on this side when the Breach was sealed." He scratched his head. "I mean, if it could change shape, it could have blended in..."

The gnome went silent and after a few moments, Madison once again grew impatient and gestured for Araman to continue. "And the other possibility?"

"What? Oh," the gnome replied with a shake of his head. "Well... if it wasn't here from when the Breach got sealed, the only other logical explanation would be.... That the Seal on the Breach is weakening and Fey are starting to slip through."

"That doesn't sound good." Madison frowned.

"No... no it doesn't," the sage replied. He furrowed his brow. "You say this creature you think was a Fey was in the burrow?"

Madison nodded. "Yes, it was in the room with the commander..." She paused. No, that wasn't true. It had come into the commander's room from the door they'd come in through. From the treasure vault. Thinking back, she remembered there had been another door on the opposite side of the vault. Had it come from there?

"Actually," Madison continued. "It came from one of the other rooms near the commander. Maybe further into the Artoshian ruins."

Araman turned back to the fire, staring into the crackling flames as he rubbed the stubble on his chin. He turned back to her. "If that was a Fey and it was in those ruins, there must be a reason. I would suggest going back in there and seeing if you can retrace its steps and figure out what it was after."

You have received a new quest "In the Fey's Footsteps"
Araman Blackpipe is worried that the Fey you encountered in the gnoll burrow may have been up to something. To alleviate his fears, he would like you to further investigate the Artoshian.
Explore Deeper into the Artoshian Ruins
Ruins Explored (0/1)
Reward: +1000 reputation with Araman Blackpipe.
Accept quest (yes or no)?

Madison looked at the quest and accepted it. Truth be told, she was curious now too. "We'll do it."

The gnome flashed her a worried look. "Hopefully, it is only nothing. But be careful in there."

"I think we can take care of the gnolls," she said confidently.

Araman shook his head. "Not the gnolls. The ruins. If those are Artoshian ruins, then they may have wards against those of the Valharian empire. At the time, that included humans and... well... Drakkar."

"You're saying there might be boobytraps for me and

the guys?" she asked. This new revelation was just one more thing they'd have to worry about now. "The other person in our party is an elf."

The sage shook his head. "It might not matter. Remember, there are no true Artoshians any longer. They were all affected by the Curse. They are shadows of true Artoshians. It might not recognize her either."

"Well, that stinks!" Madison growled.

"Be careful," the gnome repeated.

Madison nodded and stood up from the chair. The dogs' eyes followed her, but they didn't bother to even lift their heads. "I have to get back to my group now."

Araman nodded. "Good luck and..."

"Be careful," Madison finished with a smile. "We will."

The sage didn't bother to get up and see her out, so Madison walked over to the door. She opened and started to step through. Pausing, she turned to the little gnome. "Thank you."

He nodded back to her and then twisted in his chair. The gnome patted the seat she had just been occupying and both dogs jumped to their feet. The two of them hopped into the chair and after a moment, settled back into a lying position.

Smiling to herself, Madison left the house and closed the door behind her. She had a lot to tell everyone.

31

"Well," Rose said with a smile as she finished up a bite of blueberry pancakes. "It's got to be a unique quest. I have four or five hours - uh, real time - before I have to go to bed. That might be another $20 or $30!"

Madison took a bite of her own pancakes, soaked in maple syrup. They tasted so real, it was easy to forget this was just a game. She sighed contentedly and was happy the inn served breakfast. She looked over at Cole and Michael.

Both of the boys had their heads in their hands, staring down at the table and moaning. The moment they'd logged in, they'd learned that virtual hangovers were a thing in the game.

Grinning, she held out some of her pancakes on her fork. "Are you sure neither of you wants some. They're REALLY good."

"Uhhhh," Cole moaned. "Get it away. I never want to see in-game food again."

Michael had at least ordered a small plate of sausages and every so often, handed one down to Buddy. The little cub snapped it out of his hand, shook it around and then dropped it on the floor and ate it.

"I can't imagine that anyone else has gotten the quest from Araman," Madison agreed. "We should get some money from that. Plus, there might be some new monsters too. Boobytraps too - but I don't know if they will give us money."

"These pancakes are so good!" Rose said as she finished chewing. "Hopefully we can make at least $50-$60. Then my parents can't say anything about me playing. Altogether, that would be more than I can make in almost a week working part-time."

Madison finished up her pancakes and smiled. "Those were so good! We need to eat here every morning! Uh... game morning."

"I'm game!" Rose agreed.

Cole made an unintelligible noise. Michael didn't reply at all.

"You guys better eat something," Madison scolded them. "Otherwise, your characters will get hungry."

"To go," Cole managed. Michael nodded.

"Fine," Madison replied. She felt a bit of satisfaction and vindication watching her brother and cousin suffer after their debauchery earlier. But, at the same time, she also felt sympathy for them.

After all, this was a game. It was supposed to be fun. It wasn't supposed to be something you logged in and then felt terrible. That was too much like real life. But apparently, there were consequences to actions in the game. Madison just wondered what other actions would hold consequences.

ANOTHER HOUR and another order of pancakes later, the group was ready to go. Her brother and cousin were both feeling better. When she asked about them, Cole explained.

"We had a debuff called Severe Hangover," her brother said. "It was like -30 to all stats and some other stuff…."

"Like nausea," Michael added.

"Like nausea," Cole agreed with a sour expression. "And vertigo. But that's gone. Now it just says Hangover and it's a -10 to stats."

Michael looked over and nodded. "And the nausea and vertigo are gone thankfully."

Her brother bobbed his head in agreement.

Madison was so tempted to tell them "I told you so" but somehow, she resisted. Watching them be miserable for the last hour - and missing out on adventuring time - she didn't want to add insult to injury.

"Alright, what's the plan?" Madison asked. "For the gnolls?"

"We'll have to play it by ear." Cole shrugged. "Without knowing how they might have reacted to the death of the Commander and that shaman thing, it's hard to formulate a plan."

"I only caught about half of what you were saying earlier," her brother said, glancing over at her. "You said that was some sort of dark Fey? And something about them being from another world or dimension or something?"

"Yes." Madison nodded. "That's what Araman..."

"The gnome."

"That's what Araman the gnome said," she continued. "The Fey invaded from somewhere and wanted to take over this world. And the two big superpowers at the time combined forces and drove them out."

"Like little lion robots combining together to form a giant robot," Michael said with a grin.

Not understanding the reference, but sure it was a reference to some show, movie or anime, Madison just shrugged.

"And you said they cursed us, right?" Rose asked. "I mean, elves."

"Yes. You used to be Artoshians," Madison confirmed. "Which were like some super elves or something. But the Fey cast some sort of curse on your ancestors and it caused them to split or morph or something into high elves, wood elves and night elves."

"You're Transformers!" Michael grinned. He immediately began singing the theme song to an animated TV show about robots that turned into cars and other vehicles. Cole quickly joined in.

Rose and Madison exchanged annoyed glances. They waited until the boys had finished the song - or more likely, couldn't remember the words to the rest of the song.

"Anyway," Madison said loudly. "Araman thinks there might be traps down there."

Cole snapped his fingers. "That's what we're missing! A thief!"

"A thief?" Madison inquired.

"You know," her brother retorted. "Someone with stealth skills, lockpicking ability and trap detection."

"And what happens if we don't have a person like that?" Rose asked.

"Boom!" Michael made an explosion motion with his hands.

"We'll have to be extra careful," Cole said.

"That's what Araman said too," Madison remembered.

"Then we should be doubly careful," her brother noted. "Oftentimes, if the NPCs make note of something specific, it's a clue that it's important. If the gnome said to be careful more than once, it's probably the game letting us know that there are definitely traps."

"Actually," Michael said, scratching his head. "Just the fact that the NPC mentioned traps probably means traps. The fact that he said be careful twice, probably means they're deadly traps. Or maybe deadly at our level."

"Yeah," Rose said, her forehead furrowed. "But we can just respawn, right?"

Cole and Michael looked at each other grimly. "Sure, we can. But what if the trap is a 100-foot-deep pit with acid at the bottom. How would we get our bodies and our loot?"

Rose's eyes went big. "ACID?!"

Madison waved off the guys' talk. "I'm sure they're exaggerating."

Her brother looked and Rose and shrugged. "Maybe, but that doesn't mean we'll always be able to recover our corpses and our stuff."

"We need a bank to store things in," Michael pointed out.

"A bank?" Rose asked. "Why?"

"In most games, the bank allows you to store money and items and then those things are accessible at any other bank in the world," Cole explained.

"Then we could get money and items from the bank if we were ever in a situation where we lost our corpses and our stuff," Madison reasoned.

"Right!" Michael said with a smile. "It's saved me a few times in other games."

"Do you think there's a bank in Fisherton?" Rose asked, obviously liking the security of having some money and items stored away.

"I didn't see one," Madison admitted. "But we didn't really explore the entire town."

"When we get back, we should look for one," her elven cousin suggested.

"Hopefully," Cole chimed in, "when we go back, we'll have more money and more items."

"With great risk," Michael said, "comes great reward."

"Or great death!" Cole countered.

Michael nodded with a grin. "Or great death."

The four of them lapsed into silence as they cut off the road and began moving through the forest, towards the gnoll burrow.

Madison considered what the gnome had said and what it might mean. Had the raven-hag been a Fey that had been left over from the war, thousands of years ago? If so, what had it been doing all that time? And more importantly, what had it been doing with the gnolls?

Then there was the alternative. Araman mentioned that perhaps the barrier - or whatever was keeping the Fey out of this world - might be breaking down, letting in Fey. That seemed more disturbing to Madison - but perhaps it was all part of this world or some larger story.

Now that the raven-hag was dead, there was no way to know where it had come from or what it had been doing. At least, not directly. Perhaps exploring the ruins would yield some answers.

Then again, it might just raise more questions. Frustrated, Madison continued their trek to the gnoll burrow.

32

Without the gnoll commander and the shaman, the other gnolls put up an unorganized resistance. Madison and her group were able to beat most of them and when the others barricaded themselves into the other rooms, Michael had suggested smoking them out.

It had worked, of course. With no place to go, the smoke drove the remaining gnolls out, barking and coughing. That was when things got weird.

"Are those.... children?" Rose asked, looking at the larger gnolls clutching smaller gnolls as they scrambled out of the cave.

"That's weird," Cole said. "Games don't have monster children."

"Uh," Michael said, a frown forming on his face. "This one does."

Madison swallowed, realizing what they'd just done. "I

think those are all females and children. Moms. Did we just, you know, kill off their dads?"

The group exchanged looks, none of them happy.

"That's messed up!" Rose said. "I... I...."

Her cousin trailed off, unable to continue. She just stared out at the coughing gnolls.

"And this is why they don't put children in video games!" Cole said angrily. "It creates an unnecessary ethical situation."

"You mean, like killing children?!" Rose growled. "I'm not going to kill them!"

Cole sighed. "Rose, they're not real. None of this is real. It's just a game."

Rose crossed her arms over her chest. "I'm not killing them."

Madison nodded, taking a step over to stand next to Rose. "I'm not going to kill them either."

Michael shrugged. "We can't really let them go back in. If we don't kill them, the Captain will probably send his men to finish the job."

"I won't kill them," Rose said defiantly.

"I didn't say we had to kill them," Michael shot back, holding his hands up in a placating gesture. "We just can't let them go back in - otherwise they will be killed."

Cole let out a heavy sigh. "I get it. It sucks. They look like women and children but the reality is, they're just game data. But... I get that you don't want to kill them and honestly, we don't have to. We finished the Captain's quest already."

"Can we just leave them be?" Rose asked hopefully.

"No." Cole shook his head. "Michael is right. If we go

back, the Captain will probably just send his men to finish them off. The three of them would be able to finish them off."

"We don't have to tell him!" Rose protested.

"I don't think it will work that way," Madison told her cousin. She bit her lip. "I think the game will keep giving us quests until the gnolls are completely gone."

"But we can't..." Rose started but Madison put a hand on her shoulder.

"I know," Madison told her cousin. "We can't kill them. We'll have to drive them away. Far away."

It was Rose's turn to bite her lip as she looked from the cave to the huddled group of gnolls. She nodded finally. "Fine."

Cole smiled down at Rose. "If you feel strongly about it, we can bring their stuff out here and give it to them to take with them."

Rose brightened. "Yeah! That would help them wherever they end up."

As if in response to their decision, a quest prompt appeared.

You have received a new quest "No Enemy Left Standing"
You have vanquished most of the Blackmange gnolls inhabiting the area near Fisherton. Only a few females and young gnolls remain.
You can kill them and end the gnoll threat forever or allow them to leave.
Kill The Remaining Gnolls
Remaining Gnolls Killed (0/22)

Reward: Unknown
Allow the Gnolls to Leave
Remaining Gnolls Allowed to Leave (0/22)
Reward: Unknown
Accept quest (yes or no)?

"Hmm," Cole said, his eyes glassy from looking at his HUD. "Apparently, the game is letting us decide. It just won't tell us what the rewards are for either."

Madison flashed her brother a smile and he shrugged. "Maybe it wants to give us a chance to do the right thing. And honestly, I don't really want to have dreams about slaughtering kids - gnolls or not."

"What's the plan then?" Michael asked.

"It looks like we're letting them go. First, we unblock the chimneys. Then, Madison, you and I will stay out here and make sure they don't go back in," Cole said. "When it clears out in there, Rose, you go in, grab their stuff and bring it out."

"We're going to have to make it clear that they shouldn't come back," Michael added.

Madison sighed. "I know. I'll try to communicate with them."

"Do you think you can?" Cole asked.

"I'll try," she replied.

Michael chuckled. "It won't take much. I mean, we're dumping their stuff on the lawn and screaming for them to leave. Like, isn't that the classic way someone gets kicked out of their place?"

Madison and Rose rolled their eyes at Michael but he just grinned and shrugged. "It's true!"

The group put their plan into action. They cleared the chimneys and then stood guard in front of the entrance.

The gnolls, for their part, just sat huddled in a circle. The smaller gnolls remained in the protective circle of the larger adult gnolls. They glared and barked at the group but didn't make any threatening moves.

After nearly an hour, the cave cleared out enough that Rose could go into the cave and begin bringing stuff out. She made trip after trip without complaining, bringing armloads of furs, cooking utensils and even foodstuffs. Her cousin dumped the items in a pile between the two groups and continued to make trips for another half hour.

Finally, she came up, out of breath, with empty arms. "That's all I can carry. Most of the other stuff looks like maybe they built it inside. Even if I could lift it, it won't even fit through the door."

"Now what?" Michael asked, looking at Madison.

"Now I try to make them understand they need to leave their home," Madison replied, feeling sick to her stomach. She felt like a slumlord about to evict a family because they couldn't pay rent. She cursed the game. Why would it even have stuff like this?!

Walking over to the pile, she picked up a pot and tossed it at the feet of the gnolls. The gnolls scrambled back a bit, maintaining their protective circle.

Madison sighed. She walked forward, eliciting some growls from the larger gnolls. Picking up the pot, she took a step towards them and thrust it out.

The gnoll in front of her looked down at the pot and then back up at Madison. Then it looked back at the others and barked something at them. Other gnolls barked back at it. The gnoll turned back to Madison and growled.

Rolling her eyes, she repeated the gesture, this time pushing it into the gnoll's stomach. This time, the gnoll brought its hands down and Madison let go of the pot so it fell into the creature's hands. The gnoll looked down at the pot and then up at Madison in what appeared to be confusion.

Madison pointed at the pile of stuff and then at the gnolls, then she pointed in what she thought was north. "You have to leave!"

The gnolls barked at each other for a moment and Madison repeated her gesturing. "You have to leave!"

"I don't think they understand you," Cole said from behind her.

After thinking a moment, Madison walked over to the pile. She pointed to the gnolls, then pointed at the pile. Then, she picked up a handful of stuff and pointed north. Then she began to walk north. After a dozen steps, she stopped and looked back at the gnolls.

"You have to leave!" She pointed to the gnolls then back north.

The gnolls looked around at each other and then from Madison to the others, then down at the gnoll children. They barked some more at each other before going quiet.

One of the gnolls crept away from the circle towards the pile. The gnoll's eyes darted from Madison to the others and then back. It crouched at the pile and grabbed a few things before retreating back.

There was more barking and then the gnolls began

coming in groups of two. They went over to the pile, picked out some items and retreated near the kids.

When all of them had made at least one trip, they glanced around, alternating from Madison to the group.

Once again, Madison pointed north. "You have to leave! You can't stay here!"

Still, the gnolls did not move.

Madison walked back to her group, biting her lip. She frowned at what she was about to say. "Everyone take out your weapons..."

"I'm not going to..." Rose started but Madison held up a palm.

"We're not going to hurt them, we just need to look threatening so they think we might hurt them," Madison explained.

All of them brought out their weapons and the gnolls cowered protectively over the children.

"Take a step whenever I take a step," she told them.

Madison pointed north and took a step. "Go!"

She heard everyone shuffling behind her and she repeated it. Once more she took a step and pointed north. "Go!"

She took another step... then another... then another.

Finally, the gnolls seemed to get the message. They barked and growled at the group but they began moving to the north. As they did, Madison stopped moving towards them.

The gnolls kept moving, eventually disappearing into the woods. As they disappeared into the trees, a new message appeared.

Quest "No Enemy Left Standing" Complete.
You have gained experience!
Your reputation with Residents of Fisherton has decreased.
Your reputation with Guards of Fisherton has decreased.
You have gained +1 Karma.
Congratulations! You were the first group on the server to complete the quest No Enemy Left Standing. A Reward has been added to your account.
You may check your rewards by going to Character Menu-> Profile -> Rewards -> Early Access Awards

"Ugh!" Michael said, reading the message. "Your reputation decreased with Fisherton."

"Hopefully, it will be offset by the other quest we have to turn in," Cole suggested.

"We did the right thing," Rose said with a smile. "That's more important."

Madison cocked her head. "And what is a Karma point?"

"No idea," Cole replied. He gestured to the cave. "But now it's time to do the other quest and explore those ruins."

As one, the group turned to stare into the entrance to the gnoll burrow. For some reason, it looked just a bit more foreboding now.

33

The group made their way through the rooms the gnolls had inhabited. Madison counted ten additional rooms, not including the commander's room and the vault, that the gnoll tribe had used. All of them were missing the stone doors they'd encountered in the treasure vault.

One of the rooms with a chimney had obviously been a kitchen and/or eating hall. The giant kettle still stood suspended on a strange tripod the gnolls had rigged up. When they reached the second room with a chimney, they were unsurprised to find that it was a brewery. The smell of hops still permeated the entire room.

"I thought that smell was hops," Madison said, wrinkling her nose. She saw Michael and her brother make a face and guessed the virtual hangover they'd experienced had caused their appetite for beer and ale to wane.

"It looks like a distillery too," Michael said, pointing to

a metal contraption with several pipes. "I think that's what it is."

Cole nodded. "Yeah, it looks like one of those hillbilly stills from that show."

"The moonshine show?" Michael asked, nodding. "Yeah! It does!"

They started to move to the next room, but Madison stopped suddenly and looked around.

"What?" Cole asked, tensing. His eyes darted around the room, looking for danger.

"Nothing." Madison shook her head. "It's just that... well... if there were traps in these ruins, wouldn't the gnolls have triggered them too? I mean, these rooms are part of the ruins."

"For all we know, they did," Michael replied with a grin. He made an explosion gesture with his hands. "Traps could have killed a ton of them when they first moved in."

Rose frowned. "You would think that would have dissuaded them."

"Maybe they had nowhere else to go," Madison said ruefully. She thought about the female gnolls and children now wandering around looking for a new place to live.

"Or maybe this is where the game designers put them," Cole stated. "Remember, it's just a game."

Madison did have to remind herself of that. She was one of those people who really got involved in a book she was reading or a movie she was watching. Apparently, now she was getting into a video game. Well, technically, a virtual reality game.

The conversation died out as they reached the commander's room. The battle with the shaman and the commander was still fresh in all of their minds. Madison smiled to herself as she remembered using her dragon breath ability. It was really cool. Too bad she could only use it once a day.

Michael whistled, snapping Madison out of her thoughts.

"Wow," her cousin said, pointing at the wrecked stone door. "They really did a number on the door."

Cole chuckled. "Well, we did bust the door handle... or open switch... or whatever that is."

"Good thing they didn't catch us," Rose muttered.

The group went through the shattered doorway and into the room that had previously been the treasure vault. Now that she knew this was an Artoshian ruin, she wondered what the original purposes of the various rooms had been.

Unfortunately, with the rooms the gnolls occupied, any trace of what the room's former purpose was had been stripped away. Even the treasure vault was now just a huge, empty room.

"I wonder what this room was used for," Madison wondered aloud.

"Puppet shows?" Michael said with a silly grin. He brought his hands up and made them move like mouths.

"I'm the gnoll commander..." he said using his left hand.

"I'm Madison the dragon girl...." he said with the right hand. He made the right mouth open wide. "Zappppp! Now you're EXTRA Crispy Cream!"

Madison rolled her eyes. "Oh... Ha... ha..."

"Join us again next week, same Madison time, same Madison channel," he said with his hands and then tucked them away.

"Sounded just like her." Cole smirked.

"It did not!" Madison protested.

"Maybe a little bit," Rose agreed with a wink.

Madison realized they were giving her a hard time and she opened her mouth to rebut their ridiculous assertions but Cole suddenly stopped and held up a hand for silence.

Everyone froze, looking at Cole and then looking around, trying to figure out what had set him off.

Then Madison heard it. There was a buzzing sound, just for a second, and then it was gone. "I heard it too."

"Me too!"

"I heard it."

Madison looked to her brother. "What do you think it is?"

Cole frowned. "I'm not sure. I don't remember hearing that before."

"You mean last time we were here? Right before putting the smack down on commander gnoll and his flunkies?" Michael asked with a grin.

"And the shaman," Rose added. "Don't forget the shaman... or well, the raven-hag or whatever it was."

Madison did remember the raven-hag/shaman. She remembered how utterly sick and disgusting that spell had made her feel. It was like an instant case of the worst flu ever. She perked up suddenly, remembering something. "Wait a minute! The raven-hag came from this room." She pointed up to the hole in the ceiling. "And I don't think it came in the way we did."

Everyone turned and looked at the opposite door. The direction that the sound was coming from. There was silence for a moment as the buzzing sound repeated.

"Wooooooo!" Michael said loudly in a ghostly voice, while wiggling his fingers. "Spooooky!"

Cole chuckled but Rose and Madison both turned and punched him in the arms. Rose growled at Michael. "Don't do that!"

Michael rubbed his arms in mock hurt but his grin betrayed him. "Ow! Geez! It's just a game!"

"I don't care!" Rose shot back. "Don't do that! This place is spooky enough now that I know it was made by dead people."

"I see dead peo..." Michael started but a glare from Rose made him shut his mouth. "You guys are no fun."

"Anyway! Back to the shaman/raven-hag," Madison said loudly, getting their attention. She pointed to the door opposite the commander's chamber. "The shaman must have come through that door. The question is: what was it doing?"

"Do you think there are more gnolls in there?" Rose asked.

"Nah," Cole said. "I don't think they would have let us send away their women and children if there were any left."

"That's weird," Michael said, cocking his head. He looked serious for a change.

"What's weird?" Rose said cautiously, obviously expecting it to turn into some sort of joke.

"Well,"—Michael pointed up at the hole—"the smoke wouldn't have gone past this room, right?"

Everyone gave him a blank stare. Even Madison furrowed her scaly brow. "What do you mean?"

"You know," he said with a grin, pointing up at the hole. "That's basically like a chimney. The smoke would have gone up there. They could have come in here, gone through this door and been safe from the smoke."

Cole nodded, looking back at the shattered door of the commander's room. "That's right. All the other doors had been busted down or jammed open."

"Right." Michael nodded. "So why not retreat down here and wait out the smoke."

Madison looked from the hole to the closed door. She frowned. Michael had a point. Why wouldn't they have done that?

"Maybe there's something bad behind the door," Rose suggested.

Michael nodded with a superior-looking grin. "Exactly! They knew something we don't. And they didn't want to go in there."

Rose frowned at the door. "Like what?"

"Like a trap... or a monster," Cole said.

"Or both!" Michael grinned.

"But the shaman had to have come through this door," Rose argued. "There's no other place for it to have come from."

"So then," Cole said, looking thoughtful. "There's something in there that the gnolls were afraid of or wanted to avoid, but not the crone."

"Let's find out!" Michael said, taking a step towards the door.

"Are you crazy?!" Rose blurted out, grabbing his arm.

Michael just grinned bigger and held his fingers out about an inch apart. "Maybe a little. But let's face it. It's just a game. Unlike the gnolls, if we die, we'll respawn."

"That's true," Madison admitted. "But we'll be pretty much naked, right?"

"True," Michael admitted with a shrug. "But who cares. We run back and grab our stuff and keep going."

"The ruins aren't going to explore themselves," Cole said. "Either we go through this door, or we go back."

"Fine," Rose huffed, crossing her arms over her chest. "I don't like it. This place is starting to give me the creeps."

Madison had noticed it too. Since the gnolls had left, the entire thing seemed a bit more foreboding. Was that just because the unknown lay ahead, or was it some feature of the game?

"We can do it, Rose," Madison told her cousin. "And to make sure, we'll let the boys go first."

"What about ladies first?" Michael protested.

Rose and Madison both shook their heads. Rose smiled innocently at him. "That's just in the real world. In the game, in a dungeon... boys first!"

34

"I'll go first!" Cole said, ending the debate. "After all, I'm the tank and I have more health than anyone else. Hopefully, if something happens, I'll survive it."

Everyone quickly lined up behind Cole in front of the door. Madison blinked. "Wait!"

"What?" Cole growled, hand hovering just over the plate to open the door.

"Uh," Madison said, gesturing to them in a straight line. The same sort of straight line that had allowed her to use her lightning breath attack to devastating effect. "We're all in a straight line! What if... like... a lightning bolt comes flying out when you open the door."

"A bunch of idiots standing in a line," Michael said with a grin. He patted Cole on the back. "We're all counting on you!"

Michael then hopped to the side and put his back against the wall to the right of the door. Buddy looked around and then pounced after him. He crouched down behind Michael, ready to attack anything the door revealed.

Rose and Madison moved off to the left side, putting their backs against the wall. Her automated guardian glided to the side with her. Madison gave Cole a thumbs up. "Go for it!"

Her brother rolled his eyes and then slapped the panel that opened the door. There was a brief hesitation and her brother grimaced as he braced himself. Then, the stone door slid to the side.

Nothing happened.

Her brother looked up and through the door. He relaxed his posture. "It's an empty hallway."

"All that and it's just a hallway!" Michael chuckled, peeking around the corner. He nodded. "Yep. It's a hallway."

Since it seemed to be clear, Madison stepped around the corner and looked down the hallway. It was a five-foot-wide stone hallway about twenty feet long. At the end of the hall was another door.

Rose peeked over her shoulder. "I guess we go down the hallway."

Madison frowned. "That puts us in a line again."

"It also doesn't give us much room to maneuver if there's any enemies past that door," Cole commented.

"That might be the point," Michael suggested.

"Bottle us up and then release monsters," Cole said sarcastically. "Surely, no game designer would ever do that."

The two boys shared a chuckle, but Madison

frowned as she listened. She heard the buzzing sound again. This time, it sounded like it came from behind the door at the end of the tunnel. "Shh! Do you hear that?"

Everyone went quiet and after a bit, they all heard the sound again. Once again, it sounded familiar to Madison, but she couldn't quite place it.

"What is that?" Rose asked. "Is it... bees?"

Michael screwed up his face. "I don't think so. Doesn't quite sound like bees."

"Maybe giant bees!" Cole suggested and Madison elbowed him in the ribs.

"Don't even say that!" she told him. Madison been sixteen when she'd accidentally walked over a hornet nest in their yard. The bees had swarmed out of the nest and stung her all over her body. It had been excruciating and she really didn't want anything to do with bees, wasps or stinging insects of any type. Especially not giant stinging insects!

Michael grinned. "Only one way to find out!"

Madison was still looking down the hallway when she noticed a detail she'd missed before. The floor was covered in dust but in the dust was a series of dog-like footprints going to and from the door at the far end of the hall. She pointed at the floor. "Hey, do you see the floor? Footprints."

They all looked down at the floor to see what Madison meant. Rose cocked her head and furrowed her brow. "So gnolls were already here?"

"It looks like it," Cole said. "Or maybe..."

"Dark Shaman," Rose interrupted. "I see its footprints

with my tracking skill. The others aren't showing, so they must be old."

"Does that mean the shaman was here several times? Or were others here earlier and then the shaman recently?" Michael wondered aloud.

Rose shrugged. "No idea. When my tracking kicks in, I see the highlighted set of prints with a name next to them. I only see one set of prints highlighted and one name, Dark Shaman."

"Perhaps they found something, like that buzzing, that scared them away and prevented them from going further into the ruins," Madison suggested. It made sense to her. The gnolls must have explored further in but stopped shortly after the vault room. Otherwise, they moved into the area. Or at the very least, would have retreated here when the smoke started. That begged the question: What was beyond the next door?

"Could be," Cole agreed. He looked down at the far door. "Either some sort of monster or some trap."

The group looked down the hall at the door. Rose shuddered. "This is getting spooky!"

"Maybe the dark shaman already killed whatever monster is there," Michael said with a grin. "Or disabled the trap."

Madison shook her head. "I don't think so. When the shaman showed up, it said something about not letting me kill the commander because it wasn't done with him. I have a feeling whatever it is, the shaman couldn't get past it."

"That's not good," Cole said, but then looked around at the others. "But then again, it was one gnoll, or fey, or whatever it was. There are four of us, so we will hopefully be able to handle it."

"Hopefully. If not, we'll all die... and then respawn," Michael said. He shot Madison a look. "NAKED! We can go streaking through Fisherton!"

"Let's just go find out whatever is beyond that door." Madison took a deep breath and shook her head. "We can worry about streaking the townspeople later."

Michael stuck his tongue out. "Party pooper!"

"Madison is right," Cole said. "We're wasting time. Let's go!"

Cole marched down the hallway, his feet kicking up dust and leaving new tracks on the floor. Madison went after him and Michael and Rose fell in behind them.

The group stopped in front of the door. Cole was once again in front of the door, while everyone else pressed themselves along the side of the hallway.

"Ready?" Cole asked, bracing himself with his sword ready.

"Ready!"

"Ready!"

"Buddy is ready!" Michael said with a grin, and the tiger cub made a sound that sounded like something between a growl and a chirp.

Cole slapped the panel to open the door, and, after a pause, the door slid open. At the same time, a sound behind them alerted them that the door they'd come through closed with a thud. That seemed foreboding.

"Ack!" Cole said, covering his nose and mouth with a hand.

Madison's forked tongue flicked out and she instantly

knew what he meant. The foul, putrid stench of decay wafted to them from the new room.

But the smell wasn't the only thing revealed by the opening door. Standing on the opposite side of the doorway was a tall, broad man dressed from head to toe in rusted full plate armor. In the man's hand was some sort of weapon that Madison didn't recognize. It was a spiked iron ball on a long chain, connected to a thick metal rod.

Madison glanced behind the giant man to the room beyond to see if there were anyone else. She grimaced as she saw the bodies of six gnolls lying on the floor inside. They were bloated and seemed to be the source of decay.

At least now they knew why the gnolls hadn't ventured past this door. The armored man had killed a half dozen gnolls. And apparently, the man was even formidable enough to hold off the shaman/raven-hag.

If he had killed gnolls and held off a raven-hag. Maybe they could team up with him. Madison held up her hands. "We're enemies of the gnolls too! Maybe we can work together."

Before the words were even out of her mouth, the man made a buzzing sound from somewhere in his armor. It was the same buzzing noise they'd heard earlier. Then, without warning, visible electricity washed over the entire suit of armor, across the metal shaft of his weapon, down the chain and across the spiked iron ball.

Her brother jumped back. "What the heck was that?!"

Before anyone could venture an answer, the armored man started to take a step into the hall. As he did, he lifted his weapon.

"Shut the door! Shut the door!" Cole yelled.

Rose reached for the plate next to the door to close it but the man twisted his head to stare at her and she froze. She started to move again a moment later, but by then, it was too late. The man was already in the doorway.

The armored figure brought his weapon up and then lashed out at Rose. Luckily, she had already been scrambling away and the spiked ball hit the wall instead of her. Where the ball hit the stone wall, sparks erupted.

It appeared the man didn't want to join forces. It looked like he wanted a fight. So be it.

"Get him!" Madison yelled.

35

"Come on, tin man! Fight me!" Cole yelled his taunt, but the man did not turn. He stared after Rose, who continued to backpedal.

The armored man brought back his weapon for another strike at Rose but Cole stepped between them.

At the same time, responding to her command, her animated guardian glided forward. It slashed at the man just as Michael and Buddy reached him and did the same.

Animated Guardian slams Armored Sentinel for 0 damage.
Armored Sentinel absorbs 5 damage.
Animated Guardian slashes Armored Sentinel for 3 damage.
Armored Sentinel absorbs 5 damage.
Zachatolus Catfriend kicks Armored Sentinel for 1 damage.
Armored Sentinel absorbs 5 damage.

Zachatolus Catfriend crushes Armored Sentinel for 2 damage.
Armored Sentinel absorbs 5 damage.
Buddy bites Armored Sentinel for 2 damage.
Armored Sentinel absorbs 5 damage.
Buddy claws Armored Sentinel for 0 damage.
Armored Sentinel absorbs 5 damage.

"Oh man!" Michael yelled. "He's got some sort of damage resistance! I'm barely making a dent!"

Brothar Snowbear slashes Armored Sentinel for 5 damage.
Armored Sentinel absorbs 5 damage.
Brothar Snowbear bashes Armored Sentinel for 2 damage.
Armored Sentinel absorbs 5 damage.
Brothar Snowbear slams Armored Sentinel for 1 damage.
Armored Sentinel absorbs 5 damage.

"Man! You ain't kidding!" Cole growled. "This is going to take forever!"

The armored man, now focused on Cole, brought his weapon back and lashed out with the spiked ball, catching her brother in the chest. As the weapon hit him, the buzzing sound returned and electricity ran up and down the man's armor, down the chain and into Cole.

Armored Sentinel crushes Brothar Snowbear for 5 damage.

Armored Sentinel pierces Brothar Snowbear for 4 damage.
Brothar Snowbear takes 11 points of lightning damage.

Cole shuddered for a moment, almost dropping his sword, before the electricity disappeared from the man.

"OWW!" he cried out. "That really hurt. For a moment, all my muscles seized up!"

"Like a stun gun," Michael said. "You know, the ones that are supposed to incapacitate an attacker."

"Yeah," her brother growled. "If that was the real me, that would have done it."

Rose, now several paces behind Cole, quickly cast a heal on him.

Plays-With-Animals heals Brothar Snowbear for 9 damage.

Madison, unsure what else to do, slammed her staff down on the sentinel.

You crush Armored Sentinel for 3 damage.
Armored Sentinel absorbs 5 damage.

"I don't know you'll be able to keep up with the damage," Cole said. "And the way this guy absorbs damage, it will take a long time to take him down."

"I can't cast any faster, sorry," Rose cried.

Animated Guardian slashes Armored Sentinel for 2 damage.

Armored Sentinel absorbs 5 damage.
Zachatolus Catfriend crushes Armored Sentinel for 3 damage.
Armored Sentinel absorbs 5 damage.
Buddy bites Armored Sentinel for 1 damage.
Armored Sentinel absorbs 5 damage.
Brothar Snowbear slashes Armored Sentinel for 6 damage.
Armored Sentinel absorbs 5 damage.

The armored man brought his weapon down again, this time catching Cole in the shoulder. Luckily, there was no electric shock this time.

Armored Sentinel crushes Brothar Snowbear for 3 damage.
Armored Sentinel pierces Brothar Snowbear for 4 damage.

Her brother let out a sigh of relief. "Okay, that wasn't so bad. Maybe we can heal through this. Keep attacking everyone!"

They did, but this time, as they struck, the lightning danced across the sentinel's body.

Animated Guardian slashes Armored Sentinel for 2 damage.
Armored Sentinel absorbs 5 damage.
Animated Guardian takes 7 points of lightning damage.
Zachatolus Catfriend crushes Armored Sentinel for 2 damage.

Armored Sentinel absorbs 5 damage.
Zachatolus Catfriend takes 6 points of lightning damage.
Buddy bites Armored Sentinel for 2 damage.
Armored Sentinel absorbs 5 damage.
Buddy takes 5 points of lightning damage.
Brothar Snowbear slashes Armored Sentinel for 8 damage.
Armored Sentinel absorbs 5 damage.
Brothar Snowbear takes 7 points of lightning damage.
You crush Armored Sentinel for 3 damage.
Armored Sentinel absorbs 5 damage.

"Yikes!" Michael cried out, withdrawing his weapons and shaking himself. "That really stings!"

"Told you so!" Cole grimaced.

Plays-With-Animals heals Brothar Snowbear for 10 damage.

Madison bit her lip. "It didn't affect me. I didn't get shocked."

"Seriously?" Her brother shot a glance over at her. "Not at all?!"

She shook her head. "Maybe because I'm part blue dragon."

"Or because you're using a wooden weapon," Rose suggested. "Wood isn't conductive, right? You know, like rubber."

Madison shrugged. "I have no idea."

"Give me your quarterstaff!" Michael said, holding his

hand out. "We'll test it."

Rose handed her cousin the staff and Michael twirled it once before starting his attack.

They all attacked again, but this time, the electricity didn't happen when they struck. Instead, it went off just before its attack on Cole. Luckily, it was gone before the sentinel's attack actually landed.

The next attack was the same but on the third attack, the electricity went off just as they attacked again.

Animated Guardian slams Armored Sentinel for 1 damage.
Armored Sentinel absorbs 5 damage.
Animated Guardian takes 6 points of lightning damage.
Animated Guardian slashes Armored Sentinel for 3 damage.
Armored Sentinel absorbs 5 damage.
Animated Guardian takes 6 points of lightning damage.
Zachatolus Catfriend kicks Armored Sentinel for 2 damage.
Armored Sentinel absorbs 5 damage.
Zachatolus Catfriend takes 7 points of lightning damage.
Zachatolus Catfriend crushes Armored Sentinel for 4 damage.
Armored Sentinel absorbs 5 damage.
Buddy bites Armored Sentinel for 2 damage.
Armored Sentinel absorbs 5 damage.
Buddy takes 7 points of lightning damage.
Buddy claws Armored Sentinel for 0 damage.
Armored Sentinel absorbs 5 damage.

Buddy takes 6 points of lightning damage.
Brothar Snowbear slashes Armored Sentinel for 6 damage.
Armored Sentinel absorbs 5 damage.
Brothar Snowbear takes 5 points of lightning damage.
Brothar Snowbear bashes Armored Sentinel for 1 damage.
Armored Sentinel absorbs 5 damage.
Brothar Snowbear takes 6 points of lightning damage.
Brothar Snowbear slams Armored Sentinel for 1 damage.
Armored Sentinel absorbs 5 damage.
Brothar Snowbear takes 5 points of lightning damage.

"Argh! That was stupid!" her brother gasped as he stopped spasming. "No more multi-attack. Geez!"

"Hey!" Michael said with a grin. "My leg got shocked from the kick, but I didn't feel anything from the staff. Rose's right. It's non-conductive!"

"Everyone look through their inventory!" Cole yelled. "Find me a club or quarterstaff and a wooden shield! Quick!"

Plays-With-Animals heals Brothar Snowbear for 9 damage.

Everyone did as he said and between the three of them, they found a quarterstaff and a small wooden shield.

Sheathing his two-handed sword on his back, Cole equipped the wooden shield and the quarterstaff.

"I'm having Buddy back off," Michael told the group. "All of his attacks are absorbing the electricity. He's already down below 50% of his health and he's barely doing any damage."

"That's fine!" Cole yelled out.

Animated Guardian slashes Armored Sentinel for 2 damage.
Armored Sentinel absorbs 5 damage.
Zachatolus Catfriend crushes Armored Sentinel for 3 damage.
Armored Sentinel absorbs 5 damage.
Brothar Snowbear crushes Armored Sentinel for 6 damage.
Armored Sentinel absorbs 5 damage.
You crush Armored Sentinel for 5 damage.
Armored Sentinel absorbs 5 damage.

The sentinel lashed out and his body was washed in electricity. This time, however, Cole was able to catch it on his wooden shield.

Armored Sentinel crushes Brothar Snowbear for 3 damage.
Armored Sentinel pierces Brothar Snowbear for 3 damage.
Wood shield absorbs 1 crushing damage.
Wood shield absorbs 1 piercing damage.

"It worked!" Cole yelled. "Rose! You're a genius!"

Rose beamed and cast her healing spell.

Plays-With-Animals heals Brothar Snowbear for 11 damage.

"So now we just keep hammering him?" Madison asked.

"Oh yeah!" Cole grinned with a nod.

The group did just that. They continued to hammer at the armored man for what seemed like an hour but was probably only a few minutes. Her Animated Guardian had dissipated, its attacks hitting the electrified man's armored body too many times. Now, it was just the four of them hammering on the man. Until his arm fell off.

"We knocked his arm off!" Rose cried out.

"Yeah, but it's just a flesh wound!" Michael snickered with a big grin.

Looking down at the arm, Madison saw that there was no blood. In fact, there wasn't even an arm. The armor was empty. She looked at the man's body, at the shoulder where the arm had fallen from. There was nothing inside the armor. It was empty. This was no man. It was an animation, like her Animated Guardian.

"It's not a man!" she yelled to the group. "It's an animation!"

"Geez! No wonder it's so hard to take down," Michael growled. Then he grinned. "It's terminator armor! I will dub it... the T-001!"

"Wait!" Madison said, bringing up her spells in her HUD. "I think... I think I might have something that will work!"

Scrolling through her spells, she found the one she

was searching for. As the others attacked it, she cast her spell, targeting the animation.

You cast Siphon Energy on Armored Sentinel.
Armored Sentinel takes 21 damage.
You recover 11 Mana.

The sentinel shuddered for a moment but then continued its attack.

"It worked!" Madison exclaimed.

"What did you do?!" Michael asked.

"The siphon spell I told you about! It doesn't just work on my animation! It looks like it works on any animation!" she replied.

"Sweet!" Cole cried. "Now keep doing it!"

Madison did. And with the spell returning more Mana than the spell cost, she kept casting it over and over until the creature suddenly shuddered and collapsed onto the floor in a pile of armor.

You have killed Armored Sentinel.
You have gained experience!
Congratulations! You were the first group on the server to kill an Armored Sentinel. A Reward has been added to your account.
You may check your rewards by going to Character Menu-> Profile -> Rewards -> Early Access Awards

They all let out a sigh and looked down at the remains of the guardian.

"Dibs on the armor!" Cole said with a grin.

36

While Cole stripped the armor from the construct, the rest of them looked around the room the creature had come from.

The room the construct had been inhabiting was a 15x15-foot chamber with hallways leading off each of the three other walls. The hallway to the left was completely collapsed about ten feet in, but the other two were intact.

The design of the room was similar to the other rooms they'd seen. Unlike the other gnoll rooms, this one was littered with a half dozen gnoll corpses and decayed bones from victims much older.

Madison thought it was interesting that when they killed a monster, like a gnoll, and looted it, the body disappeared. When another NPC killed an NPC, they stayed. Or this was window dressing from the developers.

Just in case, they searched the bodies but found no lootable items. Yet, despite having no items, the bodies remained.

"These are gnolls," Rose said, pointing at the dead dog men. "But what are these others?"

"No way to know," Madison answered. "The remains are too decayed. The skulls definitely look humanoid though."

"So, they all came in here and this thing killed them," Michael noted. "I get it. That the thing is some sort of guardian. The question is - what was it guarding?" A huge grin broke out on his face. "Treasure?"

"What treasure?" Cole asked from behind them. Madison looked back and saw that her brother was now clad head to foot in the sentinel's plate armor. He held his arms out and slowly turned around. "How do I look?"

"You look good," Madison said with a small nod of her head. "It fits well."

It actually did fit well, almost perfectly. Madison assumed that had to do less with her brother and the sentinel being the same size and more with game mechanics.

"You look like a knight!" Rose said.

"Not too shabby," Michael told him and gave Cole a fist bump. "Look at you rockin' the plate mail! Does it have much better stats?"

Cole's smile faltered. He sighed. "Not that much better."

Her brother read off the stats to parts of the new armor:

Ancient Sentinel Plate Cuirass
Type: Metal
Location: Chest

Skill: Heavy Armor
Size: Medium
Armor: 5
Quality: Poor

Ancient Sentinel Plate Chausses
Type: Metal
Location: Legs
Skill: Heavy Armor
Size: Medium
Armor: 5
Quality: Poor

"It's better than the rawhide stuff we've been getting!" Michael pointed out.

"True," Cole said. "But whatever was causing the electricity is gone. There's not even any electrical resistance on it."

"What about that weapon it was using?" Madison asked.

"The flail?" Cole asked. He shook his head. "It's useless. It basically fell apart on his death. Only the armor remained."

"It's still decent loot," Michael said.

"Now what?" Rose asked. She squinted down each passage. "It looks like we have two choices. Straight ahead or to the right. The one straight ahead ends in a 'T' intersection after 20 feet or so, the right one turns to the left after 20 feet."

Cole shrugged. "Doesn't matter to me."

Madison looked down both passages. Her eyes weren't

as good as Rose's elven eyes, but she could see to the end of passages too. One thing she did notice was that both passages had a thick layer of dust.

"No one's been this way for a long time," she said, pointing to the undisturbed dust. "No footprints."

"Ohh!" Rose said, eyes lighting up. "That means we might find things no one else has found! We could make more money!"

"You go, little mercenary!" Michael teased.

"I told you..." she started but Michael rolled his eyes.

"We know... we know..." he muttered. "You have to make money if you want your parents to keep letting you play."

"Exactly!" Rose said.

"Fine! Fine!" Michael said, gesturing to the two hallways. "Which one seems like it would have more money?"

"I don't know," Rose said and stuck her tongue out at Michael.

"Let's just go to the right," Madison said. "It turns in the same direction as the other hallway. They might meet up."

With Cole leading, the group started down the right passageway. The passage turned to the left and then immediately back to the same direction. Buddy began sniffing at the wall but disturbed the dust and began sneezing.

They continued following the hallway until it dead-ended in a T. The left passage opened up into a room after 10 feet while the other one turned right and disappeared around a corner about twenty feet further.

"Let's go right again," Madison called out from behind.

Shrugging, Cole turned right and followed the hallway as it turned the corner and ended in a door.

"Another door!" her brother turned and whispered. "Line up behind me and if there's another automation, we rush in. All of us will keep its attention while Madison uses her spell on it."

Madison and the others nodded their understanding and readied their weapons. Cole held up his hand and began counting down from three on his fingers.

3...2..1! Her brother slapped his hand on the activation panel.

Nothing happened. The door didn't open. Unfazed, Cole slapped the panel again. Still, nothing happened. He tried several more times, but the door didn't open.

"I guess this room's not meant to be explored," he said and motioned them to turn around. "We go back to the intersection and go across into the big room."

The group squeezed by each other and readjusted their line and retraced their steps back to the intersection and then past it to a large open room with no doors.

The room was a square room of about twenty by twenty feet. There was a door on the left wall but no other exits from the room. But the door wasn't the only thing in the room. Along the walls, on stone pedestals, were statues.

In the middle of the room was what appeared to be a circular fountain. The fountain was carved with ornate designs and might have been beautiful at one time. Now, with faded carvings and water that had long since dried up and stopped working, it looked desolate.

Madison looked around the room at the eight statues.

There were four men and four women. All of them were tall, attractive and somewhat stern-looking. They also had long, tapered ears like an elf, though they were not quite elven.

She remembered back to her conversation with Araman. The sage had said, the Artoshians had been the pure elves before the corruption. Before they devolved and split into the current elven races. "I think they're Artoshians."

"They don't look very happy," Rose noticed.

"Maybe they were teachers," Michael said and then chuckled at his own joke. "That's what my teachers look like just before they yell at me."

"I wonder..." Madison said aloud, walking over to one of the statues. She ducked down and began brushing at the dust that covered the base of the statue.

"What are you doing?" Cole asked.

"Looking for..." Madison replied and then let out a little cry of triumph as she uncovered words. "This!"

The others gathered around as she brushed.

Michael chuckled and then gave them his best old Scottish voice. "You call that archeology?"

Madison figured it was some line from one of the older movies he and Cole binge watched on the streaming service, but she couldn't think of which one. Instead, she continued brushing at the plaque until she could read it.

"Is that the same language?" Cole asked.

She nodded, reading the name and the words underneath it. "Quarion Charmaerith, General of the Northern Guard."

"Maybe it's a military museum?" Michael asked aloud.

Moving on to the next statue, she brushed away the caked-on dust and read it to the others. "Lorea Aedihle, Master Summoner of the Order."

She continued around the room, reading off the other names and stations. They were all either magic-users, generals, or one she found was a high priestess.

"Who do you think they were?" Rose asked.

"Beyond the titles I read off, I have no idea. I don't know what ties them to this room or to this place," she said. "Let's check out the door and maybe we'll find answers further in."

They started towards the door, but Michael stopped and looked around. "Has anyone seen Buddy?"

Even as he said it, Madison spotted the tiger cub in the corner, sniffing and scratching. "There he is!"

Madison cocked her head. "What is he doing over there? He doesn't like... you know... have to go?"

"No," Michael replied with a chuckle. "Luckily, the game doesn't do bodily functions for us or the pets. He's probably smelling a mouse or something."

"Come here, Buddy!" Michael called and the tiger cub poked his head up and looked at Michael. It looked back at the wall and then at Michael. Buddy did this twice more before bounding over to her cousin.

"Alright, people!" Cole said, pointing to the door. "Time to see what's behind door number one!"

37

The door opened anti-climatically into a short hallway that ended in another door. About halfway to the door, the hallway intersected another hallway to the right.

Cole looked back at the group and shrugged. He walked into the passage and stopped at the intersection. Madison noticed that as he walked, he tracked footprints in the dusty floor. But this time, there were no other footprints. They were the first ones to see this area in some time.

The group crept up next to him, leaving their own footprints, and they all looked down the hallway. The right corridor was long and disappeared into the dark after about forty feet.

Madison looked at Rose. "Can you see past forty feet?"

Rose squinted and then gave a small nod. "It looks like it opens into a room after fifty feet or so, but I can't see anything in the room."

Michael pointed to the door. "Let's check out the door first then. It's closer."

Cole moved forward to the door and stopped, waiting for everyone to get ready. When the group gave him the sign, he slammed his hand on the panel. After a moment, the door slid open, revealing a square room with shelves containing glass balls.

Madison couldn't be sure, but she thought she saw a swirling glow inside the glass balls. It was faint, but definitely present. But what was it? Why were there so many? And what did they do?

Unfortunately, that wasn't all it contained. While there were shelves on the right and left walls, in between the shelves were platforms. On those platforms, were armor. Even as they watched, the armored heads turned towards them stiffly, squeaking with disuse.

Electricity surged up from the platform, coursing around their metal bodies as they began to slowly move their limbs. They started to step off their platforms and Cole slapped the panel and the door slid shut.

"Back up!" he hissed. He slipped his sword back over his shoulder and pulled out one of the staffs from his inventory, as well as the wooden shield.

"Do you think they can open doors?" Rose asked, wide-eyed. She had produced a wooden cudgel from her inventory and brandished it awkwardly at the door.

Michael grinned. "We're about to find out. I give it 3 to 1 in favor of them opening the door!"

Madison rolled her eyes at her cousin but he just grinned more broadly. "What? I'm good for it!"

They waited tensely for several minutes before Cole

lowered his guard. He looked at Michael. "Looks like you would have lost that bet. It appears they can't open doors."

Michael shrugged but kept his grin. "Too bad no one took me up on it!"

Madison bit her lip. "But that means there are others. The one we encountered wasn't the only one here."

Her brother nodded. "I assume they're some sort of animated or automated security."

Rose made a face and looked around. "Security for what?! There's nothing in this place to protect!"

"Maybe not now," Cole agreed. "But there must have been at one time. These are constructs. Magical creatures. They withstood the test of time, even though whoever built this didn't."

"You're right," Madison confirmed. "The Artoshians built this. At least, I assume they did since that's the language on everything we've found. But they're all dead now - or evolved now." She scrunched her face. "Or maybe... devolved."

"But they left their friends behind for us to find," Michael snickered. "How thoughtful of them."

"I wonder if this is what the sage meant about traps," Madison wondered aloud. "Perhaps it's defending the place against non-Artoshians."

"Could be," her brother said. "That's three of those automatons so far. Chances are, there are more."

Michael came over and put an arm around Madison's shoulders. "Yeah, but we have our secret weapon now!"

"It worked with one of them." Cole nodded. "But that was two of them. That means we have to tank them while she drains them. And that's assuming they have the same powers the other one had and that her spell will work on the next one we fight."

"Yes, Debbie Downer!" Michael said with a roll of his eyes. He gestured around them. "This IS a VRMMORPG! Killing things is what we do!"

"And making money!" Rose reminded them.

"Why don't we explore more first, then we can come back and kill those two armored guys later," Madison suggested.

She actually was thinking about the glass balls she'd seen. She wanted to get a better look at them and find out what they were. Were they some sort of energy device? Maybe they were a weapon? Like an exploding crystal or something?

"Alright," Cole said. He looked back at the door to the room they'd just seen. "It doesn't look like they can open doors, so hopefully they won't come at us from behind."

"They can't open doors?! Didn't they say that about velociraptors in that dinosaur movie? And look what happened to them!" Michael asked, bringing his hands up to his chest like dinosaur arms and making biting motions with his mouth. "Nom! Nom! Nom!"

Madison shook her head at her cousin. "Then, we'll be careful."

"I'm pretty sure they were careful too," Michael retorted, giving her a knowing look. "And they still ended up as lunch."

"Fine," Cole said with a grin of his own. "You'll bring up the rear. Then you'll see them coming."

"Wait! What?!" Michael protested. He pouted. "Fine. More experience for Buddy and me. Right, Buddy?"

The tiger cub crouched down and gave a loud meow.

"Okay, it's me, then Rose, then Madison," her brother announced. "Michael, you and Buddy bring up the rear. We're moving down the hallway. Come on."

The group moved slowly down the hallway; Cole's vision limited by the light of the torch he carried. They crept along as quietly as possible, keeping an eye both in front and in back of them.

As they moved, Madison noticed that theirs were the only footsteps in the dust. No one else had walked the hall for a very, very long time.

When they had passed the halfway mark, Madison heard a noise and turned to see Buddy scratching at the wall to their right. She cocked her head. "He's doing that again. How come?"

Michael shrugged. "No idea. I think he smells a bug or rat or something. Probably a hole or something he can smell it through."

Madison nodded and then turned and caught up with the others. She continued until Cole and Rose stopped and then she peered around her large, armored brother. Unfortunately, his character was large, and she couldn't quite see beyond. "What's in the room?"

Cole stepped to the side and lowered his torch into the room, illuminating another 15x15-foot room, nearly identical to the other room. There was even a door heading off in the same direction. But where that room appeared to be in good shape, this one had suffered damage.

The far part of the ceiling had collapsed, and dirt and stone filled half the room. Like the previous room, there were shelves here too, but whatever had caused the ceiling to collapse, had also knocked over the shelves.

It wasn't all bad though. Part of an armored leg peeked out of some of the rubble. The collapse must have flattened one of the automatons. Against the right wall, was another platform, but it was empty.

"I wonder if this is where our friend came from," Michael mused, pointing to the platform. "One's missing."

Madison shook her head. "No. There were no footprints in the hall - just ours."

"Does that mean the one we fought came from a different room?" Rose asked.

"Probably," Cole said, still looking around the room.

Madison caught sight of glass strewn around the floor. She frowned. Had that been more of those glass balls? If so, they must have shattered when the shelves fell over.

Scanning the room, she saw that the shelf near the door still had a couple of the glass balls intact. Pushing past her brother, she walked over to the shelf.

Sure enough, there were two glass balls, about the same size as a billiards ball, but made completely of glass. Inside the glass was a swirling blue-green smoke that was in a constant state of motion.

She cocked her head. "What do you think these are?"

Michael opened his mouth, but Rose cut him off with a raised finger and a glare. "If this is a joke about balls, I don't want to hear it."

"But...but..." Michael said, obviously anxious.

Rose shook her head. "Not a word or I tell your mom."

"That's low!" Michael said with a sigh. Then he grinned. "Like a kick in the..."

"I mean it!" Rose said, putting her hands on her hips.

Rolling her eyes at her cousins, Madison reached out towards one of the orbs.

"Madison! Be careful... it could be a..." Cole began.

Her fingers had touched the smooth, cool surface of the glass orb and the green-blue smoke flared. Suddenly, Madison was being sucked into the smoke, her body dissolving as green-blue mist pulled her down... down... down... into the orb.

38

Madison was on the balcony of a tall, ivory tower. Looking around, she could see that the tower was part of a gleaming, white marble castle. The castle was situated on a hill overlooking a sprawling city below. It was unlike anything she had seen before - in the game or in real life.

"Come!" a woman's voice said from behind her.

Spinning, Madison saw a tall woman, slender and beautiful. She had long, flowing platinum-blond hair that fell below the middle of her back. Peeking through the hair were long, tapered ears. Elf ears.

The woman was dressed in an elegant gown of sapphire blue, trimmed in gold. On the top of her head was a petite golden crown in the shape of braided flowers. Madison guessed she was some sort of royalty.

The woman's face was flawless. It was the sort of supermodel face you saw on the cover of the fashion magazines, after they'd been airbrushed. She was almost too beautiful. Madison frowned. Impossibly beautiful.

"Excuse me? Where am I?" Madison said, not sure how she'd gotten here. Had the orb been some sort of transportation device? Was she in a different part of the game world now? If so, how could she get back to her brother and cousins?

The woman didn't look at her but looked towards the entrance to the balcony where another elf knelt on one knee. This elf was a man and as beautiful as the female elf was, he was just as handsome.

The male elf's features looked like they were chiseled out of marble, flawless and perfect. Like the other elf, he seemed almost too perfect. But he wasn't ruggedly handsome like many of the TV and movie stars. He was a pretty boy. He had an almost feminine quality to his face and slim body.

Madison cleared her throat. "Um... hello."

The elven man stood up and took several steps onto the balcony. When he spoke, his voice was also more feminine. Higher pitched than most men, but still with a masculine quality. "Your highness, thank you for seeing me."

Now fully in the light, she could see that the man was dressed in a glittering, silver chainmail that looked more like a light sweater than metal links. Over the armor, he wore a snow-white tabard trimmed in blue and bearing the crest of a unicorn and griffon.

"Report, General," the woman said, her voice as clear and beautiful as her face.

Looking around, Madison spotted two more elves just

past the general, at the entrance to the balcony. They stared back into the hallway without moving.

"Can either of you tell me how I got here?" Madison asked, speaking more loudly this time. Neither elf acknowledged her presence. She frowned.

"I regret to inform you, the Fey have taken Asve Ancalen, your highness," the general said, his face impassive and eyes cast down. His voice turned grim. "I have failed you."

The queen, or whatever she was, reacted only slightly to the news. For a moment, there was the slightest wrinkle in her forehead but then it disappeared. She shook her head slightly. "No, general, you have not failed me. That we kept the city as long as we did is a testament to your planning and strategy."

"And yet, it has still fallen," the man replied, his lips turning down into a frown.

"The Fey are not like other foes we have encountered on our world," the queen pointed out. "They continue to win victory after victory against us and the Valharian."

The general's frown turned into a full-blown scowl at the mention of the Valharian. "If only they targeted just the Valharian."

A small smile played across the queen's face for a brief moment, before retreating. "Even if they did, how long would it be before they conquered the Valharian and then set their sights on us?"

The general chuckled to himself. "At least they'd go first."

"Be that as it may," the queen retorted. "I think it is clear we no longer have a choice."

Eyes widened, the general's mouth fell open. He shook his head slightly, as if not believing what he was hearing. "You cannot mean what I think you mean, your highness."

The queen gave the general a withering look. "I know you spoke up about my plan before and I respected your opinion. But it is clear to me - and should be clear to you - that we cannot prevail against the Fey alone. Neither of our empires. We must seem to forge an alliance."

"An alliance with the Valharian?!" the general spat. "They would stab us in the back at the first opportunity!"

"Perhaps, perhaps." The queen turned and walked to the edge of the balcony. She put her hands on the railing and looked out at the city below. She sighed. "General, if you have some secret weapon or special strategy that you have been saving, I will entertain it now."

The general walked over and stood next to her. He too looked out at the white marble city below. "If I did, you know I would not have let a single one of our cities fall."

Turning, the queen favored him with a sad smile. "I know you wouldn't have. But without some way of defeating them, and as much as it turns my stomach to do so, I fear we must ally ourselves with the Valharians before it is too late. Perhaps together, we can find a way that the two of us cannot find alone."

Madison, who had been listening to their exchange, thought she understood what she was seeing. This was obviously the Artoshians. And from the way they were talking, this was still during the Fey war, since they hadn't allied with the Valharians yet.

She jumped up and down and waved her arms in the air. "Hello! Can anyone see or hear me?!"

No one responded. Neither the queen, nor the general even glanced her way. Nor did the two guards. Madison nodded to herself.

She wasn't really here. This was some sort of memory or playback of something that had happened during the Fey world. Madison could see and hear it but couldn't interact with anyone in the memory. Strange, but also cool. Too bad Earth history lessons weren't like this.

"You are my most trusted general," the queen spoke again. She turned and took the general's hand in her own. "You are also my only son."

The general glanced at the two guards in the hallway, but the queen made a dismissive gesture. "We're far past favoritism or nepotism, at this point. We are fighting for the survival of our people - perhaps our very world."

Nodding, the man put his own hand over hers. "What would you have me do, your high.... Mother?"

His mother gave him a warm smile that reached her eyes. She let out a small sigh. "I need you to go to the Valharian with an offer of an alliance against our common foe, the Fey."

He stiffened but her son nodded. "If it is your will, then I will see that it is done."

"I know you will. But you must be quick," she told her son and released his hand. She looked back at the two guards and then lowered her voice. "You and I both know we cannot hold out much longer."

"We can..." the general began but stopped and nodded, his own voice lowering to match his mother's. "You are right. We cannot hold much longer. I will go make preparations and leave on tomorrow's tide."

The queen smiled again. "Go with the goddess' blessing, my son. And let's hope they see reason and accept."

"As you say, your highness," her son said, returning his voice to normal volume. He backed up a step and did a bow before spinning and striding purposefully back into the hallway.

Madison watched him go and then turned back to look at the queen. As she did, she once again felt like she was falling. She blinked and the next thing she knew, she was back in the room with her brother and cousins.

"... be a trap!" Cole said.

Congratulations! You were the first group on the server to use an Artoshian Memory Globe. A Reward has been added to your account.
You may check your rewards by going to Character Menu-> Profile -> Rewards -> Early Access Awards

"What?!" she said, reorienting herself to her original surroundings. She was back in the 15x15 room and was holding the glowing glass orb in her hand. She shook her head.

Cole frowned. "You okay?"

Madison remembered the images from the orb as if they had really happened to her. They'd taken five or ten minutes, but it seemed like no time at all had passed. "How long was I gone?"

Her brother gave her a confused look. "Gone where? You haven't gone anywhere."

Biting her lip, Madison held up the orb. She had been

right. She'd experienced the entire memory in an instant. She smiled. "It's hard to explain! Hold out your hand."

Cole started to pull both his hands away. He wrinkled his brow. "Why?"

Madison put her free hand on her hip. "Just do it. Trust me."

Her brother exchanged a look with Michael, who shrugged. Reluctantly, Cole stuck out his hand.

Reaching out, she set the orb in his hand and then watched as his eyes went momentarily glassy before blinking. He looked down at his hand. "Whoa!"

"You saw it too?!" she asked.

"A female elf and a male elf walking on a balcony in some weird language? Oh yeah!" her brother replied.

Madison cocked her head. "Weird language? You mean, you didn't understand it?"

"Uh, no," he replied. "It was just nonsense."

She realized they must have been speaking in Artoshian. She must not only be able to read it, she must also be able to understand the spoken version too. "Wow."

"Wow what?" Rose asked.

Madison reached out, took her cousin's hand and placed the glass orb in it. Rose's eyes went glassy for a second before she blinked and backed away. Rose looked around the room. "Ok, that was really weird. It was like actually being there."

"Right!" Cole agreed.

"Did you understand them?" Madison asked.

Rose shook her head. "Nothing. It was all gibberish."

"I could understand them," she told them. "The orb lets you see a memory from the Fey war. They must have been speaking in Artoshian - that's why I could understand it."

"How does that help us?" Michael asked. "Did you learn anything useful?"

Madison bit her lip and then looked around the room at the shelves and then remembered the statues and the other room with shelves. "I think... I think this place is some sort of library or museum."

39

"A library?" Rose echoed, wrinkling her forehead.

Madison nodded and held up the orb. "I think these are like books, or movies..."

"Or YurTube videos," Michael offered.

"Exactly," Madison agreed.

Her brother looked at the orb and then at the shelves, and finally back to Madison. "What's the library supposed to be about? Or is it just a general library, like the public libraries back home?"

"I'm not sure." Madison bit her lip. She had a suspicion, but she needed more orbs to prove her theory. "But I need more orbs to view to see if there's a theme."

Cole pointed at the remaining intact orb on the shelf. "There's one more in here."

Madison walked back to the shelf. Stopping in front of it, she stared at the orb for a second. She hesitated for only a moment before grabbing the orb in her hand.

Immediately, she felt drawn down into the orb and her surroundings faded away.

SHE WASN'T on a balcony overlooking a beautiful city this time. Instead, she was in a small room. A large wooden table, covered in maps, dominated the room. But around the table were beings that grabbed her attention.

The elf queen Madison had previously seen was at the head of the table, with her son on her right. Another elf, this one dressed in sapphire-blue robes that almost matched the queen's gown. His robes were as decorated with trim as the gown, but also had an insignia on them. She had no idea what the insignia meant, but she guessed he was some sort of advisor or wizard.

Those three were the only elves in the room. Madison knew that, technically, they were Artoshians, but she thought of them as elves. The other "people" in the room were definitely not Artoshians. They were a collection of the other races.

"The Fey continue to overrun our combined forces!" a human growled. He was tall and slender, with dark hair and dark goatee with the first streaks of grey. Like the man to the queen's left, this human was also dressed in robes, though they looked to be made of black silk with blood-red trim.

"Trolls not able to hold back," a large creature boomed. Madison guessed it was a troll, given its dark green, warty skin, its long drooping, wide ears and disproportionately large nose. It was dressed in what she thought was alligator hides, with the skull of a giant alligator fashioned into a helmet. There were smaller alligator skulls on the troll's shoulders, like pauldrons. Given the rather large chest of the creature, Madison thought it was a female, though she would never have guessed from the deep voice. In her left hand, the troll held a staff that looked like a larger version of the shaman's staff Madison now carried.

"Ogres not hold back either," grunted an even larger creature. Given that it had just mentioned ogres, Madison was inclined to believe this was an ogre. It stood another head taller than the troll and had long, thick arms like a gorilla. This one wore rough-looking, blackened plate armor, with a red handprint on the front breastplate. On its back was strapped a wicked-looking two-handed axe whose blade glowed with a pale, sickly green light. "Too many."

"The problemssss," hissed a black-scaled Drakkar, "is the numberssss. They have them... wessss do not."

The Drakkar was slightly larger than Madison and more muscular. It wore no armor, nor did it carry any weapons. In fact, its clothes looked like something a Shaolin monk might wear and around its waist was wrapped a flowing black sash made of silk.

"That would seem to be the dilemma," a short female figure standing on a stool said. The woman couldn't be more than three and a half feet tall, with a child-like face but slightly oversized head, hands and feet. "Their portal to the dark realm allows them to continuously draw in additional military resources, which, as far as we can tell, seem to be unlimited."

"Or at least," said the black-robed wizard, "far more vast than our own military resources."

"We need a way to close the blasted portal!" shouted what could only be a dwarf. Shorter and broader than a human, this dwarf had long, red hair and a longer, matching red beard that was braided in two very neat braids that went to the dwarf's waist. He was dressed in plate mail armor, with a shield and axe strapped to his back and two more, smaller axes, hanging from his belt.

There was a chorus of grunts and then chaos as the different races tried to speak over each other. It was so loud Madison wanted to put her hands over her ears. Finally, a loud rapping of metal on wood caused the arguing to die down.

All of the creatures looked to the queen's son, who was rapping the pommel of his dagger on the table. When everyone had quieted down, he looked to his mother.

The queen smiled and nodded to the group. "Closing the portal is precisely the reason I called this meeting."

Everyone in the room became completely silent as all eyes stared at the queen.

"The archmage," the queen began, looking at the man to her left. She was suddenly interrupted by the man in black robes.

"YOUR archmage, not THE archmage," the man snarled.

The queen's brow wrinkled for only a moment before she gave the man in black robes a placating smile and a small nod. She continued in the same tone, as if she hadn't been interrupted. "Our archmage has come up with an idea to seal the portal."

Pandemonium erupted again as the various races shouted questions or growled in disbelief. Finally, a man who hadn't spoken yet, raised his hand and the others instantly quieted.

This last man was also a human but had an air of authority about him. He had short salt and pepper hair and a neatly trimmed matching beard. He wore some sort of military uniform, similar in style to the queen's son, the general.

The man exuded confidence and charisma, like a CEO of a top 10 company. He had been looking down at the maps, but he raised his head as he lowered his hand and looked at the queen. "Please, continue."

The queen gave the man a slight nod. "Thank you, Emperor. I think it would be better to let the… our… archmage explain it."

The archmage nodded and looked around the table.

Suddenly, Madison felt herself sucked out of the vision and back into her own awareness. She cried out, wanting to hear what the archmage was about to explain. "Noooo!!!"

Madison blinked. She was back in her own body, holding the second glass orb.

"No what?" Michael asked, looking around in confusion.

"Argh!" Madison growled. "I think this one was about the alliance of the Artoshians and the Valharians. The archmage was about to explain something about sealing the portal the Fey were using to enter the world."

"Huh?" Michael muttered, still looking confused. He

wasn't the only one. Her brother and Rose had blank expressions too.

Sighing, Madison launched into a brief summary of what the sage had told her about the Fey war and the Artoshian/Valharian alliance. She was certain she didn't do as good a job as Araman, but she at least told them the basics.

"So, do you think this is some sort of war museum? You know, like World War II, Korean War and Vietnam War museums in the real world?" Rose asked.

Madison shrugged. "I have no idea. Maybe. But then, why aren't there statues of the Valharians?"

Michael grinned and gestured around. "Maybe there are. Maybe we aren't in the Valharian section of the museum."

Cole rubbed his chin. "Or maybe this is the history according to the Artoshians. After all, according to the writing Madison has seen, this is an Artoshian ruin."

"True," Michael said, looking thoughtful. "Madison said they were enemies. They went back to being enemies after the Fey were dealt with, right?"

"I think so," Madison said, not quite remembering if the sage had mentioned it. Araman had mostly focused on the curse that had befallen the Artoshians after the war. She didn't remember him elaborating on the politics afterwards.

"Does any of this really matter?" Rose asked. "I mean, what's the point?"

Madison shrugged but Cole nodded. "This place seems pretty elaborate. I doubt some designer would have spent a ton of time and even made those recordings, or whatever they were, if this place didn't have some significance."

Michael frowned. "Unless some of this is AI generated. Didn't you say the world was generated with AI assistance to give it a similar level of detail as the real world. This could just be AI icing on the cake."

"You're right!" Her brother frowned. "I forgot about that. Well, there goes normal game theory right out the window."

"Game theory?" Rose asked.

"Normally, the more elaborate something is, the more time the developers spent on it, and therefore the more important it is," Cole explained.

"Right!" Michael said with a nod. "Like, if you see a plain sword, chances are it's just a plain sword. But if you see a sword with runes etched on the blade and a fancy crossguard and gem-encrusted pommel, chances are, it's important."

"So... what you're saying is," Rose shot back. "We have no idea whether any of this is important or not. It could be a red herring."

"Yup! Like communism," Michael said and gave her a big grin and nodded. "It might be a red herring!"

"No one ever expects the Spanish Inquisition!" Cole chimed in.

Cole chuckled but Rose and Madison wrinkled their foreheads. Madison rolled her eyes. "Probably some obscure movie, book or comic reference."

"Oh," Rose said. "What do we do now?"

"We keep exploring," Madison said, giving her brother and Michael a challenging stare.

"I don't see that we really have any choice," Cole said. "I mean, we're already here and we have no other quests."

"We go forward?" Rose asked.

Cole opened his mouth, but Madison talked over him. "No! We have to go back to the room with the guardian things."

Michael grumbled. "Why? I don't want to get shocked more."

"Because," Madison retorted. "There were more of these memory globe things in that room!"

40

They returned to the room with the shelves of glass orbs. Madison's brother moved forward to the door and stopped, waiting for everyone to get ready. "You know the drill, people! Wooden weapons for these bad boys."

"Do you think they're the same place we left them? Or do you think they returned to their platforms?" Michael asked, twirling his two quarterstaffs.

"No idea," Cole replied. "But we'll find out in a second. Ready?"

Cole counted down with his fingers and then slammed his hand on the panel. After a moment, the door slid open, revealing a square room they'd seen before. It also revealed the two metal automatons.

Both were by the door and began trying to step out towards her group at the same time. Unfortunately for them, they couldn't both fit at the same time and bumped into each other with a loud clang.

"Attack the right one!" Cole yelled, slamming his staff down on the creature.

Brothar Snowbear crushes Armored Sentinel for 6 damage.
Armored Sentinel absorbs 5 damage.
Zachatolus Catfriend crushes Armored Sentinel for 2 damage.
Armored Sentinel absorbs 5 damage.

As before, their weapons didn't do much to the creature since it was mostly just animated armor. Luckily, Madison was their ace in the hole. She cast her spell.

You cast Siphon Energy on Armored Sentinel.
Armored Sentinel takes 21 damage.
You recover 11 Mana.

Madison grinned. Just like before, her spell seemed to suck whatever magic animated the creature right out of it. But neither animated suit of armor was out of the fight yet.

Unlike the sentinel they'd encountered, which had carried what Michael had pointed out as a flail, neither creature carried a weapon. Instead, they both slammed their fists against her brother.

Armored Sentinel slams Brothar Snowbear for 3 damage.
Wood shield absorbs 1 crushing damage.

Armored Sentinel slams Brothar Snowbear for 4 damage.
Wood shield absorbs 1 crushing damage.
Armored Sentinel slams Brothar Snowbear for 4 damage.
Wood shield absorbs 1 crushing damage.
Armored Sentinel slams Brothar Snowbear for 4 damage.
Wood shield absorbs 1 crushing damage.

"Ow!" her brother said, the blows sending chips of wood flying from his shield. "Darn! I forgot to look at the shield's durability!"

"You'd better hope it holds up!" Michael called out.

Plays-With-Animals heals Brothar Snowbear for 11 damage.
Brothar Snowbear crushes Armored Sentinel for 5 damage.
Armored Sentinel absorbs 5 damage.
Zachatolus Catfriend crushes Armored Sentinel for 2 damage.
Armored Sentinel absorbs 5 damage.
You cast Siphon Energy on Armored Sentinel.
Armored Sentinel takes 20 damage.
You recover 11 Mana.

"At least Madison's spell is doing good damage!" Rose yelled. "More than both of you combined!"

"Keep casting it!" Cole said.

Taking her brother's advice, Madison continued to

cast her spell. Because the spell restored her Mana at the same time it did damage, she didn't have to worry about running out. Instead, she focused on how much damage she was doing.

Each spell did an average of 20 damage to the sentinel. After the sixth casting the first one fell apart into a pile. The second one took seven castings before it fell apart. It was just in time too, since Rose had almost been out of her Mana herself.

"Good thing you have that spell," Cole said, wiping sweat from his brow. "Otherwise, I don't think we'd be able to take one of them."

"Oh, we could," Michael contradicted him with a grin. "Just... not with you alive."

Cole glared. "Gee. Thanks."

Michael grinned even more broadly. "Think nothing of it."

"We killed the monsters," Rose said. "Now what?"

"Now, I look at the memory orbs," Madison replied, gesturing into the room.

Rose frowned as she spied the shelves. "That's a lot of orbs."

"Anything else in the room?" Michael asked, pushing past the two girls with Buddy trailing behind him. He stopped just inside the room. After looking around, he shrugged. "Just shelves with orbs."

"Well, you'd better let me at them," Madison said. And they did.

Once inside the room, Madison counted eight shelves. Each shelf had three orbs total, for a total of 24 orbs. That was a lot of orbs. Luckily, the viewing was nearly instantaneous. She sighed. Time to get started.

Fifteen minutes later, she'd gone through all 24 orbs while the group waited on her. As she put the last one down on the small pedestal that had held it, she blinked and shook her head. She'd seen more visions of the queen, her son and a dozen other elves in different conversations.

Madison massaged the sides of her head. She felt the beginning of a headache. It was probably from absorbing so much information so quickly. Given how fast she was already experiencing the game, it was hard to conceive just how fast she'd been viewing those memory orbs.

Unfortunately, despite a lot of interesting conversations between the elves, she really hadn't learned much new information. It was mostly just memories of the queen receiving different reports about attacks from an unknown enemy. Towards the end of the orbs, the elves had figured out the creatures attacking called themselves the Fey.

As interesting as the episodes were, they hadn't provided Madison with the answers she wanted. Namely, how were the Fey finally defeated. The sage hadn't known exactly how the Artoshians and Valharians had defeated the Fey, only that they formed an alliance and had done it.

She was no closer to knowing how they'd done it than she had been before they'd entered the room. Plus, she was getting a headache now.

"Wow," she muttered as she continued massaging her head. "That was like binge watching a show in fast forward."

"You okay?" Cole asked, genuine concern in his voice.

"I'm okay." She smiled weakly.

"You learn anything?" Rose asked.

"A lot," Madison said, rubbing her head. "Unfortunately, this was from earlier in the war with the Fey."

"Why is that unfortunate?" Michael asked.

"I was hoping to find out how they ended up defeating them," Madison answered.

Michael cocked his head. "Why?"

Madison shrugged. She actually wasn't sure why she wanted to know. Maybe because the sage hadn't known, and she hated a mystery. Hated not knowing. "I don't know, I just want to know. Don't you?"

"Wasn't that like a million years ago?" Michael asked.

"True," Cole said, scratching his head. "But we just saw a fey and weren't they supposed to all be dead?"

"Mostly," Madison agreed. "Though I got the impression from the sage that maybe they're immortal."

"Immortal?" Rose said, eyes widening. "Like... they can't be killed."

"Probably just means they don't age," Cole said. "If they couldn't die, they would have taken over back during that war."

"I guess that's true," Rose said.

"Plus, we did kill that other one," Michael pointed out.

Rose bit her lip. "Okay, fine. They can be killed."

Madison looked around the room. It was very similar to the other room they'd been in, only all of its memory orbs were intact. If this really was a library or museum, then there were probably other rooms full of orbs. Hopefully, one of them contained later memories.

"We need to keep exploring this place," she told the group. "There has to be more orbs."

"Fine," Cole said. He gestured to the door opposite the one they'd entered through. "I have a feeling this door opens into the hall we saw earlier."

Walking over to the door, he hit the panel and the door slid open. Sure, enough, there was a small hallway and the hallway to the left that led back the way they'd come. Her brother nodded. "That means this might be the center of the complex. If that's the case, the room on the opposite side of the hallway might be an orb room too."

Michael snickered. "Is that what we're calling them now? The orb rooms? Wouldn't.... BALL... ROOM make more sense."

"The Ball room?" Cole chuckled. "I like it."

"Ballroom? Seriously?" Rose rolled her eyes. "I think I'm going to disown both of you."

"Off to the ballroom!" Cole announced.

"To the ballroom!" Michael agreed, pointing towards the door across the hallway.

Rose looked to Madison for support, but she just shrugged.

"Actually, it was kind of clever," Madison admitted. She winked at Rose. "For boys."

"Maybe," Rose admitted begrudgingly. "We really have to call them ballrooms?"

"To the ballroom... to the ballroom..." chanted the boys as they marched across the hallway.

Madison sighed. "For the moment, I think we're stuck with it."

"Fine," Rose growled. "But we name the next room!"

"I think that's fair," Madison agreed. She looked down the hall at the two boys waiting at the door to the next... ballroom. "Come on, the guys will only get in trouble without us."

"So true," Rose said with a smile and the two of them hurriedly caught up with the boys.

41

There was only a single sentinel in the next "ballroom." Unfortunately, this was because the room had been mostly destroyed by a cave in. That included all of the memory orbs.

"Argh!" Madison growled in frustration as she finished digging through the rubble. "They're all destroyed!"

"Sorry, sis." Cole frowned. "I think there was a door out, but we'll never get to it, let alone get it open."

Rose cocked her head and looked from the rubble back to the way they had come. "I think... I think if we back track, we might reach the other room from the opposite direction."

Michael looked back the way they'd come. "You mean that hallway to the left we never took."

"I think so," Rose said. "I have a mental image of what this place looks like in my head."

The boys shared a glance. Michael whistled. "You're mapping the place in your mind?"

Rose smiled. "Yeah, aren't you?"

Madison exchanged looks with the two boys. She had a general idea of the room layout, but mapping places out wasn't really her thing.

"Uh, kinda," her brother said.

Michael furrowed his brow. "You're really mapping it in your head? How? Aren't you going to go to school to be a vet?"

"So?" Rose shot back. "What does that mean?"

"Well," Michael replied with a grin. "Not sure how much mapping you'll be doing with animals."

Rose shrugged. "My dad's really good with his hands. Very mechanically inclined. I guess I got it from him."

Michael slapped her on the back with a big smile. "Cool! Lead the way then."

"Uh, no," Rose replied. "I'll tell you where to go, you go first."

"Fine, fine," Michael replied. "Let's go see if you're right!"

The group left the room the way they had come, then went back to the first room and took the left hallway. Like the right hallway, it turned fifteen feet in, turned again and continued the same direction until it ended in a stone door.

"Let's see what's behind door number one," Cole said, looking back at the group to make sure everyone was ready.

Slapping his hand down on the plate, Cole got ready to rush in as soon as the door opened. Only the door didn't open right away. There was a grating sound and it started to open, then it stuttered and then opened a bit more. Then, spiders began pouring out of the room.

"Ah!" Michael yelled. "Spiders!"

Large spiders poured through the opening door and into the corridor their party occupied. The creatures were larger than any real-life spider. With their legs, the spiders were the size of dinner plates. They were also a bright-green color, with orange spots on their backs.

The spiders didn't pause but went right for Cole, who backpedaled into the rest of the group. "That's not sentinels!"

"Kill them! Kill them all!" Michael yelled and he and Buddy rushed forward. As he did, Madison saw his weapons shift to the metal clubs she'd gotten him. Cole's weapons changed too, his shield and staff disappearing, replaced by his two-handed sword.

Brothar Snowbear slams Forest Spider for 11 damage.
You have killed Forest Spider.
You have gained experience!
Congratulations! You were the first group on the server to kill a Forest Spider. A Reward has been added to your account.
You may check your rewards by going to Character Menu-> Profile -> Rewards -> Early Access Awards
Brothar Snowbear bashes Forest Spider for 12 damage.
You have killed Forest Spider.
You have gained experience!
Brothar Snowbear slashes Forest Spider for 19 damage.
You have killed Forest Spider.
You have gained experience!

Zachatolus Catfriend crushes Forest Spider for 7 damage.
You have killed Forest Spider.
You have gained experience!
Zachatolus Catfriend kicks Forest Spider for 6 damage.
You have killed Forest Spider.
You have gained experience!
Buddy claws Forest Spider for 6 damage.
You have killed Forest Spider.
You have gained experience!
Buddy bites Forest Spider for 8 damage.
You have killed Forest Spider.
You have gained experience!

Knowing the spell she used on the sentinels wouldn't affect the spiders, Madison slammed her staff down on a spider that was coming at her.

Buddy bites Forest Spider for 8 damage.
You have killed Forest Spider.
You have gained experience!

The spider died with a satisfying splat, leaving green ichor all over the passageway floor. The spiders all seemed to die with only a single hit, which was good. Unfortunately, more continued to scramble through the open door.

Running directly at her and her party, as soon as the spider reached someone, they crawled up their leg and bit them.

Forest Spider bites Brothar Snowbear for 0 damage.
Ancient Sentinel Plate Greaves absorb 5 damage.
Forest Spider bites Brothar Snowbear for 0 damage.
Ancient Sentinel Plate Greaves absorb 5 damage.
Forest Spider bites Brothar Snowbear for 0 damage.
Ancient Sentinel Plate Greaves absorb 5 damage.

The spiders who climbed up her brother, didn't seem to be able to pierce the metal armor that now encased him. Unfortunately, the same couldn't be said for the rest of them.

Forest Spider bites Buddy for 3 damage.
Buddy is Poisoned.
Forest Spider bites Buddy for 2 damage.
Buddy is Poisoned.
Forest Spider bites Buddy for 3 damage.
Buddy is Poisoned.
Forest Spider bites Zachatolus Catfriend for 3 damage.
Zachatolus Catfriend is Poisoned.
Forest Spider bites Zachatolus Catfriend for 2 damage.
Zachatolus Catfriend is Poisoned.
Forest Spider bites Zachatolus Catfriend for 2 damage.
Zachatolus Catfriend is Poisoned.
Forest Spider bites Zachatolus Catfriend for 3 damage.
Zachatolus Catfriend is Poisoned.
Forest Spider bites Plays-With-Animals for 3 damage.
Plays-With-Animals is Poisoned.
Forest Spider bites Plays-With-Animals for 3 damage.
Plays-With-Animals is Poisoned.

Rose screamed and backed away as the spiders came for her, but two managed to climb up her legs and attack. Unfortunately, three managed to get onto Madison as well and she felt the sharp pains in her legs as the spiders bit into her.

Forest Spider bites you for 3 damage.
You are Poisoned.
Forest Spider bites you but misses.
Forest Spider bites you for 3 damage.
You are Poisoned.

Immediately after the bites, Madison began to feel a lethargy in her legs, making it difficult for her to move back, out of range. She began to panic. It must be the spider poison. Was it paralyzing her legs?

"I'm poisoned!" she cried out.

"We all are!" Michael growled. "I can barely move my legs!"

Madison mentally went through her list of spells but there were too many spiders for Daydream and the spell she used on the animations wouldn't work against living creatures. Then she got an idea!

"Eyes closed now!" she yelled and cast Color Blast.

A flash of multicolored light erupted from Madison. Even through closed eyes, the bright lights left afterimages on her retinas. But the messages she received made her smile.

You critically stun Forest Spider.
You critically stun Forest Spider.

You critically stun Forest Spider.
You critically stun Forest Spider.
You critically stun Forest Spider.
You critically stun Forest Spider.
You critically stun Forest Spider.
You critically stun Forest Spider.
You critically stun Forest Spider.
You critically stun Forest Spider.
You critically stun Forest Spider.
You critically stun Forest Spider.
You critically stun Forest Spider.
You critically stun Forest Spider.
You critically stun Forest Spider.

She looked down as the spiders which had been clinging to her fell to the ground, limbs twitching. The eyes! Spiders had eight eyes so they must have been really affected.

"Nice job!" Cole yelled. "Kill them while they're stunned!"

Cole, Michael, Buddy and Madison began stomping, bashing and otherwise squashing the spiders while Rose cast cure poison spells on all of them.

Luckily, the stunned spiders climbing out of the door had blocked any other spiders from entering the hallway until they finished killing the ones lying on the ground. Once the ones in the doorway were cleared, more began coming through.

Once again, the spiders swarmed the group until Madison cast her stun spell, then the spiders fell twitching to the ground and they quickly killed them. Then they repeated the same thing with the next wave.

This went on for several minutes before no more spiders came out of the room. Even then, they waited for several more minutes before Cole finally walked over to the door and, with a show of strength, finished pushing the door all the way open.

With the door completely open, the group was able to see into the large room beyond. It was completely covered in long, thick webbing. It was a spider nest. A spider nest they needed to go into.

Madison swallowed hard.

42

Everyone just stood around for a long minute, staring into the web-filled room. Even in the dim light of the torches, they could all see that things still moved among the webs. More spiders.

Finally, Rose spoke up. "Am I the only one who doesn't want to go in there?"

"It's just spiders," Michael said with a grin. "I thought you wanted to be a vet?"

"I do," Rose shot back. "But I'm not going to be treating spiders!"

Michael's grin grew even wider. "What about a pet tarantula?!"

"Uh, they can find another vet!" Rose retorted and crossed her arms over her chest.

Madison looked away from her two cousins and peered into the room. She shuddered involuntarily as she thought of that movie about aliens who had taken over part of a planet and had captured all of the colonists and laid eggs inside them. Space marines had gone in to save them, only to get mostly slaughtered themselves. "This is like the part in the horror movie where you call the characters on the screen idiots for going into the monster's lair."

Michael made a stabbing motion with his hand. He hummed the music to one of the psycho thriller movies.

Cole chuckled halfheartedly at Michael and then followed Madison's stare into the mess of spider webs and shrugged. "It is like walking into the dragon's lair... but it's still just a game."

"It's not just a game, it's an adventure," Michael said cockily. He was bent down, scratching Buddy's neck. The cat was purring, but his eyes didn't leave the doorway and his ears twitched constantly. "I say we nuke it from orbit. Probably the only way we'll be sure we get all the spiders."

Cole snickered, obviously getting some reference her cousin was making. He looked back at the others. "Actually, that's not such a bad idea."

Michael cocked his head and wrinkled his brow. "Really?"

"I don't suppose we have any fire spells we could use to burn the webs - and maybe the spiders too?" her brother asked.

"I don't have any fire spells." Madison, who had actually been thinking the same thing, shook her head. The idea of burning the web first really appealed to her. Unfortunately, they lacked any magical means of creating fire.

Rose shook her head and pointed to the torch in Cole's

hand and then to the other torch being carried by Michael. "What's wrong with the torches we have?"

"We can use them," her brother replied, looking at his torch. "But if we throw them and they go out, then Michael and I can't see. Besides, it would be nice to have something we can... you know... shoot into the spooky-looking spider lair."

"Ha!" Rose snorted. "Then you think it's spooky too!"

"I'm not going to lie," he replied, looking back inside the web-covered room. "I don't like the idea of walking into a place where things can jump out at you from any direction - including above you."

Madison liked the idea of setting the place on fire. The nice thing about the glass orbs was that they would be fireproof - theoretically, at least. She thought back to the gnoll areas they'd passed. "What about the torches from the areas the gnolls were living in?"

Her brother arched an eyebrow. "Go back, grab them, light them up and throw them inside?"

"Why not?" she replied with a shrug. "Maybe they have some lamp oil or something we can use too."

"Molotov cocktails!" Michael said evilly, rubbing his hands together. "Mawahahaha!"

"Actually," Cole said, rubbing his chin. "That might not be a bad idea."

"Don't tell me they taught you how to make Molotov cocktails in chemical engineering class," Rose said, hands on hips. "Please don't tell me that's what our tax dollars are going for..."

"It's not high school..." Cole protested but Rose rolled her eyes.

"You guys are going to state college," she pointed out. "It's paid for by the state."

"Focus," Madison said, waving her hands in the air to get everyone's attention. "Focus on the problem at hand before more spiders decide to eat out. Cole, you and I will go search the gnoll area. Michael and Rose, you stay here."

"Why do I have to..." Michael protested but Madison didn't let him finish.

"Because Cole is studying to be a chemical engineer, so he might know what will be flammable. You're on a soccer scholarship. You haven't even picked a major," Madison responded.

Michael put his hand over his heart and pretended to be wounded. "Human relations is a major!"

"Human relations?" Rose said snarkily. "You mean... dating?"

"Ouch! Et tu, Brute?" Michael smirked, casting a glance at their cousin. "Fine! Fine! I'll stay here with little Miss Muffet!"

Frowning at her cousins, Madison furrowed her brow. "Just behave and keep an eye out!"

Giving them one last look, Madison motioned for her brother to follow her. She quickly led them back to the main corridor, then back to the treasure vault and finally into the main gnoll area. As they went along, they searched the various chambers.

They did find a few torches, but the real haul came when they visited the room the gnolls used as a brewery. Her brother moved past her into the room and began to knock on various kegs and then examined the shelves and then the still itself.

"This might work!" he said excitedly.

"I hope you're not thinking about drinking it!' Madison objected. Hadn't they learned their lesson about drinking in-game alcohol earlier in the day?

"Blackmange stout? No, I don't think so!" Her brother chuckled and then dripped a bit more of the alcohol into his hand. He stood up and walked over to her, holding out his hand. "Smell!"

Narrowing her eyes suspiciously at her brother, she nonetheless took a whiff of the liquid. She wrinkled her nose at the bitter, antiseptic-like smell to it. "Smells like rubbing alcohol!"

"It's definitely high-proof spirits."

"What can we do with it?" Madison asked, looking at the still. "Make a bomb?"

"Not exactly," he said. "High-proof alcohol does burn, but it probably won't stay lit long. We need something to mix it with to make it spread and stick to things. Some sort of oil would work best."

"What about the mess hall? Maybe they have some cooking fat," she replied.

"A lard bomb," Cole joked.

"As long as it works, who cares," she told him.

Madison and Cole went between the mess hall and the brewery several times until they finally had enough materials to create their makeshift Molotov cocktails. They gathered several hollow gourds, some rags and some of the cooking fat - which did resemble lard.

After collecting all of the "ingredients," the two of

them made their way back to the mess hall to assemble them.

"I'm going to need you to start a fire, heat up some of the lard and then we'll mix it with the alcohol," Cole told her.

"Just dump it all into the kettle?" she asked.

"No!" Cole said loudly. "We don't want to heat up the alcohol. One, that could cause the actual alcohol to evaporate. Second, it might become volatile enough to blow up in our face."

"Okay already," she retorted.

Working together, they heated up the fat until it was a liquid, then poured in carefully into the gourds. Then, they combined it with the alcohol, carefully mixed it and added the rags that they soaked in the mixture. In the end, they had a half dozen of the makeshift Molotov cocktails.

"And what? We just light them and throw them?" Madison asked her brother.

"Basically," he replied with a nod.

"And they're not going to blow up in our hands?" Madison asked, eyeing the gourds.

"I hope not," her brother replied with a shrug. "I have no idea whether or not normal physics and chemistry will work in the game world. Hopefully they won't blow up in our hands - but I can't guarantee anything."

"Oh, great!" Madison growled. "Way to inspire confidence."

Cole shrugged. "You wanted bombs, I made you bombs!"

"The question is...will they work?" Madison wondered aloud.

"There's only one way to know for sure," Cole said with a grin. "We have to try them!"

"Okay," Madison replied. She walked over and stopped in front of the gourds. "Let's take them back and fry up some spiders."

They each carefully grabbed some of the gourds and then quickly made their way back to their waiting cousins.

43

Eyes wide with excitement, Michael made a "give me motion" with his hands after Cole explained what the gourds were. "Come to papa!"

Cole, Madison and Rose all exchanged looks before simultaneously replying. "No!"

Michael feigned a look of hurt. "Why not?!"

"Because you'll probably use it to blow something up!" Rose responded.

"Me?!" he replied with an evil grin. "Would I blow something up with a homemade Molotov cocktail?!"

Once again, the three others exchanged looks before again simultaneously replying. "Yes!"

"You're probably right." Michael chuckled to himself and then shrugged. "But that's the whole point? Right?"

"I'll handle them for now," Cole told Michael, turning towards the door that led to the spider room.

"No more spiders came through?" Madison asked, looking past her brother into the room. With her enhanced eyes, she could still see spiders moving among the webs inside the room. But why weren't they attacking?

"Not since you left," Rose replied.

"I wonder why they aren't attacking?" Madison wondered aloud.

"No idea." Rose shrugged. Then, she looked at everyone looking at her and made a face. "I WANT to be a vet. I haven't even graduated high school yet, so obviously I haven't taken any vet courses, let alone a course called Psychology of Spiders 101!"

"Sorry." Madison smiled at her cousin. "I mean, you love animals, and you work at the shelter on weekends..."

"CAT SHELTER," Rose said slowly. "CAT SHELTER! No spiders allowed!"

"Yeah... yeah... she doesn't know anything about spiders," Michael smirked. He grinned evilly and rubbed his hands together. "Let's throw some bombs!"

Cole looked at Madison questioningly.

"Why not?" Madison replied.

After all, what was their other option? Go in first? That seemed as stupid now as it did before. Not only would they be walking into the spider's lair, they'd also be surrounded by webbing if they decided to use the fire-bombs Cole had made. She was certain that meant they'd take damage too.

And depending how deep they were into the spider's lair, the more damage they might take. For all she knew, they'd create an inferno around themselves. Burning alive seemed a terrible way to die - even if they would respawn.

"Let me! Let me!" Michael begged.

Cole looked at Madison, who frowned. Knowing their

cousin, if they didn't let him use one, he'd either sulk or keep bugging them. Best to get it over with now. She shrugged. "Go ahead. Give him one."

Madison gave Michael a stern look. "Be careful!"

"You know me!" Michael replied cockily. He handed his torch to Rose and then held out his hands eagerly.

"We do know you," Rose said, taking a step away from him with the torch.

"That's why I said it," Madison agreed, giving Rose a nod.

Michael rolled his eyes. "I'll be careful.... Mostly..."

Cole held out one of the gourds to Michael.

Taking the offered gourd, Michael walked over to the doorway. He peered into the room. He looked first one way, then the other. He cocked his head one way, then the other. Next, he held out his opposite hand, thumb out, like he was sighting a camera.

"Just throw it already!" Rose cried.

Michael turned his head and grinned. He nodded. "Okay, light me up!"

Madison took a deep breath and then nodded to Rose, who was holding the torch. She took a step forward and began to lower the torch.

"BOOM!" Michael yelled, startling everyone.

Madison nearly had a heart attack until she realized he had been joking. She took a deep breath to stop herself from punching Michael in the face - or electrocuting him with her breath weapon. Or both!

"You little...." Rose started but bit her tongue. Neither of her parents allowed her to curse and she was probably afraid they'd somehow find out she'd done it in game.

"Nice one!" Cole laughed.

"The next time I see you, I'm going to smack you across the head, Michael!" Madison growled.

Michael was laughing at all of them. "You should have seen your faces!"

"Okay! Okay!" Rose snarled. She suddenly thrust the torch at the gourd's wick and the thing immediately caught fire.

Looking down at the now-lit Molotov cocktail, it was Michael's turn to be surprised. "You lit it! Oh shoot!"

Turning, he did an overhand throw of the gourd into the room. A moment later, there was the sound of something shattering, along with a whooshing sound. Then a high-pitched squealing started.

Madison flinched as the high-pitched squealing continued, sounding like fingernails against a chalkboard. She looked around and saw that everyone was cringing.

At Michael's feet, Buddy let out a pitiful wail. The cat looked from side to side, as if seeking someplace to run off to.

"Is that the spiders?" Rose asked, hands over her ears. "It's horrible!"

Messages had begun scrolling in her HUD and Madison took a moment to look at them.

You have killed Forest Spider.
You have gained experience!
You have killed Forest Spider.
You have gained experience!
You have killed Forest Spider.
You have gained experience!

You have killed Forest Spider.
You have gained experience!

"It looks like it's working," Madison told her group. "The spiders are dying and we're getting experience."

Cole opened his mouth to talk but then made a face. Madison was about to ask what it was but then the smell reached her. And smell wasn't the right word. It was a stench. A rotting, burning, putrid odor smell that made all of them gag.

"Ugh!" Michael said, wrinkling his nose. "That's foul!"

Madison was about to reply but the thick, inky smoke coming from the room made her cough. As she struggled to catch her breath, she noticed the others were having the same reaction.

"We need to... get back... to the vault," Cole told them between coughs.

Still coughing and eyes starting to burn from the acrid smoke, the group retraced their steps back to the vault. When they reached it, they gulped in deep breaths of clean air.

"Hopefully, the smoke will go up and not go past this room," Cole said.

"Smoke rises, right?" Madison asked, blinking her stinging eyes.

"In the real world... it does," Cole said.

Michael opened his mouth to say something, then coughed. He tried again but broke into another coughing fit. Finally, he seemed to master his breathing. "That... wasn't... me. I just threw it... against... some webs."

"That must just be the way... they burn," Madison agreed.

"I say... it's his fault..." Rose coughed while smiling.

"Obviously, it was a good thing we threw the first one into the room and didn't try to use it from inside the room," Cole said. "You two weren't looking, but it went up quick!"

Rose shivered. "I just remember that squealing sound. It was horrible! I'm pretty sure spiders don't squeal in real life."

"And you said you weren't a vet yet," Michael teased. He shivered. "But you're right, that sound gave me the chills."

A flash in her HUD gave Madison a start and she brought it up to read a very welcome message. Even as she read it, more spider death messages scrolled by.

You have killed Forest Spider.
You have gained experience!
Congratulations! You have gained a level!
You are now level 5.
You have gained a new Ability Slot.
You have killed Forest Spider.
You have gained experience!
You have killed Forest Spider.
You have gained experience!

Madison grinned as she read the new message.

"What is it?" Rose asked, looking at Madison.

"I just got level 5!" Madison smiled.

"No fair!" Michael protested.

"You all are about 1000 experience behind me," she told them. "So, it shouldn't be long."

Cole's eyes went glassy for a moment and he nodded. "The spider deaths seem to still be coming, so maybe we'll get our level soon."

"I got an Ability Slot!" she told them.

"An ability slot?" Rose repeated excitedly. Then, she frowned and wrinkled her forehead. "What's that for?"

"I'm pretty sure those are what we use to choose special abilities," Madison replied. "Like we did during character creation. I think that's how I got that lightning attack."

"Oh, cool!" Rose replied.

"Lucky you," Michael said. "What are you going to choose?"

Madison shrugged. She honestly hadn't given any thought to it, since she hadn't realized she would get the opportunity to choose another ability. "I don't know."

"More lightning would be nice! Or breathing fire!" Michael grinned wickedly. He looked thoughtful. "I wish I could breathe fire! Yeah! That's what I want!"

"No!" the rest of the group said at the same time.

"What?!" Michael retorted, the grin never leaving his face.

44

While they waited for the smoke to clear, Madison brought up her HUD and looked at her character sheet. She navigated through the screens until she found the spot to spend her newly earned Ability Slot.

Similar to character creation, she received a categorized list of items. She quickly scanned through the categories, hoping something popped out at her.

Background
Combat
Magic
Profession
Racial
Skills

She looked through the Background category first. Unfortunately, most of them were grayed out with a small note next to it.

Only available at character creation.

Madison sighed. So much for those items. She wished she would have paid more attention at character creation. If she had known certain abilities were only available once, she might have chosen differently.

Even though the game seemed to mostly revolve around fighting, she moved past the Combat category. It might be helpful, but she just wasn't feeling it right now. She didn't even open it up.

Magic was intriguing. She was an enchantress after all. She expanded the category and started reading through the available options. Sadly, there were only a few of them but those few were intriguing.

Illusionary Form I
Create a realistic illusion of a targeted bipedal creature of roughly the same size. You appear as an exact copy of that creature. This may fool others of its kind but will not fool the targeted creature, who will become instantly hostile at seeing its doppelganger.
Note: Does not convey any special abilities, language or breathing mechanism of the form.

Invisibility I
Create a constantly shifting illusion of the background to render you invisible. The invisibility lasts for as long as you have Mana.

Note: Does not hide you from any other senses. Some creatures can pierce the veil of invisibility.

Minor Enchantment I
Infuse a touched, non-magical object with Mana to create a known spell effect from yourself or a person/creature/item you are touching. Enchantment persists for 1 hour for every 10 points of Mana used, up to a maximum of 24 hours.

MADISON HAD to read all three options several times. She could think of many uses for each one.

Illusionary form could have helped them with the gnolls, but also might have helped her in the town. Of course, there were drawbacks too. She had to emulate a specific person or creature. There could be unforeseen consequences if someone who knew that person or creature met her while she was impersonating them.

Invisibility seemed extremely useful as well, though its biggest weakness was that it only seemed to hide her visually. She would still make sounds and give off a scent. While possibly useful around humans and other humanoids, she wasn't sure it would work so well against monsters who could smell her.

Then there was minor enchantment. The ability to put an enchantment on items seemed extremely useful but she immediately realized the downside would be time. Each enchantment would require minutes of rest to restore her Mana. She could spend an hour or more just enchanting a few items for the day. If she tried enchanting an entire suit of armor for each of them - that was many hours.

It was a tough decision, and she hadn't even looked at the other categories yet. Reluctantly, she opened the next category: Profession.

This opened a list of various professions that seemed to give skill bonuses and other specific abilities. Most were grayed out. After looking more closely, she seemed to lack the prerequisite skills needed for them. But there were a few that were available.

Archaeologist
You have made your life's work the exploration of ancient cultures, their history and their impact on the world. Through your devotion, you have gained a better understanding of the historical impact of those cultures.
Prerequisites: History, Archeology
Bonuses: +5 History, +5 Archeology, choose 2 ancient languages, special ability: Decipher

Decipher
Through years of study of ancient languages and history, you are able to decipher a percentage of any unknown language (based on level of your history and archeology skills).
Note: This only applies to magical languages if you can cast arcane spells.

Artificer

You have devoted your life to the study and understanding of ancient magical artifacts. Through study and experimentation, you have mastered a deep understanding of the process of their creation and use.
Prerequisites: History, Runes, Archeology, Enchanter
Bonuses: Special ability: Discern Use

Discern Use
You are able to understand ancient technologies and how they work. Because of this, you automatically identify one power of a magical object and how to activate it. Once identified, and as long as the object's ability is able to be activated, it can be used as if the artificer had access to that spell.

Treasure Seeker
You have made it your life's work to discover and recover ancient items of cultural and intrinsic value. It is up to you what you do with the items once you recover them.
Prerequisites: History, Archeology, Appraise
Bonuses: +5 Special Ability: Trap Sense, Special ability: Sense Treasure

Trap Sense
When in a ruin, burial site or other ancient site, you have an unnatural ability to sense hidden danger and traps. In all other ways, this works like the Rogue's Trap Sense ability.

Sense Treasure

When in a ruin, burial site or other ancient site, you have a knack for finding hidden treasure caches. This ability works even through physical and magical barriers, though does not provide a way through those barriers.

Madison perked up at the professions. They all sounded very interesting, especially considering the ruin they were currently in. The Treasure Seeker's abilities seemed like they might be able to help them find treasure that might otherwise be hidden - possibly winning some real-life money.

On the other hand, the Archeologist profession might allow her to decipher languages no one could read, which might also win them real money for being the first one to read them.

And then there was Artificer. That profession seemed to align very closely with her Enchanter abilities. It also had the bonus of allowing her to figure out how to make ancient magical items work.

In fact, if she could take both the Minor Enchantment and the Artificer profession, it sounded like she could actually enchant their own items to do the same thing as any magic items they found. That seemed incredibly useful. Though once again, she ran into the Mana issue. Too bad she could only choose one.

She looked through the Racial and Skill categories but only one thing stood out to her.

Draconic Ancestry II
Your draconic ancestry continues to manifest itself.

Your scales thicken, providing damage reduction while your breath weapon ability becomes usable twice a day.

Draconic Ancestry II sounded very nice. Her lightning breath was powerful and being able to use it twice a day would be extremely helpful. Not only that but having scales that reduced her damage would really help her stay alive longer. It would be like wearing armor.

She groaned. Too many decisions. And without knowing if and when she might get additional Ability Slots, it made this choice even more important.

After debating for several minutes, Madison finally made the decision to go with Draconic Ancestry II. The Minor Enchantment and Artificer would be nice, but she would only get the biggest benefit if she took both. Since she had no idea whether she could take one now and the other later, it seemed a safer bet to go with Draconic Ancestry. At least it gave tangible benefits in the short term.

Madison shut down her HUD so she could run her choice by her brother but when she looked around, she saw everyone else's eyes were vacant as well. They must have made level 5 and were busy making their own choices. So be it.

Bringing up her choice menu again, she reviewed the three choices again before selecting Draconic Ancestry II. As soon as she did, she received a new message.

You have selected Draconic Ancestry II. Do you wish to purchase this ability with an Ability Slot or with a Karma Point?

Madison blinked and read the message a second time. Did it really mean what she thought it meant? She felt herself growing excited.

Did this mean she could take both Minor Enchantment and Artificer?! She quickly backed out of her choice. Biting her lip and hoping it meant what she thought it meant, she chose Minor Enchantment I. Once more she received a choice.

You have selected Minor Enchantment I. Do you wish to purchase this ability with an Ability Slot or with a Karma Point?

Holding her breath, Madison chose Karma Point.

You have gained a new ability: Minor Enchantment I.
Karma Points: 0
Ability Slots: 1

So far, so good. She quickly selected Artificer. This time, no choice appeared. Instead, she received a new message.

You have gained a new ability: Artificer.
Karma Points: 0
Ability Slots: 0

Madison let out a cry of joy. She'd gotten both! She could now identify enchantments and enchant objects! She couldn't wait to tell the others.

45

It took several minutes before everyone was done selecting their own abilities. Michael was first and it immediately became evident that he had chosen some sort of ability that enhanced Buddy, because the tiger was now fully grown.

In fact, the tiger looked even larger than a full-grown tiger, if Madison's memory served her. She'd only seen tigers up close in a zoo a few times, but Buddy looked a good head taller than a normal tiger. Then there was the fact that Michael was grinning ear to ear.

"What did you do?" Madison asked him, not even waiting for the others to finish.

Michael continued to smile as he scratched the extra-large tiger on the chin. Buddy rumbled a loud purr in response to the scratches. "I got two abilities - I assume we all did with that karma point - so I chose Enhanced Companion and Companion Steed!"

Madison blinked. "Wait! What? Companion Steed?"

"Oh yeah." Head bobbing up and down, Michael's Cheshire Cat grin grew even larger. "I can now ride Buddy!"

Madison cocked her head and smiled despite herself. Riding a tiger. That actually sounded really neat. "That's so cool, Michael!"

"Right!" Michael exclaimed, hugging the enormous cat to him. Her cousin looked around the cat as he hugged him. "I think I have to find a saddle though."

"Probably," she agreed.

"Oh wow," came Rose's voice from behind her. "Buddy's huge!"

Madison half expected a "that's what she said" joke from her cousin but Michael was too busy grinning and nodding.

Turning towards Rose, Madison raised an eyebrow. "What did you choose?"

Rose bit her lip and looked down. Madison furrowed her brow at her cousin. Why the sudden shyness? "Go on, tell us."

"I really wanted a pet like Michael," Rose said, still looking down. "But none of the abilities really had anything to do with pets..."

"And?" Madison prompted when her cousin trailed off.

"Yeah," Michael prodded. "Don't keep us in suspense. Just tell us what you chose!"

Rose still wasn't looking up. Instead, she seemed completely fascinated by her shoes. "I chose a special ability called Summon Swarm... and then another ability called Enhanced Swarm."

"Swarm?!" Michael shivered. "Like a swarm of ants? Or bees? Or spiders?!"

Her head still down, Rose raised her eyes to look up at them. Even with her head down, Madison saw a smile on her cousin's face. "I got to pick the animal swarm."

"Oh?" Madison asked, gesturing for Rose to go on.

Raising her head, Rose gave them both defiant looks before announcing her choice. "I chose Kitten Swarm!"

Madison just blinked at her cousin; sure she must have misunderstood. At the same time, Michael burst out laughing, dropping over and holding his stomach.

"Kitten.... Swarm..." he choked between laughing. "I love it.... I love it... beware... the kitten swarm!"

"Kitten swarm?" Madison repeated slowly. "You're serious?"

"Well," Rose retorted defensively. "I like cats! Especially kittens!"

"Kitten.... Swarm..." Michael continued to hold his stomach as he laughed, tears running down his cheeks.

"But... you're going to summon... a swarm of kittens... to attack an enemy?" Madison said slowly.

"Yes!" Rose snapped. "What's wrong with that? It's better than bees or spiders!"

"Swarm... of... cats..." Michael was starting to wheeze from laughing so hard and Buddy walked over and prodded at him with his nose.

"But... kittens... attacking an enemy?" Madison said again, still trying to wrap her head around exactly how that would work.

"Whatever!" Rose growled. "I wanted some cats!"

Madison held her palms up. "That's fine. That's fine. I

was just trying to figure out how that would work logistically. I mean... where do the cats come from?"

Rose shrugged. "It doesn't say. It just says the swarm will answer my call and come from all around to attack my designated enemy."

"Kitten... swarm..." Michael gasped, trying to suck in lungfuls of air. He was still smiling, despite tears coming from his eyes. "I... love... it."

"What does he love?" Cole asked. Her brother looked around. His eyes stopped on Buddy. "Nice! You made Buddy stronger!"

Still trying to suck in air, Michael could only nod as he wiped tears from his eyes.

"And what does Michael love so much it has him crying?" her brother asked, looking between Madison and Rose.

"My special ability," Rose said, putting her hands on her hips. "Kitten Swarm!"

Madison half expected her brother to break down laughing too but instead he just nodded. "A swarm? How much damage does it do?"

"It's based on my level and the number of cats I summon," Rose replied, relaxing her posture at Cole's serious question. "I think it's 1 point of damage per level per kitten and I summon 10 cats per level."

"Wow." Cole whistled. "At level 5, that's 50 cats, each doing 5 points. That's 250 damage. That's good damage for our level."

Rose beamed and then turned and stuck her tongue out at Michael. "See!"

Michael was finally standing but still struggled to

catch his breath and stop the tears. "Killed by kittens, I just want to see that on the log. Seriously. I can't wait."

Cole pointed to Michael. "Enhanced companion..."

"And companion steed!" Michael added.

Cole's eyes widened and he grinned. "Nice! We just need to get you a big sword and a castle called Grayskull!"

"Right!" Michael grinned. "I didn't even think of that!"

"And kitten swarm!" Her brother pointed to Rose.

She nodded.

Turning to Madison, Cole cocked an eyebrow. "And you?"

"You first," Madison shot back.

"I chose Armor Mastery," he replied. "Which raises the damage reduction of any armor I wear by 25% and an ability called My Sword is my Shield, which allows me to use my sword as a shield of the same material."

"Wow," Michael said, finally sounding normal. "That's some serious defense. I thought you might enhance that sword-throwing ability."

"I haven't really had much use for it so far," Cole replied, regret seeping into his voice. "Mostly I've just been tanking. So, I figured I'd max out that part of my character."

"We'll call you the man of steel," Michael teased.

"Hey, as long as it keeps us alive," Cole said. Her brother turned to her. "Okay, that's mine. What's yours?"

Madison took a deep breath. "I took an ability called Minor Enchantment I, which allows me to enchant items..."

She saw excited looks from everyone, but especially Cole and Michael. She held up her hand. "But only for a certain period of time... uh... 1 hour for every 10 points of mana I use, maximum of 24 hours."

The looks of excitement waned but were quickly replaced by thoughtful looks. No doubt, Michael and Cole were both running the numbers in their heads to min-max her skill. She sighed.

"The other ability is ... uh... actually a profession... Artificer," she continued.

Cole cocked his head. "Artificer?"

"As in, someone who makes artifacts?!" Michael said, eyes widening in excitement.

"What's an artifact?" Rose asked, obviously unfamiliar with the term. "You mean, like something from Egypt?"

"In games," Cole explained, "they're usually old and powerful magic items."

"Oh," Rose said and turned to Madison. "You can make them?!"

Madison sighed and shook her head. "No, it's more like an expert in them. Like, I can tell what they do and how to activate them."

"Oh," Rose said, excitement gone. "That doesn't seem very good."

"Actually," Cole contradicted her with a raised finger. "It might be VERY good. It's possible we won't know the powers of artifacts we find. We might not even recognize it as an artifact. Her ability might allow us to identify them - which might mean earning rewards for being the first person to do so."

Now Rose's eyes lit up. "Oh! That would be good!"

"I think..." Madison started and took a deep breath. "I think if I identify an enchantment from an artifact... I think I can use it to enchant an item to do the same thing..."

Rose frowned, brow wrinkling, but Cole and Michael both blinked.

"Are you serious?" Michael said, mouth open. "You can use an artifact as a template to enchant other items?!"

"Geez," Cole gasped. "Do you have any idea how powerful that could be?"

Michael shook his head. "There's got to be some sort of limit on that. There's no way they'd allow that."

Madison shrugged. "That's what it says."

"Michael's right," Cole said, shaking his head. "That could be totally OP. There must be some limiting factor."

Madison, feeling better about her choice, just shrugged again. "I guess we'll find out - once we find an artifact."

Cole smiled at the group. "The smoke's clear. Let's see if we can go find us one!"

46

Madison and the others soon discovered that although the smoke was mostly cleared away, the stench remained. It was a nauseating stench that she simply had no comparison for. It wasn't even close to anything she'd smelled before.

The further they went back towards the spider area, the worse it became. They began to gag at the smell. First Rose, then Michael, then Cole and finally even Madison was struggling. The only reason she held out so long was that she smelled with her forked tongue and it was easier to keep that in her mouth than it was for the others to not breathe through their noses.

They reached the spider room where they had started the fire. The group stopped and, at Rose's insistence, fashioned masks from one of the cloth garments Madison still had in her inventory. Their makeshift masks helped but didn't eliminate the odor completely.

"Remember this," Madison told Michael. "The next time you want to firebomb something."

Michael shrugged. "It's still better than fighting all those little buggers."

The room Michael had thrown his Molotov cocktails into was littered with smoking corpses of the large spiders they'd fought. Most of the damage had been done to that room, with the floors, ceiling and walls blackened.

But the singed remains of Madison guessed were tendrils of webs led out of that room and through a doorway at the far end of the room. Her enhanced eyes let her see more dead spider corpses through the open doorway.

Judging by the soot and burn marks along the floors and ceiling, the web strands had burned and the fire had gone from this room into the next room. "There's another room past the door."

Grunting and one hand covering his mouth overtop the mask, Cole raised his torch and looked to the far side of the room. "Man! This smell sucks!"

"I like the smell of burnt spider in the morning!" Michael said in a strange voice Madison didn't recognize and she guessed it was some movie or video game reference.

If her brother got the reference, he didn't indicate it. Instead, he walked over to the doorway. As he did, the crispy remains of spiders crunched under his feet, causing Madison to shiver. Holding up his torch, he peered in.

"I see burned shelves in there," Rose said, throwing a sideways glance at Madison.

Squinting, Madison saw them too. They were blackened and the shelves had all collapsed. Fearing the worst, she moved directly behind Cole and searched the floor with her eyes. Just as she had feared, she saw the broken glass fragments scattered across the room.

She bit back a curse as she looked around the room. All the shelves had either been shattered by the fire or had broken some time ago. Either way, none of the glass orbs had survived.

Her brother looked over at her. "Sorry, doesn't look like the memory orbs survived."

Madison didn't reply. She had been hoping to find another room full of the orbs so she could understand more of the story. Whatever history these orbs had contained was now lost forever.

"Come on," Cole said and, kicking some burned spider web husks out of the way, he moved into the next room.

Madison went in after him, followed by Rose and finally Michael and Buddy. They entered the next room, which seemed exactly the same as the previous room. It was a square 15x15 room, but instead of leading to another room, this one led into a hallway.

"If this mirrors the other side," Cole said. "Then the hallway out of this room will lead to a T intersection."

Carefully picking his way across the charred spider remains, her brother moved closer to the hallway out of the room. As he moved the light closer, Madison saw that he was right. After ten feet, the hallway dead ended in a T intersection. The scorch marks along the walls, floors and ceilings told her that webs had once covered the area.

Coughing behind his mask, Michael grumbled. "Man, this stuff stinks. I think I would rather have fought them."

"Remember that next time, before you go all pyromaniac," Rose shot back.

"Hey, I didn't..." Michael started to retort but Rose held up her hand at the same time that Buddy lowered his head to the floor with his ears back.

"Shh! I hear something," Rose said, holding up a hand.

Everyone stopped moving and didn't make a sound. They did move their heads though, looking into every corner of the room, back the way they came and then forward down the corridor in front of them. But there was nothing.

Rose moved her head one way, then the other.

Madison could hear her heart thudding in her chest. She didn't see or hear anything. She glanced at Rose. "What did you hear?"

"Shh!" Rose repeated, cocking her head to the right. She bit her lip and then cocked it to the left. "I thought... I thought I heard... skittering."

"Skittering?" Cole said. "Like what? More spiders?"

Rose shook her head. "No. I heard them earlier. This wasn't them. This was something louder. Ah... probably larger."

Michael, who had been looking down at Buddy, snapped his head towards Rose. "A larger spider?" He turned back to Buddy, whose ears were still back. "Is that what you hear, Buddy? Is that why you're afraid? Is it a big spider?"

Buddy didn't give any indication that he understood

Michael. From what she guessed, Michael and the cat shared some sort of bond, but not telepathy. They could maybe sense what each other was feeling, but not communicate on a human intelligence level.

"I don't think he understands you, Michael," Madison said.

"But Buddy is afraid of something," Cole said. "And given how big Buddy is now, that worries me."

Michael glanced at her brother and cocked her head. "What? Like some sort of boss?"

Cole shrugged. "Probably. I mean, it would follow normal MMORPG standards, right?"

Madison furrowed her brow. "What do you mean?"

"Hold on," Cole said, and his eyes went glassy.

"What's he doing?" Rose asked, her head still pivoting to look in front and in back of them.

Michael gave a knowing nod. "He's checking the logs."

"Why?" Rose asked.

"If there is a boss," he replied. "Then it will be in the logs. I don't remember seeing one."

"There wasn't," Madison said.

"Are you sure?" Michael asked.

"Yeah," she replied. "Otherwise, we would have gotten another reward, right? I mean, it would be another unique monster kill, so we'd get a prize."

Michael opened his mouth and then snapped it closed and smiled. "Right! Good call!"

Cole blinked. "I didn't see a..."

"We know." Michael chuckled. "Madison pointed out that we didn't get a new reward for killing a unique monster."

"Oh, right," Cole said. "I keep remembering that."

"Then... there's something ahead of us?" Rose asked. "Some sort of giant spider?"

"Not necessarily," Cole replied, looking down the passageway in front of them. "It could be anything."

"Like a giant cockroach," Michael suggested.

"That's... terrifying," Rose muttered with a shiver.

"We've beaten everything so far," Cole said softly. "If we stick together, we can beat another boss."

"Yeah," Michael whispered with a grin. "We have Madison, the secret spider-stunning weapon."

Madison said nothing. It was true that her stun spell seemed to work well against spiders. But would it work against a giant spider? And what if it wasn't a spider? What if it was something without eyes and her stun spell didn't work at all?

"How far is the noise?" Cole asked.

Rose shrugged. "I can't tell. Too many tunnels and stuff. I just heard it, but I also heard echoes of it. I tried, but I can't pinpoint a direction or how far it is."

"It could be just around the corner," Michael whispered with mock fright.

"Shut up, Michael!" Rose said, craning her neck as if that would allow her to see around corners.

"Both of you be quiet," Cole said. He moved his torch one way and then the other, illuminating the tunnel in front of them from multiple directions. Finally, he looked back.

"Okay," Cole said, gesturing to them to follow him. "Let's move forward slowly - single file. Keep your eyes open...."

"And look up!" Madison declared.

Cole turned to her and wrinkled his forehead. "What?"

"Spiders, right? They can climb on ceilings. So, look up too?" Madison pointed out, gesturing up at the ceiling with her hand.

Looking up, Cole nodded his head. "Good point. Madison, you keep your eyes up. Everyone else, look front, back and to either side."

Everyone nodded their understanding.

"Alright," her brother said, gesturing to them to follow him. "Let's move out. Single file. And stay alert!"

Following Cole, the small procession slowly moved forward towards the T-intersection. Madison kept her eyes up, looking for a giant spider, giant cockroach or anything else. She had a bad feeling that she couldn't shake.

47

The group went forward to a "T" intersection. The left side was blocked off by what appeared to be a cave-in. Dirt and stone had completely obliterated the passageway. The only way to go was right.

"Nothing creepy about this," Rose whispered, giving voice to Madison's thoughts.

Madison was picturing herself in a horror movie with something about to jump out at them all. Her eyes constantly roved the sides of the passage and the ceiling. After all, wasn't that usually where the bad guy or alien, or whatever, came from? She bit her lip. Or did it come from behind?

Casting a glance over her shoulder, Madison suppressed saying something very unlady-like. She hated movies like this! And now she was basically in one! She just knew something was going to jump out at them at any moment.

"You see anything?" Madison whispered to her brother.

Cole shrugged and held his torch up higher. "Just this long corridor. You can probably see further than I can."

Moving up closer behind her brother's hulking form, she glanced around him, down the corridor in front of them. Like the previous room, the walls were scorched, and the floor was littered with the crispy corpses of spiders.

Madison thought she saw an opening to the right, about twenty feet down. Was that another passage? The hallway they were in also continued another twenty or so feet, but that was the limit of her vision with the current torchlight.

She started as she spotted four sets of eyes glittering in the dark, at the very limits of her vision. Madison blinked and they were gone. Had that been real, or had she imagined it?

"Did anyone else just hear some skittering?" Rose asked from behind her. "Because I think I did."

Suppressing another shiver, Madison realized the skittering had probably come from whatever she'd seen in the dark. That meant it was real. Given the size of the eyes she'd seen, the spider at the end of the hallway must be huge.

"Uh," Madison muttered, coming to a halt. "There's something really big at the end of this hall."

Everyone else stopped moving and she heard a small growl from Buddy. Cole glanced back over his shoulder. He spoke in a hushed tone. "What is it?"

Madison shrugged. Like Cole, she kept her voice low.

"I'm not completely sure, but I think it's a really, really big spider."

"Probably the Queen or something," Michael said as he moved up into their huddle.

"How big?" Rose asked, wide-eyed. "Like bigger than the ones we already faced?"

Flashing her cousin an apologetic look, she nodded. "Much bigger. Like… huge."

She saw Rose swallow reflexively, her head straining to see down the hall now. "I don't see anything."

"Probably hiding," Michael said in a low, spooky tone. "Just waiting to sink its fangs into some tasty little elf meat."

"I'm going to whack you, Michael!" Rose growled.

The big cat, now larger than a real tiger, glared at her and gave her a deep, warning growl. Rose turned her glare on Buddy. "Fine, if you don't want me to do it. You whack him."

Buddy cocked his head and looked at Rose, then turned and looked at Michael. In an expression that might have been a shrug, the cat smacked Michael with one of his huge paws. The cat kept his claws retracted but the force of the blow sent Michael stumbling into the wall.

"Traitor!" Michael said as he stood up. "No fish for you when we get back to town."

The tiger dipped his head and let out a pitiful meow that seemed like something a housecat would make. Buddy then dropped to the ground and rolled over, showing his belly to Michael.

Trying to suppress a laugh, but grinning like a maniac,

Michael bent down and scratched the big cat's belly, earning some deep purrs. "Fine! Fine! You'll get fishes!"

The cat sat up and began licking Michael on the face.

"Ugh!" Michael groaned. "His tongue is really like sandpaper now!"

"Keep it down," Cole said, rolling his eyes at the exchange between man and cat.

"Why?" Michael looked down the hallway. "It's a spider. It's not like it can understand us."

The girls looked from Michael to Cole.

"No," Cole shot back, his face serious. "But I don't want it coming down here to investigate the noise before we have a plan."

They moved their gaze from Cole to Michael.

"What plan?" Michael retorted. "We go in, you tank, the rest of us beat on it. Madison stuns it if stuns work on bosses."

The girls looked from one boy to the other, trying to see who would win the argument. Neither of them particularly cared at this point. Let the boys decide. Madison just wanted to find more memory orbs - or an artifact that she could use to enchant.

"We don't know what special abilities it might have," Cole pointed out.

"And we won't find out until we fight her," Michael countered. "It's not like we can look it up on the forums. Hopefully, no one's defeated this boss before."

"And that means more money for us!" Rose said.

Madison turned to her cousin. "Is that all you really care about, the money?"

Rose gave a small shrug of her shoulders. "I like

playing this with you and the boys. Hanging out with you all is cool. But this game really isn't for me. I'm pretty sure my parents would disapprove if they found out about all the fighting."

"Why? They let you watch movies with more fighting than this," Madison reminded her.

"True," Rose agreed. "But in the movies, I'm not doing the killing."

"Good point," Madison conceded. "Do you think they'd make you stop playing?"

Rose frowned. "Probably. But if I earn enough money, they won't say anything. Well, probably not. Plus, if I make money doing this, then I don't have to get a job and I can spend time volunteering at the shelter."

Madison furrowed her brow. "Is that the only reason you're playing this? So, you can work at the shelter instead of getting a job?"

"It's not the only reason." Rose grinned mischievously. "Someone's got to keep an eye on Michael."

"Huh? What?" Michael said, turning to the two girls. They both giggled.

"Did you guys figure out a plan yet?" Madison asked the confused-looking Michael.

Cole looked at Michael and then rolled his eyes. "It looks like we're going to just rush in and pound on it."

Madison frowned. "Seriously? That's the big idea you two came up with?"

"Without knowing what to expect," he replied, gesturing down the hallway. "It's hard to formulate a plan."

"Yeah," Michael said with his customary grin. "We'll just have to play it by ear."

Shaking her head, Madison gave Michael and her brother an incredulous look. "Play it by ear?"

"Hey, the worst that can happen is, we die," Michael told her. "Then we respawn and try again - but this time, we'll have an idea of what she can do."

"That's the big plan?" Madison repeated.

Cole shrugged. "It's a tried-and-true method of figuring out how to take down a boss. You try different strategies, see what abilities they have, how often they can use them, etc."

"In the other games," she growled, remembering her own brush with death. More than anything else, she remembered the embarrassment of being in nothing but a string bikini. And this wasn't even her real body! "Do you respawn with your equipment or are you butt naked?"

The two boys exchanged looks. "That's a good point."

Cole made a face but then his eyes lit up. "Let's go back to the treasure room. We can leave our extra gear there. That way, if we die, we'll still have something for a second try."

Madison sighed but nodded. She wouldn't like running all the way back here in her underwear, but at least they'd have some backup gear.

"Let's hope this works," Rose said.

"And if not," Madison growled at the boys. "It had better work the second time. Otherwise, we'll be trying to fight her naked."

"Spring break... Adventurers Gone Wild!" Michael said a bit too loud before everyone shushed him.

"Come on! Let's get back there before the spider comes and eats Michael... and I let it," Madison said, stomping off towards the entrance.

Michael stood there unmoving. He shrugged. "What?!"

48

Thirty minutes later, the group had dropped off some of their equipment in the vault room. They could tell from the hole in the ceiling that it was dark out. They'd been exploring the area for quite some time.

With some of their spare equipment left in the room, in the case of their untimely deaths, they were once again back in the hallway where Madison had seen the spider eyes. Her brother stopped them at the point they'd stopped before and turned to face them, voice low.

"Okay," he started. "We're going to rush in, and I will taunt the big spider. I'll spin so her back is to you and you begin beating her. Rose, keep me healed. Madison, you see if your stun works on it. It's a boss, so it might not. And, Michael..."

Michael grinned. "I know... Michael smash!"

"Uh, right," Cole replied with a nod. "DPS it!" Her brother turned to look at them all. "Everyone got it?"

"What about special abilities?" Michael asked. "If it's a boss, it's got to have some sort of special ability."

Madison frowned. "What kind of special abilities?"

Her brother shrugged. "It could be anything."

"The boss could shoot unicorns from its butt!" Michael teased.

Cole shook his head. "This isn't one of those kinds of games."

"Everything so far has been based on reality," Rose pointed out. "Or as close to reality as a fantasy game can be."

Madison thought back to the creatures they'd faced. It was true. All of their abilities were based on real-world physics or abilities. Well, except for the creatures like the Fey, who wielded magic. Magic had its own rules. "Except for magic. Would a spider have magic though?"

Her brother looked thoughtful for a second, then shrugged again. "It might. Some bosses are larger and more intelligent versions of the lesser monsters. It IS possible the queen could be some sort of caster."

"That could be," Cole admitted slowly. "But more likely, Rose is right. If it has special abilities, then they're probably based on real spider abilities."

"You're the vet." Michael turned to Rose. "What are spider abilities?"

Rose growled at him. "I'm not a vet. I'm still in high school. I haven't taken any animal courses and I'm not going to be doing first aid on spiders."

"Yeah, but..." Michael tried but Rose cut him off.

"No, not even a pet spider! They can go somewhere else," Rose shot back.

Michael rolled his eyes at his cousin. "Well, what good are you then?"

Rose opened her mouth to retort but Madison held up her hand. "Some spiders make holes and jump out to surprise them. I think they pull them back inside."

They all looked at Madison, but she just smiled. "Uh... nature videos."

Cole nodded. "Right. They're like... trapdoor spiders... or something like that. What else?"

"Poison," Rose said, her eyes drifting to her legs where the spiders had bitten her - bitten them all.

The group unconsciously looked down at their own legs and then they all nodded. Her brother held up a second finger. "Okay, poison. We can probably count on that."

"And count on it being much worse than the spiders we encountered." Michael made a face.

"They jump too," Rose offered. "Right? Some spiders jump?"

Her brother held up a third finger. "Okay. So, trap-doors, poison and jumping. What else?"

They all exchanged glances as they racked their brains for more spider abilities. Cole snapped his fingers. "Some of them fling their hairs!"

Michael furrowed his brow. "Throw... their hairs?"

"Like a porcupine," Cole said and held up another finger. He shot a grin at Madison. "I saw it on one of those nature videos."

"Okay, so four possibilities," Michael said. "That's not bad."

"We'll have to watch for any tell-tale signs that it's

about to use a special ability," Cole said. "Watch for any behavior changes or sudden, weird movements."

"Like what?" Rose asked. Madison was wondering the same thing. It wasn't like she sat there watching spiders. How would they know what was normal and what was some special attack?

"I have no idea," Cole told them. "Just look for something out of the ordinary or a sudden change in the way it's attacking."

"Sudden change," Madison repeated. "Got it."

"And if you do notice something," Michael said, his voice going serious for a change. "Call it out."

"Right! Call it out and generally back away, roll away or in some other way get out of the way," Cole agreed with a nod. "Once we figure out what the spider can do, we can call out the exact ability when we see the tell."

Michael nodded and after exchanging glances with Rose, Madison and her cousin nodded as well. Rose's face had told her that her cousin, like Madison, didn't really understand, but they'd watch the boys and figure it out as they went.

"So, we have a plan," Cole said. "That means it's go time. Everyone ready?"

The group nodded and a large grin spread across Michael's face.

"All right... on 3..." Cole said and held up a fist. He began holding up fingers. "1... 2... 3... Go!"

Her brother charged forward, followed by Michael, then Rose and finally Madison. They rushed up the hallway and after fifteen or so feet, Madison heard splashing from the floor.

Looking down, Madison could see that they were splashing through small puddles of water the closer they got to the room with the big spider. She thought it was odd that there were puddles in a stone complex.

Madison glanced to either side of the passage and noticed that the further they got to the room, the more webbing there was on the wall and the moister the webbing looked. She guessed that was the reason the webbing in this area hadn't burned. Something had wet the area. But what?

There had been no sign of any sort of plumbing in any of the other rooms they'd explored. Glancing up at the walls, she saw no piping in this hallway and no indications of any sort of break in the ceiling where moisture might have seeped through.

Before Madison had much of a chance to think about the water, the group was bursting into the room. And then they were screaming.

They were screaming because her brother fell through the floor, followed by Michael and Buddy, and then Rose. Madison was right behind them and managed to slow herself slightly, but not enough that she could stop before she too fell through a floor that seemed to be nothing more than dead, wet leaves.

As she fell, Madison managed to grab onto a solid piece of the floor. At first, she thought it might be some sort of wooden beam, but it gave slightly as she clung to it. Then, as she tried to climb atop the beam, she realized the truth. It wasn't a beam. It was a very thick piece of webbing.

Wide-eyed, Madison looked around the irregularly

shaped circular room to see that there really didn't appear to be a floor. Nor was there a ceiling. Both must have collapsed at some point, giving way to a large hole in the ground. Through the webbing above them, she caught a glimpse of stars and a sliver of the moon above them.

The sound of water caused her to follow the sound to the corner, where water poured down the corner of the room and disappeared into the darkness below them.

Rose's scream brought Madison back to the moment and she glanced around the floor she now knew was nothing but sticky strands of one large, giant web. And she was caught in it like the proverbial fly in a spider's web.

Searching the area with her eyes, Madison first noticed her brother and Michael. The two boys were several feet below her, also caught on large strands of webs. Buddy was a few feet further down slightly off to the side. The big cat was caught and attempting to struggle against the webs. This only served to further entwine the cat in more of the sticky strands.

Then Madison spotted Rose struggling near the big cat. She was about to tell her cousin to stop it when movement caught her eye. Then she spotted the reason Rose and the cat were both struggling so hard.

A dozen feet from them was a huge spider. Madison couldn't be sure, but the thing's body had to be the size of a large dog. With its legs, it was easily the size of a car. And it was coming closer to them.

The enormous spider, who had been moving extremely slowly, suddenly shot forward and grabbed Buddy. Madison saw the spider move its mandibles in close and heard a yelp of pain from the big cat. Then Buddy went limp.

Forest Spider Matriarch bites Buddy for 11 damage.
Buddy is poisoned.

Michael yelled a curse at the spider but the creature didn't react. Madison saw messages flash by as the poison continued to do damage.

Forest Spider Matriarch venom poisons Buddy for 11 damage.
Forest Spider Matriarch venom poisons Buddy for 11 damage.
Forest Spider Matriarch venom poisons Buddy for 11 damage.

The spider wasted no time. In a series of motions that seemed almost too quick to follow, the spider cocooned Buddy. Then, with a deft motion, the spider matriarch hung the cat on one of the nearby strands. Then she turned to Rose.

"Rose!" Madison yelled. "Cut yourself free!"

"I can't! I can't get my weapon…" Rose started but the Spider Matriarch rushed forward and sank her fangs into Rose. Her cousin screamed for an instant and then her body went limp, just like Buddy had.

Forest Spider Matriarch bites Plays-With-Animals for 9 damage.
Plays-With-Animals is poisoned.

The spider queen wasted no time and quickly wrapped up Rose in a cocoon before hanging her on a nearby strand. Then, the queen skittered up the webs towards Michael. Madison saw damage messages from the poison continue to scroll through the screen, slowly killing Buddy and Rose.

Michael wasn't taking it lying down and he and Cole were close enough that they both were able to get shots in before the spider reached them.

Zachatolus Catfriend crushes Forest Spider Matriarch for 6 damage.
Brothar Snowbear slashes Forest Spider Matriarch for 11 damage.

Unfortunately, the blows did little to dissuade the matriarch. She flinched back for a moment, then shot forward and bit Michael.

Forest Spider Matriarch bites Zachatolus Catfriend for 7 damage.
Zachatolus Catfriend is poisoned.

Michael immediately stopped moving. The spider matriarch scrambled to the side, out of the reach of Cole. She then pulled Michael to her and cocooned her cousin before hanging his unmoving body on another strand of web.

"Cole!" Madison yelled as the spider shot towards her brother. She wanted to do something but there was nothing she could do but watch.

Her brother got in a good strike with his sword and another hit with the hilt of the weapon in the spider's face, just below her eyes.

Brothar Snowbear slashes Forest Spider Matriarch for 14 damage.
Brothar Snowbear critically bashes Forest Spider Matriarch for 13 damage.

The spider flinched back again, but only briefly. She struck out and managed to find a gap in her brother's armor. She sank her fangs in and her brother stopped moving.

Forest Spider Matriarch bites Brothar Snowbear for 7 damage.
Sentinel Plate Armor absorbs 5 damage.
Brothar Snowbear is poisoned.

"Cole!" Madison screamed again but was helpless to do anything but watch as the giant spider cocooned her brother and hung him on a web strand. Then she turned to her.

The spider matriarch hurried towards her and Madison screamed again and did the only thing she could think of. She triggered her Color Blast spell.

Forest Spider Matriarch is stunned.

The spider queen froze in place, unmoving for several

seconds. Madison rejoiced slightly in finding out that her spell worked.

But after only a few seconds, the spider quivered, seeming to shake off the effects of the spell. She started to move forward again and Madison triggered her spell.

Forest Spider Matriarch is stunned.

Madison knew she was only prolonging it, since none of her other spells had a chance of killing the giant spider. Yet, she kept stunning the spider until she was out of mana. Then, the queen came for her.

Forest Spider Matriarch bites you for 9 damage.
You are poisoned.
You are paralyzed.

A burning sensation flowed into her from the wound in her leg where the spider queen had bit her. At the same time, she felt all of her muscles suddenly go useless and she flopped in the web like a rag doll.

Forest Spider Matriarch venom poisons you for 11 damage.

She saw her surroundings change and realized the spider had grabbed hold of her and pulled her from the web. Madison couldn't feel the spider touching her. She couldn't feel anything but she could see the queen, as her eyes were still open.

Forest Spider Matriarch venom poisons you for 11 damage.

Then, Madison watched dizzily as her surroundings began to rotate. She realized the matriarch was cocooning her!

Forest Spider Matriarch venom poisons you for 11 damage.

Round and round she went until at last, the webbing reached her eyes and she was no longer able to see anything except darkness.

Forest Spider Matriarch venom poisons you for 11 damage.

All she could feel now was the burning of the venom as it spread across her entire body. She wanted to scream but she couldn't. Nothing worked. Even breathing was becoming more difficult.

Forest Spider Matriarch venom poisons you for 11 damage.

Madison desperately wanted to do something - anything.

Forest Spider Matriarch venom poisons you for 11 damage.

But there was nothing but the darkness and the pain. And then, even that faded away.

Forest Spider Matriarch venom poisons you for 11 damage.
Forest Spider Matriarch venom poisons you for 11 damage.
You have died.
Your equipment has suffered damage.
Part of your soul has been left behind. You will suffer penalties until your soul is reunited.

The darkness dissolved, replaced by a familiar sight. Madison was back in that place where she'd started. The other world or afterlife or whatever it was called in this game.

The familiar pillars and the fog were there, as was the golden gate. This time, the goddess was there again, but more substantial than before. She spoke, but her words came out as a ghostly whisper.

"I cannot interfere, but you must defeat this enemy," the goddess told her. "Something of great importance lies past her. You must retrieve it..."

Madison opened her mouth to ask the goddess about what she needed to retrieve but like dust in the wind, the ghostly visage faded away.

Frowning, she looked around the area to see if there was any other sign of the goddess. Madison growled in frustration and turned towards the gate. She needed to tell the others about it.

Then she stopped. Maybe the goddess had already spoken to them. Knowing there was only one way to find out, she took a deep breath. Madison plunged into the glowing portal and the world dissolved into shimmering light.

49

Madison emerged from the portal back on a familiar beach. Looking around, she saw the rest of her group lying down on the sand - groaning. Buddy was there too, lying next to Michael, licking his face. Then it hit her.

You are suffering from Death Penalty.
Death Penalty: -10% to all stats, -10% to Maximum Health, -10% to Maximum Mana
Time left: 59 minutes 59 seconds

A feeling of nausea and cramping in all of her muscles caused Madison to fall to her knees. She let out an involuntary groan. She wrapped her arms around her chest, overcome by what felt like a very bad case of the flu.

"Welcome to the club," Michael groaned, trying to grin through the pain.

"Do we have an hour of this?" Rose whined. "I feel like I'm going to be sick."

Madison was immediately sympathetic with her cousin. This feeling was terrible. Why would they put this in the game? What was the point? A punishment for failure? To her, it seemed unnecessarily harsh.

As she thought about it, Madison decided she had better things to do than roll around on a beach and be sick. Besides, time passed more quickly in the game. She only had to log out for a few minutes and then the penalty should be over. She made up her mind.

"I'm logging out," Madison told the others.

"Me too," Rose agreed. "There's no point in sticking around for pain."

"You know, I agree with you there," Michael chimed in.

Rolling over so she faced her brother, she asked him. "You logging out too, Cole?"

Cole didn't say anything for a long moment but finally shook his head. "I'm going to stay in."

"You want to stay in?" Madison felt her eyebrows furrowing. She thought she might have heard him wrong. "Why would you want to stay in?"

Grunting and groaning even more loudly, Cole pushed himself up to his knees. His face was ashen but was also determined. "Because I want to start heading back."

"Back to the spider that just killed us all?" Rose said incredulously. "Why?"

He didn't move for a moment, appearing to summon his strength. He turned to the others. "We have to go back and kill that thing."

"Uh... why?" Rose asked, her forehead wrinkled in confusion.

"Because it's guarding something we need to get," he growled.

Madison blinked. Wasn't that the same thing the goddess had said? Something about something of great importance past the spider. She'd almost forgotten when she'd appeared back at the beach and the wave of sickness had hit her. "Did the goddess tell you that?"

Cole looked at her, beads of sweat on his forehead as he pushed himself to his feet. "Goddess? What goddess? No, Thorakar told me when I was in the afterlife or whatever that is when we die. It looked like the same place I was in during character creation." He looked around at the others. "Did you see him?"

"I saw him at character creation," Michael said, "but not this time." Gritting his teeth, Michael sat up and Buddy sat up too, continuing to lick Michael's face. The cat didn't seem to be under any distress, so maybe animal companions didn't get Death Penalty. Lucky them.

Madison let out a groan, as she rolled over and pushed herself upright. A wave of nausea hit her, but it passed quickly. She kept her mouth closed for a moment longer, just in case. Finally, she thought it was safe to talk. "I saw a goddess during character creation."

"So did I," Rose groaned. She was still lying on the ground. Her cousin made no attempt to sit up with the others. "Maybe it's a girl thing. But I didn't see her this past time."

"That's weird," Cole said.

"That I saw a goddess and you saw a god?" Rose retorted.

"No." Her brother shook his head. "Why did Madison and I see them this time and you two didn't?"

The group exchanged glances, but no one offered any explanation.

"It could be completely random," Michael suggested. "Like we triggered some event or something and so each time we die, we each might have a random chance to have someone tell us about it. You know... to encourage us to go further with the quest."

Cole frowned. He tried pushing himself to his feet, failed, and sat down hard on the sand. "Okay. That's not happening for a bit longer."

Rose looked thoughtful. "So, if it's a goddess speaking to us. Do you think that means it's important? You know... like a unique quest?"

"And more money!" Michael grinned and rubbed his fingers together. "That's our Rose. Always thinking with her wallet!"

"Purse actually," Rose replied and stuck her tongue out at Michael.

"There might be some truth to that," Cole said. He tried pushing himself up again but once again ended in a sitting position.

"Why this quest and not any of the others?" Madison wondered aloud. If anything, it did seem to give credence to Rose's theory that this might be a unique or important quest. But what could the big spider be guarding? Some more memory globes?

Memory globes might make sense. Perhaps there was some part of the previous story she'd witnessed which would start a quest or lead them to a quest. Madison wasn't sure.

Unfortunately, she had really seen much of the room - if that could really be considered a room. It was more like a giant sinkhole the spider matriarch had claimed for her own. And that meant, the memory orbs could be anywhere in the webs or perhaps, down at the bottom of the area.

"Madison?" Cole said and she looked up.

Madison realized she'd gotten lost in her thoughts and that someone had been speaking. "What?"

"I said, we should try to go back and figure out a way to beat the queen," Cole repeated.

"We could wait until the death thingy is done with," Rose suggested.

"True," Cole said, turning to face Rose. "But by then, someone else could have gotten or even completed the quest and we won't be the first."

Rose furrowed her brow. "How? We haven't seen any other players?"

"Not here," Cole said with a shake of his head. "Some of these quests may not be unique to this area. This quest could be in multiple areas. In which case, the first one to complete it gets the money."

Madison narrowed her eyes at her brother. She wasn't completely sure he was telling the truth, but judging by Rose's reaction, he knew the right buttons to press.

"No!" she growled. "What if it's a lot of money!"

Cole nodded solemnly and Madison knew he was hamming it up. He shook his head. "Who knows how much money we'd lose if we wait."

Rose bit her lip and snarled as she pushed herself up to her knees and then, with a Herculean effort, managed to stand on shaky legs. She wobbled for a moment and looked like she might be sick, but she stayed standing.

Looking around at the others, she put her hands on her hips. "Well, come on! We need to go do this quest before someone else does it and steals our money."

Madison caught Cole giving Michael a wink and knew this had been her brother's plan all along. She'd chide him, but she was impressed that her brother had it in him to be that manipulative. Not that she would ever admit that to Cole.

Struggling against the feeling of nausea and the muscle cramps, the rest of the group slowly got to their feet. They just stood there for several minutes.

In addition to the nausea and body aches, there was also some vertigo. Madison really felt like she could actually feel the planet moving and she struggled to stay on her feet. But the longer she pushed through it, the less prevalent the effects became.

After a few minutes, the group looked around at each other. Madison shrugged. "Is it just me, or are the effects mostly gone?"

Cole's eyes went glassy. "The penalties are still there, but I do feel better."

Michael screwed up his face. "Do you think it was us getting up... or was it just timed?"

"No way to know now," he replied. "But we should get going."

Madison cleared her throat as she gestured around at their avatars. She had been in too much pain before, but now she noticed it and was trying not to blush. "Uh... guys... we're naked."

50

"Why do you even have breasts?" Rose asked suddenly, not bothering to cover herself at all. She looked Madison up and down. "You're a reptile. Reptiles don't nurse their young."

"Because, little miss veterinarian, chances are, the designer was a guy," Michael answered with a grin. His avatar was wearing nothing more than a loincloth, but he wasn't bothered at all by it. Neither was her brother.

"I'm not a vet..." Rose started to retort but Madison cut her off.

"None of you are concerned we're naked?" Madison asked, her arms crossed over her breasts, hiding them as much as she could. Sure, she had the equivalent of a string bikini on, but she never wore such things in real life, and it felt awkward wearing one in a game.

Cole shrugged. "I'm lying-in bed in sweatpants and a t-shirt. This isn't me."

"And technically, we're not naked. We're... scantily clad." Rose shivered. "It is a bit cold though."

Madison squinted at her cousin and then raised her scaly eyebrows. "Do you have goosebumps?"

Looking down at herself, Rose nodded. "Wow. I do. That's weird."

"They really went all in on the level of detail," Cole remarked, looking over the goosebumps on Rose's skin.

"Yes. They got the chilly thing down." Rose rubbed her arms. "Can we get our clothes now? And go find this quest before someone else does it."

"It's a long walk back," Michael frowned. Then he did a mock yawn. "For you guys, I mean. Me, I'll be riding my trusty mount."

With that, Michael went over to Buddy and threw his leg over his back. He held up his hand like he had a sword in it. "By the power of gray..."

"Don't..." Rose said dryly. "Just... don't."

"What?!" Michael grinned back.

Rose shook her head. "Come on, let's go get our stuff."

The group set off, skirting the town. None of them were sure whether the NPCs would react to their lack of clothing and didn't want to risk it. After all, they were trying to build up their reputation with the town.

Cole and Rose quickly realized that their soft, human-like skin was not proof against sharp sticks and rocks - especially on their feet.

"We have to walk all the way back there in bare feet!" growled Rose, flinching as she stepped on another sharp stone.

"Buddy's not complaining," Michael replied with his

typical grin. He bent over and scratched the big cat behind the ears. "You don't mind it, do you, big boy?"

Buddy just leaned his head back in the scratches as his response, a low rumbling purr coming from his chest.

The stones didn't bother Madison either. Like the rest of her body, her feet were covered in scales. She walked normally, the stones not even a slight inconvenience to her.

Madison had also quickly gotten used to the running around naked. Or maybe, it wasn't that she had gotten used to it, but rather, she didn't feel so conspicuous when everyone else was naked too.

IT TOOK them over an hour to get back to the vault room. Luckily, by the time they did, their death penalty was gone, and their stats were back to normal.

Cole and Rose had complained most of the way and their feet had been sliced up by stones and briars. If this was reality, the two would barely be able to walk. But, in the game, their natural healing factor kept them from any lasting damage.

On their trip back, there hadn't been much conversation about a new strategy for overcoming the spider that had killed them. Neither Cole nor Michael had offered anything, and Madison hadn't pressed them. But it had weighed heavily on her mind.

The spider had killed them so quickly last time - and that was with their best gear. Now, they had their old gear or the stuff they'd found along the way. How could they hope to defeat it with second-hand equipment if they couldn't defeat it with their best equipment?

Cole seemed to sense her thoughts. "Anyone come up with any bright ideas for killing the spider matriarch?"

"Uh... kill it first?" Michael offered with a grin.

"The first step is probably not to get caught in its web," Madison suggested. That was one thing that seemed self-evident.

"No." Michael shook his head. "I think we should all run in there again and throw ourselves headfirst into the webs. I had so much fun last time."

Rose rolled her eyes and then bit her lip before speaking. "That was horrible. If there wasn't some big quest involved, I wouldn't go back there."

"We don't know for certain there's a quest," Cole pointed out. "There was just something about an item or something past the spider."

"It's got to be a quest, right?" Rose countered. "I mean, a god and a goddess both spoke to you."

Michael nodded. "It does seem likely. Though, that's almost like railroading us into the quest. And this is supposed to be open world."

"Open world?" Rose frowned, looking over at Michael with a furrowed brow.

"It means the world is designed so that we explore it however we want," Cole replied, probably seeing that Michael was getting ready to give them a smart alec answer. "Most MMOs are open world, not linear like regular computer games. Michael is right, it seems strange that we'd have gods and goddesses basically telling us what to do."

Madison thought back to the visions she'd seen with the memory orbs. Those conversations had been important. Historical. It had been about the Fey war. And the museum or whatever this place was, seemed to be devoted to the Fey war. It made sense that whatever the spider was guarding had something to do with the Fey or the Fey war.

Then, there was the Fey itself. An actual Fey had been here, masquerading as a gnoll shaman. It had obviously been looking for something. But what? Was it trying to destroy the memory orbs? Was there something in them that the Fey didn't want them to know?

"Maybe it's a memory orb," Madison offered, giving voice to her thoughts. Everyone turned to look at her skeptically. She raised her palms. "Hear me out. The other orbs had to do with the Fey war. What if there is an orb with some special knowledge? You know, like what they did to defeat the Fey. Maybe that's what that shaman-Fey was after."

Cole looked thoughtful. "It could be. Maybe viewing the orb starts a quest."

"Whatever it is, we need to find it," Rose told them. "Before someone else gets the quest!"

"Calm down there, mercenary-girl," Michael said. He glanced at the doorway that led back to the museum. "There's still the little issue of the giant freaking spider."

Rose put her hands on her hips and looked between Cole and Michael. "You two are the gamers. Figure it out."

Madison gave her brother a smile. "Yeah, you two, figure it out."

"It's not that easy," Cole growled. "That's a real boss.

Not like that gnoll we fought earlier. Well, maybe just a higher level. But it was fast and that poison is deadly."

"Yes," Madison agreed. "But we were also separated and stuck! We literally walked into the spider's lair."

"Like flies," Michael commented.

Her brother nodded. "The webs give her a huge advantage and us a huge disadvantage. We need to get rid of the webs. Burn them, maybe."

Madison shook her head. "The webs were all wet. I don't think they will burn. Water is leaking into that room from the outside."

"Yeah," Michael added. "I saw that too. It looks like the top of the place collapsed in. That's probably what allowed her to get there to begin with. It's not like she waltzed in through the front door, past all the gnolls."

"Maybe we can lure her outside," Rose suggested.

"Maybe," Cole said, looking thoughtful. "We'll need to investigate the outside. We might be able to use a large open space to our advantage."

"Maybe we can build a trap and lure her into it," Madison said aloud. She remembered some stupid show Cole loved to watch with one of those old action stars.

Everyone turned to her, expectantly. Her brother raised an eyebrow. "Oh?"

"Remember that movie you like, the one with the former governor of California and the alien?" she asked.

Cole screwed up his face. "You know about an Arnold movie?"

"Get to the Choppa!" Michael said in a low, accented voice.

"You've watched it so many times, I think I've seen the

whole thing just walking by the living room," she shot back. "Anyway, didn't that guy build a trap for the alien?"

"Yeah, but it didn't work," Michael chuckled.

"I thought it killed the alien?" Madison replied, trying to remember the scene. She thought something heavy dropped down and flattened the alien.

"Well," Cole said, scratching his head. "Technically, the counterweight was what killed it, but I think I see your point. If we can lure it outside..."

"Then maybe we can build some traps and do some serious damage to it," Michael finished with a grin. "I like it."

"But how do we lure it out?" Rose asked.

"One thing at a time," Madison replied. "First, we need to investigate the outside and see if that's even an option."

There was a muttering of approvals and Madison began walking towards the door. They had the beginnings of a plan. She just hoped they could figure out how to actually make it work.

51

"I'm not going in there," Rose said, staring at the mass of webs spread across the trees.

The group had gone outside and walked past the area where they'd found the back entrance to the vault. Only fifty yards beyond that, obscured by a cluster of thick pine trees, was a giant spider nest.

"We're definitely not luring it out." Cole whistled. "Not if we have to go into that to do it."

Webs covered the trees beyond for several hundred feet in either direction, effectively walling off the area from outsiders. Madison shuddered as she saw hundreds of the smaller spiders moving around the webs. "How did we not see this before? I mean, we cut down a tree right over there."

"I'm glad we didn't see it before," Rose said, staring wide-eyed at the webbed area. "I wouldn't have come anywhere near it."

"I don't think Buddy's so thrilled about it either,"

Michael muttered, stroking the big cat's back. The large tiger was crouched low, a low growl escaping his mouth.

Her brother pointed to a stream that was trickling out from the webs. "Look!"

They all looked at the stream. Madison noticed that although only a stream of water was coming out of the webbed area, the riverbed was almost twice as large. "I'll bet that's why the webs are all wet down there, part of the river must be blocked by webs. The water is probably all over the ground inside."

Cole shook his head. "I'm guessing the designers made it this way specifically to make it harder for someone like us to just wipe out the entire spider colony with a little fire."

Michael nodded. "They did a good job. Even without the water, if we tried to cut through those webs, all those little spiders would swarm us."

"No way to go over it either," Madison commented, pointing at the top of the webs. They didn't reach to the top of the trees but did go up.

"You sure you can't fly up there?" Michael asked, nodding to her wings.

"No, I can't fly. Just glide." Madison replied. She stretched out her wings. Keeping them tucked behind her back like a cloak, it was easy to forget she even had wings. Unfortunately, she couldn't actually fly with them - they were more like a parachute than anything else, slowing her fall and possibly allowing her to glide short distances.

"Too bad," her brother lamented. "Having air support would be nice."

"Right!" Michael chuckled. "Just hover up there and

drop some bombs or oil or whatever. They couldn't touch you!"

Rose nodded her approval. "That would make things easy."

"But I can't," Madison said with a shrug. "And we don't have any oil or bombs."

"Actually, I think we have two more of the Molotov cocktails left," Cole corrected here.

"We could use them to set these webs on fire too," Rose said with a wicked grin.

Michael grinned and held up his hand for Rose to slap. "You go, girl!"

"And take out the whole forest." Madison shook her head and gestured to the huge swath of webbed forest. "If this stuff burns like the other webs, it will set the trees on fire. If they go up..."

"It could spread to the trees around us," Rose finished dejectedly, dropping the hand that was about to slap Michael's hand.

"Only you," Michael said in a deep voice and pointed to Rose. "Can prevent forest fires!"

"Madison is right," Cole growled in frustration. "That might make things easier and kill the spiders, but there's a good chance it would set the entire forest on fire. The ground inside is probably wet from the water in the river, but the trees themselves look dry. They'll go up quickly."

"Not to sound insensitive." Michael scratched his head and then shrugged at them. "Why do we care what happens to the forest?"

Everyone turned to stare at Michael, but he just shrugged. "Guys, it's just a game. These aren't real trees, and this isn't a real forest. Does it really matter if we burn the whole thing down?"

The group exchanged glances. Madison bit her lip. They might not be actual trees, but it didn't feel right to her. It might be a simulation, but the forest was beautiful - well, when not infested by spiders. The idea of destroying it just didn't sit well.

Madison thought of another reason not to. "The forest goes all the way back to the farms around the city. If we set the whole forest on fire, it will reach the town. If that happens, it could burn down the crops - maybe even the homes. I know... I know... they're not real homes, but still. Plus, I'm sure the townspeople won't thank us for that."

"Valid point," Cole pointed out. He looked around. "Not to mention... we're in the forest. Who's to say we can outrun a forest fire. It could kill us and destroy our loot."

Rose made a face and then gave Michael a stern look. "I don't feel like being burned alive."

Michael put his hands up. "Hey, burning it was your idea!"

"I didn't say to burn the whole forest down!" Rose objected.

Madison sighed and looked around while her cousins had some back-and-forth banter about whose idea it was to set the forest on fire. From where they stood, she could see the remnants of the tree they had cut down. Madison thought back to how they'd felled the tree and blocked the chimneys.

They'd been so careful cutting the tree. They'd done it just right so that it landed exactly where they wanted - or close enough. She suppressed a giggle as she remembered

Michael waiting until the last minute to get out of the way of the falling tree. Madison had thought for sure he'd be flattened.

Stopping her train of thought, Madison cocked her head and looked at the tree. Then she turned and looked at the other trees around the area. She held her fingers up, lining up the trees' trajectories. She smiled. "Hey guys. I have an idea.

"What if we chop down a couple of trees so that they fall on spider-ville over there," she said.

"Spiderville!" Michael grinned. "I love the name!"

Ignoring her cousin, Madison continued. "We can chop them down, so they fall on the spider nest over there."

"Spiderville... spiderville..." Michael sang softly. "Does whatever a spiderville can..."

Cole looked skeptical. "That's not going to do much. Maybe just flatten a few spiders that happen to get caught under it."

"... can you get caught, in a web," Michael continued quietly. "Yes you can, it's a spiderville. Look out... here comes the spiderville."

"Michael!" Rose hissed, hands on her hips. "Listen up."

Her cousin rolled his eyes. "Fine. Tell us about cutting down trees."

"As I was about to say," Madison continued. "What if we cut the tops of the tree, but not all the way. Then, when they crash down, the tops will break off and fall into that hole where the matriarch was."

Cole made a face. "I don't know if that'll work... I

mean, we'd have to cut it at just the right spot, so that the top snaps off when it hits and goes into the hole." He looked skeptical and pointed to the wall of webbing. "We can't see past the webs."

"We still have rope, right?" Michael asked with a mischievous grin.

They all looked at him suspiciously. Even Cole arched an eyebrow. "Yes."

Michael's grin grew even larger. "I'm thinking... tree flail."

Rose screwed up her face. "Tree flail?"

"Tree flail," Michael confirmed with a nod. "A flail is basically a stick with a ball attached to it with a chain. So, instead of cutting the tree at the top, we tie ropes around it. At the end of the ropes, we can put logs. Or better yet, spiked logs!"

Cole's eyes lit up. "Right! The tree falls, the logs on the ropes swing down into the pit!"

"Whack! Whack! Whack!" Michael rocked his hand back and forth, emulating the movement of a pendulum. "Even if we don't get her, it should really wreck the spider-webs in there."

Rose gave them a skeptical look. "Do we have enough rope?"

Madison nodded. "We have some and I remember seeing more in the gnoll cave."

"And then what? We hit her with a... tree flail... and she'll come up to investigate?" Rose asked.

"That's the plan, right? Lure her out and fight her up in the open?" Michael asked.

"Good point," Rose agreed but still looked wary.

Madison bit her lip. “The problem is. We have to place the ropes at just the right height so the logs swing into the pit. If we’re too high or too low, they’ll miss.”

Rose shrugged. “Can’t one of us just climb the tree and figure it out?”

“We probably only have enough rope for one try - two at the most. I think we’ll need something better than eyeballing it,” Cole commented.

“Like what?” Rose asked.

“We could,” Madison began as an idea came to her, “measure the distance with a rope. Then we pull the rope back here and use it to measure how far up the tree we need to put our... uh... flail ropes... or... whatever they are called. You know, like a measuring tape.”

Rose’s eyes opened wide. “You mean... go... in there... into the spider nest?”

“Not spider nest... Spiderville,” Michael corrected with a grin and began humming some tune Madison couldn’t quite place.

“Uh... that’s suicide,” Rose gasped. “Those spiders would kill anyone going in there really quick.”

“Normally, you would be right.” Madison smiled. “Whoever we send, it will need to be someone fast.” She looked over at Michael, who was looking down at Buddy. “Someone maneuverable. Maybe... someone with a mount...”

Michael’s head popped up and he looked at her wide eyed. “Woah! Woah! Woah! Wait... what? You want me and Buddy to go into spiderville?”

Cole clapped Michael on the back. “Well, you ARE the only one with a mount.”

"Yeah but..."

"And you're fast," Rose added with a smile.

"Well.. yes... but..."

Madison mirrored Michael's normal grin. "And maneuverable."

"Not to mention, it will be easier for you to get back here from the town if they kill you," Cole added.

"Which they probably will!" Michael retorted. He looked around at the others and his shoulders sagged. "I'm not going to be able to talk my way out of this, am I?"

"Nope!" they all responded at nearly the same time.

"Fine!" Michael growled but then he put on his normal grin. "But if I'm going into spiderville... I'm going naked!"

"Eww," Rose said, her face twisting in disgust. "Are you serious?"

Michael rolled his eyes. "Don't get your loincloth all twisted. I meant, someone needs to hold my stuff so I don't lose it when I die."

"Then we have a plan," Madison said. "Michael holds one end of the rope; he breaks into the webs and goes to the edge of the pit and then drops the rope. We mark this side of the rope, then pull it back and use it to measure how high up on the tree we need to put the... flail ropes... flail arms?"

"And Michael gets eaten by spiders," Rose said with just a bit too much enthusiasm.

52

Madison and the others watched Michael as he surveyed spiderville. He had stripped down to his loin cloth and now sat atop Buddy. He frowned. "Go in there, find the edge of the pit and drop the rope. That's all, right?"

"That's it," Cole confirmed. "Just go in there and get to the pit."

The group had moved closer to the spider webs to make sure their length of rope reached the edge of the pit. They'd staked down the rope so none of them actually needed to be nearby when Michael started his run.

Madison shuddered. From here, the spiders moving around the webs were much more evident. She remembered the spiders from the tunnel and all of the bites. It wasn't something she wished to repeat.

"And then get eaten," Rose added.

"Uh, yeah," Michael retorted. "Try not to sound so happy."

Rose just grinned in return.

Michael frowned. "And what if the rope doesn't make it to the edge of the pit?"

Madison shrugged. "It should. It can't be that far in there."

"If that rope is tight against the stake," Rose suggested. "We'll wait until you return. You can tell us how far past the edge of the rope the pit is."

"I guess," Michael replied, his frown still in place.

It was hard to fault him. Michael knew he was going in there to get bit over and over again. Madison wasn't sure she'd be willing to do the same in his place. Yet despite his mischievous nature, she knew Michael had a heart of gold and would do anything for his cousins.

"You can do it, Michael," Madison told him, patting him on the back. "Go be a hero!"

"That's me... Spider-snack," he replied with a grin. "The hero."

"Alright, Spider-snack," Cole said, slapping him on the back. "You'd better get going."

Taking a deep breath, he nodded and sighed. "While I'm coming back from the village, you guys get the tree ready. When I get back, I want some serious payback on those spiders."

"You'll get it," Madison promised.

"I'd better," Michael snapped and took the end of the rope from Madison. "Otherwise, the next time you need something measured - one of you gets to go to spiderville!"

Making a loud clicking sound, Michael dug his heels into Buddy. "Hi-ho, Buddy, away!"

The big cat let out a roar and then leaped forward. They cleared the twenty feet to the webs in two bounds and then leaped through. They punched a hole through the spider web curtain that surrounded spiderville and then disappeared inside. The entire time, Michael sang at the top of his lungs. "Spiderville! Spiderville! Does whatever a spiderville can!..."

As Michael and Buddy disappeared into the webbed area, the spiders they could see stopped what they were doing and scrambled after him. That's when the messages started.

Forest Spider bites Zachatolus Catfriend for 3 damage.
Zachatolus Catfriend is Poisoned.
Forest Spider bites Buddy for 2 damage.
Buddy is Poisoned.
Forest Spider bites Zachatolus Catfriend for 3 damage.
Zachatolus Catfriend is Poisoned.
Forest Spider bites Buddy for 3 damage.
Buddy is Poisoned.
Forest Spider bites Zachatolus Catfriend for 4 damage.
Zachatolus Catfriend is Poisoned.
Forest Spider bites Buddy for 2 damage.
Buddy is Poisoned.
Forest Spider bites Zachatolus Catfriend for 3 damage.
Zachatolus Catfriend is Poisoned.
Forest Spider bites Buddy for 3 damage.
Buddy is Poisoned.

Madison gritted her teeth, wanting to look away but knowing she could not. There were so many bites.

Knowing what the hornet stings felt like, she sympathized with Buddy and her cousin.

Glancing at the others, she saw that Cole and Rose were glassy eyed too. They were watching the messages scroll by in their HUDs. They kept scrolling. And Michael kept belching out his "Spiderville" song.

Forest Spider bites Zachatolus Catfriend for 4 damage.
Zachatolus Catfriend is Poisoned.
Forest Spider bites Buddy for 3 damage.
Buddy is Poisoned.
Forest Spider bites Zachatolus Catfriend for 4 damage.
Zachatolus Catfriend is Poisoned.
Forest Spider bites Buddy for 3 damage.
Buddy is Poisoned.
Forest Spider bites Zachatolus Catfriend for 3 damage.
Zachatolus Catfriend is Poisoned.
Forest Spider bites Buddy for 2 damage.
Buddy is Poisoned.

Looking down, she watched the rope as it uncoiled. It had gone quickly until they entered but now had slowed down. And kept slowing down. But Michael was still pulling it. He and Buddy were still moving.

Forest Spider bites Zachatolus Catfriend for 4 damage.
Zachatolus Catfriend is Poisoned.
Forest Spider bites Buddy for 3 damage.
Buddy is Poisoned.
Forest Spider bites Zachatolus Catfriend for 3 damage.
Zachatolus Catfriend is Poisoned.

Forest Spider bites Buddy for 3 damage.
Buddy is Poisoned.
Forest Spider bites Zachatolus Catfriend for 4 damage.
Zachatolus Catfriend is Poisoned.
Forest Spider bites Buddy for 2 damage.
Buddy is Poisoned.

Just before the rope had all but used up, they heard a shout from inside the web. "FOUND IT!"

Forest Spider bites Zachatolus Catfriend for 4 damage.
Zachatolus Catfriend is Poisoned.
Forest Spider bites Buddy for 3 damage.
Buddy is Poisoned.
Forest Spider bites Zachatolus Catfriend for 3 damage.
Zachatolus Catfriend is Poisoned.
Forest Spider bites Buddy for 3 damage.
Buddy is Poisoned.
Forest Spider bites Zachatolus Catfriend for 4 damage.
Zachatolus Catfriend is Poisoned.
Forest Spider bites Buddy for 2 damage.
Buddy is Poisoned.

And then the rope went slack and his "Spiderville" song resumed, although weaker this time. The messages kept on scrolling but they had no idea where he was. Would Michael somehow make it back? Then she saw the messages they had all known were inevitable.

Zachatolus Catfriend has died.
Buddy has died.

Everyone was quiet for a long moment. Michael had been a trooper. He had managed to make it through who knew how many spiders, all the way to the pit. And he'd done it while being bitten over and over.

"Well, at least he did it," Rose said soberly. "I knew he would."

Madison furrowed her brow at her cousin. "You knew?"

"I wasn't going to tell him that," Rose replied with a grin that rivaled Michael's.

Rolling her eyes at the elf, Madison bent down and marked the rope with a piece of charcoal they'd taken from the gnoll area.

"Okay, Michael will be heading back once he respawns," she told the other two. "Let's haul the rope back and then get started on making the flail arms... or whatever they're called."

Cole and Rose nodded, and the group quickly rolled up the rope. Madison was just happy no spiders came along with it. Once they had the rope, it was her turn to climb the tree and mark the spot on the tree based on the length of the rope.

She'd volunteered, but Madison didn't really care for climbing trees. This was especially true of the one they'd chosen. It was the closest to the spider area, but it seemed to have fewer handholds than the trees around it. Still, if she fell, at least she had wings to allow her to glide down. The other two had nothing to break their fall.

Madison carried the rope with her, tucked into the belt at her waist. Her end was tied to a second rope, which was also tucked into her belt along with the remaining strands of rope they could find in the gnoll area.

Cole was at the bottom, watching for the mark. As soon as he saw it, her brother yelled up to her. "Right about there!"

Hanging onto the tree with one hand, she carefully pulled out the charcoal and marked a thick line across the trunk. Next, she took the ropes she'd tied together and slipped them over a thick branch. She let the other end drop to the ground. With any luck, they'd be able to use it like a winch to hoist the thick logs up.

"Rope secure!" Madison yelled down. "Give it a try!"

She saw and heard the rope being pulled by her brother and watched it zip along the branch. "It's working!"

"Awesome!" Cole yelled. "Tie off the other ropes while Rose and I chop logs! Once we're done, we'll tie it onto the winch and haul it up to you."

"Ok!" she yelled down. Anchoring herself between two branches, she used a smaller length of rope and wrapped it around the tree trunk and then around herself. She tied it off, securing herself against the tree.

After testing the rope several times, she began tying off the ropes that would be used to hold the logs. By the time Michael and Buddy finally joined them, they already had three sharpened logs attached to the tree.

53

An hour later, Madison's group had eight of the sharpened logs tied securely to the tree at alternating heights above the line she marked.

After the first three, they'd realized that the branches around the area might interfere with the logs. Once they had all of the logs tied onto the tree, Madison had cut all of the branches above her mark for a good ten feet. Now there was a conspicuous bald spot on the tree where all the ropes were tied.

In theory, the tree should fall, and the logs would swing down and into the pit, taking out much of the webbing and possibly even killing the spider queen herself. Of course, they couldn't count on that happening. At the very least, they hoped the attack would draw the matriarch out of the pit and into the open where they had a chance.

Madison returned to the ground with the others, and they all looked up at their handiwork.

"Think it'll work?" Rose asked skeptically.

"It'll work," Michael assured her. He smacked his fist into his open hand twice. "Bam! Bam! Dead spider queen!"

"What if it doesn't work? What if we have to fight it?" Rose looked around at the group. "It kicked our butt last time."

"We'll be out of the webs," Madison reminded her cousin. "This time we can actually fight back."

Rose frowned. "That poison paralyzed us instantly."

"But you can cure poison," Cole countered. "So, I will tank it, you heal and cure me while the rest of us beat it down."

"And that'll work?" Rose asked.

Cole shrugged.

"What about our special abilities?" Madison asked. "If this is a boss. We should use everything we have. My lightning and Rose's...uh... kitten swarm."

"Kitten swarm!" Michael chuckled.

Rose glared at him but nodded. "I can do that. It's only usable once a day, but Madison is right. We should use it."

Cole smacked his head. "I had forgotten about those. Yes. Use them. I'd say use them as soon as the spider queen attacks - or better yet, before she attacks. Between your two special abilities, we might be able to take her down before she even gets into combat."

Rose and Madison both nodded. Madison remembered how effective her lightning had been against the last boss. She could only hope it would do as much damage to the spider matriarch.

"Okay," her brother told the group. "We lure it back

here, I tank it and then we beat it down as quickly as possible. If Rose has to heal and cure, I have no idea how long her mana will hold out. We need to burn this down as quickly as possible."

"Don't forget," Madison reminded her brother. "I can stun it."

"Wait." Cole blinked. "Your stun worked on the boss? You're sure?!"

Madison smacked her scaly head with her palm. With the death sickness after respawn, she'd completely forgotten to tell the group she was able to stun the spider matriarch. "Yes. I stunned it many times until my mana got low. Then it killed me."

"Well, that changes things a bit!" Michael said. "Maybe we actually have a chance!"

Her brother nodded. "Oh yeah. If you can keep it stunned, that's less damage she can do to me."

"Right, keep stunning it," Madison affirmed. "Got it."

"Sounds like we have a plan!" Michael said with a grin. "Time to kick some spider butt!"

The group nodded in agreement.

"Good," Cole said with a grin. He looked up at their tree flail. "Let's chop down a tree!"

"TIMBER!" Michael yelled as a loud groan and crack filled the air and the tree started to fall over.

The boys had very carefully cut away at the side facing the pit so that the tree began to fall precisely where they wanted it. Madison watched from the side as the tree fell.

It crashed through the webbed area and hit the ground with a crash.

At the last second, they'd lost sight of the tree and couldn't tell whether or not the flail branches had actually hit the pit. Then the messages began coming in.

Forest Spider is crushed for 133 damage.
Forest Spider dies.
Forest Spider is crushed for 141 damage.
Forest Spider dies.
Forest Spider is crushed for 138 damage.
Forest Spider dies.
Forest Spider is crushed for 131 damage.
Forest Spider dies.
Forest Spider is crushed for 136 damage.
Forest Spider dies.
Forest Spider is crushed for 141 damage.
Forest Spider dies.
Forest Spider is crushed for 142 damage.
Forest Spider dies.
Forest Spider is crushed for 137 damage.
Forest Spider dies.
Forest Spider Matriarch is crushed for 63 damage.
Forest Spider Matriarch is pierced for 42 damage.
Forest Spider Matriarch is crushed for 51 damage.
Forest Spider Matriarch is pierced for 39 damage.
Forest Spider Matriarch is crushed for 58 damage.
Forest Spider Matriarch is pierced for 41 damage.

"Woohoo!" Michael yelled, throwing his hands in the air. "We got her good! It's gonna be a piece of..."

Her cousin trailed off as he saw a sea of spiders pouring out of the spider nest. They were headed directly for her group.

"Um... spiders!" Michael pointed and yelled. "Spiders!"

Cole swore. "I didn't think they'd leave the nest!"

Madison looked out at the hundred or more spiders that were quickly closing on the group. She spun towards her brother. "What do we do?!"

"I... ah..." he started and then shook his head and cursed. "I think we may need to fall back."

"I know what to do." Rose stepped out in front of the group. She raised her hands and called out in a loud voice, "KITTEN SWARM!"

And nothing happened.

A second ticked by and then another. Rose looked back at the group, confusion etched in her features. "Why didn't it..."

"Meow!" came a small, high-pitched sound from behind them.

Madison turned to see a small black and white tuxedo kitten appear between some plants. It looked at the group. "Meow!"

Then another meow sounded to the left and a calico kitten appeared. Then a tabby. Then more kittens. Meowing, the kittens rushed forward. More and more seemed to appear from behind trees or beneath plants. The kittens continued to appear and rush at the spiders.

When the swarm of kittens reached the spiders, they hissed and pounced on the eight-legged creatures, biting and clawing. More and more kittens appeared, running past the stunned group and attacking the spiders.

As many spiders as there were, there seemed to be more kittens. And these weren't ordinary kittens. They fought fiercely, clawing at the spiders' eyes and pouncing on their backs where the spiders couldn't reach them. Some of the cats somehow flipped over the spiders and attacked their soft underbellies with claws and teeth.

Madison and the other watched open mouthed as the cute, adorable kittens tore the spiders to shreds. It was surreal and, if Madison had to admit it, a bit frightening. Who knew kittens could be so vicious!

In minutes, the spiders had been routed and the kittens broke off and darted back into the forest, where they disappeared.

Everyone was quiet as they surveyed the field of dead spider bodies.

"Kitten swarm rocks!" Michael shouted suddenly.

"That was crazy!" Madison admitted.

Cole shook his head. "I have to admit, I was not expecting that."

"It was so cool!" Rose grinned broadly. "And did you see all the kittens!"

Madison smiled at her cousin. "That was more kittens than I've ever seen at one time!"

Michael screwed up his face. "That ability seems really OP."

"OP?" Rose frowned.

"Overpowered," Michael explained. "I mean. Look at what it did."

"It might be more effective against a lot of smaller

foes," Cole theorized. "I wonder how much damage it would do against a larger opponent."

Michael shrugged. "I guess we won't find out now. We can't use it on the boss. It's on cooldown for 24 hours, right?"

Rose frowned again and nodded. "Sorry, I just thought..."

"No, Rose," Madison told her cousin. "You did the right thing. I'm not sure we would have survived a fight with all of those spiders."

"Yes," Cole agreed. "That was quick thinking."

Rose beamed and opened her mouth to say something else but stopped at the sound of tree branches snapping.

The group turned towards the sound, somewhere inside the webbed area. They watched silently as more cracking sounds followed and then silence.

"I got a bad feeling about this," Michael muttered.

The spider matriarch silently climbed over the tree and into the gap the tree had created. The queen paused, seeming to look over the field of her dead children. Madison could swear the matriarch was glaring at them.

"Uh-oh," Madison breathed. "I think mommy's angry."

Then the spider matriarch charged forward.

54

The group reacted quickly. Cole rushed forward carrying his two-handed sword. Rose raced after him, ready to heal him. Michael, already mounted on Buddy, urged the big cat forward as he brought out his two striking sticks. Madison hesitated for just a moment before rushing forward as well.

The spider matriarch reached Cole and seemed intent on barreling him over with her greater size. That is, until Cole brought his two-handed sword down on what Madison thought of as the spider's face.

Brothar Snowbear slashes Forest Spider Matriarch for 23 damage.

The giant spider rocked to a stop, scrambling back from the fierce blow.

"Come on, eight-legged freak!" Cole taunted. "Fight me!"

At the same time, Michael and Buddy raced around the large spider, landing a few blows on her rear abdomen.

Zachatolus Catfriend crushes Forest Spider Matriarch for 6 damage.

Buddy snapped at one of the matriarch's legs but didn't seem to be able to penetrate the hard carapace.

The giant spider recovered quickly and darted forward just as Madison reached them. "Eyes shut!"

She then cast Color Blast, filling her vision with intense, multicolored swirls of color.

You cast Color Blast.
Forest Spider Matriarch is stunned.

Cole and Michael both took the opportunity to attack her again, stepping in closer to get all of their attacks in.

Brothar Snowbear slashes Forest Spider Matriarch for 21 damage.
Brothar Snowbear slams Forest Spider Matriarch for 9 damage.
Brothar Snowbear bashes Forest Spider Matriarch for 8 damage.
Zachatolus Catfriend crushes Forest Spider Matriarch for 7 damage.
Zachatolus Catfriend kicks Forest Spider Matriarch for 6 damage.

Like before, the stun didn't last long and the matriarch shuddered and then launched herself forward, biting at Cole.

Forest Spider Matriarch bites Brothar Snowbear for 2 damage.
Sentinel Plate Armor absorbs 5 damage.
Sword is my Shield absorbs 5 damage.
Brothar Snowbear is poisoned.

Her brother went stiff, his muscles seeming unable to respond. He didn't even seem to be able to talk.

"Cole!" Madison yelled, but Rose was already casting her spell.

Plays-With-Animals cast Cure Poison on Brothar Snowbear.
Brothar Snowbear is no longer poisoned.

The queen moved in on Cole. Remembering their last encounter, Madison guessed the queen was about to cocoon her brother. Luckily, he was no longer paralyzed.

Brothar Snowbear slashes Forest Spider Matriarch for 23 damage.

The giant spider flinched away from the strike to her head. She seemed momentarily confused as to why her prey was still fighting.

Before the queen could try and attack her brother again, Madison stepped closer.

"Eyes shut!" she warned the group and then cast Color Blast.

You cast Color Blast.
Forest Spider Matriarch is stunned.

Once again, the spider was dazed and the group moved in to attack.

Brothar Snowbear slashes Forest Spider Matriarch for 24 damage.
Brothar Snowbear slams Forest Spider Matriarch for 7 damage.
Brothar Snowbear bashes Forest Spider Matriarch for 7 damage.
Zachatolus Catfriend crushes Forest Spider Matriarch for 6 damage.
Zachatolus Catfriend kicks Forest Spider Matriarch for 7 damage.

"Keep pounding it!" Cole yelled.

Brothar Snowbear slashes Forest Spider Matriarch for 22 damage.
Forest Spider Matriarch has become enraged.
Forest Spider Matriarch is healed.

The giant spider's eyes glowed red as the stun wore off; she spun towards Madison. Ignoring her brother, the queen came directly after her.

"I think we activated some sort of special ability!"

Michael yelled as he and Buddy bounded after the spider. "The stupid spider healed up!"

"Fight me!" Cole taunted and made an obscene gesture at the matriarch. Ignoring the taunt, the spider queen continued towards Madison.

Seeing the spider getting closer, Madison began to desperately backpedal, trying to stay away from her. She realized she would need to stun the queen and use the time to get away. "Eyes shut!"

You cast Color Blast.
Forest Spider Matriarch is immune to stun.

Madison blinked as she read the message. She was immune to stun?! Since when? She screamed as the enormous spider bore down on her. The queen halted less than a foot from her, mandibles snapping and dripping a foul, green liquid.

"Get over here!" Cole yelled, muscles bulging.

Looking past the spider, which stopped in confusion, Madison saw that Cole had thrown his two-handed sword into the spider's rear abdomen and was using his Sword Chain ability to hold it at bay.

The spider seemed to decide something and then tried going for Madison again like she had some single-minded vendetta against her. The spider's eight legs tried to propel Madison forward and she moved slightly. Madison saw her brother's huge arms bulging as he groaned and held onto the chain attached to his sword, trying to pull the spider back - or at least keep her from getting to his sister.

"Can't... pull... it... back!" Cole grunted. "Can barely... keep it... from moving... forward!"

Michael swooped in on Buddy and held out a hand. Grabbing Madison, he pulled her onto Buddy's back behind him and moved off before coming to a stop.

"Michael Dash pick-up service!" He grinned and motioned for her to hop off. "That'll be 20 gold pieces for the fare! But we always deliver in 20 minutes or it's free!"

Not waiting for her response, Michael tapped Buddy with his heels and the two of them sped towards the spider.

The Forest Spider Matriarch was still staring murderously at Madison, trying to get to her. Little by little, the spider's larger size and eight legs working together, was dragging her brother along.

"It... must... fixate... on... a random... target," Cole spat. "Can't... taunt... it... off!"

Madison realized this might be a good time to use her lightning breath. She stepped forward and opened her mouth but then saw her brother was in the way. She couldn't risk hitting him with it. Growling with frustration, she tried to think of what else she could do. Then she remembered her other spells.

You cast Minor Telekinetic Asphyxiation.
Telekinetic Asphyxiation hits Forest Spider Matriarch.
Forest Spider Matriarch chokes for 5 damage.

It wasn't much but at least she was doing something while Cole held the thing back, Michael dodged in and hit the thing and even Rose had moved in and was slicing at the spider's abdomen with her scimitar.

The spider stalwartly ignored all of those attacks. Her attention and focus was solely on Madison. Cole continued to hold her off, but in doing so, wasn't able to attack. That left it up to the rest of them.

Michael, Rose and Madison continued to attack the spider for what seemed like a half hour but was really probably only a few minutes. Finally, Madison saw a new message.

Forest Spider Matriarch's rage has ended.

The red glow from the creature's eyes faded and she seemed to be momentarily confused. Then Cole yanked her backwards.

The matriarch skidded backwards several feet before she managed to catch herself with her eight legs. She then spun around, jerking her brother off balance. He managed to catch himself before he fell and with a flick of his wrist, his sword pulled free of the spider and came flying back to his hand.

"Come here, fly-eater!" Cole yelled and the spider hurried over to him.

As she did, Madison ran to the side and, making sure no one was on the opposite side of the spider matriarch, she let loose with her lightning breath.

You use Ancestral Breath Weapon: Lightning.
You critically electrocute Forest Spider Matriarch for 207 damage.

Her vision went white with the intensity of the lightning blast, but she thought she saw the spider's legs twitching and dancing. She blinked several times to clear her vision but then saw that the spider was still alive.

"Whoa!" Rose exclaimed. "It barely even seemed to faze it! It's still attacking!"

Michael pulled Buddy to a halt, his face a mask of frustration. "How much health does this thing have?!"

"It healed, remember!" Rose shot back.

"Stupid spiders and their stupid healing!" Michael growled. He took another swipe at the spider queen.

"Then we keep attacking it!" Cole yelled.

Madison tried to hide her disappointment. She had been really hoping that, like the gnoll boss, her lightning bolt would kill the spider. It didn't and now she couldn't use it for a full day. She ground her teeth in frustration.

After a moment, she joined the others and continued to attack the giant spider.

55

They began attacking the spider again, alternating between stuns, heals and damaging it. Still, the spider matriarch fought on. She seemed to have endless health and stamina, while their stats - especially her Mana, seemed to be getting lower and lower.

Just when they thought they were making headway, the spider became enraged again. And once more, she healed herself.

Madison noticed that not all the wounds healed, but enough healed that they all let out groans.

The spider spun around, eyes red, as she scrambled after Michael. Before she had even taken a few steps, Cole's two-handed sword buried itself into her rear. Her brother's muscles bulged as once again he strained to hold the thing back.

"I'm really low on mana," Rose said with concern.

Madison checked her own Mana. "Me too."

"I think we're all low," Michael growled. He was evidently frustrated, and possibly a bit worried as well. He didn't even try to make a joke. "I'm not sure we can take this thing."

"We can't give up now," Madison told them.

"Madison... is... right," Cole grunted. "Have to... see... how far... we can... get it down."

Michael tried to circle around to attack, but the spider mirrored his every movement. Cole yelled. "Don't... move! I can... barely... hold her... back!"

As if to emphasize his point, the spider pulled her brother another foot.

"So, I can't even attack!" Obviously frustrated, Michael threw his arms up. He looked from Madison to Rose. "It's up to you girls."

Rose had already moved up and was slicing at the spider's rear with her scimitar, leaving small bloody lines but not seeming to cause any real damage.

Madison cast her choking spell again, but her damage was pitiful too.

Forest Spider Matriarch chokes for 5 damage.

They just weren't doing enough damage. They needed to do more damage, more quickly. But how?

She thought about her other spells but other than her choking spell, none of the others did direct damage. Madison brought up her spell list.

Spells:
Minor Force Shield

Minor Telekinetic Asphyxiation
Animated Guardian
Color Blast
Daydream
Siphon Energy
Minor Gateway

Unfortunately, as far as direct damage spells went, the Minor Telekinetic Asphyxiation was it. Of course, if she still had a shield and sword, Madison could summon her Animated Guardian. Unfortunately, the extra shield was with her old body - somewhere in the pit. And that was if it hadn't been destroyed by the falling tree and the flailing logs.

Madison looked at Cole. He wasn't using his shield now that he had that new ability to use his two-handed sword as a shield. Did he still have a shield on him? If so, she could summon an Animated Guardian and at least do a bit more damage.

She skirted around the spider and stopped next to her brother. He was red-faced, hanging onto the cord that went from his gauntlet to the sword stuck in the spider.

Looking at the entire scene logically, Madison doubted such a feat would have worked in real life. Either the cord would snap, or the sword would pull out of the spider. Or her brother's arms would be yanked out of their sockets. But then again, this wasn't real life.

"Do you still have a shield?" she asked her brother.

Grimacing with the effort of holding back the giant spider, Cole flicked his eyes in her direction. "What?!"

"Do you still have a shield?" Madison repeated.

Cole, his face screwed up from the effort, nodded curtly. "One... sec... gotta...open... inventory."

A moment later, a shield dropped onto the ground next to him.

"Thanks!" she told her brother and received a grunt in return.

She looked at her inventory but realized she had no one-handed weapon to use either. It was with her body too. Madison turned to Rose. Her cousin continued to slice at the back of the spider. "Rose! Do you have an extra weapon?"

Rose looked back. "No! Just this."

Madison growled in frustration and then ran around the side of the spider where she could see Michael. "Michael, do you have an extra weapon?"

"Why?" he yelled back.

"I want to summon my guardian, and have it attack too!" she told him.

"Oh," he responded and looked at his two striking sticks. He bit his lip for a moment but then brightened. "Hey... just use one of the axes we used to chop down the tree. That would work."

Madison nodded. "The tree! Right!"

Turning around, she saw the stump of the tree they'd just recently cut down. The same one that they'd used as the "tree flail" and lured the spider matriarch out of the pit.

She cocked her head, looking at the other nearby trees. Madison looked back at the spider, then at the trees, then back at the spider. She smiled as an idea suddenly formed. "The tree! Right!"

Running over to the stump, she grabbed the axe and tossed it and the shield on the ground. Bringing up her HUD, she cast her Animated Guardian spell on the items.

In a burst of magical sparkles, the shield and axe rose in the air, arranging themselves roughly at chest level. The guardian stood there, unmoving.

Madison looked over at the trees and then back to the spider, lining up the angle. She gestured at the guardian. “Follow me.”

Leading the Animated Guardian to her chosen tree, she took out the charcoal she’d used earlier. Madison looked back at the spider and then made a mark. She turned to the Guardian. “Chop here. And keep chopping.”

Without hesitation, the Animated Guardian began chopping.

“What are you doing?!” Rose yelled.

“I’m about to give the spider a really big headache!” Madison yelled back.

From her vantage point, Madison saw the spider matriarch suddenly stop straining on the rope. Instead, she turned and scrambled back towards Cole.

Madison cursed. The spider was out of position. If the tree fell where she had planned, it would miss the matriarch completely.

Glancing back at the tree, she could see the Animated Guardian was making good progress with the chopping. It would only be a matter of minutes before the tree collapsed. She needed to get the spider back in position before the tree fell.

“Keep chopping!” she ordered and then spun and ran back to the clearing with the rest of the group.

Reaching the clearing, she lined up the tree trajectory. Once she knew where it would land, she used her heel to put an “X” on the ground. “Cole! Bring it over here!”

Cole screwed up his face. “What?!”

“My guardian is cutting down a tree! Bring her right here!” she yelled back.

Her brother went rigid as one of the spider’s bites paralyzed him but then shuddered as Rose cured him. Nodding, Cole began side-stepping towards her while batting away the spider matriarch with slashes, slams and bashes.

He got paralyzed three more times before he had the spider on the “X” she’d marked. The group heard a crack and the tree shuddered.

“Keep it there!” Madison said.

“I’m also out of Mana!” Rose shouted.

As if on cue, the spider got a bite through on her brother and he went rigid. Rose cured him almost instantly but then frowned. “I’m out! I’m out of mana!”

Another crack sounded and the tree shuddered again. Madison knew it would only be a matter of seconds. But did they have seconds?

The spider struck again and her brother went rigid. This time, no curing magic came.

“I can’t do anything,” Rose cried, nearly in tears. “I’m out! I’m out!”

With Cole unmoving, the spider moved forward and grabbed him. Madison knew what happened next. She would cocoon him.

Uttering something very unladylike, Madison ran forward to stand next to her brother. “Eyes shut!”

You cast Color Blast.
Forest Spider Matriarch is stunned.

The spider stopped what it was doing, and Madison grabbed her brother and tossed him to the side. "Grab Cole! Drag him away! Hurry!"

Rose nodded and grabbed his arm. She pulled but her brother's larger, armor-clad frame didn't move. Her cousin looked up at her. "He's too heavy! He won't budge!"

Michael came racing in and jumped off of Buddy. Without a word, he reached down and grabbed Cole's other arm. "Come on! Pull!"

They began to move him just as a huge cracking sound thundered through the area. She heard the tell-tale sound of the tree starting to fall and didn't have to look back to know it was coming.

No longer stunned, the spider began to swivel towards her when she could have sworn all eight of her eyes went wide. She sensed the danger and began to turn.

"Oh no you don't!" Madison yelled at her and cast her last stun.

You cast Color Blast.
Forest Spider Matriarch is stunned.

Knowing she had only seconds, Madison started to turn and leap out of the way. As she did, she saw it was too late. The tree was literally right on top of her. She shut her eyes, waiting for the tree to smash her into a pulp.

And then it hit her and she went sprawling across the ground.

Forest Spider Matriarch is critically crushed for 563 damage.
Forest Spider Matriarch dies.
You have gained experience!

Not quite understanding why she wasn't dead, Madison opened up her eyes. Above her, Buddy's big, feline head stared down at her. The cat cocked his head and then licked her face.

"Stop it!" She laughed at the cat, who only licked her more.

In between licks, she saw the twitching legs of the spider sticking out from under the massive tree. She smiled. They'd done it! They'd killed the spider!

56

After managing to get Buddy off her, Madison checked her log. They had a new message that they'd received a reward for being the first ones to kill the Forest Spider Matriarch. Good. That meant more money. That would certainly make Rose happy.

Now that combat was over, their stats began to regenerate, and Rose was able to cure Cole just before he died of the poison. Another minute, and he would have been walking back to them from the village.

"You know"—Michael smirked—"I honestly didn't think we'd do it."

Rose's face went red. "I thought you were all gung-ho on the plan!"

Michael shrugged. "Well, I thought we had a chance."

"Technically, I think it was my plan..." Cole tried but Rose wasn't listening to him.

"If Madison wouldn't have brought the tree down on it..." Rose retorted but Madison cut her off.

"At least we made some money," Madison interjected, trying to take Rose's mind off her anger at Michael. After all, it was just Michael being Michael. "I wonder how much?"

Rose stopped in mid-sentence and looked at Madison. Her face brightened. "We did?"

"Check your log," Madison told her.

Her cousin went glassy eyed as she looked through her HUD. Then her eyes went wide. "Guys! That boss was worth 5,000 Koyesta coins! That's $500!"

Madison blinked and the boys exchanged looks. Michael whistled. "Wow... that's like... uh... $125 each, right?"

Rose nodded, a huge grin on her face. "Sweet! At this rate, I won't have to work at all."

The group took a moment to revel in the money they'd just made. Madison had to admit, the money was nice. It would certainly help. But she was anxious to find out what it was that the spider was guarding.

After all, the goddess herself - or one of the goddesses in this game - had told her there was something past the spider. Something important. But what?

"We should go check out the pit," she announced, getting everyone's attention. "Remember, that goddess said there was something beyond the spider."

"Maybe it's ON the spider," Cole suggested. "We haven't checked it for loot yet."

Michael gestured at the legs sticking out from under the tree. He grinned. "Maybe it dropped pancakes? Spider pancakes."

Rose pouted. "You think the loot was crushed?"

"That's usually not the way it works," Cole replied, looking at the spider legs sticking out from under the tree. "But let's go find out."

The others agreed and they all walked over to the spider matriarch's flattened body. Cole turned to the group and smiled. He held up crossed fingers. "Moment of truth."

Brothar Snowbear loots Giant Spider Venom Sac (x4).
Brothar Snowbear loots Giant Spider Carapace (x8).

"That's it?" Rose asked with a frown.

"Well, it is a spider," Michael said with a shrug. "We can't expect it to have weapons and armor. And personally, I would hate to meet an armored spider who could wield weapons."

Her brother nodded. "He has a point. The monsters seem to drop loot specific to them. That means no weapons, gold or other refined goods on an insect or animal."

Rose didn't bother to show her disappointment. "But the spider queen was really tough!"

Cole looked as if he was about to respond but Madison spoke before he had the chance. "Maybe there's loot in the pit. I mean, there's SOMETHING after the spider. That's what the goddess said. Maybe there's treasure too. Or maybe what's waiting is something important AND treasure."

Her cousin brightened. "You think so?"

Madison shrugged. "We won't know until we go look."

"Then what are we waiting for?" Rose asked, turning towards the pit.

"Uh, do we even have any rope left to climb into the pit?" Michael asked.

They all exchanged glances until Madison remembered. "The rope we used as a winch. It's still intact. Plus, it's extra-long!"

"Right!" Cole agreed. "That should work!"

They retraced their steps back to the stump of the "tree flail" and found the rope they'd used to haul the logs up to the correct spot on the tree. Then they made their way through the webbed area to the edge of the pit.

As they reached it, her Animated Guardian glided behind her. She blinked. She'd forgotten about it. She smiled. "Good job, guardian."

The construct did not reply and made no acknowledgement that it had heard or understood her. She shrugged and turned back to the pit.

Madison looked over the ledge to where the pit disappeared into darkness. The fallen trunk of their "flail tree" now lay over the pit, with over a half dozen ropes hanging down into the pit. She nodded her head. "We actually calculated that out really well. All of the logs went into the pit."

"Hero's a strong word," Michael said, putting his hands on his hips and striking a superhero pose. "But you know what they say about, when the shoe fits..."

Rose rolled her eyes.

"Hey," Michael said, feigning hurt. "Buddy and I gave our lives for those measurements. If that's not a hero, I don't know what is."

"You're right," Rose shot back, and Michael grinned. "Buddy is a hero."

"Hey… what about me?!" he retorted.

"Focus, people!" Madison said, gesturing at the pit. "Pit. Treasure. Something special. All at the bottom!"

"Right, treasure!" Michael and Rose said at the same time.

"And our corpses and other gear," Cole added.

"That too," Michael said with a nod. "Well then, let's get to it."

Her brother stepped up to the side of the pit, carrying the rope. He looped it over the fallen tree and tied it. He yanked hard on the rope several times before letting it drop into the darkness. Cole looked up. "Who wants to go first."

"I volunteer Cole!" Michael said with a grin. Then his grin slipped, and he glanced down at Buddy. "Wait. How do we get Buddy down?"

Madison gave him an apologetic look. "I don't think we can. He'll have to stay up here."

Michael frowned. "But…"

"Sorry, Michael," Cole said, slapping him on the shoulder. "She's right. Buddy can't go down the rope and there's no other way to get down there."

Michael dropped down and threw his arms around the big cat. "Sorry, Buddy, you have to stay up here."

The cat cocked his head, stared at Michael and then licked his face. Her cousin laughed. "Maybe that was a yes."

Madison was getting more and more anxious about

figuring out what lay below. She let out a heavy sigh. "I'll go first."

Not wasting anymore time, Madison grabbed the rope with both hands and flung herself into the pit. She looked up at the rest of her group. "At least if I fall, I can glide down with my wings."

Not waiting for a response, Madison looked down and began to lower herself into the pit. She saw that the Animated Guardian started to follow her, coming dangerously close to the edge of the pit.

"Stay!" she commanded, and the Guardian stopped.

Letting out a sigh, she began lowering herself again. She only got a few feet before she heard Cole's voice above her. "We'll have to wait until you get all the way to the bottom."

"Why?" she looked up and asked her brother.

"The ropes are tied together, remember," he responded. "I don't know if I trust the knot to hold two people at once. We're heavier than those logs were. Just go down and then jerk on the rope three times when you're clear."

Madison looked down again. Suddenly, the idea that she would be alone at the bottom until someone made it all the way down the rope, didn't sit well with her. She bit her lip. Maybe Cole should go down first. After all, he was the better fighter.

She had a short internal debate, but her curiosity got the best of her. She really needed to know what lay down at the bottom. Madison looked down into the looming darkness below her. She let out a heavy sigh.

"Everything okay?" Cole asked from above her.

Madison looked up and smiled. "Everything's fine."

Looking back down, Madison began lowering herself into the darkness.

57

Madison's reptilian eyes were able to make out details, even in the semi-darkness. Hand over hand, she slowly descended the rope. She wasn't an architect, but as she went lower, she began to get a better idea of what had happened.

The walls were still mostly intact, and it became obvious that the "pit" had actually been a two-story room. Either that, or a room with a very high ceiling - twice as high as any other room they'd searched. Madison wondered if that large, open space was the reason the room had collapsed.

The pit smelled of decay and mold and the further down she went, the more pronounced it became. Glancing around, she saw that water ran down the walls. Not a lot, but enough to keep them moist and obviously enough to wet the webs. That dampness had been the reason they hadn't burned with the other webbing.

The moisture was most likely the reason the place

stank of mold too. Madison made a face as she got a fresh whiff of the moldy smell and she tried not to gag. She tried to keep her tongue inside her mouth so she wouldn't smell it, but that proved more difficult than she thought. She finally gave up and just kept lowering herself.

Their "tree flail" had done its job well. The first twenty feet was clear of nearly all spider webs. Unfortunately, that was where the tree flail's effectiveness ended. Madison paused as she looked down into a tangled mess of spiderwebs.

"There's more webs down here!" she yelled up.

"Any more big spiders?" Rose shouted back down.

Madison made a face, letting her eyes roam the darkness. She hadn't even considered that there might be another large spider down here. She bit her lip. Weren't they solitary creatures? Did the female kill the male or something after they mated? The last thing they needed was another boss fight!

After nearly a minute of staring beneath her and seeing nothing moving, she gave up. "I don't see anything!"

"Keep going then!" Cole told her. "Yank three times when you get to the bottom."

Letting out a frustrated breath, Madison took one last look around, looking for any sign of another big spider. There was nothing. She began lowering herself once more but stopped just as she reached the webs.

She remembered how they'd all become stuck in the webs. Those webs were incredibly strong - and sticky. Madison frowned as she looked down at the tangled strands of webs. There was no path wide enough for her to fit through and she had no desire to get stuck again.

"The webs are too thick!" she shouted up to her group.

"Can you cut them?" Cole yelled back.

"Or burn them!" Michael added.

"No!" she answered. "Nothing to cut them with."

It was true. The only bladed weapon she carried was usually a sword for her guardian. The Animated Guardian! Madison furrowed her brow and looked up. She could just make out the shield of her Guardian at the edge of the pit, still following her last order to wait.

The Animated Guardian still had the axe it had used to cut down the tree. If she could get that, she could possibly use it to cut the webbing. Madison cocked her head. Why should she cut it? After all, she had an animated construct with an axe.

Madison knew the distance was right around twenty feet. Even a human could survive a fall from twenty feet. They might break an ankle or leg, but they could survive. The real question was, could the construct survive a fall from that height? There was only one way to find out.

"Come!" she told the construct and it immediately glided forward. And then it fell straight down.

The construct fell to the beginning of the webs and then stopped abruptly. She saw a message flash in her HUD.

Animated Guardian falls for 23 damage.

The construct had taken damage, but it was still functioning! It hovered just above the webs. Swiveling, it faced

Madison and then glided over one of the thicker web strands. It stopped below her and hovered in place.

"What are you doing?" Cole yelled.

Madison smiled. "I'm going to see if the animated guardian can cut a path through the webs."

"Oh," Cole retorted. "You think that will work?"

"Only one way to find out!" she shouted. Madison looked down at the construct and pointed beneath it. "Cut a path through the webs beneath you."

Without hesitation, the Animated Guardian began chopping at the webs with its ax. The thing went about its task with mechanical efficiency. In less than a minute, it had dropped down a few feet to strands beneath it. Still, it continued to hack.

"It's working!" she yelled up to Cole.

"Cool! Let us know when you're at the bottom!" he shouted back.

Madison began lowering herself after the Animated Guardian as it cut a path through the webbing. The construct was efficient, wasting no energy on extra strokes or pausing to rest. Within ten minutes, it had cut a path another thirty feet to the bottom of the room.

The last ten feet were completely clear of webs. Rubble of what had once been the ceiling, littered the ground, making it extremely uneven.

Along with remnants of the ceiling, were bones of all sizes. And that wasn't all. The walls of the area were dotted with cocoons of all sizes. That included several newer-looking cocoons that were suspiciously around the size of her group members.

Shuddering in revulsion, Madison finished the last

few feet of her climb and then stepped onto the floor. Small bones crunched under her feet, making her shudder again. She needed to find whatever treasure was down here, but she didn't want to spend any more time here than necessary.

She looked up. From her vantage point, she only saw the light from the opening. She couldn't make out any details.

Grabbing the rope in her hand, she gave it three yanks. "I'm down!"

Madison saw someone else, possibly Michael, get onto the rope and begin to shimmy down. She held the rope to make it easier for him to climb down. After a moment, she could see that it was her cousin.

Michael dropped down next to her, more bones crunching under his feet. He grinned at her. "Piece of cake. Don't know what took YOU so long."

"Just be glad the guardian could do the chopping, or it might have been hours!" Madison rolled her eyes at Michael.

She gave the rope three more tugs, signaling the next person to come down. Rose came down next, followed by her brother. Once all four of them were down, the group surveyed the area.

"Charming," Rose said, screwing up her face in disgust.

Cole pointed to the newer cocoons. "Our old bodies have to be in these. Let's cut them open and get our stuff, then we can search for whatever treasure is down here."

They began cutting the cocoons open and they each found their old body. Madison found it a bit disconcerting to look into her own dead face but as soon as she clicked to loot the body, her old equipment showed up in her inventory and the body dissolved into sparkles.

Madison re-equipped her better gear. When she was done, she turned to see that the others had done the same. Cole and Michael had even lit torches so they could see better in the dim light.

She looked at the now-empty cocoons. Like her body, all of their bodies had disappeared after they were looted, leaving hollow shells in their place.

"Okay, we have our stuff," Rose said. She scanned the area and frowned. "Uh, where's the treasure?"

Everyone in the group looked around the room and its uneven floor. Michael shrugged. "So much for the days when there was a nice big, shiny chest waiting for you to loot."

Cole nodded grimly. "I don't think this is that sort of game. If there's treasure down here, it must be buried."

Michael groaned. "So, we have to dig for it?"

"Let's start searching!" Rose said and climbed over a large pile of nearby rubble to look behind it.

Cole chuckled. "You heard her. Let's start searching."

The group had just started to move in different directions when they heard Rose's voice. "Don't bother. I think I found it."

Michael's head snapped in her direction. "What is it?!"

Rose was quiet for a moment before poking her head around the rubble and waving them over. "You'd better see it for yourself."

58

Madison and the others followed Rose behind the rubble to where a doorway was partially blocked by a large section of collapsed ceiling. Luckily, there was enough room for them to crawl through.

"You think the treasure is in there?" Michael asked skeptically.

Rose shrugged. "Did any of you find anything else?"

"No," Cole replied. "But we really haven't looked very hard."

"We should check it out," Madison suggested. "The goddess did say that something important lies PAST the spider. Maybe it's through the doorway. Besides, we can always come back and search."

"Fine," Cole agreed reluctantly. "But let me go first. Rose, you follow behind me. Michael, you bring up the rear."

Moving forward, her brother looked through the

doorway into the darkness. He held out his torch, examining the door. After several moments, he turned sideways and, with a groan, squeezed his large frame through the partially blocked doorway.

"It's clear over here," she heard Cole say from the other side. "Some sort of hallway. Come on through."

After Cole, with his large frame, made it through, the others managed without a problem. Once all of them were on the other side, her brother led them twenty feet down the hallway to another stone door.

"Be ready for anything," he said, his hand hovering near the activation panel.

The group prepared their weapons and spells and then Cole slapped the panel. The door slid open, revealing a circular room. In the middle of the room was a pedestal. A beam of light from overhead illuminated the pedestal, revealing something shiny atop it.

"Oh, shiny!" Michael said, peeking around Madison. "Is that treasure?"

"Shh!" Cole snapped, squinting into the room. "There's... shapes in the room."

Rose's eyes went wide. "Shapes? What sort of shapes?"

Moving his head from side to side, Cole craned his neck, looking at something in the room. He held out his torch, moving it from left to right and then back. "People, I think."

"People?!" Madison gasped. "Like... real people?"

Her brother turned towards the group; his brow furrowed. "I think... I think they're statues."

"Like the ones from the other room?" Rose asked.

That was right; they had found statues in one of the

rooms. Old statues of the Artoshians. Those statues and the memory orbs had made her think this had originally been some sort of museum. She still thought that was the best possibility, despite the fact that half of it had been taken over by spiders.

Cole shook his head. "No. They're... monsters. Well, some of them, at least."

"Monsters?" Michael hissed. "Are you serious? Statues of monsters? This is a classic trap. We walk in and they come to life and kill us!"

"That's a thing?" Rose asked. "Statues coming to life? Are they like angels that cry or something?"

"It's all fun and games until they come to life and kill you," Michael warned.

Rose put her hands on her hips. "I say we volunteer Michael to check it out."

Michael shook his head. "I've already been the cat's paw today! It's someone else's turn to die."

Her brother bit his lip. "I'll go in. If they do come to life, everyone retreats back through the passage. I doubt they can get through the blocked doorway."

Madison furrowed her brow. "Are you sure?"

"Someone's got to do it," Cole said with a lopsided grin. "You guys ready?"

After everyone nodded affirmatively, Cole put one foot forward into the room. The moment he did, beams of illumination appeared in a circle around the room. Bobbing her head side to side to see around Rose and Cole, Madison was able to see the statues. They weren't monsters per se, they were the other races: Ogres, Trolls, Drakkar, Gnomes, Dwarves, Reppits, and others.

From what Madison could see, they were all standing around the pedestal, looking down at it in... was that triumph?

Her brother stood perfectly still, nervously glancing around at the statues. Rose glanced between the room and the hallway, ready to bolt. Michael just stood there, leaning against the wall and looked bored. He sighed. "Did they kill you yet?"

"Shh!" Cole hissed.

"Uh... they're statues. They have no ears... well, no real ears," Michael retorted with a grin.

Cole ignored their cousin and let out a breath. "Okay... I'm going all the way into the room."

Stepping fully into the room, Cole assumed a defensive stance and looked from statue to statue. Nothing happened. He took another step in. Then another. He turned his head around and shrugged. "I guess they're not going to come alive."

"That's what they want you to THINK!" Michael said, giving them a knowing look. "But as soon as we let down our guard - WHAP!"

Curious, Madison pushed past Rose into the room. She looked around the room, taking in all of the statues. She had been right. These were the other races in the world. The races of the Valharian empire. There were even two Artoshian statues. They were in a circle, in various poses of triumph or celebration - all facing the pedestal.

Madison moved past Cole and peered around the statue of an ogre. She looked down at the large, stone pedestal. Lying in the middle of the pedestal was an odd piece of silver. It almost looked broken.

Rose came up beside her and followed her gaze to the piece of jagged silver lying in the middle of the pedestal. Her face screwed up. "Please tell me that is not the big treasure we were supposed to find. It looks like a piece of old junk."

"Wait," Cole said, pointing to the open palm of the closest statue. "Look!"

Following his finger, Madison saw what he was pointing at. The ogre statue had one hand in the air in triumph, but the other was out in front of him. The palm of the statue was open and resting inside was a familiar shape.

"A memory orb!" Madison exclaimed. She moved her gaze from statue to statue, noticing each one had been carved with one hand cupped. All of them had memory orbs.

As she was looking at the statues, she recognized the two Artoshian statues. One was of a beautiful, regal woman and the other a handsome elf. It was the Queen and her son from the other memory orb!

"They all have memory orbs," Rose said with a furrowed brow. "What does that mean?"

Remembering her brief history lesson from the sage, she thought back to his conversation. "The Artoshians and the Valharians came together to seal the breach. Maybe that's what this represents."

Michael finally moved in and glanced around the room. "So what? The silver thing represents the breach?"

Madison moved forward towards the pedestal, but Cole grabbed her wrist. “What are you doing?”

“I’m going to check out the silver thing,” she told him.

Her brother released her wrist, eyes darting to the piece of silver that seemed to be the focal point of the room. “Be careful… and don’t move it.”

“Why not?” she asked.

“Uh, didn’t you ever see that movie with the archeologist and the golden idol?” Michael said incredulously. “It’s probably sensitive to pressure changes and if you move it a giant boulder will come rolling down.”

They all turned and stared at Michael. He just shrugged. “What?! It could happen!”

“I’ll be careful,” Madison promised and moved forward. She stopped just in front of the pedestal and bent over to get a better look at the silver fragment. As she did, a message flashed in her HUD.

Amulet of Artolean, Fragment 1
Type: Artifact
Location: Neck
Skill: Any
Size: Small
Armor: 0
Quality: Mythic
Description: The Seal of Artolean was created in the 4th Age to seal the breach to the world of the Fey. The amulet is the first of seven fragments.
Power: Three times per day, this amulet can be used to cure all wounds and negative conditions.

Congratulations! You were the first group on the server to discover a Mythic item. A Reward has been added to your account.
You may check your rewards by going to Character Menu-> Profile -> Rewards -> Early Access Awards

Congratulations! You were the first group on the server to discover Amulet of Artolean, Fragment 1. A Reward has been added to your account.
You may check your rewards by going to Character Menu-> Profile -> Rewards -> Early Access Awards

Madison blinked and read the messages twice. She turned back to the group. "Did you just see those?"

Rose was glassy eyed, mouth open. Her eyes came back into focus but were wide. Her mouth moved but no words came out.

"Spit it out!' Michael said.

"I think..." she started and then swallowed. "I think we just earned 60,000 Koyesta coins! That's $6,000!"

The rest of the group just stared at her. Michael laughed. "I think you're going cross-eyed. You mean $600, right?"

Rose stuck out her tongue. "I mean $6,000! Look for yourself!"

They did just that. Madison couldn't believe it. They had gotten 10,000 Koyesta coins for finding the first mythic item on the server and another 50,000 Koyesta for finding the Amulet of Artolean.

For the first time in a while, Michael was speechless. When his eyes came back into focus, he just shook his head for a full minute. Finally, he smirked. "That can't be real."

Rose did a little happy dance. "You know what this means, right?"

The three others looked at their cousin. "What?"

"It means I don't have to get a summer job!" she said happily, continuing to do her little dance.

Madison smiled at her cousin, but her curiosity was still piqued. She had a feeling that the memory orbs would tell her something about the amulet, and maybe about the fey breach. Walking over to the Queen's outstretched hand, she took the memory orb.

As she did, she had the familiar feeling of falling and the world around her dissolved away.

59

Madison blinked and looked around. This time, the memory orb had dropped her into a large circular, stone room with high ceilings. The stone of the walls was a dark, gray granite, very unlike the smooth, white stone of the previous castle she'd seen in her other vision.

The walls themselves were decorated with long, vertical tapestries depicting scenes from epic battles. The scenes portrayed a crowned man slaying dragons, giants and other monstrosities. It looked and felt very different from the castle whose balcony she had appeared on previously. If she had to put a word to it, Madison would have said it almost had a sinister feel to it.

"This is outrageous!" boomed a deep female voice, pulling Madison's attention to the center of the chamber.

In the middle of the room was a giant, stone table occupying the middle of the chamber. Around the table were a similar crowd to what she had seen before. Some were seated in large stone chairs, while others had leapt out of their chairs and were leaning over the table shouting.

In the middle of the table was a single, glowing object. Madison recognized it as being the same shiny, silver metal as the fragment. Straining her eyes, she saw that it wasn't a fragment, it was a full amulet. The Amulet of Artolean.

"Please sit down, Gruuda," a familiar voice said. "Let us discuss this as civilized people."

Madison recognized the Artoshian queen slumped back in one of the chairs. The queen looked haggard. She had dark circles under her eyes and her previously flawless skin was pale. She looked like Madison did after several nights of staying up to study for finals.

The other creatures around the table didn't look much better. Opposite the queen was a dwarf in dull, scratched armor sitting in one of the chairs. She wore a dark eyepatch over a blood-stained bandage. Given the blood, Madison guessed she must have recently lost the eye.

To the right of the dwarf was a smaller female figure with a child-like face and oversize hands. She was dressed in dark robes lined with silver runes. From her previous vision, Madison thought this might be a gnome.

On the dwarf's other side was a halfling. Also small, he was somewhere between the size of a dwarf and the size of a gnome. He wore stained leather clothes and used a dagger to pick at his fingernails while resting large, thick feet on the table. Of all people around the table, he looked the least concerned.

Further around the table on the left was a troll, and a

re-scaled drakkar. The right side had a large frog-like creature called a reppit, an ogre and a dark-robed man.

The man was tall and slender, with a refined look. He wore jet-black robes embroidered with ivory skulls along the sleeves. He held a staff that glowed with a pale, sickly green energy. A necromancer?

The ogre, Gruuba, had been the one who had spoken. She was garbed in bloody and battleworn armor and shook a mailed fist in the air. Her thick hair had been shaved on the right side and the left side had been decorated in dreadlocks. The ogre growled and glared at the other people around the table.

The queen let out a sigh and shook her head. "I'm just pointing out that the Artoshians created it. We are the logical choices to keep it."

The necromancer chuckled. "Your enchanters may have bound the enchantment but remember that it was me who added the necessary component to make it work. Not to mention the Emperor himself gave his life activating it."

"He blundered into a bloody ambush, you mean," the dwarf growled.

"And plunged the empire into civil war," the halfling chuckled. "Who do you propose keeps it, Mordecai, you personally?"

Mordecai gave the halfling a condescending smile. "The necromancy guild can keep it safe. Surely you're not suggesting the halflings can protect it."

The halfling shook his head. "My people don't want it. It's unnatural. But we do want it safe."

"Did you forget that it was the dwarves who forged it

and provided the Mythryll?" the dwarf shouted back. "It's worth a king's ransom in the Mythryll alone! It should come back to us. It will be safe in our deep halls."

"The gnomes can keep it safe," the gnome cried out in a high-pitched voice. "We have the best clockwork vaults in the world!"

"And look how your constructs fared against the Fey, Ednedot," Mordecai sneered. "Remind me again how many of your Death-Blossom-Destroyer-Golems are left?"

The gnome replied, "That's not fair! They had..."

"Trolls should have it," the troll bellowed, interrupting the tiny gnome. "We hide it good. Fey never find."

The table erupted into pandemonium as everyone began talking or shouting at the same time. The queen sighed as the others argued and rubbed her forehead with her fingers. She sat back in her seat, suddenly looking very old, and watched the others yelling at each other.

The arguing went on for several minutes before a loud hissing interrupted the argument. The red-scaled Drakkar kept hissing, his mouth wide open. It was loud and annoying, like nails on a chalkboard, and eventually, the group fell silent.

Snapping his mouth shut, the drakkar glared around the table. "We argue like younglings. There are still Fey in the world for us to kill."

"We need to..." the necromancer started but the drakkar immediately began hissing until he was silent.

"No!" the drakkar growled. "No one people should keep this. It would be too easily plundered by the Fey who remain. No. To keep it protected, we must split it between us. Keep it from the Fey."

"Split it? Are you mad?" the dwarf snorted. "That'll break the enchantment."

"Actually," the gnome replied, rubbing her smooth chin. "It wouldn't. The way it was designed."

The group collectively turned their heads to the queen. She bit her lip and looked thoughtful for a moment. "Ednedot is correct. Breaking apart the amulet would not break the enchantment."

"See!" Ednedot grinned. "It'll work..."

"But!" the queen interrupted. "The enchantment that powers it will slowly decay. Eventually, the pieces would need to come back together and be re-enchanted. If not, the magic will fail completely, and the Breach will be unsealed."

"Then what are we talking? Once a year? Once a month?" the dwarf asked, narrowing her one eye at the queen.

"It took an enormous amount of energy to create the enchantment," the queen replied. "It will take some time."

"How much time," Mordecai demanded.

"A thousand years. Maybe two," the queen replied.

"Ha!" the dwarf said. "A thousand years?!"

There were chuckles around the table. Only Mordecai and the queen didn't laugh. The queen looked deadly serious while the necromancer looked calculating.

"I think it's agreed then," the necromancer said in a sugary sweet voice that dripped with insincerity. "We will split the amulet and divide it among the people at this table..."

"Except me!" the halfling interrupted. "We want nothing to do with it."

"As he says," Mordecai continued. "All except the halflings. One for the Artoshians, one for the trolls, one for the ogres, one for the gnomes, one for the drakkar, one for the reppits and one for me, of course. Seven pieces."

"Seven is a lucky number," the halfling said with a grin.

"As you say." The necromancer gave the halfling a condescending nod. He slid his gaze across the others. "What say you? Divide the amulet among us?"

A loud chorus of "ayes" echoed around the room and Mordecai smiled like a snake sizing up a mouse and turned a triumphant look on the queen. "It seems the ayes have it."

The queen said nothing but simply nodded.

Madison was suddenly falling again and the next moment she was back in her body in the circular room. She blinked and looked around at the statues. She recognized them as the people in her vision.

Then her vision turned to the amulet and she reached out and picked it up, despite the gasp from Michael. The moment her fingers touched it, she received new messages.

Quest "In the Fey's Footsteps" Complete.
Ruins Explored (0/1)
You have gained experience!
Your reputation with Araman Blackpipe has increased.
Congratulations! You were the first group on the server to complete the quest In the Fey's Footsteps. A Reward has been added to your account.

You may check your rewards by going to Character Menu-> Profile -> Rewards -> Early Access Awards

Congratulations! You have gained a level!
You are now level 6.

She was about to say something about gaining a new level when another message flashed across her HUD.

You have received a new Mythic quest "Seal the Breach"
You have acquired a fragment of the Amulet of Artolean. The seal on the breach has weakened and the amulet must be recharged or it will fail completely and begin invasion from the Fey.
Reunite the fragments of the amulet and find a way to recharge the magic.
Fragments Collected (1/7)
Amulets Restored (0/1)
Amulets Recharged (0/1)
Reward: Unknown
Accept quest (yes or no)?
Note: This quest is not unique. Others may acquire the same quest by locating a fragment of the Amulet. The first person or group to complete the quest will cause all others with the quest to fail.
Congratulations! You were the first group on the server to receive a Mythic quest. A Reward has been added to your account.
You may check your rewards by going to Character Menu-> Profile -> Rewards -> Early Access Awards

60

The others took turns using the memory orb. They all saw the vision of the gathering and the decision to split the amulet.

While her group watched the initial memory orb, Madison used some of the other memory orbs that were in the hands of the various statues. The visions she received were all from the perspective of the other races. It showed a brief glimpse of what they did with their piece of the fragment.

The trolls buried theirs at the bottom of a statue of a giant troll. The ogres sealed theirs in a sarcophagus, along with the body of what appeared to be their king or leader. The other races all placed their fragments in various places.

Michael was the last one to view the memory orb. When he finished, he handed it back to Madison. "That was wild."

"And you guys saw the quest," Cole said, his face grim.

"We have a mythic quest - and it's not unique to us. Other groups could get it if they find a fragment."

"Not if we find them first!" Michael chuckled with a broad grin.

Rose practically vibrated with excitement. "We need to find them first and get the money for them! That was a lot of money!"

"You only get money for finding a certain type of item the first time," Michael reminded her. "We already found a mythic item and a fragment."

"No," Rose retorted. "Read it again. It says we received the reward for being the first to find fragment 1! The others are probably numbered too, which means we can earn another $30,000 if we can find them all!"

Michael's eyes went wide, and he sputtered but didn't actually say anything for several seconds. Finally, he shook his head. "$30,000. Are you sure?!"

"Oh yeah," she replied with a grin that rivaled Michael's normal smile. "According to the orb thing, it was split into 7 pieces. We already found one, so that means 6 more. At $5,000 each, that's $30,000."

Michael whistled. "That's a lot of money."

Cole nodded but his face was serious. "But only IF we find them."

"Why wouldn't we?" Rose said, brow furrowing. "I mean, what else are we going to do to earn that much money? I mean, I know this is just a game and all, but if we can earn that much money, why wouldn't we do that? Why wouldn't we go after them?!"

"That's not what I mean," Cole said with a sigh. "I mean, read the quest again. It's not unique. Some other group can get it. That means they might be trying to get the fragments too."

"But no one has gotten it yet!" Rose argued.

"We don't know that," Michael said.

Madison cocked her head. She smiled. "Yes, we do."

Everyone looked at Madison. Cole furrowed his brow. "How do we know that?"

"Because we just got a reward for getting the quest, one for getting the first mythic item and one for being the first party to get a mythic quest," she replied triumphantly. "If someone else would have found a fragment, they would have been the first to get a mythic item reward. Same with the quest."

Rose flashed Madison a grin and she gave her cousin a wink.

Cole considered her answer and nodded. "That may be true. But we have no idea where the others are."

"Actually, we do," Madison replied. She held up a handful of the other memory orbs. "These other orbs show what happened to the other fragments."

"Oh?" Michael peaked an eyebrow. "Where are they?"

Madison bit her lip. "I'm not sure."

"I thought you said you knew where they were," Rose asked with a frown.

"Well," Madison admitted. "It shows me what they did with it, but I don't really have any context. I think... I think they're in whatever lands the other races live."

Michael whistled. "Have you seen the map of this place? It's huge! And the races are really spread out."

"Not to mention," Cole added. "We wouldn't be welcome in some countries."

"You mean, like how they killed Madison when we first got here?" Rose asked.

Madison cringed at the memory. It hadn't been a good start to the game.

"Exactly," her brother replied. "Only, in the evil countries, it would be the three of us who were KoS."

"KOS?" Rose frowned.

"Kill on sight," Michael said, sliding his finger across his throat. "Persona non grata."

Rose's frown deepened, but then she brightened. "But she was able to be accepted by killing the gnolls, right? We could do something similar!"

Cole nodded. "True. But that's a decent amount of work."

"For $30,000?!" Rose snapped.

Madison nodded. "She has a point. Is there really a better use of our time?"

Michael and her brother exchanged glances. Michael grinned. "Not if we can make that sort of cash."

"Keep in mind," Cole said. "The monetary rewards are only valid during early access. That means we would only have 3 weeks."

"Minus a day," Michael added. "Not a lot of time."

"The accelerated time frame would work in our favor," Madison pointed out. "Three weeks of real-world time is like... what... "

"A regular day to us is like 6 days in game time," Michael replied.

"Seriously?" Rose asked, cocking her head.

Michael looked sheepish. "As far as I can figure."

Rose's face grew excited again. "That's great! That's like 20 real days, which is 120 days of game time!"

Madison did some quick calculations. "Minus time for us to sleep."

"Oh." Rose's face sank. "So, what, like a third less time?"

"Probably, not to mention meals, etc." Madison replied.

Michael scratched his head. "Figure we lose at least 2 game days, each day... so, that's like 40 game days total."

Rose pouted. "So only 80 days?"

"Wait," Michael said with a huge grin. "Are we saying... we've got to go around the world in 80 days?!"

Madison rolled her eyes at the reference to the classic 19th century book called Around the World in 80 Days, though she was secretly impressed that Michael actually knew what the book was. She guessed there must have been a movie version of it.

"Come on! We have to at least get all the fragments we can!" Rose argued. "Right?"

"There's no point in not doing it," Madison agreed. "I mean, it's money - always good. And we get to explore the world and do more quests and stuff."

She didn't tell the others, but she really was interested in finding the various fragments and finding out more of the story about the Breach and how it was sealed. The quest actually sounded really interesting, and she was certain she would learn more of the lore.

"You had me at money," Michael said solemnly. "You had me at money."

Cole slapped Michael hard on the back. "Madison is

right. We'll get to explore the game world and even start building reputation with the other factions. Even once the early access is over, that'll help us."

"So, we're going to do it?" Rose asked, her face beaming.

They all exchanged glances and nodded. Madison smiled. "It looks like it."

Rose bounced up and down and clapped her hands together. "Excellent!"

"If that's what we're going to do," Cole said, gesturing around. "Then we should finish searching this place, go back to town and then log out for the night. We can get a fresh start first thing tomorrow morning."

They all muttered agreements before turning their attention on searching the rest of the room.

61

"My mom wasn't happy I had been on my bed all day," Rose said over their online video chat. "But she stopped complaining when I told her how much we earned. She wanted to know how."

"Did you tell her we killed a bunch of gnolls and then a giant spider and then got sent on an epic quest?" Michael asked just before a yawn overtook him.

Rose rolled her eyes. "No. I just told her we were playing a video game and won some money."

"And she was fine with it?" Cole asked.

"Well." Rose bit her lip. "Once I convinced her I wasn't doing online gambling or something... uh... not appropriate."

Madison raised an eyebrow. "She thought you were... well.... You know."

Rose nodded gravely. "Finally, I convinced her it was just a game that I was playing with you guys."

She remembered the call between Rose's mom calling her and drilling her about the game and what they had done. Madison had kept things as vague as possible and eventually her mom had seemed to accept her story. "Yeah, I know."

"Sorry about that," her cousin replied sheepishly.

"What about your parents, Michael?" Madison asked. "Did they say anything?"

Michael grinned and shrugged. "I'm down here all the time playing video games anyhow, so today was no different. I told my mom and dad I earned some money online playing a new game. They thought it was cool."

Rose let out a sigh. "Must be nice."

"It was." Michael grinned.

"How about you?" Rose asked Madison. "Did your mom say anything?"

Madison shook her head. "Mom was at her job all day. She just got back a little while ago."

"She's really working a lot," Michael commented.

"Some sort of state inspection or something," she replied. "She has to do all of this stuff to get ready for it."

In fact, Madison knew the inspection was a really big deal. Her mom ran a daycare and the state had recently passed some new regulations. It meant rearranging part of the daycare. That mean she had to spend a lot of money to get things renovated. It also meant long hours overseeing the men doing the work.

When that was done, her mom would come home and take her online courses to finish up her degree in early education. That was some other requirement of the state.

They had to have so many people per x number of children with degrees.

"Wait," Rose said with a frown. "Does that mean you didn't tell her about the money?"

Cole answered before she could. "Nah. She was really tired when she got home. We'll tell her tomorrow before she goes to work."

"If we get all of it, that's enough to buy you a new car," Michael told Cole.

Her brother shook his head. "Nah, gotta save it for school."

"Yeah, but it's $30,000!" Michael retorted.

"He doesn't get the whole $30,000!" Rose broke in. "Remember, we each get a quarter. Hopefully, we'll each get around $10,000 when everything's said and done."

Michael grinned. "I'll take $10,000!"

"So will I," Cole said, sharing their cousin's smile.

Madison hated to curb their enthusiasm, but she felt like she needed to be the voice of reason. "Remember, that's if... IF... we find all of the other pieces."

"We will," Rose said confidently. Madison wasn't sure if it was real confidence or desperation. She knew her cousin didn't want to work a minimum wage job.

All her cousin really wanted to do was spend the summer volunteering at the no-kill animal shelter. Rose loved animals and that was her dream job. Unfortunately, it was on a volunteer basis - so no pay.

If they did get all the money - or even most of it - Rose was counting on her parents letting her volunteer. Madison hoped she was right. Working at the shelter was something her cousin was really passionate about. She hoped she got to do it.

"Alright," Michael said. "I'm gonna watch a movie and then go to bed. See you guys tomorrow. 8am, right?"

They all nodded. "8am and we meet in the game to figure out which fragment we go after next."

"Sounds good!"

"Alright!"

"See you then!"

They said their goodbyes and then shut down the connection. Madison heard footsteps and looked up to see her brother. He smiled.

"Admit it," he said with a smile. "You had fun."

"I guess so." Madison shrugged. In truth, it had been fun. She hadn't thought it would be at first, but it had. The best part had been learning about the history of the place and discovering how the people had come together to seal the breach.

She cocked her head. Of course, it was all made up. It was just a game. But was it really? It almost seemed more like an interactive novel. There was action, excitement, mystery - all the elements of a good book.

But unlike a book, it felt so real. She shook her head. Of course, it seemed real. She'd just lived it! At least, she'd lived it in the game.

"You okay?" Cole asked, concern etched on his features.

She looked up at him and nodded. "I'm fine. And yes, it was fun."

Cole's look of concern turned into a grin. "I thought so. You and Rose did good..."

"For girls," Madison teased.

"For newbies! I wasn't going to say girls!" he shot back. "You did good for someone who hadn't played VRMMORPGs."

Madison smiled. "Thanks."

Her brother nodded and then turned around and padded back to his room, leaving Madison alone in her bed. A minute later, the light in her brother's bedroom went out.

She reached over and switched off her own lamp. For a moment, she half expected to be able to see in the dark - like she did in the game. She couldn't. Madison chuckled at herself, turned over, and closed her eyes.

Tomorrow was another day. And another adventure.

JOIN THE ADVENTURE

Thank you for reading this book! If you enjoyed it, please consider leaving a review on Amazon or tagging me on social media.

Reviews help readers like you find this book. More readers means more sales, and more sales help independent authors like me to be able to write more books!

To learn more about the author and his other books and projects, visit the author's website at:
https://www.johnecressman.com
Or visit our Facebook Page
https://www.facebook.com/authorjohncressman/

OTHER SERIES BY THIS AUTHOR

If you enjoyed this book, please check out other series by John Cressman:

The Abduction Cycles - Books 1-6
Check Out The Series on Amazon
Imagine waking up in a world where magic is real! One minute Ethan Gower was an average computer technician, playing online games with his friends. Now he's been abducted and dropped into a strange world with others who have been taken from their homes. And magic and monsters are real.
Now, Ethan is a wizard and must convince his new companions to band together in order to survive in this strange new world as they level up, gain abilities and try to unravel the mystery of why they were abducted and how to find a way home.
But things are never easy and soon he and his friends find

themselves in the middle of a conflict that could spell disaster to their new home.
Oh, and there might be something murdering wizards and sucking out their brains.
Could things get any worse?

***

The Veil Online Trilogy (Second Edition) - Books 1-3
Check Out The Series on Amazon
Junior programmer Jace Burton is your average computer geek. By day he works on the most popular VR game in the world and by night, he slay dragons and saves damsels.
Not any more.
Today he woke up inside the game and there's no way out. Worse, he's not even his high level avatar. He's a monster. And every time he dies, he jumps into another monster body.
Something is wrong. Seriously wrong.
Join Jace on a mind-blowing adventure as he desperately tries to unravel the mystery of what has happened to him and most importantly, is he even alive any more?

LITRPG

To learn more about LitRPG, talk to authors including myself, and just have an awesome time, please join the LitRPG Group.

MORE LITRPG

For more information on this book and other exciting LitRPG/GameLit books, please visit the following Facebook groups:

LitRPG Books

https://www.facebook.com/groups/LitRPG.books/

and

GameLit Society

https://www.facebook.com/groups/LitRPGsociety/

ACKNOWLEDGMENTS

I'd like to acknowledge all the members of the LitRPG Authors' Guild who helped me in so many ways! Without your help, I could never have gotten this far!

I also want to acknowledge the 20Booksto50K Facebook group! I've received lots of help and inspiration from them and I recommend the group to new and experienced authors.

Also, a big thank you for everyone who had bought one of my books. Your support really means a lot to me.

ABOUT THE AUTHOR

Paige Fallbright is student and aspiring author. She lives with mother, sister, brother and - not to be forgotten - her dog.

The two things she enjoys most are reading and singing. Her passions include history and unique art. Known as the "retro chic," she enjoys an eclectic taste in music.

In the future, she hopes to achieve a fulfilled life of success and fun!

John E. Cressman is an author, magician, mentalist, hypnotist, programmer, and longtime lover of roleplaying games and fantasy/sci-fi books.

As a teen, he wasted long hours creating D&D fantasy campaigns for his friends to play. He has tried several pen and paper roleplaying games from the original Dungeons and Dragons, Traveler and Star Frontiers to the new Pathfinder games.

He still enjoys computer RPGs and MMORPGs, with his current favorite being Elder Scrolls Online. He used to play Skyrim, but then he took an arrow to the knee.

Made in the USA
Monee, IL
30 June 2022